For Mc

with love from

Shirley Turner.

Feb. 2001

SHOOTING AT STARS

Shirley Turner

INTERNATIONAL CONSULTANCY SERVICES
GRAVESEND
KENT DA11 0LP

SHOOTING AT STARS

ISBN: 0 9539985 0 9

First Published December 00 by

INTERNATIONAL CONSULTANCY SERVICES
GRAVESEND
KENT DA11 0LP

Printed in Great Britain by Unity Print Ltd

SHOOTING AT STARS

This book is dedicated to my late mother Constance…and all my friends who have heard about it for so long.
It is for my daughters Heather, Melanie and JoAnna. Last, but by no means least, my husband Martin, without whose help and encouragement it would never have been completed.

Thanks for help and advice go to:-

John Hooton

Melanie Green

Marjorie Pryce

Lyn Norris

Brenda Eamus

Marion Sherwood

Acknowledgements

William Shakespeare

William Wordsworth

Charles Kingsley

Dictionary of Astronomy

Shooting at Stars

Time is….

Too slow for those who wait
…
Too swift for those who fear
…
Too long for those who grieve
…
Too short for those who rejoice
…
But for those who love….

Time

is

Eternity

SHOOTING AT STARS

By Shirley Turner

Shooting at Stars

Prologue — *January 1942*

The blizzard that had started as a pretty flutter, had thickened making visibility almost non-existent, and the swiftness with which the drifts were forming was quite frightening. As she looked out of the window she saw that the snow was almost waist high and a chill ran down her spine. She threw the window open; with difficulty, for the snow was rapidly trying to engulf it; then, thrusting her head out she turned it upwards towards the grey sky and felt the flakes as they dropped on to her face. The silence was unbelievable to ears that were usually being assailed by many other sounds. She closed the window again making sure that the catch was firmly secured against the encroaching weather. Almost at once a sudden gripping pain low down in her abdomen caused her to wince.

"I can do without that at the moment thank you, " she said patting her stomach, "You've a whole month to lie in state so make the most of it baby dear".

The words were hardly out of her mouth, however, when another contraction more powerful this time, made her grip the windowsill behind her.

"No…no…please God….not now…"

Making her way slowly to a chair she sat on it and tried to relax the tenseness in her body. She lay there with her eyes closed, breathing deeply, in a controlled rhythm.

A while later, when she hoped the danger had passed, she stood cautiously. Her worst fears were confirmed as she felt the warm rush of water….without any doubt she was in the first stage of labour, and about to experience the birth of her first child…… As she stood there clasping her hands, her eyes fell on the green emerald on her finger. She thought of her husband Angus…….recognising at once, that wherever he was there was no possibility of him reaching her tonight……

Another contraction doubled her body.

"Dear God – please help me.." she said knowing (with complete awareness), that indeed the only help from the outside – would have to come from the hand of God….. For like it or not – prepared or not – the child within her was determined to be born. There was no stopping it now, for its journey into the world had begun…and she was alone…..

Shooting at Stars

Book 1 Chapter 1
'Alpha' – In the Beginning *October 1984*

The man sat, his head buried in his hands with his arms resting on a large, leather-bound old bible; just part of the clutter of the desk top in front of him. The ornate chandelier was off; the only illumination coming from two lamps standing at the corners of the desk, their angled shades sending showers of light downwards that only dimly lit the rest of the room.

The room itself was large, and lined on three sides by tall bookcases. Row upon row of every size and shape of book was there, and every shelf was filled to capacity. The ceiling was high and its decoration gave the room an air of opulence about it, with the white sculptured corners just visible in the gloom.

Behind the man was a large window. It looked black, but was totally reflective; every book, and every other detail was there giving the room an ethereal quality, mirroring a scene of peace and tranquillity.

The picture etched on the man's face when he raised it was far from tranquil. A sadness seemed to hang over him, making him look as if he had all the cares of the world on his shoulders. The dark, slightly greying hair surrounding his face was dishevelled; and made him look older than his years.

Turning around in the Captain's chair he stood in one movement. Now he faced the window, and himself. As he stood looking at his reflection he thought of his father; who was a totally unfathomable old man, whose presence in the family home had changed, both his, and more obviously, his wife Angela's life. A second stroke had struck him down some three years earlier and his dependency had grown daily. A father like a helpless baby was no joy, and that fact coupled with the repetitious phrase 'What is the answer?' that was constantly on his lips, made life unbearable at times. For it was a question neither he nor Angela could ever answer.

He put both hands on the window and put his weight on them. He found himself sighing when recalling his father's efforts at communication, in fact he felt himself becoming quite claustrophobic. The trouble being that his father had become obsessed by something the stroke had triggered, and now there was no way of stopping it. For long years they endured it; there had been no respite. The same words were spoken over and over again.....never changing. The pain of the laboured breath was always followed by the same four faltering words.

"What ...is...the...answer?"

The man sighed again and took his hands from the window watching the imprint of his fingers as they faded and finally disappeared. Taking a deep breath he looked again at his reflection, then moved to the window, his face nearly touching the glass. It was dark now and the lights of the town were glowing yellow.

"They look like Wordsworth's daffodils," he thought "twinkling in the dark instead of dancing in the breeze."

As free afternoons were precious to him, he felt a pang of guilt as he stood there.

"This is just hopeless, I'd better pack up and go home". His thoughts were tumbling about in his head.

"God help me, I'm at the end of my tether. I'm frightened for the future and just don't know what I can do....."

At that moment something extraordinary happened in the room. The man was quite still .. too still. His eyes looking outward, were not seeing. His hands hovered an inch above the glass, transfixed; and there was no rise and fall on his chest. He was not breathing. There was an eerie silence in the room, as if it was waiting, holding it's breath for something.....

There was no ventilation of any sort, no draught to move the emptiness around. Then, without warning the air was cut by a soft sound. A flick, flick, flick. The man, still entombed within himself did not hear, for he was as stone. The flick, flick continued behind him. It was coming from the large leather-bound book that lay open on the table. The pages were whirring, faster and faster. Suddenly they stopped, leaving the page open at Genesis. The first words seemed to be briefly illuminated. 'In the beginning...' As the pages came to rest the man and the room came to life. He rested his hands on the cold window glass momentarily before straightening up, closing the book, switching the lamps off before departing. He was oblivious of the strange occurrence that had robbed him of a few seconds of his life. Somewhere below, a clock chimed the hour of five, the muffled sounds drifting up into the now dark and empty room.

The Homecoming

It was quite dark when he arrived home. He cut across the lawn, which was wet and slippery and made for the lighted window.

The house looked quite beautiful, standing proudly silhouetted against the neon sky and although Angela and he were well aware of its drawbacks, they both loved it and the rambling garden. As it truly was a haven in the concrete jungle about them, they called the house 'Oasis'.

He reached the window, and leaning across the narrow flowerbed supported himself on the ivy covered windowsill, and looked into the room. It was a familiar scene. His father was sitting, propped up and motionless on a chaise-longue, that had seen better days. He looked so small and frail, lying there. His eyes were bright and darting, as if to capture every movement, and every time he saw Angela he started the same old words again.

Having heard them a hundred times and more, she didn't answer him, but smiled and touched his arm. Looking in on the scene he couldn't hear any of the domestic sounds within the room…so was spared the sound of his father's plaintive voice. However tea was on the table and as Angela glanced at the clock he knew he must go in.

He reached the back door where a lamp showed him the way. Turning his key he entered the kitchen and crossed at once to his wife and took her into his arms.

"Any change today m'love?"

Angela shook her head, "No, worse than usual if anything Peter, but Sarah came in, it hasn't been all bad."

He kissed her gently on the mouth, then glanced at the partly open door of the sitting room.

"Go on in" she said and mouthed the words, "I love you", as he hesitated at the doorway.

His father's eyes pounced on his own at once. Then the words rang again…

"What…is…the…answer?"

Peter made his way to him and kneeling by his side, took his frailty into his own strong arms.

"Oh father, father," he said.

Angela came to the door and watched as she had many times before. It never failed to move her. In her mind she called it...the ritual of the words.

The older man searched out the eyes of the younger. Saliva dribbling from the corner of his twisted mouth. It was so hard for him to speak. Then laboriously the words again...

"What...is...the...answer?" he said, as his eyes filled with tears.

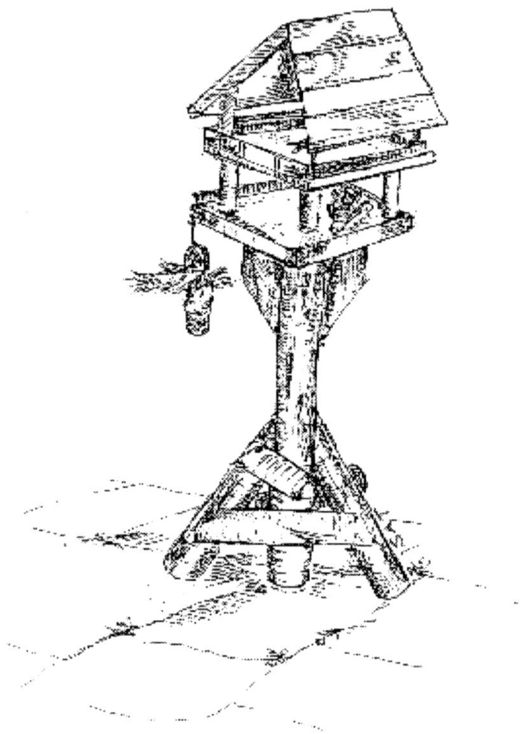

Angela *October 1984*

Angela stood looking out of the kitchen window. She was a fine looking woman, tall and graceful and Peter always said that .... "Moneypenny's lips had nothing on hers, for she had the most kissable ones without any doubt!" At the present time, however, her lips were drawn up into an unfamiliar straight line, causing the usually friendly face to take on a disgruntled look.

The dark brown shoulder length curls shook with more than a little annoyance, as she looked out of the kitchen window at the bird tray. The starlings were greedily squawking and fighting their way through the food. Then, all at once,(as if by an invisible signal), they all flew upwards, leaving the almost bare tray behind them, with not a thought for their insignificant brothers. Slowly, and with caution, the smaller birds were now attacking the remnants with relish and making the most of the few crumbs.

"How unfair," she thought, "that the largest, noisiest and definitely the most bad tempered, get the best and the most."

Having had their fill, the starlings were sitting high on the tall trees, preening and clustering together.

The family unit all together, she thought, mother, father, sister, brother, child all sitting and swaying together...She broke off her thoughts of the birds and concentrated on her morning. Her father-in-law was already washed and dressed, and as ready to face the day as he could be. He now sat awaiting his breakfast, although, she felt sure that he couldn't care about it, one way or the other.

It was nine o'clock in the morning, and the day was overcast and gloomy. Rain was falling in a steady downpour, and, since it was late October, she felt the day would disappear into night rather quicker than usual.

I mustn't get depressed, she thought, not at nine o'clock in the morning. The egg and bacon was cooked and ready, so she put it to keep warm until she was ready for it.

As she entered the room with the tray, the old man looked at her. She crossed and set it down beside him. His eyes looked at her.

"What...is...the...answer?"

"My love, I don't know…please don't cry." She wiped his tears, and then sat down and prepared to feed him. Her own eyes brimmed up again so that she was looking through a blur of water.

Why, oh why do I do this? I see and hear him all day long, why can't I just learn to ignore him?

Porridge all gone, now for the egg and bacon. She stirred the mixture around, ground down now and quite unrecognisable from it's beginnings. She fed him like a baby.

Just like a baby, she thought, while scooping up that which had slipped from the corners of his mouth.

How she longed for a baby. God's gift it seemed was not for her and Peter. Perhaps with her father-in-law like this, it was right not to have a baby in the house; but it didn't stop the longing that she felt from time to time for a child of their own.

She was thirty-eight now and Peter was forty-three. They had been married for thirteen years. Years that had been filled to capacity with…life. Happy, busy and fulfilled years. She had been a nurse before and during the first part of their marriage, and that had helped her a great deal over the trying months with father. Peter had been busy from the word go. Even today, he had roused himself at the crack of dawn; to get to the local radio station, where he was to be the 'Voice of the common man' on a chat show called…'How the modern family copes with living in the eighties'.

It was only a recording she knew, but judging by other recording sessions that he had been asked to attend, she guessed that he was bound to be involved until late afternoon, and when he did get home, he would be closeted up in his study, for quite a long time. All these thoughts raced around in her mind as she was feeding, then cleaning, the old man.

He suddenly gripped her hand, snatching at her fingers, and holding them tight with a movement that she had thought was impossible for him. It made her draw her breath in as she was quite unprepared for the sudden movement. She looked into his face.

"What…is…the…answer?" he said with a voice that she didn't recognise as his. It was harsh and toneless, but more demanding than ever.

"What…is…the…answer?" he said again.

She shook her head. This time she shed no tears.

"Hurry home, Peter" she said quietly, and closed her eyes.

Angela looked through the kitchen door towards father. Although the house was pleasantly warm, she had switched on the fire's artificial flame to make the room more cosy. It was very effective. It flickered realistically in the room, glinting on the framework of the metal chair and, on father himself.

On the corner of a side table, at an angle, was a photograph. The light played on this too, and the old man's face was focused on it. The picture was of a smiling woman and two children, one of them a baby. The photograph was of Peter with his mother and brother.

Angela was sure that the only real pleasure Peter's father had in his life, was looking at the picture. Although his wife and younger son, were a long time dead, the old man still seemed to get immense pleasure, or what passed for pleasure, from looking at it.

He was still asking them for the answer, but it was as elusive as ever. Lately the knowledge that he so desperately wanted, seemed to have taken on a strange urgency; for his look was more intense, his voice more impatient, as though he felt that time was running short.

She prayed each day that an answer would be found for his troubled brain, so that he could gain some peace, with some gentle, pleasurable reminiscences of the past, instead of the ongoing, unrelenting experience that was currently permeating his brain, just something…something for Christmas.

Although Christmas was close now, it was going to be a relatively quiet one for them. Because neither Angela nor Peter had any close family they would be staying at 'Oasis' the whole time.

Before the event though, both of them were going to be extremely busy. Angela in charge of the meal that was to take place at the local 'Evergreen Club'. All the committee were more than willing to shed that particular responsibility. Being aware of the home circumstances, her friends admired her dedication to both the job in hand and to her husband's father. As well as everything else Peter had to do, he was involved with an outdoor Carol Service, which was proving to be more complicated than he had at first envisaged. Because he was involved with the youth of the town, in trouble or not, it was felt that he would be the ideal person for the job. And since the head of the local constabulary had suggested it, and offered the police band to play – how could he refuse?

Angela was taking a quiet breather from father, by putting the shopping away, before making a cup of tea for them both. It had not been a good day with him. His voice had seemed to violate every quiet space. He had started the day with a terrible coughing fit which left him gasping and silent, but not for long, because the old question was soon ringing in her ears, again .. and again. She put her floral mug on the tray next to father's beaker. She hoped that in his hazy mind, if he knew it was a feeder, he would not feel it too demeaning, for it was the most practical way of helping him.

She spoke to him gently,

"Here I am with our afternoon tea, sorry I've been so long, but I've been putting the shopping away and having to sort out the freezer."

She put the tray down, and released the handbrake on the chair, and turned her father-in-law towards the fire, positioning it close to her own. The old man's eyes sought out hers at once. She tried not to look at him at first, and concentrated on getting the napkin and beaker ready.

At last she could put off their eyes meeting no longer, the words were being formed once again. Saliva droplets fell from the corner of his mouth on to the waiting napkin. Still and straight his eyes caught hers with a hypnotic and magnetic pull.

"What…is..the..answer?" He said, his eyes filling with tears before starting to dart about wildly. She tried to console him.

"We're trying, father, honestly we are, we are trying to help you – don't worry, everything will be alright. Come, try to have a sip of tea…."

She picked the beaker up to place it in his lips. Once again his face had become a blur, for, once again, her own eyes had filled with tears.

Although Peter was usually late on a Friday, tonight was different, and he was due home at any moment. She longed to hear his key in the lock…….

The events in the room had taken only seconds of time, but to Angela, each second had seemed like an eternity.

Shooting at Stars

Book 2 – Chapter 1
The Accident *January 1939*

The air hit him in the face and shocked him.

"Boy, it really is cold tonight" he thought as he made his way down the long flight of steps. Because they were unlit and it was very dark, he went down in mechanical fashion, sight playing little part in his progress.

Then to his horror, the steps seemed to fall away and he felt himself falling headlong. He shot his hands out, trying frantically to dig his fingers into the swiftly moving ground – but it was hard and unyielding. Finally it was too late for any act of self-preservation, for his head hit the ground with tremendous force and sent him instantly into the blackness of unconsciousness. How long time was suspended he had no idea, but as he started to come through the fog on his return to the world, he was aware of muffled sounds.

"Can you hear me?"

He felt a hand on his face, then the voice again, more urgently asking.

"Can you hear me?"

He tried to nod but pain shot through his head. He opened his eyes. Blurred shapes danced before them but gradually the shapeless mass took form, and all at once the voice had a face.

"Can – you – hear – me?" It said once again.

He found himself looking up at a woman's face, a face framed by a cloud of fair hair encased in dark blue. She smiled at him.

"Just about." He said.

As if from nowhere, she produced a glass of water. He tried to sip it, but didn't feel anything pass beyond his lips. Trying to prop himself up, he was aware of a group of men looking down on him.

"You went a right wallop there son and no mistake." said one, "Drunk and disorderly at twenty Missie, you'd better have a good talk to him."

As he spoke the man shrugged his shoulders, then convinced that the boy was not too seriously hurt. The men who had shown concern laughed on their way back into the pub, leaving the young woman to her 'good works'.

"How do you feel now? Can you stand up yet do you think?" She held out her hand to him. "You can hold on to me".

He took it and staggered to his feet, taking an involuntary step sideways as he did so.

"I'm not drunk, honestly I'm not. I just missed my footing on the steps. I put my foot down and…just missed them." His voice trailed off in a rather pathetic way.

"Don't worry, lean on me, we'll take it slowly and you can sit down for a while.

He nodded but said nothing. They walked slowly into the saloon bar of 'The Moon'.

The smoke hung like a heavy curtain about him, and it made him gasp. The young woman sat him down on a chair just inside the door. She turned her eyes towards him and started to speak.

"What beautiful eyes," he thought, hardly hearing her voice.

"I'll stay with you till you feel up to leaving. Where were you going in such a hurry anyway? My name's Laura by the way, what's yours?"

He thought for a long moment.

"It's….it's…"

She didn't press for an answer, but tried the first question again.

"Well, where were you going, you must have been in quite a hurry?"

His mind was a complete blank.

"I don't know," he said softly, "I don't even recognise where I am…I know that must sound silly…but I just don't know. I don't know my name …or anything." He looked into the lovely eyes and then lowered his head into his hands. She touched his shoulder and said gently,

"What about where you live?"

He didn't move, just remained with his head in his hands. She looked at him, he did look a fright. The dishevelled hair – the dirt – as well as the sight of rapidly appearing red at the side of his face. She knelt at his side and put a comforting arm around his shoulder.

"Well, where do I live?" A feeling of panic was whirling around in his stomach, and as it grew, he found himself starting to breathe rapidly. He raised his head.

"I don't know, I can't remember…anything," he added lamely, putting his head once more into his hands.

"Well, you did fall hard, and you do look very battered, it's not too surprising that you feel dazed and forgetful, is it?" she added kindly.

"Yes, that's it, perhaps I hit my head on the steps, that must be it. It's still a bit frightening though, not to remember your name or anything."

The girl looked at him, thinking

"He must be hallucinating or something, there are no steps there, never have been, still he has taken quite a fall so it's not surprising that he is so confused." Giving attention to the young man again she said,

"Look in your pockets, there may be something in them that will jog your memory."

He put his clammy hands into his pockets. Laura watched him. Beads of sweat were forming on his forehead and upper lip, and his hair swung to and fro as he searched. As she watched his hands racing from pocket to pocket, she could see that he was becoming more and more panic-stricken. The jacket itself didn't help it was so baggy. The look on his face was a look of hopelessness.

She felt very sorry for him, for his fear was quite obvious. The search was fruitless.

"Stop, don't look anymore...you're coming home with me,...then when you're feeling better, well...we'll sort things out. Give me your arm, and I'll help you."

They made their way to the door. The gangling young man, slightly bent, and the young woman, straight and confident. She pushed the door open and they stepped out into the coldness of the evening.

"I'm sorry, my brain seems to be asleep and I can't piece anything together," he said putting his hand to his head.

"Well, hold on to me, and I'll help you find your missing pieces....if I can."

As the door shut behind them and they were enveloped by cold, he realised just how light- headed he was. He swayed and the young woman stopped.

"How stupid of me to think that I could manage you on my own..." but before she could say any more, the face of Regular Joe was at their side.

"Well, Missie, you seem to have your arms full, and the young fella seems to need a bit more strength than you have."

As he was speaking, he took the weight of the young man from her, and half carried him.

"Oh Joe, thank you so much, the quicker I can get him into the warm, the better I will like it."

They made their ungainly way to her home. She found her key and opened the door. All three went into the room. As Joe turned to go he gave Laura a wink and a smile,

"Well, that's one way of making sure I don't drink any more tonight isn't it Missie?"

Then he went out into the night, closing the door with a bang.

"Aunt Mary," she called, sitting him down.

"I feel so guilty, putting you to all this trouble..."

Aunt Mary's head appeared at the door.

"What's all this then? Who's this young man?"

Laura stood up and undid her bonnet. He stood up slowly, and then sat rather quickly.

"Well, Auntie, he fell outside the 'Moon'..." Aunt Mary's eyebrows arched up, and she frowned.

"No Auntie, he's not drunk, come and see."

"I'm so...sorry...for all the trouble..." he began again. Laura shook her head. Aunt Mary came closer.

"Pleased to meet you," she said looking at him more closely. He certainly did look a sight. There was a large blue bruise, at his right temple, with a livid red graze running down. Another large swelling was discovered as Aunt Mary ran her hands over his head, it was behind his right ear, obscured by his hair. His nose was swollen and had been bleeding, and the whole of his face was streaked with dirt and blood.

"Laura, go and fetch some warm water. You'd better put some Izal in it too. Then you can come and sponge this dirt off."

Aunt Mary looked at the clock on the mantelpiece. She wondered if she could catch the doctor.

When Laura came back, Aunt Mary said,

"I'm going to the surgery Laura. I'll feel a good deal happier if Doctor Andrews could come tonight." She managed to do up her coat and ram her hat on her head on her way out of the door. Looking back over her shoulder she said, "You and your waifs and strays!"

Laura looked at the battered young man before he eased off his coat.

"Auntie is a lovely lady. She was a nurse in her working life so I respect her judgement, and if she says it's the doctor – then it's a doctor."

As she was speaking she was washing his swollen face. There was nothing visible that could account for all the blood that she could see. Where had the blood come from? She soon had her question answered for, as she moved his hair from the side of his face, she found it had stuck to his skin. It was his ear that had bled. She soaked off the strands adhering to his face and saw with relief that there was no sign of any fresh flow.

His head seemed empty. His right ear was thumping and his nose felt as if he had walked into a brick wall. He watched the girl, as if from afar. She was speaking to him now and again, but he wasn't really listening. He glanced down at the bowl of water. Dirt and grit seemed to be on the bottom of the white enamel and as the water swirled, it made it go round and round. That's just how I feel, he thought. He laid his head back again and closed his eyes.

Laura saw him lay his head back and hoped Auntie was in time. She gazed at him. His hands were filthy, the nails were black and broken.

"I'll have to wash these hands," she said taking them into her own.

"Thanks," he said before drifting away again.

The doctor was washing his hands.

"Thank you for coming so quickly, I was worried about the lad."

"That's quite alright Mrs. Anderson , I knew that if you asked me to call there must be a good reason."

He sat down on one of the tall-backed chairs at the table, took out his fountain pen and began to write on a pad.

The young man was looking at the ceiling as the doctor came over to him.

"Well, I've had a good look at you my boy. Concussion – that's your trouble – concussion. Loss of memory is quite common in these types of cases; no consolation to you I know, but usually it clears up in a few days. The ear…well that's a different matter…you will certainly find yourself deaf, for the time anyway. What I want you to do now - is to rest, don't force yourself to remember…try to be patient. Of course, you will be very sore and stiff for quite a long time; but there are no bones broken. I know you are in good hands, in fact you couldn't have done better if you had chosen these two good people yourself."

He smiled. While the doctor was speaking, he had picked up his bag, hat and coat, before putting his hand on the shoulder of the still figure.

"Now heed my words, try not to push yourself to remember, just rest and let your body get over the shock. Have patience my boy. I'll come in and see you tomorrow."

Aunt Mary walked to the door with the doctor.

"I think he may be permanently deaf in the right ear. It's a bit too early to say anything for sure, but it must have been a tremendous fall and he could have burst an eardrum; I'll examine it again when the pain has subsided. There's nothing to be done at the moment. Rest is what he needs, rest and care. As for his memory, well, that's a tricky one. It could come back tomorrow, on the other hand…" The doctor just shook his head. Aunt Mary looked grave.

"Doctor, what can we do with him? What with all this talk of war, do you think he's in the services? Perhaps trying to get out of going or something?… It's all very worrying." She added shaking her head.

"Well, all I can say is that there is no recent sign of any smallpox vaccination on him…all recruits have to be vaccinated, but having said that, anything else would have to be speculation I'm afraid. One thing is certain anyway, there is no way I could pass him A1 at the moment…if ever. Do your good deed and keep him for the time being if you can. It will help his recovery no end if he is being cared for in a proper home, rather than the impersonal atmosphere of hospital."

Aunt Mary replied that of course they would take care of him, until such time that he was fit enough, to move on. The doctor raised his hat and bade her goodnight, as she closed the door. The lad sat bolt upright as Laura cleaned his hands.

"As soon as you have finished Laura, we will make up a bed on the settee."

At that she disappeared with a swish, behind a chenille curtained door. A couple of moments later, she returned; carrying pyjamas, pillows, sheets and an eiderdown, it was bright pink, slippery and dropped on the floor by Laura's feet.

"When you go out to the kitchen, could you put the kettle on Laura, please? I'm sure we could all do with a nice cup of tea."

"Let's make you more comfortable my lad, by getting you into these pyjamas and respectable before Laura comes back. This is a job for me, not a tender unmarried young lady. I'll help you when you can't manage, it won't worry me if I see your bits and pieces. After all I was a nurse...and a married woman."

He was tenderly....'made respectable'. He did the best that he could, but it was too much effort and so Aunt Mary had to do the lion's share of the whole operation

By the time Laura came back with the tray, he was propped up, smelling vaguely of Izal and looking decidedly peaky. He didn't do justice to the tea of course, just a swallow was all he could manage.

Aunt Mary adjusted the gaslight. He was oblivious of this, or of Laura as she went through the chenille curtains. Darkness had overcome him and he drifted into an uneasy sleep.

He awoke to see violet blue eyes looking into his own.

"How are you this morning?"

"I feel a bit better, but I can't hear very well," he touched behind his ear as he spoke. "I feel bruised all over, and so stiff you wouldn't believe...I can only remember yesterday in snatches. I remember you though, and your eyes. They are beautiful."

Laura seemed embarrassed at his remarks, although others had commented on the colour of them, coming from a man so close, just made her blush.

"Well you do sound a little better I must say...and I thank you for your compliment I'm off to do some detective work on your behalf now but I'll be home soon. Auntie is here so you won't be on your own, and the doctor is calling again later on. Take it easy. See you later. I must fly..."

She was gone, leaving a faint perfume of...he knew not. It was a fragrance he recalled from last night. Just the fragrance of...Laura. He lay back on the pillows. Where am I? What am I doing here? Who am I? I don't even know what day it is. Do I know the days of the week? He thought for a moment...Yes, just about.

The panic he felt would not be stifled. I just don't remember anything. He closed his eyes. An inner voice was screaming, Help me, help me...help me. He was sweating and could feel, his temple pulse banging in his head like a drum beating out a rhythm. He was gasping and frightened. He didn't hear the doctor come or go. He felt as though he was falling, floating and falling at the same time, if that were possible. Then darkness overpowered him again.

When he awoke the house was quiet. He lay on his back, staring upwards. The sun had made a shaft of light, like a golden road, and it cut the ceiling in two. His eyes followed it, from the curtain edge to the central gas bracket. It slowly faded, then quickly reappeared, to shine as brightly as ever. This is so unreal. I feel I'm caught up in the beam and have no choice but to fade or shine. He lay, eyes fixed on that sunny line. Its intensity was going now; and the glow not quite so bright and clear. It's my life, he thought, if that light goes, I..I..will die. Beads of sweat washed over his battered face. His closed eyes filled with uncontrollable tears. He felt them spill out from under his eyelids in heavy droplets, near his good ear.

When he opened his wet lids again, the sunlight shaft was gone, in despair he closed them again. A door banged. Aunt Mary crossed the room and looked at him. She saw the tear stained face.

"Oh my dear, my dear, don't worry so."

She sat beside him, lifted his body and held him like a baby; rocking oh so gently, his head resting on the flowered apron that covered her bosom. He reached up and held on to her, much as a child might have done. He put his arms around her waist, and realised that…miracle of miracles, he was not dead, but alive, and loved.

"Thank you God," he said, and fell into a natural sleep for the first time since the accident. Aunt Mary sat cradling the sleeping body knowing that she would not relinquish her charge until the moment was right. The clock struck twelve noon. Aunt Mary, slowly lowered the sleeping boy from her arms. She put her hand on her back to support it as she stretched. It was only then that she realised that she had been sitting there for nearly two hours. She went to the kitchen, and stood at the sink. Resting her hands on the cold stone, she looked into the small garden. What happens now? She thought. What happens now?

Laura didn't get home until one o'clock.

"Sorry I'm late Auntie but I called in to get some clothes for our guest – I do hope they fit; in any case they will have to do for now. How is he?"

Over a cup of tea Aunt Mary told her everything that had happened. Speaking softly Laura said,

"Well, I think we should think of him as a missing person in reverse. I have been to the Police Station, and I called in to see Captain Fuller too. No answers yet of course but surely somebody somewhere must miss him. He's a good looking chap isn't he Auntie?" she said glancing over to the settee as she spoke.

The sleeping figure, the focus of their attention stirred. He slowly turned his head, and looked at the two women seated at the table; one so young and pretty, and the other so motherly and kind.

"I feel better again." He said.

They both looked at him and smiled, their bodies coming quickly to life again. Laura went across to him.

"Hello stranger." She said.

He sat up, slowly at first, then, when he found that his head had stopped reeling, he pushed the covers back and swung his legs to the floor.

"Slow down," Aunt Mary said, "don't go so fast, we don't want you falling over again."

He cautiously stood for his first solo expedition. He was thankful that he was able to walk on his own and become independent again. Laura handed him the clothes that she had brought home.

"Here you are, try these on for size. Your own things are in so much of a mess that I am going to take them to the cleaners for you as soon as I can." She smiled as she added, "Can you manage?"

He gave her a wry smile as he made his way slowly, but with growing confidence, to the small bathroom. When he emerged some time later, a complete transformation had come over him. The shirt, jacket and trousers were a remarkably good fit and although his face still bore the signs of a fall, he did look much better.

"I feel good, really good, except..." The two women looked at him with dismay again, He went on,

"I can't hear in my right ear." He put his head into his hands as he was speaking, and turned it from side to side.

"Yes, I'm quite sure, I can only hear the clock ticking on one side."

Aunt Mary, trying to make light of the situation said,

"Well, don't worry too much about that. I'm sure that it can be put right later on. Now you must be hungry. I'll get us all something."

With that she disappeared into the kitchen.

Laura questioningly said,

"Well, are you hungry?" He looked at her, tipped his head on one side,

"Yes I am,...I am" As if he was surprised by his own answer.

His smile lit up his whole face. For the first time he looks really happy, she thought. A little later Aunt Mary came into the room and lit the gas. It popped, flooding the whole room with light. As she adjusted the brightness, he gazed at her, and the whole proceeding – with complete wonder. He couldn't recall seeing anyone – anywhere – at any time – light a gaslight before. As the light shone out, his spirits lifted. Now I can start living, he thought.

After the meal was over and cleared away, the three of them sat around the fire. The first thing they agreed on was that he had to have a name.

"We can't go on calling you....nothing. Can we?"

"I suppose not, but what can I say? What would you like to call me?" He looked into the lovely eyes again, and then at Aunt Mary.

"Jonathan," Aunt Mary said, "What about that? It's a good name."

Laura said the name over.

"Or William," Aunt Mary's voice came again.

"No – it's not quite right, I don't know why, but they're just not right."

Suddenly Aunt Mary jumped to her feet.

"My goodness, with all the excitement of the day, I nearly forgot that I promised to sit with Ted Davis for an hour or so 'til May gets back."

As she was talking she was rushing about the room.

"Now look you two, this name business must be sorted out by the time that I get back." Looking into the mirror and adjusting the angle of her hat, she went on "We'll have a deal of work to do on Monday morning – registering the lad with the police, and all the paperwork that goes with it, as well as all the questions. We must at least have a name, just for the time being of course…but I'm sure it won't be very long before you recall your own…still, 'til then…I'll call in at the Police Station again on my way back, just to see if they have heard anything more about…" She looked at him…"Mr X," she said.

And they all laughed as she went out of the door.

They sat in the stillness of the room, looking into the fire. Laura was the first to speak.

"I belong to the Salvation Army. Do you remember me in my uniform last night?" He nodded. She went on, "I must ask you, do you know about God?"

Without any hesitation he answered her at once,

"Yes."

Then she went on,

"Are you familiar with the Bible?"

Again he answered her with assurance.

"Well, not word for word, but yes, miraculously, I do recall things, and I know I have a faith in God."

"Well then", said Laura "what about a name from the Good Book? Any suggestions for yourself?"

Whilst he was thinking, Laura took the poker and prodded the fire; making way for some new pieces of coal that she took out of a brass bucket with a long pair of tongs.

The fire, still hot, was blackened by the new coal, and seemed to resent the new intruders, and set about the task of removing them from the glowing furnace. It spat and hissed, and moved the position of the shiny black lumps. At last one piece fell down, out of it's position, on to the hearth with a loud crack. Laura's voice brought him out of his thoughts, and back to reality.

"Oh! Quick." He leaned towards the tongs, took them, and quickly replaced the coal, tapping it down. This time it stayed in place.

"Well?" she said, "Have you thought?"

He nodded,

"What about Simon?"

Laura said the name aloud a few times.

"Simon, Simon…yes, I like it, it's just right for you. Hello Simon."

"Hello Laura, so very pleased to meet you."

They both laughed, and then fell into silence. Once again Laura spoke first.

"Now we need a surname…any idea for that?"

He shook his head.

"Well, I've an idea, don't laugh, will you? What about Moon? After all that is where I found you, albeit you were flat on your back at the time!"

Resting her elbows on her knees, she cupped her chin in her hands and looked at his face for his reaction. She went on,

"Simon Moon. I like the sound of it. What do you think?"

"Simon Moon…Simon Moon….yes I like the sound of it too. That's me then….Simon Moon. Do you think your Aunt Mary will approve?"

As he awaited her reply, he inclined his head in her direction. It was a movement that she would get used to in the weeks, and months to come. But at this moment, he reminded her of a cheeky bird, with it's head on one side whilst awaiting a crumb.

She thought, the only crumbs he will get are the crumbs of his memory. I pray that I can help him to catch the crumbs so he may be made whole again. She placed a gentle kiss on his forehead and looking into his face, lightened now by a small smile, said,

"Yes, I know she will…Simon Moon."

Sunday Morning

The doctor came and went. The two pieces of information he gave to Simon were, as he put it,….."not very helpful". They were: one, that he estimated his age to be approximately eighteen years, therefore, his birth was about nineteen-twenty-one, and two, that he may be permanently deaf in his right ear. He went on to say that there were some more tests that he wanted to do, but that he mustn't get too hopeful about the results.

All three of them talked over what the doctor had said once he had gone. They all decided it was quite useful to be able to choose one's own birthday and agreed that it was no good worrying about his deaf ear. The doctor could be wrong and even if he were not there was really nothing they could do about it.

Laura turned to him, and trying to keep her voice as cheerful as possible said,

"As it's Sunday morning, I usually go to church about now…would you like to come? I will quite understand if you say no."

“Yes, I’ll come if I can stay with you all the time. I don’t know anything about the service though.”

“Oh don’t worry about that and, or course, you can stay with me.”

With a smile she left the room, closely followed by Aunt Mary.

He stood up and looked at himself in the mirror. It was quite a sight. It was then that he realised that he didn’t even know his own face properly, for a stranger was looking at him. It looked thin, and the livid red graze made it look white, showing up the bad bruising down the side from temple to jaw. His neck protruded from his shirt collar, rather like a bird craning for food from the nest. The nest, he then concluded, was tipped up and placed on the top of his head, for the brown coloured hair, was sticking out in all directions. In fact, a bird’s nest would be neater. He patted it down best way that he could.

“Well, my friend,” he spoke to his reflection, “you were born on a January day in 1939 aged believe it or not, eighteen years, or thereabout. You have no parents, at the moment, you don’t know who you are – where you are- you have no memory, and I have no idea if you have a job.”

He broke off his soliloquy to turn his right ear to the clock. He covered his left ear and listened. Then he put his hand down, and continued his speech... “and you are completely deaf in your right ear."

Before he could continue, Laura returned, dressed in her uniform. Her eyes were shining. She looked so beautiful, he thought.

“Shall we go?” she said, offering her hand to him.

With gratitude he took it, and then her arm.

“I know what I have though…” he said aloud to the mirror, whilst Laura stood looking puzzled…”the prettiest friend ever.”

New World – New Beginning *August 1939*

It was a whole new world to Simon. The day seven months ago that he had started working in the little grocer's shop had been nerve-racking.

He had learned how to weigh and pack sugar and currants, cut and wrap cheese and butter, and make up orders. He had to sort orders at first because he had no knowledge of, or had forgotten, all about...money. Now after seven months he understood everything about it, from the white flimsy, fivers, to the pennies, halfpennies and farthings. Tanners, half-crowns and ten-bob notes held no fears for him now. It was as if he had always had the knowledge. Mr. B and his wife Rosie, had been very kind and understanding towards him as he had struggled in the first few weeks and had done all they could to help him.

His cheery disposition when he made his bike deliveries made him a welcome figure in the neighbourhood and, in fact, Mr. Bartholomew (Mr. B. for short), the owner of the shop, was sure that sales had gone up since he had arrived on the scene.

Rosie had a soft spot for Simon, he was a helpful and pleasant boy, and more than that – he made her laugh.

On the whole Simon found that life was good, but he couldn't help but be worried about all the talk of war. He honestly didn't understand it, and so was apprehensive about the future, but what about the past?

He knew no more about his past today, than he did all those months ago when he had first met Laura. He still reported regularly to the local police station (by now they knew him very well) and although they could shed no light on his missing relations, they always had a cheerful word for him and encouraged him.. "to look on the bright side." In fact, everywhere he went in Amleth, the people were always co-operative and friendly towards him.

On the evenings that Aunt Mary and Laura were at the Salvation Army, Simon found great enjoyment in exploring the locale in more detail. He seemed to learn something new every day and he didn't feel so much of an outsider any more.

It was Thursday, early closing day.

"You can go off Simon, when you have finished with the biscuits. I'm staying on with Rosie this afternoon to do a bit of stock-taking, but there is no need for you to, so you can cut along."

Mr. B. was wiping down the bacon-slicer's blades as he was speaking, concentrating hard not even raising his head as he spoke.

"Thanks Mr. B." he said, putting the lids on and thumping them to make sure they were on tight, "I was planning a lazy stroll this afternoon but by the look of the weather it's not going to stay fine for long" he added glancing out of the window.

The day was warm but overcast, and did look dismal. He stepped back and looked at the biscuit tins. There was a whole row of them, each one tilted at an angle to enable the customers to view the contents. The succulent aroma from each one was now gone, locked in until tomorrow. He was quite proud of his tidy counter and always made sure that it was just so, before he left for the day.

Because it was early closing, there were not very many people about. Simon looked up the hill to the main town. There was a tram coming down whining and swaying. By the time it had reached him it had started to brake, and he could see that it was nearly empty. The driver was standing stiffly at the controls turning the loudly clicking driving handle with one hand. Two woman were seated in the middle, and at the other end the conductor was hanging out, trying to catch as much of the breeze as was possible, whilst holding on tightly.

It clicked and clanged, screeching to a halt almost opposite Simon. He saw an elderly couple with a handicapped child clamber aboard and then the bell tinged and it whined away; gathered speed, and was soon out of sight, the sound remaining long after it had disappeared.

Today the pavements were hot, and there was very little breeze. He walked slowly past the fish shop, and although the shutters were down, the smell of the fish hung on the air, unpleasantly pungent.

Passing the large newsagents on the corner he crossed the wide road. As he stepped onto the pavement on the other side there was a loud ringing behind him. He turned and saw the smiling face of a young man who was pedalling a Walls 'Stop-me-and-buy-one' tricycle. His cap and uniform looked uncomfortable and the brown leather money pouch seemed to add to his discomfort as he chinked his way to a stop beside Simon, looking decidedly hot and bothered.

"Phew! It's hot work pushing these pedals round in this sort of weather. Sometimes I wish I could get in the box with the ice-cream"

"Good idea if you could do it." Simon commiserated whilst fishing in his pocket for some money.

"I'll have a twopenny one please, it may help to cool me down."

The young man pushed his cap back, took the money and dropped it into the leather bag. Then he flipped the lid of the ice box up, and as he did a swirl of smoke rose up into the warm, still air, cooling his face momentarily, as he reached inside for the ice cream bar. As the thick lid thudded shut, he gave a quick,

"Cheerio" and was soon gone.

Simon continued until he reached the Co-op, the largest and tallest shop on the block.

There was a milk depot at the rear and he could hear the chink, chink of the bottles as they were loaded and unloaded. Then he reached the clothing department windows, and looked in. There, resplendent in the middle of the window, was the matronly-round faced vision of...'the model'. It was the only model that the Co-op had ever possessed he was sure. He loved to see her clothing change from week to week.

There she stood, as usual, stiff and straight. The bland smiling face, with brown painted hair that moulded into stiff waves around it ended symmetrically at her perfect little ears. The eyes, wide and pale blue, had brown painted lashes, giving the face a constant surprised expression and the lips with perfect bows were painted bright orange clashing horribly with the totally unreal pink cheeks. Simon stared at her and in response she stared back although really looking nowhere and seeing nothing for all her effort. The body that matched the head seemed too large in proportion, and too matronly for the cupid bow, Simon thought. The right arm was crooked in front of her body, the left one was at her side. This attitude was never changed. This week she was a nurse. She had a white triangle tied low on to her forehead, the red cross centred between her eyebrows. Her dress was blue, matching those sightless eyes, and she had a large white bib fronted apron on, emblazoned with a large red cross. In the fingers of her crooked arm, she held a thermometer . rather precariously, and the whole window display was bedecked with bandages and safety pins.

Admittedly, there was a sign at her feet telling people to join the Red Cross, with times and places, but that was not enough - there had to be a focal point – but Simon could hardly believe his eyes when he saw it. It was a focal point alright – it was a bedpan! Propped at an angle against one of the 'Nurse's' legs. Simon could hardly control himself, he leaned against the window shaking with laughter. Then he stood back in mock admiration.

"I love it," he said aloud, "You're wonderful, I'm speechless." He was still chuckling as he crossed the main road, throwing her a kiss as he did so.

He walked through the park gates, and made his way to one of his favourite spots, a fish pond with a central fountain. He sat down on a bench seat. It was quiet and peaceful and the fountain's gentle splashing had a restful, mesmeric effect on him. He sat there for some time, getting rather introspective and maudlin. All sorts of things found themselves slipping in and out of his thoughts but, of course, inevitably he came back to his own life. Aunt Mary and Laura were as kind as could be and he loved them both dearly, but sometimes he still felt unsure of himself, and desperately lonely. Now he had war rumours to cope with too. Whether there was a war or not posed the same question. What would happen to him?

A peacock strutted in front of him on the grass, it's long tail dragging behind it, its beauty hidden from view.

The peacock's tail remained unfurled, just as his past still remained a mystery for – try as he may, he could remember nothing before last January ....He gave a little shudder as he thought, as he often did, of what would have become of him had Laura not been there to help him on that awful night.

The weather was still oppressive. It was warm, but the clouds had closed in, low and brooding. Even the breeze, which was slowly growing in power, could do nothing to shift the dark blanket above their heads, hanging like some gigantic bird of prey.

"We're in for a good storm, I think."

Simon was suddenly aware of a voice close by. He looked up and saw a Park Keeper walking towards him, his ginger-brown uniform looking hot and uncomfortable.

"I said, we're in for a storm soon I think."

"Yes, I think you're right", he said looking up at the sky "and I've only just come in here. Where do the peacocks go if it rains?"

"Oh, they usually fly up into the large trees behind you."

"Fly? I didn't know that they could fly."

'Oh my goodness yes...I won't be having them here for very much longer though, because of this damn war that's coming."

"You think there will be a war then?"

"Yes I do, 'orrible 'itler will see to that. My 'powers that be' must think so too, they are going to ship the birds down to a safe haven,

somewhere in Dorset, so make the most of them." He looked very sad as he said the words.

The peacock strutted off to join its mate under the trees as they had been speaking and Simon, watching its sedate progress, noticed the sky, that was darkening by the minute. He stood up.

"I think that I'd better get going."

"I should, and be quick about it, I think we are in for a good downpour, and at least I've a large hat …and a hut."

Simon smiled as he turned and ran up the path through the iron gates and out on to the street. Large drops of rain had started to fall on the hot pavements by this time, making them look like they were covered with brown pennies.

"Pennies from heaven," thought Simon, and he started to hum the tune to himself….

"Every time…it rains it rains…"

The rain felt warm on his face as he ran, and with his jacket swaying limply in his hand, he made a dash for home. As time passed, the droplets grew more and more frenzied, and as they fell they penetrated his shirt and felt cool on his skin. By the time he reached home, there was a steady downpour and he could hear distant rumblings of thunder.

The lightening shot across the room as he closed the door behind him.

"Simon? Simon? Is that you? Oh I'm glad that you're home." Laura's voice greeted him.

"Yes, it's me…and I'm very wet…just look at me." She studied his bedraggled state. Suddenly there was a loud clap of thunder. Simon covered his ears and slumped to his knees, thinking that his head was about to burst…Laura was at his side at once, flinging the towel that she was carrying around his shoulders before crossing to the windows to pull the curtains. As she was pulling them, a flash shot through filling the room with blinding light. Although Laura's eyes were shut she still saw the brilliance of the flash through her closed lids. At once there was another deafening peel. Quickly she ran to Simon's side crouching beside him and putting her arms around his shoulders.

She could see that the storm was having a devastating effect on him. He sat motionless on the floor, his face frozen into a mask…of sheer terror. Another tremendous crash hurled itself into the room and enveloped the two figures, quickly followed by another bright flash of lightning.

Simon shuddered, so she tightened her grip to reassure him

"It's only a storm love, it will soon pass."

Another violent crash rent their ears. The storm was now overhead, for the thunder and lightening were almost simultaneous.

"It must pass over soon," she thought.

"Aunt Mary always says that it's God way of saying He's angry with the world."... She knew she was only making small talk, but anything to try to take Simon's mind off what was happening was worth a try she thought.

At last, after what seemed an eternity, the storm finally started to abate. The crashes started to turn into benign rumbles, the rain eased off and the lightening faded away. Ominous rumblings could still be heard, but in the distance now.

Simon moved, and sat on the edge of a chair, his shirt still plastered on his skin. His face was ashen.

"Laura, I was...terrified.. I've never felt like that before and the pain in my ear was ...was just terrible."

'Don't worry, dear, there are a lot of people like you..they go and hide in cupboards, or under the stairs...and some get into bed and cover their heads over. It was the first storm that you've been in wasn't it?"

Simon nodded.

"Go and get changed, and don't worry about feeling so bad." She put her arms around him to reassure him once again.

"It's over dear, it's all over."

But as she spoke, she noticed a small trickle of blood running out of his deaf ear...

Book 1 – Chapter 2
A Set-back *January 1985*

Christmas came and went...Then early in the new year Peter's father had a setback. One morning before Peter had left the house, his father had another stroke.

After the doctor's examination, it was decided that it would be best for him to spend a while in hospital.

The arrangements had been made, and after they had seen for themselves that the old man was in good hands, they left him and made their way back home again.

In the car Angela didn't speak.

She felt empty. The worry of the past few months suddenly manifesting itself in silent, copious tears.

Once at home, Peter took off Angela's coat and helped her up to their bedroom. It was late afternoon and watery sunlight was filtering in through the windows. Angela kicked off her shoes and lay down. She closed her eyes, covering them with one of her arms and allowing the other one to drop in listless fashion over the side of the bed. Peter came and knelt beside her, taking the loose hand into both of his own.

The sun gave one last burst of light on to the still and silent couple. The only sounds in the room were the quiet ticking of a clock, and their breathing.

When at last Peter bent his head to her hand, she moved the arm that had been covering her face and laid it gently on his shoulder.

"I will miss him so Peter, will he ever come home again to us? He looked so frail and still in hospital."

Peter sat on the edge of the bed, still holding her hand.

"I don't know m'luv, he is in the Lord's hands at the moment, and out of ours...isn't he? They fell silent again.

"I've been selfish...I've been thoughtless, so close yet so far from you, letting you take so much of the responsibility for father...I've stood by and let you give so much of yourself...to us both. I'm ashamed.." he concluded.

"But…but I love you both so much," she broke down sobbing, "I know why I'm so upset Peter, I'm crying not just for your father…but for…me. He's like a baby to me, the baby that we have never had…" She spoke in a soft voice, her words catching as she said, "I love him…as I would a ….baby….and now he has been ….taken from me, from us, the hollowness is so painful." Her sobs were less intense now, as she turned her face towards him. She looked into his eyes.

"Tell me Peter, will he ever come home to us again? Will he?"

She looked towards him with expectation, and he felt inadequate; so helpless to cope with this dear, sweet person in front of him. He loved her so much, and hated to see her so distressed. What could he truthfully say, in answer to her question without building up her hopes too much. Only to perhaps have them smashed again.

"I don't know the answer to your question any more than we know the answer to his. I wish I knew the answer to both of them m'luv. The one thing I do know for sure though is that I'm going to get Kenneth Reynor to replace me for a few days, and I'm going to take you out of this house."

He saw her worried expression in response to his words, and so he quickly went on,

"Just to give you a rest m'luv, so that we will both be able to cope more readily, if….when he comes home again."

She seemed to accept what he was saying,

"Yes maybe we should get away for a bit, just so that I can be refreshed for his homecoming."

The room was sunless now, and they sat, arms entwined around each other in the gathering gloom. Angela's head was leaning on her husband's broad shoulder.

"We will find the answer for him…won't we?" she said.

"I will do my best," he looked at her and corrected himself, "We will do our best, won't we? If only we knew the question…that elusive question. If only we knew we might be able to find the answer for him. We must find the answer…we must." He added.

"Together we will, I know we will." Angela added, smiling for the first time that afternoon.

They did get away. Their friends, Martin and Phillipa Blake had let them borrow their small country cottage in York. It was nothing grand they had told them, just a place to get away from it all, a place to relax and let your spirits soar, a quiet retreat from the hurly burly of usual life. They first saw the cottage through the trees as they drove up a narrow lane. Although it was winter the scenery was still beautiful and quite different from the murkiness that sometimes surrounded 'Oasis' at this time of the year.

As they left the car and made their way to the front door Angela had the feeling that this was going to be a special place. A retreat indeed. Outside it was bitter cold, but inside it was warm and comfortable, Martin had said it would be all ready for them and Phillipa had instructed them to take nothing but personal things, as everything else would be there. Their friends had not exaggerated in any way, and the lady that they had an arrangement with in the village had done them proud, even to the extent of leaving a posy of spring flowers on the table.

"Oh Peter, it's just lovely…."

"Yes, I think it is just what we both need, and it's what you especially have been in need of for quite a while." He opened his arms and Angela snuggled into them, nodding in agreement.

Now that the pressure was off her, she realised for the first time, just how tense she must have been for the past few weeks. She had been under enormous pressure, and now that had been taken away, she felt quite strange, as calmness and freedom started taking over.

After a light meal they sat for a long time talking in the warm, cosy kitchen. Peter cleared the supper things away whilst Angela was in the bathroom, and then he sat down again at the table, where he rested his head in his hands. There were small unaccustomed sounds – water running through pipes, and gurgling away through unseen hollows, and a clock ticking away somewhere; but Peter heard none of it; he sat motionless for a good five minutes, before he stood. He went to the back door and opened it, stepping outside into the cold.

He stood looking up into the night sky, alive and brilliant with a myriad of stars, stars so low that he felt he could touch them. Suddenly he saw a shooting star, visible in the inky blackness for only a second, and then invisible for eternity. The moon, that had been hidden by the corner of the house slipped quietly into view, flooding the garden as does the sunlight during the day. The row of spruce trees at the edge of the lawn, were silhouetted like a line of black spears, pointed to the heavens.

A light went on inside the cottage, and was extinguished again. Peter's train of thought had been broken, so he turned back into the kitchen, locked the door behind him, flipped the light switch off, and made his way up the twisting stairs.

After a while he entered the room where Angela lay, he found her propped up on a flowery pillow, with her eyes closed. The small table lamp was glowing softly, throwing shadows into the room. Peter pulled back the curtains and looked out. The moon was shining as if it were made of polished silver, dimming even some of the brighter stars. Angela put out the light. The moon's luminous rays filtered in, and she too could catch a glimpse of the stars.

"What a wonderful sky," he said.

"Come to bed now Peter....please. I still have the funny feeling that I should be somewhere else, and doing something else.........I'm so disorientated at the moment. Come and hold me....I feel so lonely."

He crossed the room seeing his way by the moon's light.

"Yes, I feel the same as you m'luv." So saying, he joined her in the large bed, pulled the covers up around them and held Angela in his arms next to his heart.

They took comfort one from the other, and allowed their earthly worries to fade away into the night. The moon shone on. Until at last, it too faded and made way for a bright new day.

Book 2 – Chapter 2
New World at War *August 1939*

It was August 1939, and there was political unrest at home and abroad. The names of Chamberlain and Churchill were on people's lips constantly. The other name frequently heard more and more was that of the German Chancellor, Herr Hitler.

One thing now seemed inevitable. War. Laura, a schoolteacher was not involved in the first great wave of conscription, but many women of her age had been sent to work in one of the local armament factories. Others had been moved to the country to become workers in the Women's Land Army.

At the moment though, Laura's occupation was exempt from war work. She was, however, extremely busy at school, with the organisation of the evacuation of the children. The Salvation Army were working flat out too, so she was kept very busy.

Very reluctantly Aunt Mary was preparing to go to her only brother, who lived in the country. He was eighty-nine years old, lived by himself since his wife had died some seven years earlier, and was absolutely terrified at the thought of another war.

Fortunately, Simon was a strong young man now, and Aunt Mary knew that both he and Laura would make a formidable couple. She knew that they would uphold one another, and took comfort from that.

Now the time had come, and Laura and Simon were seeing her off at the station. They stood waiting for the whistle to blow, for the departure of the train. Aunt Mary, leaning out of the Ladies Only carriage, kissed them both vigorously, not wanting to leave them….but knowing that she had to, for although she had known Simon for only nine months, he was almost as dear to her now, as Laura herself. The guard blew his whistle, and waved his flag, the train gave a violent jolt and started to move slowly away from the platform.

Aunt Mary's eyes filled with tears, and Laura had her handkerchief to her own already. The calls became louder and more urgent as each second passed and the train's speed increased.

"Goodbye…."

"Take care…."

"Write soon…."

"God Bless…."

All three of them seemed to be talking at once.

Aunt Mary stood at the window watching the fluttering handkerchief, until the train rounded the bend and the trees obscured her view. Then grasping the thick, wide leather strap, she pulled the window up halfway, the train lurching her back and forth.

Finally the momentum of the train and one last jerk of the wheels, helped her to sink down into her seat. She looked back at the two large bags that Simon had stowed, and the small bunch of everlasting flowers that he had given her, and felt the hot burning in her eyes getting worse. Hastily she started to rummage in the depths of her voluminous bag, not quite seeing what she was doing.

The carriage was empty, which was just as well, for Aunt Mary was the last person in the world to make an exhibition of herself – especially in front of complete strangers. However, had it been full it would undoubtedly have made no difference on this occasion – for now it was time for Aunt Mary to bury her head in her handkerchief.

Activity in Amleth was unprecedented, it went on day and night. The large trees that lined the main road, looked like they were having their party dresses put on, for they were having gigantic white cummerbunds painted around their girths. The trees were not the only things to have decoration, for white paint was soon adorning the edges of the pavements, steps and doorways.

There seemed to be painting going on everywhere. The large stencilled letter S, was soon a familiar sight on the fronts and sides of shelters. There was a great feeling of expectation – but not the pleasant kind, unfortunately.

Simon's job at the moment was putting brown sticky tape in a criss-cross pattern across all the windows of the shop, it was an arm aching job, not to say a bit messy. He did what he was asked – but neither he, nor anybody – knew exactly what was going on, nor what to expect next.

There was, however, a friendly ambience about, with people caring about each other, more than they had done in the past.

Sandbags sprung up from nowhere overnight and stood in neat piles in various strategic places. An air-raid siren, high up on a pole, had been in place on a spare piece of ground; next to a group of houses, before the outbreak, majestically surveying the only small patch of grass visible in the cluster of houses. Now even that was gone, under the Air Raid Warden's Post, and extra Police Station.

All three structures were surrounded to a depth of some twelve feet by the cleverly stacked, fat sand bags. The bottom ones tended to split and release the bright orange sand, allowing it to spill out, to the joy of passing children, who, Simon noticed, kicked or played with it at every opportunity.

Today both he and Laura were at the Town Hall, to collect their gas masks, identity cards, and ration books. Although all the things were in different departments, they both hoped to get everything at one fell swoop. So did many others! They spent the day, or so it seemed, in endless queues!

"Simon Moon really is a person now," he thought when he saw his name on his ration book. It was emblazoned for all the world to see. Simon Moon, followed by his address, the only one he knew. He flipped the pages of the book, and saw numbers and figures all in little boxes. He would get to know this book, and many just like it in the weeks and months to come.

Laura was speaking, she touched his arm and he inclined his head in her direction.

"Let's get back now, I must finish off the black out curtains or we will be in real trouble."

They came out of the Town Hall and ran down the steps, crossing the road and joining the queue for a tram. There were quite a few people already there and most of them were looking at their new acquisitions. The woman in front of them turned around after perusing hers.

"I reckon this is the real thing, now that they have given us these," she said as she tapped the top of the cardboard gas mask case with her ration book, "don't you?"

She didn't wait for an answer from them, because the clanking of the approaching tram took all her attention, as it came winging its way up the hill.

It stopped opposite them, and the conductor jumped down, undid the leading rein that held the black electrified pole securely above them, and pulled it away from its moorings: causing it to spark in protest; before walking, rein firmly in hand, to the other end of the tram, where he released the pole, allowing the coupler to jump with a jolt onto the downhill wire. He completed his task by anchoring the rein before jumping once again on to the running board.

The tram slowly moved over to Simon and Laura's side of the road. The methodical thud, thud of the seat backs being turned by the conductor to face down the hill, could be plainly heard (as well as his whistling rendition of..."You are my sunshine"....) telling them that it was almost time to mount the high step for the short ride home.

Laura was talking to the conductor, but Simon was watching the world pass by outside the window, just the odd ping, from the ticket punch distracted him a little, but the noise was not great enough to pervade his thoughts completely.

He looked into the clear sky, and wondered if the first real taste of war would come from there. Of course, he realised that it had to, but the sky looked so innocent. What horrors was it going to hide he thought? There was still no chance of his being called up like the other young men of his age. The blow to his head had seen to that so he would have to be content to do his war service on the home front at Amleth.

War, what would it really mean to Laura and himself?

Would it change their lives so very much? He was musing over all the possibilities when the tram screeched, and finally came to a halt. They managed to alight together with Simon gallantly holding her arm.

Mr. Chamberlain had failed to reach an agreement with the German Chancellor, Herr Hitler, and therefore England was at war with Germany.

After the declaration was announced on Sunday morning, the 3rd September 1939, there was an alarm. Simon rushed Laura to the newly planted shelter in the garden and there they sat, in that cold and dismal place, not knowing what to expect – and not knowing what to say to one another – so they just sat in silence – waiting.......

At last they heard the wail of the all clear, and nothing seemed to have happened. It later proved to be a false alarm on that first occasion. However, not knowing true from false, nobody took any chances.

The phoney war, once entered, seemed to continue........

Shooting at Stars

Book 1 – Chapter 3
Respite and Return

The telephone call that Peter made to the hospital the next morning was very encouraging. His father having had a good night was making excellent progress.

The Sister, who knew Peter well, had said that his father was improving steadily, and was on form once more, for, since he was able to communicate to them again, he was asking his 'old question', repeatedly! In fact she was of the opinion that it was probably this overriding, all powerful need for an answer, that had pulled him around and kept him going. Providing he maintained the progress that he was making at the moment, she felt sure that he would be able to go home at the end of the week.

Much relieved, Peter finished the conversation, and made his way into the kitchen, where Angela was waiting. She stood looking out across the garden. Her heart was pounding, and she was dreading what Peter might say. He crossed swiftly to her side, put his arms around her shoulders and said,

"Father's come out of the stroke Angela…thank God."

He felt the tension fall away from her taut frame as she turned and faced him. She put her arms around his neck and when she looked into his face, he could see that her eyes were shining with unshed tears.

"You mean he can come home again?"

"Yes, in a few days time, a week at the most."

"Oh darling, I'm so glad. I just couldn't imagine home being home, without your father."

"And I'm as pleased as you too, but we're going to make the most of the next few days, m'love. Do you realise that this is the first break that we have had together for a long time? Now that I have you all to myself, I'm going to make the most of you." He kissed the tip of her nose.

She responded with a kiss of her own, on his lips. Then she smiled and said,

"I 'can't believe that I don't have to share you with anyone either. I'm going to enjoy being with you, and having you, selfishly all to myself."

Time passed very quickly for them, and soon the days of respite were rapidly ending. Since the 'phone calls they had been making to the hospital had brought nothing but good news, they were able to put away difficulties, and enjoy their diminishing hours without worry. Now, on the last day, they found themselves refreshed, for the unaccustomed freedom of the past few days had renewed them greatly.

They found that they could talk about father objectively, and about the problems they would have to encounter on their return home. One decision was that they must make every attempt, and use every idea at their disposal to find an answer for him. At least trying in a positive manner would give hope and encourage them to go forward. Then, one day in the not too distant future, those ideas might, just might, give father his long awaited answer. They had tried contacting old colleagues of his, some time back – but that had proved fruitless. Although the gentleman that had dealt with them had been understanding and sympathetic, (unfortunately), there was little that he could do for them. Some of his friends it transpired, had been killed quite early on in the war, and there were no others alive, who could be of any help to them.

So now they had to think of some other forms of detective work to help. Just to dismiss the old man's question as a mere figment of his imagination was just too cruel to contemplate. With these things on their minds, they prepared to leave their quiet haven.

She looked back once as they left. The cottage was dappled with sunlight, and serene…a serenity that she felt at the moment herself.

They didn't speak much on the journey home. Silence for them was truly golden.

When she saw Peter's car coming up the driveway with father, her heart gave a leap. No matter what sort of heartache he gave them, he was still a dear old man.

Once inside the house, Angela was quickly in the old routine, but of course Peter was here tonight, and with his help father was soon in his room once more, and from all they could tell, happy. On strict instructions from the hospital, he had to have a sleeping draught to help him get over the trip, and to settle him for the night, so Angela stayed with him. His frail frame seemed to be as delicate as ever, but his eyes….

He started to fall asleep quite quickly whilst looking into Angela's face. Yet, even with his eyes closing he was painstakingly asking his old question.

"What...is...the...answer?"

She kissed him lightly on the forehead, and quietly left the room.

When she arrived downstairs she found Peter had dragged out a few unopened boxes that they had been storing, ever since father had come to live with them. No time like the present, she thought, as she crossed to him hoping that the anticipation she felt was not too premature. Peter had opened one of them. He was sitting in an easy chair with the boxes at his side; the open one revealed that it was full of books. He had taken some out already, examining each with care.

"Nothing to report at the moment", he said tipping yet another book, leaves down and shaking it.

"Early days, darling, early days." She came and sat on the floor next to him, and started to sort through the other box.

"Hello, what's this then?" she said as she tipped a book downwards and something pink fluttered out. Peter looked at her with anticipation.

"Oh, it's only a ticket," she went on as she held it in her fingers, up to the light, and peered through the hole that was punched in it. Although it was undoubtedly old, it looked new, but she thought, probably its only claim to fame , was that at one time it had been used as a bookmark. However, it was just a ticket – an old relic, so she put it carefully back into the book once more, knowing that it was of no use to them in their search.

Peter looked disappointed and a little defeated.

"I suppose it was too much to ask for so soon."

"We will find something I'm sure, just keep on looking.'

They both resumed their task, the pile of books growing higher as they inspected each one with care. By nine fifteen two boxes of books had been examined in detail and they all proved to be of no help in their quest. The third box was just bric-a-brac and of no importance at all.

The last box they were going to look at tonight was smaller than the other three. Peter held it on his lap, and saw that it was well taped up.

"Before we open this one I'll go and make us a cup of coffee, shall I?"

"Good idea m'love, we need something to keep us going."

"Before I do though, I'm going to peep in on father."

"Shall I go and do that?"

"No, don't worry, it will only take me a moment love."

Peter looked at the box and turned it over in his hands. It was made of silvery cardboard, the silver had long since tarnished and flaked off in places, leaving large patches of brown cardboard showing and the tape was drawn tightly around the body of the box. He tried to run his fingernail along it to find a weak spot – but couldn't. It looks as if it has no beginning or end, he thought to himself. He heard Angela in the kitchen and called out to her.

"I need the scissors m'love, this one just doesn't want to be opened."

"Don't worry, I'll bring them with me, I'm just about to come anyway."

Minutes later, they were both looking at the box.

"I'm sure I recognise this one, or at least feel I should, but I just can't remember what's in it."

He took the scissors and cut with great difficulty into the tight tape, first on one side and then on the other. Then all at once the lid shot into the air as if propelled by a bullet, or as if a spring had pushed it upwards; taking with it a flurry of photographs.

Angela gave a little gasp as they tumbled at her feet and into her lap.

"Well….that was a surprise, if you like."

"Of course, how stupid of me, I remember now, of course…of course, it was the old snaps box. I remember it from when I was a boy. Of course…of course." He bent down and collected the photographs that had showered over them both in the explosion, and Laura did the same.

"I've never seen so many in one place before, Peter, there must be a hundred here. How on earth they all fitted into such a small box I'll never know. It's a mystery to me!"

After they had finished their coffee, they started to look at the photographs in more detail. Some had writing on the back, usually in pencil…and usually unreadable.

There were pictures of smiling men and women, none of whom Peter recognised, except those of his mother and father, and his grandparents. There were a great many of children and groups, and a few landscapes, of places he knew not. There were some glossy prints that had cracked, and some even older ones in a sepia finish. Smiling faces of friends and relatives, Peter guessed.

One picture in particular caught Angela's eye. It was of Peter's mother and father on their wedding day.

"Your father was a good looking man in those days darling, they made a lovely couple."

"Well, that's where I get all my good looks from don't you know", he added, giving her a wink, and touching the 'distinguished ' hair at his temples.

"There's just one thing," she said, trying to keep a straight face, "I don't see even a teensy weency sign of …" she broke off and pointed to his stomach, "in the picture of this handsome man."

Peter laughed and looked at the print again.

"Do you think that father would prefer this one of him with mother to the one that he has?"

"Oh no, I don't think so, look." She held out a copy of the one that was in the frame. It was smaller and had obviously been in a wallet for it was quite dog-eared, "I think he loves that one best, don't let's change it."

They went through the box meticulously and scanned photograph after photograph on both sides. They both longed to find something that would help them.

They faced the fact that they didn't know exactly what they were looking for. After all, when you were looking for a needle in a haystack, at least you knew what the needle looked like! However, they were more determined than ever to find that elusive something, or someone, that seemed so near….yet so far….They both had the overwhelming feeling that they would find the answer, they had to, for all their sakes, and with God on their side they would succeed.

Now, here she was with the old man again. Sometimes she felt quite guilty…for even thinking…"Is there any answer?" Then she would push those rather negative thoughts out of her mind, as she always concluded,

"Yes…there is an answer…somewhere…"

She gazed at the questioning face that was before her. She dropped down on one knee.

"What…is…the…answer?"

"Soon dear….we'll know soon…"

Book 2 – Chapter 3
The Meeting *October 1939*

Although there had been odd sightings of mysterious vapour trails in the sky and puffs of cloud, the war had not taken hold properly yet. Everyone was very aware of the tense situation, but life had to go on.

The barrage balloons sent up when a raid was imminent, became part of the new skyline by day, and the searchlight beams the accustomed sight in the night.

Many schools were being evacuated with their teachers, and Laura's was no exception, but since there was no possibility of her going she happily transferred to a school where the children were not, for the moment, earmarked for the evacuee labels.

The carefree months before the declaration seemed to be in a different age and time – like a fast fading dream, and life had changed so quickly for Simon particularly in the ten months since he had arrived in Amleth.

His past was still an enigma to him, of course, the same old mystery that it had always been and no amount of searching either by his own efforts, or the efforts of the police and the Salvation Army, had brought forth any results, Laura had worked so hard for him in that respect, but all to no avail.

Nothing…. It seemed to Simon that he was not known to anyone, and worse, not missed by any other living soul. This fact weighed heavily on him if he gave himself time to dwell on it, and because of that he knew that he had to keep himself busy. He made friends easily and had a terrific sense of fun, which in the present dark days, helped when it came to taking his mind off his own troubles. He went to church with Laura, where he was popular and well liked. He willingly helped with all the ongoing war effort and projects that the church, and consequently Laura, were involved with; no matter whether it was street, house to house, salvage, clothes, or any other collections.

Laura knew that she could rely on him at all times and could not imagine life without – or before – him. Aunt Mary wrote often to them always imploring them to… 'take care of each other', for her, and they did because of the way they felt. For as well as the protectiveness over the past months they found they had a great deal in common when it came to their likes and dislikes and they never argued …well hardly ever!

They also had the knack of being able to judge each other's moods and actions and that alone enabled them to have a harmonious relationship. Added to which the consideration they felt for each other amounted to one thing – love. They did love each other, there was no doubt about that, but in brotherly and sisterly fashion. Because of this happy relationship, they were able to journey forward, and share their lives together.

More men had been called up, but Simon was still not in that category. Instead he was able to join the A.R.P., which entailed many and varied duties. Today, Thursday, had found him on the roof of the Co-op in the late afternoon. He had just finished his watch and after completing the hand-over, he ran down the four flights of stairs and walked to the front of the building. There, in all her glory, was his favourite model.

This week she was representing a member of the Women's Land Army by being dressed in breeches, shirt, pullover, round Baden Powell type hat and neckerchief. In her crooked fingers, the handle of a large garden fork had been pushed at an impossible angle. Simon looked at the black moulded shoes with a sensible heel that were fixed into a solid round base poking out, and smiled. The shoes could never be changed whatever her dress and so, of course today was no exception, and because socks and boots could not be put on the unmoveable feet, straw lay thickly around the offending imperfections – piled high in an effort to obtain the much hoped for invisibility, but, unfortunately, not reaching full submergence!

He looked again at the breeches and smiled,

"If the feet don't move, how on earth were they put on? He asked himself.

Determined to get to the bottom of this question, he moved his position to the side of the window. There was the answer staring him in the face. The window dresser must be some sort of genius without any doubt. He shook his head in disbelief. There were two pairs of breeches, pinned in strategic places; to give the impression of one pair.

"It's a good job they are so large", he thought, for, as a final touch, the dresser had pulled them out at the sides, giving the overall impression (unwittingly, of course,) of a clown!

He looked again at the enigmatic smile,

"You don't care do you? If you did, you wouldn't be smiling!"

Laura was in when Simon arrived home.

"Hello, how were the skies?"

"Fine when I left my post, no problems as far as I know, thank God...but if it's news you're after, well...I did see my favourite girl on the way home, you know the one I mean don't you? The one in the Co-op window."

"Oh no, not again." Laura grimaced.

"Yes...there she was, she's in the Land Army this week. Have you by any chance seen it...hem, I mean her?"

"No, I haven't had that pleasure yet." She said, trying hard to keep a straight face.

He put on a mock voice of adoration, and graphically went on to describe his favourite girl, in great detail. Then, only pausing long enough to give a stupid smile, he went on,

"Oh how handsome she looks standing there in her great clown's trousers and boy scout's hat."

Laura couldn't contain herself any longer, and she exploded into uncontrollable laughter.

"Stop it....please Simon, my ribs are aching..."

She flung herself onto the settee and buried her head in the cushion; trying to blot out his silly voice, and to stop herself from laughing. It was hopeless, Simon made a lunge for the offending cushion, his silly voice droning on.

"Come along, my dear, you know that you would like the whole outfit.."

He fell next to the giggling girl and it took them a few minutes to get their composure back

"If only Auntie could see us now," she smiled "she would think we were really bonkers, wouldn't she?"

"I don't know so much. I've a feeling that there would be three of us here, instead of two giggling, and being stupid. I only wish she were here with us, I miss, her don't you?"

"I do miss her.....especially her lovely bread pud"

"Oh you...you're hopeless," she threw another cushion in his direction as she went over to pull the blackout.

"Why so early?"

"So I don't fumble with them when I come home later. It's the last collection at the locals tonight – well for a while anyway. Will you come with me?"

"Of course I will, I don't like you going to some of them alone anyway ...and in the pitch dark too."

"Oh no, sorry your worship, what am I thinking of? How could I go without my shadow? By the way, can you guess where the last call will be?"

"Well, my pub of course, 'The Moon'."

"That's right," she said placing two collecting boxes on the table. "I'm going up to get changed now. You must wrap up too, it's quite foggy tonight."

"Perhaps old jerry will keep away then...here's hoping."

She went through the curtained door nodding in agreement as it closed behind her.

They set off at a good pace, and by the time they had reached the 'Moon', it was about eight thirty.

"We've done quite well, Simon, haven't we? Considering." She shook the box in her hand, it was quite weighty. "Even if it's all pennies there must be quite a few shillings here."

They entered the saloon bar, Simon clinking his box. He was a good collector, and most people gave something.

Laura walked before him through the door into the public bar, and went up to the landlord, speaking to him briefly. He inclined his head to the group of men at the far end of the bar when he answered her,

"Well, they're in fine form tonight Sister, although it's all rather sad. They have decided to abandon their club until the war's over, so it's their last match, for quite a while I reckon. Half the men have their call up papers now, and more have got to report tomorrow; so the few remaining – well, they just haven't the heart to go on. Never mind, the end of the match is in sight and I'm sure your collection box will do well – they're in good humour, considering, and, as you can hear, in high spirits."

Laura nodded as she made her way to the end of the bar. She stood on tiptoe behind the outer circle of men. She couldn't see very much even then, but the men saw her. Regular Joe detached himself from the nub of them and came and spoke to her.

"Hello Missie, here again with your old collecting box...all for a good cause though eh? Give us a bit o'time, and I guess we'll fill it up for you if you're lucky," he added, giving her a little nudge.

Then he turned round again and they both stood listening to the soft dib.. dib, of the darts as they hit the board.

Simon, whilst all this was going on, was standing back, surveying the scene and the other occupants of the bar.

There were three tables along the left side of the elongated room against the windows, that were draped in long widow's weeds; ensuring that not one chink of light exposed itself brazenly to the darkened street outside. The large group of men were at the end of the room and the highly polished bar ran the whole length to his right.

Seated at the table nearest the door were two army officers, deep in conversation. The second table was empty. The third had a young couple holding hands, with their heads together, and they were deeply engrossed with each other.

"Well, I'll just have to try my best with these four. I'll start at the front first," he said to himself, as he moved to the table and spoke to the couple. The man put his hand in his pocket at once, pulled out a handful of change, and put it into Simon's box. The woman didn't say a word, but just held on to her companion's other hand, as if it were fused to her own.

"Thanks chum," Simon said, "all the best to you."

"Thanks, you just caught me in time, I'm off tomorrow with the other lads," the man said, casting a glance at the sorrowful face of his companion. Simon could see that the young woman was very upset, so he made his way back up the room, leaving them to themselves.

He now turned his attention to the occupants of the first table. They were two youngish men in army uniform. They were wearing officers' clothes, Simon was sure, but of what rank, he had no idea. They looked up at his approach but at that moment there was a shout from the end of the room and all three of them looked in the direction of the darts players.

Stepping up to the table, holding his box, and the sheaf of 'War Crys' he offered both to them. They declined the paper, but at once put their hands into their pockets. One man dropped a couple of silver coins into the box. The other, taking out a brown ten-shilling note in his fingers, folded it carefully, then glancing up the room said,

"I think I would rather give it to the young lady, if you don't mind, old man." So saying, he stood up and walked to the group.

All went quiet, the end of the match was near… He stood silently for a split second before bending his head close to Laura's left ear, and whispering

"What's a nice girl like you doing in a place like this?"

She turned at once, surprised by his voice. She just had time to look into a pair of sparkling, clear eyes; shining out of a handsome face before she heard a tremendous roar behind her. As she had looked into those eyes she experienced something that she couldn't quite understand…She opened her mouth to speak, but before she could, she was swept up shoulder high, her arm sticking out at an awkward angle with the collecting box in her hand.

The soldier quickly put the ten-shilling note in, and then Laura was whisked away into the centre of the group, disappearing from his sight. The huddle of jostling men placed her gently before them.

"Well we won the match then Missie – so the 'Moon' men are best after all."

There were jocular calls behind him.

"Not for long mate."

"Only this time."

"We'll go and beat old Hitler, then we'll come back and beat you."

"Hear, hear." The losers all cheered at this last suggestion, and the winners willingly agreeing to accept their challenge with equal readiness.

"Now lads, quieten down…quiet…please." It was Regular Joe speaking,"the little lady has been very patient, let's make it worth her while, after all it's for a good cause."

He took Laura's box and held it aloft, and then passed it around.

The mood was jolly. Even the losers had now conceded gracefully – happily contributing to the collection.

"If I take your money now Joe, you won't be able to spend it on any more drink, will you? There's a method in it isn't there?"

"Well Missie, it won't be for the first time that you have stopped me…will it?" He looked over the heads to where Simon was standing…

"It was him not so long ago wasn't it? He stopped me having my last pint.."

Laura nodded and tried to see over the bobbing heads of the men in front of her. Then at last a gap appeared and she was able to make her way out of the merry throng. There was no one between her and Simon now.

The soldier had gone.

Simon watched, as the soldier folded the ten shilling note and walked the length of the room. He had seen him stop behind Laura and say something – something that had made her turn around.

"Oh no", the other soldier had said "we really haven't the time to get involved with girls, no matter how charitable they may be....no offence meant....in fact we should be going now," he said glancing down at his watch as he spoke. There was a beep from outside.

"That's for us," he said, jumping to his feet.....

At that same instant the great whoop of joy had rung out from the far end of the room. Simon had seen Laura swept up by the jubilant crowd of men, and the soldier depositing the money into the fast receding box in her hand. The soldier that had been at Simon's side had suddenly leapt to his feet, and was rushing forward towards his friend, saying,

"The taxi's here, here's your hat, let's go – and quick."

As they were hurriedly making for the door, the soldier with the bright eyes, looked from Simon to the other end of the room where Laura was, although invisible, and said,

"Tell her she's a knockout."

He never had time to say anything else, because he was pulled through the door and away.

Somewhere in England a train rumbled into the night. The carriage was full and quiet, for all the occupants seemed to be in a sombre mood.

The two friends sat together, one leaning his weight on his companion's shoulder with his hat tipped over his eyes, the other man staring straight ahead of him. Thinking. The lights were dim and the blinds were down. No glass to reflect his thoughts. He was filling his mind with mental pictures. The picture he had at the moment was that of a face; a face of a girl in a pub. When he had spoken those few words to her, and she had turned – he had been quite unprepared for what he had seen. The beautiful, violet blue eyes with their thick lashes, the pretty mouth, the curling fair hair each side of her ears, and lastly – framing it all the bonnet.

In that fleeting second, she had reminded him of a flower – the flower danced before his eyes. A pansy, yes a pansy. I don't know her name, but that's what I'll call her. He pictured the lovely face.

"That's my girl," he thought. "My Pansy."

Then he fell asleep.

Somewhere in England a train rumbled on into the night...

"I've a message for you from a soldier," Simon said when they reached home.

"You're a knockout,' that's what he said."

Laura had a peculiar feeling again.

"He was quite a knockout himself," she replied. The feeling that she had had earlier grew stronger, as she thought of him. She could still hear his voice in her head, whispering those few words in her ear,

"What's a nice girl like you doing in a place like this?"

Then, as she thought of them again, she was surprised to find a glow somewhere by her heart, that didn't go away.

Waning 1939

They had experienced a few false alarms so far in the war, the one on the morning of September sixth had found Laura and Simon hurrying down to the shelter. Although it had not lasted, it was long enough for the corrugated iron to start to sweat, with little beads of moisture sprouting like blisters on a burn. There was still the pungent smell of earth that wafted through unseen joints and cracks, too. They had no idea at that time just how long, or how often they would find themselves there, sitting perhaps for hours at a time in that musty dugout.

During the next few weeks they attempted to make the place more liveable and by the time Simon had fixed up the lighting system with night lights, torches and a tin box and they had their bedding and a shelf and a chair, it was far more friendly.

Aunt Mary still wanted them to go to the country with her, but they really didn't want to. Not that they didn't want to see her – far from it: but Laura was still at school, the lessons were being somewhat curtailed, but were still very important. As for Simon, he would never leave Laura, nor his contribution to the war effort. He really was pulling his weight with all his A.R.P. duties and working in the shop. Of course, they had friends there too, and they both felt that, had they gone, it would have been like running away, and one thing was certain, they had no intention of allowing Hitler to get them on the run. So going to the country was definitely 'OUT'.

One Thursday afternoon, when he had finished at the shop, Laura stood outside waiting for him. She had been worried about him lately. He had been so quiet and introspective, not his old self at all. She knew that he was pondering over something, and she just had to get to the bottom of it. Today had presented itself as a golden opportunity, for the expected driving lesson she was supposed to be having, had been cancelled.

"What a lovely surprise.... I didn't expect to see you here this afternoon. Thrown out of your class?" His face broke into a cheery grin, or what passed for one, when he asked the question.

"Never mind the grin, this brooding has gone on long enough for me, and I have to get to the bottom of it," she thought to herself. Aloud she said,

"Yes, the ambulances were all being used, not much point in my staying there to have a lesson if there wasn't one was there? Anyway, don't be so cheeky! I thought that we might go for a quick walk, what do you think? Let's make the most of what's left of the day."

"I'm game, what about going up to the park? I know it won't be for long, because it seems to be getting dark already."

Laura agreed at once, and linking her arm through his they set off, their gas mask cases slapping at their hips as they made their way quickly up the hill to Amleth Park. Slit trenches had been dug at various places in the park, to jump into for protection, if there happened to be a raid. Pretty dangerous, they both agree, if you didn't know their exact positions, especially in the twilight, as it was now.

There was a gauzy mist about and the trees were slowly dripping the accumulated vapour back into the atmosphere. Some of the larger ones had the now familiar wide white bands painted around them to prevent unexpected collisions.

Laura drew closer to Simon. Neither of them said much. They just walked on in spooky silence, strangely bringing them closer together. At last Laura spoke,

"Penny for your thoughts?"

"Oh, just thinking about the world in general – and us, and what will become of us? What will become of me? .... Don't you think it's strange Laura, that nobody has every come forward to even ask about me? ... Even after all the inquiries. It's not possible surely that nobody knows or cares about me. I'm in a very difficult position, aren't I? I must be unique. I have been giving the whole thing some serious thought...." He broke off for a moment and Laura tried to speak...

"Simon..."

"No, please Laura, let me finish.... I'm finding this...so hard...I've been thinking over the past weeks.. I...I...I could be a spy, couldn't I? After all, what do you know about me deep down? ...Nothing! Where did I come from? What do I know about myself? .....Where do I belong? I could be a spy, couldn't I?" He blurted out the last words all in a rush, hardly pausing for breath.

Laura stopped dead in her tracks. She turned to face him. She thought he might be smiling...but he wasn't. He was deadly serious.

"Is this why you have been so moody and sombre lately? Worrying yourself to death...and all over nothing." She tried to keep the tone of her voice light-hearted as she answered him.

"Just what would you be spying on? What great secrets do you have to pass on? More than that, to whom would you give this information?"

He thought for a moment, and then said,

"Well, there are the gun emplacements. I know where quite a few of them are... I know about them; what type they are...I know how many soldiers are involved with them.... I know about the local munition's factories, roughly how many people are employed in them... As for whom I should tell...well, I don't know...I don't know anything any more. All I know is that my mind has been in turmoil, with all this talk of spies in our midst, and about the walls having ears... Do you think I am a spy? Do you thing I was sent here to spy on...anything?"

"No I don't think you are a spy, I don't think that you were sent here to spy on anything. Don't you think that the police would have had you in by now if they had the slightest suspicion that you were up to anything? Think about it, Simon; the police have known about you from the first day that you were with us...there is clearly no need to worry about it. Promise me you will forget all these fanciful ideas. It just isn't so."

"Yes, alright, I guess you're right. Forgive my going on so, I was so worried and unhappy. I just don't seem to belong anywhere, to anyone, do I?"

"Yes you do, you belong here, with me, and all your friends, including the police." She gave his arm a squeeze. "Come on," she went on, "I'll race you home." She took to her heels with Simon in hot pursuit.

He never mentioned the conversation again, to Laura or anyone else.

"Fine spy he'd make," she thought, "when he has no memory and no contacts to give his pathetic information to, a highly unlikely way to tackle espionage!"

She also put the whole incident out of her mind, and never mentioned it to him again.

Book 1 – Chapter 4
Bleak House *June 1985*

Because of Peter's heavy involvement with young people in the district, and the special way he had with them, he had been asked to head up a new committee. It was to be involved with after-care of minor offenders and to make the homelessness of the young in the district a top priority. Of course, he wasn't involved all the time with these projects, but, with his own duties, his life was unbelievably busy.

Angela also had been co-opted on to the local branch of the Association for the Handicapped Society. This had been a blessing in disguise, for it had made her aware that… 'trying to go it alone' was not the answer with father; and that help was available, and that she was going to take advantage of this help – in a very practical way, in the very near future.

So, both their lives had changed, quite dramatically in the last few months. During one of Angela's meetings, it had been decided that a group from their branch would take both helpers and the chair-bound, for a week's holiday, to the sea. So Angela was going with father, leaving Peter to fend for himself!

There were to be ten in the party in all, and they would journey together in a hired mini-bus for the sixty miles to Broadstairs, in Kent. As it was to be the first venture for their group, they were all filled with anticipation and high hopes.

Peter was quite astonished to find that the very week, indeed the very day, that Angela was to leave, coincided with a journey that he had to make to Leeds.

The night before the respective trips were to take place, the hassle of packing over, and father being in bed, Angela and Peter sat together. Peter's arm was around his wife, and her head was resting on his shoulder. He started to speak quietly to her.

"I'm so pleased that things are falling into place for us, even our trips have worked out well, haven't they?"

Her eyes were closed as he slowly stroked her bare arm, from finger tip to elbow, and then back to her finger tips once again as he continued,

"I will miss you though, you know that don't you?"

"Oh I'm sure that you will be far too busy to miss me darling," she answered without even opening her eyes. Then suddenly, before he could answer her, she sat up; and looked into his rather crestfallen face.

Hurriedly he went on,

"I will miss you, truly I will, you must believe me m'love…I will".

He spoke with such earnest feeling in his voice, and looked so sad, she just had to smile at him.

"I know you will, and I'll miss you, too."

He stood up and held his hands out to her. She took them and was gently pulled into a warm embrace, responding at once to his strength and touch.

Although the light was fading fast, they crossed the room to the french windows, and opening them, stepped out into the sultry evening. Arms entwined, they walked slowly around the garden.

"I won't be able to give it even half an hour this week," he said, looking down at the fast growing weeds in the flowerbeds.

"Don't worry about that, Dick Harper said that he would look in for us this week; you see, I have every thing under control…so… don't worry about me, or father, the house, the garden, or all the people in Asbury."

As she turned to him, she was smiling her lovely smile, and he knew that she was teasing him just a little, about his worrying nature. He took her into his arms again and kissed her with a tender passion, which she returned. In those few precious seconds both of them felt the wonderful warmth of love, spilling over them. The sensual feeling of love and longing remained with them long after they had made their way back into the house.

Later that night in the quiet of their room, when physical passion and uncontrolled emotions had ebbed from their bodies, they lay together, still and quiet, in each others arms, content and happy. Peter caressed her hair tenderly, brushing a wispy curl towards her temple as he spoke her name softly;

"Angela…I truly thank God for giving you to me, my dear, dear, love."

"And I give thanks for you too, my darling."

They slept, each content that the wonderful gift of love was theirs.

The journey down to Kent had been uneventful, although hot and tiring. Peter's father had slept part of the way, but as soon as he was awake, his old question was asked over and over again, wearing everybody out. Most of the time he received kindly... "there, there's" from the other helpers. They all knew of the problem that he had, and so each of them dealt with it in his, or her, own way.

The boarding house itself was wonderful, and the dedicated staff were on hand the whole time to make life much easier for them all. Although the day was grey at the start, it was warm, and Angela decided to take father for a walk along the cliff path, so that he could hear the sounds of the sea and gulls, and feel the warm breeze.

They set off after lunch, and by the time they had reached the cliff tops, the sun had broken through the clouds. She turned the chair towards the sea and applied the brake.

"Do you hear the gulls father? I love to hear them calling."

She turned her eyes, and watched as the birds first circled and hovered above, and then dipped gracefully to the sea.

Father looked at her, and his eyes brimmed with tears, "What...is...the...answer...tell ...me?"

Angela was both surprised, shocked and excited... "tell me".. Two small words more. Would they lead to others? Excitedly she looked into his eyes and wiped away his tears.

"What is it father? What do you need to know? Tell me, try, try."

He looked back at her, his head lolling on one side, his lips twitching, words were forming, oh so painfully in his head again, before the great battle of getting them out of his mouth.

"What...is...the...answer?"

Angela sat down on the grass at his side with a sigh. She looked out at the sea and felt the excitement of the moment slowly ebbing away.......

The next day Angela was free... Father would be cared for all day and she could do as she wished.

She walked down to the jetty and saw the men fishing from the sea wall, casting their lines into the deep, dark waters below. Young boys were there, as well as the men, all of them pitting their skills against the elusive silver darts.

The wind was blowing now, not cold, but blustering around: making the rigging on the little fishing-boats ting, and the tarpaulins flap, as well as blowing her own hair around her face; sending strands into her eyes and mouth, the lips of which she could now feel were quite salty to the taste.

Turning away from the jetty, she looked up and saw the house perched on the cliff top. It looked for all the world as if it was…. waiting. She made her way up the hill to it. Charles Dickens' house, Bleak House, the house that gave it's name to the book of the same title.

Having paid her entrance fee, she moved into the hall. There was a room set aside as a museum for sea relics and such like – it was light and airy (although it had a slight smell of mustiness about it) with a high ceiling and ornate coving.

There were other people there too and, like Angela, they were all soon engrossed in reading about the life and death struggles that took place along the coast. There were plenty of drawings, models and photographs, dating from way back to fairly modern times, as well as the other visible memorabilia. The huge size of some of the shells displayed made her realise just how deep and dangerous the sea could be and how fickle; one moment giving pleasure – the next, giving grief.

She moved out of the museum, along the hall and up the stairs that were bedecked with feathers, driftwood and shells. The brown woodwork was gleaming and kept that way, by unseen hands. Into a bedroom next. The high bed, quite small, she thought, had a brass head and foot rail; with a white coverlet thrown over it. There were fringes and dried flower arrangements too. Clothes were laid on the bed, and casually hung on the backs of chairs, giving the impression that the owner of them had just stepped out of the room. The sweet, musty smell and the artefacts of the bygone age were all too much in the smallish room, too cluttered… and yet, she still felt as if she were intruding into somebody else's life, a voyeur even though the occupants of the room had long since departed.

Turning she found what was to be the best room in the house – for her.

It was very small with tall sash windows that overlooked the sea and in the bay there stood a high wooden desk. She ran her hands over the much used top (resting them there for a moment) and thought of the man who had sat there, looking out at the same view that she now saw; and of all the writings that were penned there, some discarded, perhaps never to be finished. She looked out to sea…. The wind was boisterously blowing the tall grasses and trees that were in the garden below. The sea gulls, separated only by the glass in the window-panes from her hands, were lying on the air supported by that obvious, yet unseen element – the wind.

The windows, old and much painted, rattled in their ill-fitting frames, the unseen element outside, buffeting them into life and Angela, back from the engulfing past, into present reality.

Intruders came now into her thoughts. A group of noisy children wanting her space – her room – her moment. They jostled into the tiny area, making her have to squeeze her way out.

She turned into the minute hall and descended some narrow twisting stairs, looking, as she did so, at the many and varied cuttings and pictures on the walls. There were variety bills, brown now at the edges and imprisoned behind pass-par-tout frames. One of them said "WANTED" in bold type and then there was some smaller script below which Angela didn't bother to read. Next to it was another poster. It was a pen and ink drawing; a print of a smiling man holding a banjo. The bold type beneath the picture said simply "BANJO". Something registered in her mind for a moment, and then the words were forgotten.

The last room that she entered in the house was the dining room. The sun was streaming in through the windows setting the wooden furniture gleaming and, on sideboards full of china, porcelain, ornaments and glass.

The table was set for a meal, with all the finery of an almost forgotten age. Set for unseen guests.

"Victoriana at its best, and worst," she thought, as she envisaged the amount of time that would have to be spent – on dusting alone! Having paused only to purchase a post-card of the house, Angela was soon out again, into the blustering wind and the sunlight. She stopped in the garden, and looked out over the sea. She watched for a few moments, as the white horses came roaring in, whipped now by a strong wind that had sprung up, only to dash themselves to destruction on the beach far below.

She made her way down the hill. When she reached the bottom, she looked back.

"Lovely, lovely old house," she thought to herself.

Without realising it, she suddenly found herself thinking about the two words that she had read earlier.

"Wanted – Banjo.' Why on earth should I think of that again?" She didn't know, so she dismissed it again.

Later that same evening, when she was sitting with father before he went to sleep, she told him all about the house. As she was speaking her thoughts were racing ahead of her words. Banjo – at last she made the connection that triggered off her memory. Banjo… she had remembered seeing the pencilled word on the back of one of the photographs that she had looked at with Peter all that time ago.

She said aloud, "Banjo…Banjo". The old man, whom she thought was nearly asleep, suddenly stirred, and his eyes flew open. She was sorry to have woken him in that way, but she could not help herself.

"Banjo, Banjo, father, does it mean something? Was he your friend? Is he the answer?"

She looked into his eyes. She knew it was a possibility, remote yes, but still a possibility. All her hopes were there in his face. She waited silently in anticipation for an answer.

His eyes for once were not darting about. They just looked at her, still and sad. He made to speak to her, as two large tears dropped from the now still eyes.

"What … is … the… answer …tell …me."

Angela fell forward to the bed, the covers muffling the sounds of her crying that she could no longer control. The old man closed his eyes again.

Somewhere outside, the gulls were crying, too.

It was a lovely day on Sunday, the local church had made provision for all of them, wheelchairs included. The people were friendly and made them all feel most welcome.

Angela prayed her private thoughts, and felt so much compassion for father-in-law who, unable to stop himself, asked his question throughout the service, even at the very quiet times.

The minister spoke to them both as they were leaving.

"I'm sorry about the interruptions," she said quietly, not wishing to hurt father's feelings (if he could understand).

"No need to be sorry, my dear, or make apologies. We all have a question somewhere in our hearts that we would like an answer for, I suspect. Oh, perhaps we don't utter it aloud, but it's still there, unanswered. People often ask me questions, one in particular, is… 'Why?' I can never fully understand… nor answer fully myself. I'll keep you and your family in my thoughts and prayers, and one day, I sincerely hope the dear man will get the answer to his question. I'm sure we all will!"

He knelt down beside the wheel-chair and took the old man's hands into his own.

"God bless you my friend." He said, and to Angela's surprise…father just looked, her ears could hardly believe it, he just looked.

The minister stood upright again,

"Goodbye" he said and turned his attention to the other members of the congregation.

Angela quickly knelt down herself beside him. She looked into his face.

"What…is…the…answer?" the laboured question assailed her ears once again.

"There, there." She said, taking the brake off the chair and patting his arm.

Book 2 – Chapter 4
Changes Before Christmas *November 1939*

Laura opened the door.

"Why Captain, what a surprise, come in do."

Captain Fuller stepped into the sitting room, removing his hat as he did so.

"Hello Laura, I thought that I would find you home at this time. I can see that you are busy though." He inclined his head to the table that was strewn with papers.

"Oh yes, it's all to do with the evacuation. One more class is off at the end of the week and there are a couple of lists that I have to give to the head as soon as possible."

"So, I've chosen a bad time to call then?"

"No, I'm not so busy that I can't spare you some time. Captain, what brings you around here?"

"Well, Laura, two things really. Firstly, the sad news about Ted Davis. Ted and May were good friends of your Aunt Mary's and yours, weren't they?"

"Yes, they are…I mean, they were…I mean…"

"Yes, I know exactly what you mean, but Ted, poor fellow, has had such bad times over the years with his asthma … and when he developed pneumonia…well, we were all so terribly sorry at his passing…very sad, very sad."

"Yes, it is ..was, very sad, especially for poor May. They've been together since they were about fourteen years old. Did you know? Her daughter from Camberley is still here with her at the moment. Both of them stayed with us after the funeral …Simon was so helpful to me at that time, and he was so supportive to May..."

"Yes, I did know that she was still here, and as for Simon, well he is a good lad no doubt about that…in fact he is the other matter that I want to talk to you about." The Captain cleared his throat. "You are very fond of him aren't you?"

"Well, yes I am, I did find him remember and I feel somehow responsible for him … even after all this time. He still worries so much about himself, and about his past – his parentage. Have you found out something for us? Is it good news?"

The Captain shook his head.

"No my dear, I'm afraid not. No news in that direction at all – in fact – a total blank."

He cleared his throat again, and Laura looked despondently at him. His face was flushed and his collar appeared to be too tight around his neck, he cleared his throat again, running his finger round the offending material, as if to make it easier for him to breathe. He was clearly – very uncomfortable.

"How rude of me, do please sit down," she said, thinking, "Why on earth is he like this? It's so out of character for him."

Captain Fuller sat down, with some measure of relief.

"Now Laura, I have something to say. Please allow me to finish before you say anything."

His voice was quite firm as he spoke, and he seemed to regain his old composure. Laura just sat and nodded her compliance to his request.

"Now it's almost a year since Simon arrived in Amleth, and you, quite rightly and most charitably, did, and are doing your best for him now, as I'm sure you will continue to do. He's a charming and fine young man, a credit to you and your Aunt. He seems to be a very sincere young fellow, and every time I speak with him, I'm staggered by his reasoning power, and his perception of the world around him. I myself find him charming, and there is no doubt about his charisma; all the ladies, without exception, have taken to him. As my wife says.... 'he's very loveable."

The Captain paused briefly, mopping his brow with a large handkerchief, again he cleared his throat.

"Now Laura," he started again "you are a fine looking young lady," his face grew redder than ever, if that were possible!

He looked so awkward and embarrassed she felt quite sorry for him. What on earth was it all about?

"Well Laura, to get right to the point"

At last, she thought!

"I don't think that Simon should stay here with you ... I mean the two of you together... here."

Laura opened her mouth to speak, but Captain Fuller put his finger to his lips and shook his head.

"Let me finish, Laura. I know how you have helped him over some very rough patches, and maybe will in the future; but it's now that I'm thinking about. I know that we are at war, and that everyone is drawn together in friendly companionship, but I just don't think for him to remain here would be right, not here in this house unchaperoned."

Laura could remain silent no longer.

"Captain ... I don't love Simon, well I do love him, but I have a brotherly love for him ...and it's not in the least ..." she wanted to say sexual, but she felt that had she done so, the Captain would probably have fallen off his chair! Instead she said, "not in the least romantic, honestly there is no romance in our closeness Captain, you must believe me."

"I do child, I do, but I just don't want you to be compromised in this way, but you know how some people can be really nasty ... and cruel. I do feel most strongly about it, and I'm sure that Simon will feel the same way when he knows. He wouldn't want to do anything that might make you vulnerable to any sort of gossip. Knowing how he feels about you, and also knowing him too, I'm sure he will agree with what I'm saying."

"He still needs me Captain. He still has so many irrational and real fears to deal with."

"Yes, I know Laura, that's why I have a proposition to put to you. May's daughter is going back to Camberley this weekend, having unsuccessfully tried to get her mother to go back with her. Mind you she is still trying, but I know May too well...she won't go, even though her daughter is so worried about her being on her own in the house, and more so now with the worry of the war...."

He didn't have to finish speaking. Laura's face lit up.

"Yes, of course ... she must come here. It's a wonderful idea. Will she come Captain? Will she?"

"Well it's not quite..."

She was almost willing the right answer to come from the Captain's lips.

"Well, I did take the liberty of speaking to her and I know she will be very grateful for any arrangement ..."

"Grateful to me? It should be the other way round. I should be, and am, grateful to her for agreeing to come here."

Captain Fuller, his suggestion totally misunderstood, smiled at her,

"I'm sure May will be only too pleased to fall in with any plan that means that she is not left alone. This way your beloved Simon is still safely with you ... isn't he?

Her eyes were full of relief and love.

"Yes... oh yes, thank you so much for caring about us both. I didn't give it a thought and I know that Simon didn't either. Yes, we are very close... but we never dreamed that people might think ...."

"Well Laura, I must go."

"Oh do please stay and see Simon. He won't be long now and we can have some tea. You will stay for a cup at least, won't you?"

"No thank you my dear, I really must go now. As for Simon, we haven't given up the search … no, not at all, but of course, it will be made more difficult – because of the war. Never mind, keep your chin up, we'll win on all fronts, you'll see."

He took his leave of her hugging her tightly.

"God bless you, my dear girl, and remember me to that 'brother' of yours."

"Good-bye Captain, and thank you for everything."

Captain Fuller waved to her without turning round as he marched off into the dusk.

Life went on in Amleth. Enemy planes had been spotted over South East England, and gunfire had been heard as they were followed down the river by sure-sighted gunners, until the thwarted planes had finally disappeared from sight. Evacuation had become a priority, and the movement of children to safer areas took on great urgency.

Saturday had soon come. Simon had already left for the shop and Laura was now leaving home, to go to the school to see the children off, making sure that she had her handkerchief with her, for she knew that she would need it. She slammed the door and made her way to the meeting point.

There were to be three double-decker buses to take the children, and the few remaining teachers, to the main line railway station, the headmaster was relieved to see that both teachers and buses were early.

Now the children and parents had started to arrive. The teachers scooped up the children to their classrooms, to do a headcount, and make sure everything was going to plan: that all the labels were correct, and that everyone had their gas masks. The parents were only onlookers at this point, waiting for the children to come back to them, for a final goodbye.

Soon the formalities were over, and the long column of children made its way to the waiting parents and buses. The terrible pain of parting was made worse for the adults for, to try and make light of their children's 'holiday', they had to fight back their own tears and smile. There was much hugging and kissing, and soon the harrowing scenes were over, the last goodbyes had been said – and the buses had disappeared from sight. Laura dried her own tears and made her way home again,

Today was going to be special in another way, today May Davis was coming to stay.

Simon had been quite shocked by Captain Fuller's revelations that anybody could have thought badly of himself and Laura. On reflection though, he realised that anything that might hurt Laura couldn't possibly be right. He was more than happy that May Davis was coming to stay with them, for her sake as well as theirs. She would help to fill the void that had been left in the house when Aunt Mary had gone away. May could never replace Aunt Mary, but she was a pleasant lady and she was in need of a good deal of support just now herself. Maybe they would all help each other with the traumas of life and death that they might be facing – in the not too distant future, and hopefully they would sustain each other's needs, in the days to come.

Christmas was a very busy one for Laura, Simon and May. They decided to spend their Christmas helping those less fortunate than themselves, the lonely and the old. A large soup kitchen had been set up in the church hall. It was manned by the Salvation Army, and volunteers, for the three days of Christmas. It was a hectic, but happy time. Of course, Simon was on night watch some of the time, so, in fact, he had to sleep part of his Christmas away; however, they all managed to get together at one of the special Christmas services, in between their culinary duties!

There they were able to greet each other with hopes for a better future.

That first Christmas of the war had seen a great number of people in the church, many of them for the first time, and maybe, for the first time in their lives.

The atmosphere inside was hard to describe. Although they were like one family, friendly and warm, they soon became a great army, strong and resolute in their prayers. There was a common feeling of unity amongst them, and they were determined as one, that they would pray for a blanket of good to cover the evil that was now creeping over the earth.

They prayed for the strength that they knew they would have to have, to continue their fight for the right, with God's help they knew that they would succeed…but when? Only God knew the answer to that.

After the service Simon and Laura walked home arm in arm, down the darkened streets, both of them thinking their own thoughts. The news that had been emitting from the wireless, had been less than favourable of late, and both of them knew that they were going to face some terrible times ahead. They heard somebody laugh behind them. It lifted their thoughts and they both picked up their step.

"Let's just think of now, shall we?" he said.

"Just what I was thinking," she replied, her luminous disc on her lapel bobbing up and down, as their steps quickened. They saw other greenish glowing discs, and heard – and gave "Merry Christmas" greetings along their way.

May was already at home when they arrived.

"Come on in, it's bitter out there." She said as they walked into the cosy room the silver strips amongst the decorations glinting like polished steel in the firelight.

"Brrr, you're quite right May, it sure is cold," he said taking their coats and hanging them up.

Once they were settled May spoke again.

"Merry Christmas, my two very dear friends, there's not much left of Nineteen thirty nine now, and I for one won't be too sorry to see it go. I know I've lost my dear Ted this year, but I'm glad that he won't have to suffer this beastly war, he's suffered enough over the past years. My two dears, I can't thank you both enough for all that you have done for me."

She came to where they were both standing, and embraced them both. They all stood, arms around each other for a few seconds, then Simon broke the silence.

"Merry Christmas to you too, dear May. Let's try to look forward with hope for the future, and do our best not to look back, perhaps the new year will bring something good for all of us. Not forgetting Aunt Mary either, of course," he added, "Roll on Nineteen Forty, we are all ready and waiting….."

"Amen to that", said Laura.

"Yes, indeed, we won't be beat Mr. Hitler … just you try us and see."

Forget Me Not

It was April, and there was a real spring feeling about, the gardens and trees were in flower, and the Anderson shelter that had been put at the bottom of the garden some months before, was looking good, Laura thought.

Simon had worked long and hard over the past months to cover the thing, using the earth that had been dug out when it had first been installed, the final artistic touches had been achieved by the planting of bulbs and wallflowers.

Now their beautifications were at their peak, for the shelter had disappeared from view, replaced now by this shining mound of brilliance, making the small garden quite a work of art.

Even works of art have to have some considerations though, and today Laura was giving her attention to the weeding and tidying up while she had the spare time.

May, too, was gardening but at her own house, because since she had moved in with Simon and Laura, her own home and garden had not had much attention. Fortunately, gardens in winter don't need too much work, but now with spring in the air, May felt that she had to make the effort. Vegetable planting was the order of the day.

Laura had been working for about an hour and a half, when she stood back and admired her handiwork.

" Yes," she said to herself, "I think that Auntie would approve of all our efforts."

With the scent of the flowers, and the beautiful blue sky above, she was suddenly aware of how idyllic and peaceful the whole scene was, and how pointless and hateful was the war. Oh the stupidity of man's aggression against his brother. She shook her head sadly as she made her way into the kitchen.

She intended to make herself a cup of tea, and take it into the garden, to soak up the sun while she was able; however, before she could do this, she had to get rid of some of the 'garden' down the sink. She put some water in a bowl and started to scrub at her hands.

"Yes Auntie, I know now that I should have put on the old gloves," she said.

As she was scrubbing her mind wandered back to the time, so long ago it now seemed, when she had cleaned Simon's nails (though not so harshly), in the same way.

She went on thinking about him.

“Poor Simon, I know that he still feels abandoned, even though he tries his hardest to be happy. Tracing his relatives seems such a thankless task.”

As she was drying her hands, she looked down the garden again, and gazed at the flowers that had so lovingly been planted by his hands.

“Still, what would I do without him? He really is a love.”

Suddenly there came a knock at the door.

“That’s May, forgotten her key again I expect,” she said to herself as she hurried to it…

”Coming,” she called.

She opened it. It was not May.

She stood and looked at the caller. Her mouth opened to speak…nothing, but nothing came out of it.

She felt her face flushing. A strange feeling started at her feet, and slowly crept up over her whole body, finally engulfing her with the weirdest sensation. While this had been going on, her heart seemed to have taken flight, right into her throat. It was her soldier.

He stood back a little from the front door, his hat being held under one arm by his hand and in the other he held a small bunch of forget-me-nots.

“Hello, remember me?”

Smiling a bewildered smile at him, she said simply “Hello” and was relieved to hear that her power of speech had returned, although it was almost inaudible.

As he had neared the house, James had begun to wonder if this was folly of the first order. Seven months is a long time, and after all he had seen the girl for only about two minutes. Did he really mean to spend the rest of his life, with somebody of such brief acquaintance?

He had thought about her constantly for all of those months.

“But what makes me think that she will even remember me? A colossal cheek on my part, to even think that she would, and as for being interested in me…well? At least through the kindness of Captain Fuller, I do know that she is neither engaged, nor married, that must put me in with a chance. Mustn’t it? Maybe, just maybe…”

He was realising that he was walking too fast.

“Slow down you chump – don’t be too eager to get the old heave-ho.” He thought to himself as he reached the gate.

Unable to talk himself out of his seemingly rash action, he had walked up the path and knocked on the door. His nerve seemed to be cracking fast.

“What have I come for? What if she’s out?” He desperately wanted her to be in, but was terrified of her reaction.

He was looking down at the flowers in his hand when she started to open the door. He raised his head, and looked into the disbelieving and dishevelled countenance of …the girl. Her fair hair was in disarray, she had dirt on her face and was wearing dark blue dungarees. She was spectacular!

Her eyes were open wide with surprise, and the colour of them was far more vibrant than he had remembered, the thick lashes surrounding them gave her a startled look; and as she opened her mouth to speak, he heard his own voice speaking instead. His heart was thumping, he thought, “Now I know why I came…I love her.”

“Hello,” she answered him “where have you come from?… I mean what are you doing here? I mean…I mean….” In fact she didn’t know what she meant. She felt completely overcome and tongue-tied…. “After all this time….?”

“I’ve come to give you these.”

He thrust the small bunch of flowers towards her. Was his voice his own? It sounded distinctly peculiar.

“Oh forget-me-nots, I love forget-me-nots.” She took the flowers from his outstretched hand, and lifted them to her face.

“I brought them because I rather hoped that you… hadn’t forgotten …me,” he added lamely.

“No, I hadn’t,” she felt her cheeks burning with embarrassment and her voice was still playing tricks.

She looked at the tiny blue flowers, grateful to be able to avert her eyes from his, just for the moment, because his were so piercing and bright, they seemed to be able to read her like a book; and, since at that moment she was thinking how handsome he was, it was all very unnerving… Looking up she regained her composure again after the initial shock of seeing him

“I would be for ever in your debt, if you would allow me to become acquainted with you ma’am.” Then switching off his military tone he added, “Would it help in your decision making if I told you that I had been with Captain Fuller for the past hour or so? In fact, it was he that allowed me to pick the flowers for you…. from his garden!”

Laura held the door open wide,

“Come in,” she said, “I’ve been working in my garden and was just about to make a pot of tea, but with the rationing, it’s much better to share the pot for two than one…come on through to the kitchen.”

He stepped over the threshold and felt a complete sense of joy within himself. He wanted to shout out…he didn't know quite what, but he just wanted the whole world to know how happy he was. His eyes watched the slight dungareed figure as he followed behind her. He saw her pause at the sideboard briefly, to collect a small cut glass vase.

"I must put these in water quickly before they wilt. They're so pretty…thank you so much," she added, filling the vase and placing it on the table, knowing that her every move was being watched.

She knew that she was speaking too fast and that her breath was acting as if she had just run in a hundred yards race, but there was nothing she could do about it. He watched her arrange the flowers, her slim fingers dextrously guiding the thin stems into place. They were pretty enough, as she had said, but not a patch on her. He wanted, at that moment, to do nothing more than pull her to him and hold her close… He stood awkwardly and felt in the way. She was speaking…suddenly she was standing in front of him.

"I said, why don't you go into the garden? Take a couple of kitchen chairs for us, and I'll make the tea, and bring it out."

She looked into his face, questioningly, and expected some sort of reply or action from him. Her voice brought him out of his daydream, and he pulled himself together. What on earth would she make of him if he stood around like a lemon, he thought.

"Of course, of course," he replied quickly.

He laid his hat and pack on the table next to the flowers, undid his jacket and took the two chairs out into the sunshine. She watched him through the open window, and smiled at him when he glanced in her direction. When he smiled back at her she thought her heart would burst as it seemed to skip a beat.

She tidied herself before she went out into the garden. He stood at her approach, taking the tray from her and setting it down between them, on the grass.

They sat at an angle, facing one another, but with a good view of the now hidden shelter before them, the flowers dancing gently in the almost still air.

Neither of them spoke for a moment, then they both started at once. They laughed and it seemed to break the ice.

"Ladies first," he said bowing his head to Laura.

"Well, before we go any further, I feel we should introduce ourselves. My name is Laura Anthony, and I live…here, with two very good friends. My Aunt usually lives here with me but she is in the country at the moment. Instead I have her very good friend staying, a lady, then of course there is a young man - Simon, I'll tell you about him later, perhaps. His story is very complicated and very personal. More about me.. I'm a school teacher – part-time ambulance driver and, as you well know, a member of the Salvation Army," she finished speaking in a rush, "And you?"

"Well, my name is James Aston, I'm a major in the Royal Engineers. I live, by his Majesty's command in barracks, I can't say where. My home, my roots if you like, are in Wiltshire and…thank goodness, you are a member of the Salvation Army, or I never would have found you, because that is how I tracked you down. I first went to the Citadel, and I was then directed to the home of your Captain Fuller. He took the liberty, after I described you and where I had seen you first, of giving me your name and address. I hope you will forgive him for that...I was pretty persuasive. Then, when I explained that I needed an introduction and spoke to him about the flowers, he graciously allowed me to pick the little bunch I gave you. Will you forgive my devious actions? Please say that you will – I just had to meet you."

He reached out and took her hand.

"How do you do, Laura? I'm so very pleased to meet you."

"How do you do, James? Likewise I'm sure."

"I have thought of you so much over the past months and had it not been for the war, I would have tried to contact you long before this. Will you ever forgive me for being so forward? Time is precious, don't you agree?"

She looked into his eyes feeling relaxed and happy – no, more than happy – different.

She extended her hand to him again and he took it eagerly into his own.

"I forgive you… everything."

They released hands after what seemed an eternity but, in fact, was only an instant of time. They didn't say anything more until the tea had been poured and drunk.

They sat, content just to be in each other's presence, looking out at the landscape, which, in Laura's eyes, was more beautiful than ever.

The sun was shining, and for a little while they forgot the war, and were at peace with the world.

Later on that evening, when May and Simon were at home, they all became properly acquainted.

At the end of the evening they knew a great deal about James and James knew more about them. The amazing thing, as they remarked later, was that it was as if they had always known one another, because there seemed to spring an immediate bond of friendship between them all.

He felt as if he had walked into a ready-made family that had welcomed him so warmly and with open arms. It made him even more aware of what he had lacked in his own family life, which was at the moment, as it had always been, to some degree non-existent.

Now he had to go – he hated the idea. Being with Laura these few hours had been wonderful, even though he had to share her for the best part of them.

By about ten o'clock, reluctantly, he had to leave. He promised them, that if it were at all possible, duties allowing, he would be back within the week. The only reason for his non-appearance, would be the obvious one, with no need to mention.

He put his jacket on, and slung his pack over his shoulder. Laura said that she would see him to the gate. He picked up his hat and she slipped a cardigan around her shoulders as they made their way to the door.

Simon dimmed the gas, whilst they pulled the curtain aside, to enable them to open the front door, without the escape of telltale light. The door closed behind them.

"Well, I don't believe it!" Laura said, looking heavenwards.

"It's lighter out here than in the sitting room."

The night sky was glowing and into this glow there appeared to be tiny pin-pricks of light.

"It looks for all the world like a gigantic pin cushion, don't you think James?"

He nodded. They walked the few steps to the gate and just stood looking at the sky and listening to the silence.

He looked at her face shining in the light, the stars reflected in the dark depths of her beautiful eyes. The fragrance of her hair was close to him now, and he knew – without any doubt at all, that he loved her.

She looked into his face, and saw that he was gazing at her in a way that made her heart pound. She knew, without any shadow of a doubt in her mind, that she loved this man, although reason told her that surely this was an impossible deduction, having known him for such a short time.

“When love is in, reason goes out of the window,” she said to herself, “ I know I love him.”

He opened the gate and stepped through, clicking it shut behind him.

“Well, goodnight James, till next time…I’m so very glad you came.”

“Let’s say au revoir, because I’ll be back, war or no war…I will be back.”

“I loved the flowers, I will think of you when ever I see them now.”

“Please don’t forget me Laura.”

“I won’t do that, James, I promise you.”

She gave him her hand and he put it to his lips.

“Goodnight,” he said, and left her.

The feeling she was experiencing inside herself was just as it was when their eyes had met for the first time, all those months ago.

The sensation she had experienced then had left an inner after-glow but the glow this time was stronger …much stronger. She found herself gripping on to the wooden gate with both hands, as if to steady the heady feeling she felt.

He turned around just once and waved and she waved back. Then he turned the corner…and was gone.

Back indoors again, Simon started talking at once.

“Oh yes, I recognised him at once, what a sleuth he is, eh? The way he looked at you Laura…I think you have stolen his heart.”

Laura found herself blushing and busied herself by clearing the rest of the table, so that he would not have the satisfaction of seeing her blazing cheeks!

“Oh the things you say Simon, stop embarrassing the girl do.” May said, giving him a playful slap. “Mind you,” she went on, “I do think that he is attracted to you Laura, not much doubt about that.”

“I can’t hear you,” Laura sang out from the kitchen, a small smile escaping from her lips.

“Well then, you won’t be able to hear my news…”

It was Simon speaking this time. Laura was back in the room in an instant.

“What news? Good news? News? Tell us what news?”

“So you’re interested in me again, are you?”

Laura found herself blushing and said,

“Get on with it, and stop being so mysterious, will you?” She flicked a towel in his direction and said with deliberation “What news?”

Laura was getting exasperated with him now. He was tantalising them both – and he knew it.

"Well, it was like this. I was going past the Co-op on my way home and I stopped to see my favourite girl…"

"If this is your news Simon…well I'm going to bed…," May said. "Hearing about your favourite model is not my idea of news."

"Well, it's all to do with my favourite girl first…then my big news."

"Hurry up and tell us then."

Simon looked at Laura as she finished speaking and put his hand to his good ear, and inclined it towards her direction…and waited. "Pleeeeeeeease" she said.

Simon cleared his throat,

"Well, as I was saying, I was standing outside the Co-op…"

"That's it" May said, "I'm off to bed, I can't go all through that again at this time of night, it's alright for you youngsters, but I'm off. I'll have to hear your big news tomorrow Simon."

Looking at Laura she said quietly,

"I think that your new friend is very nice, and very good looking." Louder she said, "I'll take my leave of you two now if you don't mind." She made her way to the curtained door. "Forgive me Simon, but I do feel quite tired out, I've had a pretty hard day myself. Good night both of you, see you in the morning. God bless."

"Alright May, see you tomorrow, but do you think that you will be able to sleep? I mean…because of the excitement of… not knowing my news?"

He put his arm around May's waist and gave it a squeeze.

"Get away with you," she laughed and pushed him away. "I think that I will survive the night. Goodnight again."

"Goodnight"

"Goodnight"

At last the chenille-curtained door swished closed leaving them alone.

"Come on Simon, I'm dying to hear this news…but it's getting so late, please hurry up…"

"I must start at the beginning"

"Alright, start at the beginning, but START"

"Well, I was outside the Co-op looking in at my favourite girl, she is a housewife this week by the way," he started to describe the model.

"Picture her here before you" he extended his arm to the imaginary form as he spoke. "She is standing in her usual way…thus," he adopted the same stance and then went on, "She is wearing a large floral wrap-around apron, and in her crooked arm, she holds…a baby. The ugliest thing I have ever seen. It's painted eyes are squint and it's rosy cheeks make it look as if it has a very bad case of scarlet fever."

Laura covered her face at this point, to stop herself from laughing. The thought of that 'baby' was just too much, but it wasn't over yet...

"The knitted bonnet is lopsided, making it look a tinsy winsy bit drunk. Whether the child is male or female is anybody's guess, because the hideous, mustard coloured coat, knitted of course to match the bonnet, completely obliterates any sign of romper or dress." Simon took no notice of the sounds coming from Laura's direction, and just went on without hardly a pause.

"From the hand of her left arm, which as you may remember, is hanging down at her side, dangles a rattle. The whole sight is totally uninspiring to say the least. In the window with her are a bucket, floor mop and broom, and a very small pile of tea towels. Not the best display in the world, eh? Plus the fact that it's all behind the prison bars of the brown sticky tape."

Laura was trying not to make too much noise with her laughter, for fear of waking May, but laugh she just had to.

"Do you think that anyone is ever tempted to buy anything from there?"

"That's just what she said."

"She...?"

"Yes, that's where my good news comes in. I've made a date with Netta."

"Netta?....Netta Phillips? The one from church?"

"That's the one."

"Oh Simon, I'm so pleased for you, she is a lovely girl. I've known her for a long time, she is very nice."

She went over to him and put her arms around his waist. Looking up into his face she said,

"It's high time a handsome young man like you had a girl friend. Although I feel a little bit jealous...you and I seem to have been friends forever, don't we?"

"I don't think that you will miss me, or my antics. Firstly, I'm not going anywhere, and second, I think that you will have your time taken up with James, if tonight is anything to go by. I think he's great by the way...and really smitten...I can tell these things you know," he added, giving her a knowing wink.

Laura felt herself colour up a little. He spoke again.

"Perhaps we can all go out together, that is if Hitler gives us a chance" he added wistfully.

"I think you are rushing things a bit…but, yes, it sounds a good idea. I'm so pleased that you like him…because I think James is…" she paused to think of a good adjective to describe him.

"Indescribable?" Simon interjected.

"Oh you're hopeless, come on it's high time we were clearing up. Come and dry."

"I'm really pleased for you Laura…you looked so happy tonight. Perhaps I'm the one who should be a little jealous," he said as he put his arms around her shoulders.

Her hands were in water, so she turned her head in his direction and looked at him.

"I'm so pleased for you too Simon, but I'm not going anywhere either…"

April turned into May. There was still no word from James. Laura tried hard not to worry about him too much, but she thought of him constantly.

She was kept very busy all around, and she worked very hard in the evenings too and this helped her keep her mind occupied. Simon and Netta Phillips had been seeing each other for some time; but since she was a nurse, her hours didn't always fit in with his, and his didn't always fit in with hers. However, they seemed quite happy with the way things were working out, and their friendship flourished, despite the difficulties they sometimes encountered.

Simon had found another passion – crossword puzzles. As with all his passing phases, when he was keen on something, all of the household became involved too. He was always doing them, whenever he had a spare moment, and gave the excuse that….

"It helps me with my education, which is still sadly lacking, and makes my brain cells do some work…"

One of the most annoying things about this new craze, from Laura and May's point of view was, that he was always wanting help with his clues! He even made up his own, and left them about for the two women to ponder over. Netta, of course, aided and abetted him at every opportunity…which made things worse. Still, it was all light hearted nonsense, and they did need something to take their minds off the worsening developments that were delivered to them each day by the wireless, war news was never good news after all.

Laura saw a gradual change come over Simon. It was as if the old Simon was dying away and a new, more assured person was taking his place. He became less demanding and dependent on her. She felt slightly hurt at first, but then realised that it was a good sign, and that she must learn to let him go, if that was what he wanted.

As far as she was concerned, he was her brother, and as such, she loved him dearly, and she knew she always would. His funny ways, his head cocked on one side, the cheeky grin and his sense of humour, were as endearing to her as ever. She knew that she would always be there for him, even if he decided to leave home, a prospect, which at the moment, had never entered his head. It was apparent that Netta also shared his sense of fun, and was also very fond of him, so she couldn't be anything but pleased, for them both.

The news from Europe was bad. Rationing had begun to take a real hold, and the world was in a dark mood. Therefore Simon's happy disposition helped to keep people's spirits up. Laura had just been to the little grocers and heard, yet again, how pleased Mr. B. was with him and that he..."never regretted taking him on, not for a moment, and nor did Rosie...."

At last it was Saturday (quite late in the afternoon now thanks to her encounter with Mr.B), she didn't have to rush home. She took the long route back, and walked past the sports ground. Of course, there was not much sport on, since the whole ground had been commandeered by the R.A.F. and Army a long time ago.

The WAAF's and soldiers were conspicuous by their absence at the moment, however, and the sole inhabitants, or so it seemed to her, were the barrage balloons. They were tethered at housetop height at the moment, and looked, Laura thought, like a troupe of overweight ballerinas, waiting for their big moment to come.

She hoped that they would continue to wait in the wings. For she was well aware that when an air-raid was imminent, they would be sent soaring – high into the sky. Sometimes they would float with the sun behind them, making them look like so many dark ink blots. Other times the sun would glint on them, as they strained on their moorings. Today, however, the overweight chorus girls were slumbering, still awaiting their moments of glory.

"Thank goodness," she thought, as she continued to walk home.

As she was nearing the house, she started to think about James, and it made her heart beat faster.

"Where are you James? Where are you?"

She turned into the path, and the gate clicked behind her. It made her remember the night the he had left her, especially the moment when he had lifted her hand to his lips as they were saying goodbye……..

As she opened the door, there sitting with May at the table was – James. He stood immediately and came to greet her, hands outstretched.

"Hello," he said, "I told you I would be back Laura – and here I am!"

With the colour flooding her cheeks, and legs feeling slightly detached from her body, she walked toward him and took his hands into her own.

"I'm so pleased to see you, I'm so pleased you came back"…….

Shooting at Stars

Book 1 – Chapter 5
Strong as Crystal *June 1985*

On her return to Asbury, Angela knew that drastic changes had to be made in the house. Peter was in favour, of course, for he could see that it made good sense.

Because of the holiday home they had just left, Angela realised that, with a few changes, life could be made much easier for them all. All the lifting and carrying up and down stairs was much too much of a strain for them, and things were bound to get worse rather than better with poor father. They hated to admit it – but it was true.

The main task of bringing the bedroom furniture downstairs, and taking Peter's large oak desk, bookcases and filing cabinets up, was soon accomplished; by a group of good friends.

The move was finished. Peter's lovely study was now his father's bed-sit, and father's old room had made a more sensibly sized study for him.

"What it is to have friends," he said as he flopped down into a chair. Angela came over and sat on his knee.

"Yes, they were wonderful, weren't they? It's a jolly good job very well done…and so speedily too. You can relax now, I can cope with everything else…with the exception of your room, of course…especially your paperwork! It will be a real blessing to have your father on the ground floor…why we never thought of it before, I have no idea."

"That's just it… we never did… think."

"It won't present any problems when you have a visitor either, because they can just go straight up the back stairs."

"In fact, it will be better – because they won't have to disturb you… no it's going to be great, I'm sure – good for us – and more comfortable for father too" he added, giving her a squeeze.

"I'll put the coffee maker in there, and once the telephone extension is connected, you will be quite self-sufficient. Perhaps I will have to make an appointment to see you myself."

She leaned forward and placed a kiss on his forehead. He put his arms around her waist and held her in a tight grip.

"Never…never…," he said giving her a hug and a kiss.

She freed herself from the friendly embrace and crossed the room to the old man as he sat in his chair.

Bending down, so that her face was on a level with his, she said,

"Father, we have been making a new bedroom for you across the...," she said no more because the old man's eyes darted, and then locked on to her face as he said,

"What...is...the...answer?"

"The answer, father," Angela continued, "will be a much easier time for us all, and a more dignified way of life for you."

She brushed his hair away from his eyes, and plumped his cushions again, making him more comfortable, then she knelt down at his side, his eyes following her every movement. His old question rang out again.

"If only we knew, dear, if only we knew."

She took both his hands that were lying limp on the rug that covered his knees, and lifted them to her face, holding them there for a moment; they felt cool on her cheek. She laid them down again and covered them.

"What...is...the...answer...please...tell...me?"

Startled, she turned to Peter.

"Did you hear that?"

"Yes, I did m'love"

He was at her side in an instant. He knelt next to her and faced his father.

"Father, listen to me."

The old man's eyes darted from Peter's face to Angela's and then back again to Peter's

"We are trying to help you, we love you, and we are trying to help you. Can you help us?"

The old man said nothing, just turned his eyes first to his photograph, and then to them.

"What...is...the...answer?"

Peter patted his father's shoulder, and then they both stood up.

"Well, he is improving...isn't he, darling? There were three extra words, there...meaningful, and used correctly."

Angela was trying to sound hopeful. Peter shook his head.

"Maybe, but we're no nearer now than we were months ago, even after all our enquiries...and after all our efforts. We're still no nearer to finding the answer to his question, when it comes to it...are we? Just look at him, he is still in some sort of torment, - and we can't do anything about it...can we?" He looked from Angela to the photograph, "That picture seems to be the only thing in his life."

"Well, he did love your mother very much, didn't he? It's only natural that he wants to be reminded of her."

"Yes, but you notice, he never asks her the question, does he? He sits and gazes at her all day long, but he never – never – asks HER!"

"She's not here with him, is she? We are, that's the simple explanation for that, surely..."

Peter looked at his father's motionless frame and said despondently,

"Or, maybe he knows – that she doesn't know it either..."

His father turned his eyes from the photograph and looked at the couple.

"What...is...the...answer?" He said, and then turned his attention once more to the silver-framed photograph.

The woman and the two children smiled down on the old man's face, as two fat tears rolled down his sallow cheeks.

The move had been very successful for all. Angela had put the final touches to the bed sitting room, and was very pleased with the result. Peter's study was slowly getting tidy, but as it had been a heaven sent opportunity to clear a backlog of papers, it was taking longer than he thought.

Of course, the fact that he was the only person who could do the sorting made things that much more difficult and, as the thing he needed most of – time – was a commodity that he found most demanding, the whole thing was tending to drag on...and on.

After a short downpour of rain Angela was looking out of the french windows. About eight feet from the house was a gracefully slender silver birch tree. Now the rain had ceased, the sun was struggling to shine through patchy clouds; when it did, it reflected the full beauty of the tree.

Each branch was left with row upon row, of what looked like symmetrically perfect crystal beads, shimmering in the sunlight. The rain beads clung on, even though they were being buffeted gently by the rhythmically, intermittent breeze.

"How very beautiful," she thought, "and how incredible that they have the power to stay on."

Suddenly she was distracted by a sound from father's room. She ran quickly to it and was alarmed by what she saw.

His face was flushed, and he was trying hard to catch his breath, and not succeeding very well.

She propped him up and stayed with him until the bout had passed and then she rang the doctor's surgery. She decided not to ring Peter until the doctor had been and she had more to report.

Now all she could do was wait. Whilst sitting there with the old man, she gently sponged his face and tried to comfort him. Because of the difficulty with his breathing, there were no questions, just the pitiful sounds of him trying to suck in his breath, and the equally distressing sounds of the painful exhaling of the same.

"How could this have happened so quickly," she thought, as she sat there saying a silent prayer. Aloud she said to him,

"Cling on father, you're much stronger than a raindrop."

"Bronchitis…How? …. Why?" Now it was their turn to ask the questions.

Tender nursing and modern medication were needed for quite a long time. Angela's patience and love for the old man were superseded only by her dogged will to pull him through the illness.

How she longed to hear his old question again…..

Book 2 – Chapter 5
Winning Ways *May 1940*

After the initial pleasantries, and May's seemingly unending cups of weak tea, Simon said,

"Why don't you take off for a walk. I'm on duty tonight, so I'll watch over the sky for you both. It all seems very quiet at the moment, and James told us before you came in that a car is picking him up at eight thirty, so you won't have long."

Laura glanced at the clock on the mantel that told her it was a quarter to seven…

"and," he went on "I'm sure you have a great deal to talk about." He looked across at James and gave him a wink… "What about taking him up to the castle?"

"Oh yes, that's a good idea, Simon. Why not go up to the castle?" May echoed.

Having agreed that it was a good idea, Laura was soon saying that she was ready to go.

"Don't go without this," May said as she handed Laura her gasmask case.

"Oh yes, that definitely gives the final touch to your Paris outfit" Simon said as he was dodging just out of reach of Laura's playful slap.

"See you both later?" James asked.

"Not me chum, I'm stargazing tonight. If you see me from the castle, give me a wave."

Laura nodded, and although James was somewhat perplexed by the remark, he nodded too.

"I'll see you both later." May said as she bustled them to the door,

"Off you go now, or you won't have time to see anything at all," she added, closing the door behind them.

They left the house and started to walk up the road. James crossing behind her to walk on the outside.

"I must keep my sword hand free to protect my lady."

He swung his arm with a flourish as he was speaking and, doing so, brushed Laura's hand. They looked at each other, smiled, and then each offered a hand to the other.

Their fingers met, cautiously at first, then each sensing the other's acceptance, quickly entwined. James gave Laura's hand a squeeze.

When their fingers touched for the first time, she felt a warmth flood over her that owed nothing to the temperature of the evening air, and as their fingers laced together she felt such joy. He was squeezing her hand now, and bring her down to earth by speaking to her.

"What's this castle that you have all been talking about? Tell me about it"

Laura explained that there was a park with a very steep hill and on the top was a castle; not a huge one, but rather like a chess-board castle. It was a towering monument and a replica of one in Madeira, and she added, that only the extremely fit should undertake the arduous journey to the top.

"I see, well, lead on my fair lady, I'm fit and ready for the challenge."

Just then, coming down the path towards them, they saw two young people with a dog on a leash.

"The mist's just trying to get up," they said as they passed them. James was completely intrigued.

"Nearly there now, last long haul coming up," she said breathlessly, as she pulled James up the narrow pathway, and through the rock garden that was filled with small flowers of all colours.

Huge rhododendron shrubs in full flower stood at the summit, proudly surrounding the castle, like so many soldiers. The evening was still with not a breath of wind disturbing the flowers, and their flaming reds and pinks, were as if a cushion for the tower to gently sit on.

"So this is the famous castle?"

"Yes, we are at the back of it at the moment. There should be a tea room inside, but since the war started, it's all been boarded up, and left rather neglected."

She led him around the path at the base of the circular turret, and then he saw it.

An immense panoramic view spread out before them. Laura spoke first.

"I'll never get tired of this view – never. It's London, and the suburbs, and on a clear day you can see the river, and St. Paul's."

There was a slight mist on the horizon now, and a shimmering heat haze was on the rest of the view in the distance. Laura continued to point out landmarks that were still visible, and, occasionally, they saw a glint of sun on metal or water.

"Simon is down there somewhere too, on a roof," she waved, "I know that he won't see me, but I did promise, so I'll wave anyway."

James was still drinking in the view, when he said quietly

"Earth has not anything to show more fair: Dull would he be of soul who could pass by a sight so touching in it's majesty…"

Laura, picking out some more lines from the same sonnet continued –

"…..Ships, towers, domes, theatres and temples lie, Open unto the fields, and to the sky…" She pointed animatedly as she spoke the lines, and they both finished in unison…

"Dear God, the very houses seem asleep,
and all that mighty heart is lying still."

She looked at him, "You like poetry then?"

"A few poets – a few poems – yes."

"What do you think that Wordsworth would have made of this view?"

James pursed his lips together thoughtfully, then uttered the lines…

"Earth has not anything to show more fair, than very fat barrage balloons hanging in the air!!"

She laughed and they both turned and sat on the bench. They sat quietly, holding hands, and viewing the now quite hazy scene. The grassy bank fell away steeply before them, and eventually turned into a doll's house valley; with even mighty chestnut trees taking on the guise of insignificant stalks and bushes.

The landscape had the look of an enormous patchwork quilt, with tiny houses, roads and gardens, blending together, making some sort of uniformity.

The reddening sky was dotted now with silhouetted buildings, looking black against the magenta horizon. The barrage balloons, hanging low, were like menacing birds of prey…waiting. Everything seemed so quiet and still. Laura was the first to break the spell.

"Tell me some more about yourself, and your family."

Speaking slowly and thoughtfully, with his eyes still firmly on the valley below, he said

"I never knew my parents at all."

"But I thought you said that they lived in Wiltshire?"

"Oh yes, the people that I call mother and father, and whom I regard as such, do live in Wiltshire, but my real parents are dead."

"I'm so sorry," Laura squeezed his hand with a gesture of sympathy.

"Well, it <u>was</u> a long time ago. My actual parents were missionaries. I was born in Nigeria, thirty four years ago. I'm quite an old man aren't I!

I lived there with them until I was nearly two...It's a tragic story really. I'll tell it to you as I heard it. Evidently we were all moving up river to a new village. All our worldly possessions were packed and then stacked on to one of the local craft. Once everything was ready, the native boys that were in charge of the embarkation, jumped aboard with my mother, father and me. The journey began quite uneventfully, then, out of nowhere, which can happen, I've since been told, a squall suddenly hit our little craft. It must have been a truly terrible time. The boat was so laden down, it became top heavy, making it unstable. It turned turtle in just a few moments. In the rushing torrent my mother, father and two of the native boys were washed overboard and swept away. The two boys that survived were so brave...diving and diving until they exhausted themselves." Laura laid her head on his shoulder.

"Anyway, one of them saved my life. My loose clothing billowed out and gave me a few seconds of buoyancy as I was washed down stream. The boy that I owed by life to, evidently, carried me to the shore in his teeth!"

"Do you remember anything of that terrible experience?"

"No, incredibly...nothing. I would have thought that such a traumatic happening would have etched itself indelibly on my mind, but thankfully, I remember nothing of the incident."

"What happened to the native boy that rescued you? Do you know?"

"Well, after I was shipped home to my mother's sister, and many years later, I was told that he had become a pastor himself and, would you believe, at the same village that my folks had set out to go to on that awful day."

As he continued his story, he turned and faced her.

"Anyway, mother and father in Wiltshire were able to send me to a rather good school because of a trust fund that had been arranged for me through the Missionary Society, where I did quite well. It was whilst I was there that I decided that I would like to make the Army my career." James laid his arm along the back of the seat, his hand resting lightly on Laura's shoulder, then he turned his eyes to the rapidly disappearing dolls house valley again.

"As I was growing up, I found coming to terms with my loss very hard, especially when I learned what a loving, compassionate couple they were.... I did come through my bereavement at last, but it took quite a while, and by then, I knew that I didn't have the call from God to follow in their footsteps."

He fell silent for a moment...

“I just feel – just know, that God has been with me all through my life. Oh I may have lost sight of Him from time to time, but deep down I’m sure that He has never given up on me, and now – He’s sent me an angel.”

His fingers tightened on her shoulder, and she felt her heart pounding.

“Anyway, that’s enough about me. What about you?”

“Well, you will just not believe it when I tell you that my parents were also killed in a freak accident…but unlike you, I remember it all…I was nine at the time, and we were in Ireland. There was some sort of mission going on, and because my parents were married officers, they were heavily involved with the setting-up of something or other. I never really knew the full in’s and out’s of it,” she paused, because remembering still brought a sadness to her… “On the fateful day, I was taken to some friends of my parents. They thought that it would be better for me to stay there with them because they had some children that I could play with – rather than take me, to what would be, a very boring day. My dear mother and father set off in a pony and trap….I heard afterwards what happened… Evidently they were wending their way along one of the lanes when a cow, in some sort of frenzy broke through the fencing of its field. It ran headlong across their path…the poor pony was terrified, it shied and then galloped on in terror…the trap overturned and fell down the bank. Both my parents were killed instantly… even the poor pony had to be destroyed because it’s legs were broken…” Laura’s eyes filled with tears at the recollection of the events.

“Oh my dear, I am so sorry, I should never have pried into your life. Please forgive me…whatever was I thinking of?”

“No, James, there’s nothing to forgive – anyway I want you to know about me – and my life.” She pushed a tear away with her hand and continued.

“Even at the age of nine, I accepted that God wanted them both so badly in heaven that He had to take them from me…Then when I came home again, my dear Aunt Mary and Uncle John were waiting for me. I lived with them both until Uncle John died. They had no children themselves, so I simply slipped into their lives as the daughter they never had, and I loved them as much as they loved me. Once Uncle John died, there was just Auntie and me. Then, of course, the war came along and Auntie had to leave Amleth…but not before the appearance of Simon. He, quite literally, seemed to drop out of the sky. Everyone has done everything and tried every way to contact his family, but we have all drawn a complete blank. He is a real-life Sherlock Holmes mystery, there's no doubt about that…and I'm sure that Sherlock Holmes is the only fellow to solve it. I love him dearly, and whatever comes for me in the future, I will never abandon him. I still worry about him and his funny moods. He is such a tonic though, lively and so outwardly happy. He is so willing to learn, and he has had to learn so much in this past year…he was so caring and kind when May lost her husband last year, and has taken her right under his wing."

"I can tell that I have some real competition from that young man, and although I don't really know him, we have somehow hit it off. We seem to have found an instant rapport. What I know of him I like very much and I know that you do too."

"You're right, because you see, he may look confident and assured but underneath he is just a lonely and confused boy, with so many unknowns. I know that he is about nineteen and I'm only twenty four, but somehow I feel very protective towards him, maybe that's because I found him… but that's another story for another day."

Laura stood up, and as she did so, she almost overbalanced. James stood quickly and put his hands on her shoulders to steady her. At the same time, her hands moved forward to his forearms to help her regain her balance.

"Ooh, thanks," she said.

At that instant their eyes met. He bent his head down and brushed her lips with his own. Each of them waiting expectantly for the other's response.

Laura put her arms around him, her hands slipping beneath his open jacket and coming to rest on the back of his shirt where she felt the warmth of his body as he held her close. They spoke not.

For they were in a timeless, wordless moment, shared throughout the ages by lovers – and known only to them. When their lips touched again, each felt a great surge deep within…engulfing them in a rapture that was theirs alone. When at last the intimacy of their embrace was broken, Laura held her face down. She felt nervous and somewhat embarrassed, for the response she had given him was of total love – and this man was almost a stranger to her. She felt herself tremble at the thought of his kiss. James looked down on the top of her head, and at the fair hair being stirred softly by a tiny breeze. He felt her tremble. Tilting her head with his hands, he sought her eyes with his own. The sight of them now, brimming with emotion as they were, melted what was left of his heart. He said with great tenderness,

"My dearest, I love you so very, very much."

The tears fell from Laura's eyes without hindrance and a sob escaped from her throat.

She clung to him as she replied with the words that he longed to hear.

"I love you too James, I have always loved you…I love you so." She was sobbing quite openly now, so much that James became quite concerned.

"My dearest…my dear…don't cry. What is it?"

"I'm sooo…so….happy."

She tried to laugh as he gave her his handkerchief, the voluminous khaki thing nearly covered her face, as she snuffled into it, and finally dried her eyes. When the emotion of the moment had passed and the tears had dried up, she patted her hair and said,

"I must look a fright."

He took her hands and held her at arms length, taking in every part of her, with his eyes. He wanted to remember this moment all his life. He looked at her, and saw her fair hair tumbling about her face, that was slightly flushed now, and very beautiful to him. Her light summer frock was clinging to, and enhancing her slight figure.

"I want to remember this moment for ever," he said, "You look so gorgeous, I could eat you."

He pulled her to him, and they kissed again, with a long passionate embrace. Afterward, he smiled at her that special smile, the one that made her heart skip a beat…the one that she would never forget. Because they had been totally consumed by their newly found love, it seemed cruel that time – and the harsh reality of the world, had to break into their freshly discovered enchantment, but break in it did.

Incredibly, when James looked at his watch, he saw that it said eight twenty.

"Oh no. Can we get home in ten minutes, love?"

"Yes, if we run all the way," she said.

Negotiating the narrow path, they ran easily down the hill, the breeze cooling their faces as they ran. Eventually, they reached the bottom, slightly dishevelled, but with time still on their side.

As they approached the last corner, James suddenly stopped and drew Laura to him into another lingering kiss, not caring what the world might think…for the world was theirs.

His only two thoughts at that moment were, one that he was totally head over heels in love with the sweet and beautiful girl in his arms and two, that he was completely overwhelmed by the fact that she loved him too.

As they turned into the road, they saw the staff car ahead of them, waiting for him. May was at the side of it speaking to the driver. They called out, and she turned, beckoning to them and calling

"Hurry up, hurry up".

When they reached the car, they were only five minutes late. May stood back and James jumped into it, pulling Laura in after him.

"Not a word, Corp. I know I'm a bit late, but don't you think she's worth it?"

The Corporal gave a knowing and approving nod by way of an answer and tactfully changed the angle of the rear view mirror.

James took Laura into his arms again, and held her tenderly. Laura said wistfully,

"We are always saying goodbye, aren't we?"

He took her hands into his own and pressed them to his lips and kissed them. He looked into her face and the lovelight that he saw in them prompted him to have the courage to speak.

"Laura…Laura – will you marry me? I know it's a cheek to ask you such a think after such a short time, but I love you so much. Will you consider my proposal? Will you?"

His handsome face, so full of love, faced her, the eyes clear and shining. There was no hesitation in her heart, or on her lips, when she gave the only answer possible.

"Yes my darling, yes, of course I'll marry you."

The car whined into life. They kissed briefly as she got out.

"Goodbye May," he said and then to Laura, "Au revoir my sweet love…I'll be back .." He blew a kiss and the car sped away down the road and was soon gone.

As the car sped away from them, Laura turned and faced May. She threw her arms around the smiling woman.

"Oh May, May, he's so wonderful…he loves me, he loves me, and he's just asked me to marry him…and I've said yes. I'm so happy. Be happy for me May."

The glow on Laura's face told May that she had, indeed, quite obviously found the love of her life. May had known the same feeling herself long ago, so she could feel nothing but happiness for the excited girl before her. Marriage? Well, that remained to be seen, but love? There was no doubt about that at all.

They linked arms, and May gave her a hug. "He's a smashing chap love. Of course, I'm happy for you." They went through the gate and it clicked shut behind them.

"He'll be back May, I know he'll be back."

That night Laura sat and wrote a long letter to Aunt Mary. She wrote often, but this letter was special. As she finished it, and was screwing the top on the ink-bottle, Simon came home. She stood up and threw her arms around him and hugged him.

"Oh Simon, I've such wonderful news to tell you."

"Steady on, I've got to go back on duty in an hour."

He stood back from Laura and put his hands on her shoulders. She looked radiant, and he could see that she was bursting to tell him something.

"Come on then, tell me what it is"

"James has asked me to marry him, isn't it wonderful?"

Simon's face clouded for an instant, then he lifted Laura off her feet and holding her close, he twirled and whirled them both around in a little circle. May became quite agitated, and was worried that they might knock something over.

"Careful, Simon now, be careful."

Laura threw her head back and laughed, and he set her down again.

"You are pleased then…aren't you?"

"For you of course, yes, for me….?" He went silent for a moment, "Well, if you love him…and not me…" he pulled a mock sad face.

"Of course I love you, but I love James."

"I'm only teasing you Laura, honestly. I think James is smashing but are you really sure that he's the one for you? After all marriage is a big step and we don't know that much about him, do we?"

He looked at Laura – the shine in her beautiful eyes – the joy on her face, and answered his own question.

"Yes, you're sure alright."

His emotions were mixed, however. The happiness he felt for dear Laura was tempered with, and overshadowed, by his own recurring insecurities.

"What would happen to him when Laura was married?"

He couldn't think of life without her, she was his friend, and she had saved him from…he knew not what.

Later on that evening whilst he was walking back to go on duty, he found himself reliving, once more, the terror that he had felt on the night that he had fallen, and when he had first met Laura. She had been there with him during his darkest moments. Self-pity swept over him, like a dark cloud, when he thought of losing her. He stopped in the doorway of a shop for a while, and leaned back into the darkness.

"What am I going to do without her? What am I going to do?"

A tram rattled and clanged past his dark refuge and brought his mind back to the job he had to do. Swallowing hard and standing straight, he quickly left the sanctuary of the doorway, and put his unnerving thoughts behind him.

He strode towards the A.R.P. station.

"Forget self," he thought, "Just think of Laura and James….and be happy for them"

He was smiling when he reached the door.

"Hello chaps. I'm back again, and old jerry had better look out….the mood I'm in!"

Book 1 – Chapter 6
Back at the Oasis *July 1985*

The bronchitis continued for well over a month. There were a few disturbed nights, but on the whole, father was a model patient. The antibiotics had made a terrific difference to him, but to regain his original state of health was still taking patience and time.

By the beginning of July he was well enough to sit, for part of the day, in the garden again. He was quiet and calm whilst dozing and daydreaming alone but he still had his old traumas when somebody approached him. At least there was no struggle for breath now, just the old, old struggle of trying to form the words – and then the horrendous task of speaking them. The phrase incorporating the whole sentence had never been heard again, by Angela, Peter or by anyone else, but they all lived in hopes!

Angela had been feeling a little under the weather herself of late, the worry and strain of father's illness had left her feeling drained over the past month, but tonight was going to be different. Once father had settled and she was able to relax, she intended to spoil herself with a luxuriously lazy bath. Since Peter's homecomings were so unpredictable, casseroles seemed to be on the menu most days but tonight it was an Italian recipe that had been slowly cooking for some time, permeating the air with its delicious aroma.

Most of all she was looking forward to enjoying Peter's birthday gift for her. It had been such a lovely surprise when she had opened the package to find a video of her favourite opera – Tosca, inside. Tonight was to be the first opportunity that they had to view it. Yes, she was looking forward to this evening very much.

On her way upstairs to run her bath, she peeped in on the old man and was surprised to see that he was still awake. She pulled a chair close to the bedside.

"Hello, my love, are you alright?"

She looked at him, he seemed smaller than ever, laying back on the pillow. His eyes were wide open and staring at the ceiling. He turned them to her when he heard her voice. Saliva had trickled from his mouth and made a round dark patch on the pillow. He looked sad.

He spoke as usual, but with a weary look in his eyes.

"What..is..the answer? Tell…me…please."

The whole sentence again, that must be an improvement surely?

"Please" she thought,…"he added please. Now he's pleading." She sighed as she placed some clean tissues on the pillow after first wiping his face, and then leaned over and kissed him on the forehead.

"Dear Lord," she said aloud, still looking into his face.. "if only I knew how to answer him, to help him get some peace."

As she stood upright again, her head spun, and the old man's face blurred momentarily. She quietly left the room, and made her way upstairs to the bathroom.

She buried her face in the towelling robe that she was holding, and leaned back against the bathroom door. She still had a queasy feeling,

"Looks as if I'm going to give my dinner a miss tonight…after all", she said, as she turned on the bath taps and threw bath crystals into the steaming stream of water.

The evening passed very happily as they sat, close together on the settee, watching the unfolding drama on the screen before them. The music and singing lifted and filled their senses, and took them gently, though briefly, into another dimension of time and place. The final scene, with Flora's famous scream as she made her tragic leap from the battlements was in their ears, when suddenly the thunderous music that was crashing out into the room was broken into by the shrill sound of the telephone ringing.

Peter was on his feet instantly, and hurried to quell the noise. The video was finished however before he lifted the receiver to his ear. After a moment or two, he returned to Angela's side

"I know that it's late m'love, but there seems to have been some trouble in the town, and somebody has asked for me so…I've got to go down to the police station…I'm sure I won't be too long …don't wait up for me, just in case. You did enjoy the video, didn't you?"

"Oh yes, it was lovely, I cried again in all the right places – as usual. Take care darling…poor Flora, I feel sorry for her every time – parted from her lover by a trick – and then never seeing him alive again."

"M'love, don't take on so, I will be back, before you know it. The quicker I go, the quicker I will be back again."

"I know dear, I'm being silly, it's only the emotion of the opera flowing out into real life. Of course you must go."

She stood up and went with him as he put on his coat.

"You're needed by others as well as me, I know that. I'll be waiting for you."

Slipping his car keys into his pocket, he drew Angela to him. She had a sweet fragrance about her and he kissed her lovingly on her perfect lips, then he went out into the night.

She closed the door behind her husband and leaned against it. Suddenly she felt very tired, and just a little lonely. Since Peter had become involved with a home for teenagers with drug problems, life had become even busier than usual for him and, if he had been able to have his way, Oasis would have become Shangri-la to them all - home to all the misfits and socially deprived. At the moment, however, he was content to take one step at a time with one particular teenager called Terri.

She was on a rehabilitation programme to get her off the drugs – drink merry-go-round that she had drifted into, and to help with this rehabilitation, Peter had suggested that she could help Angela – only for a few hours a week or course – just to see how she would get on.

As she stood at the door pondering over past events, Angela wondered how she had managed before Terri had come. She was certainly a rough diamond, but as the days and weeks passed, she had become an invaluable asset to them both. Peter was thrilled that the garden was looking as it should and Terri obviously liked his father very much and helped Angela with him as often as she could.

"Yes," she thought… "Terri's a good girl."

Even with Terri's help though it had been a busy day, and she now felt extremely tired. Moving away from the door at last, she picked up the two coffee cups and took them out into the kitchen.

On her way upstairs to bed, she looked in on father. They had installed not only a baby alarm, but also a night light so that as she entered the room, the cream shell threw patterns on to the ceiling, filling the room with a gentle glow.

She sat down. The old man was asleep. There was no doubt about it because she could see his face quite clearly. He was dreaming she could tell, for his eyes moved in an agitated manner beneath his closed eyelids. Back and forth – back and forth they raced. His lips twitched and then his head rolled, very slightly from side to side, but it was the closed lids that Angela was fascinated by and was watching instantly. Where was he in his dreams? What was he seeing? If only she knew.

She leaned forward and rested her folded arms on to the bedclothes and then laying her head on them she continued to gaze at the face on the pillow; unlined now…and somehow…young. The eyes never stopped moving under the closed eyelids.

"I wish I could see what you are seeing," she thought, "what dreams do you have locked in the prison of your mind? Dreams that you can never tell?"

Her own eyelids were becoming heavy too, although she didn't realise it. Soon, therefore, there were two people with dreams; two dreamers with, perhaps, fear and love entwining them both in some strange and wonderful fantasy and holding them both captive in another world.

Peter found the two voyaging dreamers together in slumber when he arrived home, an hour or so later.

Book 2 - Chapter 6
Letters *May 1940*

Simon tried hard to get rid of the crackle that was issuing from the wireless, because it was just about time for the news.

"Wretched thing – you would play me up right at the last minute, wouldn't you?" He addressed the whistling controls and continued to tune in to the vague voices that were escaping from it. Suddenly the air waves cleared and the familiar voice of Alva Liddell was there, reading the news. His reports that planes had been sighted and fired upon were not news, as far as Simon was concerned…

"I know that, I've seen them …yes…yes and I've heard the guns as they tracked them down river…"

Then there was the mention about the inadequate air raid warning system, and how frequent warnings had been either too late or too soon. This was like a red rag to a bull for Simon and at once he was on his high horse.

"Surely we can get it right? …. Yes….yes" He was nodding in the direction of the voice and gesticulating wildly all the time. "Remember the times we have all been caught out? I remember alright, sitting there clicking our heels. What about the people who hear the All Clear only to find the planes and guns still going at it when they come out?…..My gosh, did you hear that? People are still being stupid with their blackout…Laura's been giving some more material out round at the hall….free….there's no excuse is there?"

May could hold her peace no longer, she was totally exasperated with him.

"Simon do stop interrupting – we can't hear anything."

"Well it's all very annoying especially that bit about the warning system."

"Yes, I know it is, but I wanted to hear what they were going to do about it." The news ended. "There, you see. With all your chattering we have had a hard job to make sense of anything" she said rather crossly as she walked to the offending wireless, and turned the sound of the dance band down, as she went on, "….another thing, it's amazing to me that the dance band music is always as clear as a bell....but when I want to hear the news...well...that's a different story."

"Sorry, May." Simon looked crestfallen, "It's just that I worry about you and Laura when I'm not around....you remember, if you see or hear anything...warning or not...you get yourself down to the shelter straight away. Remember, planes, shell bursts, gun-fire, anything at all, I just want you to be safe."

May's anger had passed, after all how could you stay cross with somebody who was genuinely concerned about her welfare?

"Yes, Simon, don't fuss so, I'll be alright, and so will Laura. She can get to the shelters as easily as I can...you take care of yourself and we'll take care of ourselves. Is that a fair bargain?"

"Yes, there I go again...sorry."

"There's no need to be sorry, my dear, I know how you care for us. You're just an old fuss pot," she smiled kindly at him, "but it's early days yet, and if we start getting het up now, what will we do later? Talking of late, I wonder where Laura has got to? She's usually here by now..."

"I don't know, but I'm not going to sit here, I'm off to find her..."

Before he could get to the door though, they both heard Laura's key in the lock.

"Too late Simon, here she is now...You're rather late dear, we were worried about you – in fact Simon was just about to send out a search party – of one" she smiled.

"I'm so sorry, I had to stay and have a talk with Mr. Fisher..."

"Well the Headmaster shouldn't keep you behind without proper notification." Simon said crossly.

"No dear, it was me. <u>I</u> wanted to speak to him. In fact <u>I</u> made him late. Whatever is the matter Simon? You seem so upset and cross."

"It's the news that has started him off in his bad mood." May said.

Whilst May was speaking, Simon went over to the wireless that was now crackling again, hit it on the top and then turned it off in disgust.

"I don't like to think of May and you some place that you can't take cover, it frightens the life out of me, I can't help it, and all because of the warning system."

"They did say that there had been a couple of technical hitches...and that everything should be working well in the future."

"Yes," said Simon, looking across at May, "<u>should</u> be working well, <u>should</u> be," he angrily responded.

"Well, forget about it now dear...there's absolutely nothing we can do about it. So we'll just have to do the best that we can, won't we?"

May's words seemed to oil the troubled waters, and Simon shrugged off his bad humour as he followed Laura into the kitchen; still telling her what she should, and should not do with regard to the air raids. May gave Laura a wry smile and shook her head. As he followed Laura she stopped, turned and said,

"I know that you mean well, but you sound just like a mother hen. Am I your chick?" She smiled as she asked him the question. Her lovely eyes sparkling with fun.

"Well, yes I do like to think that I can take care of you, - for myself – and for James too. He did ask me to look out for you, you know, but I know that I'm pretty useless really."

He looked quite abashed.

"I'm sorry if I'm being too protective with you both."

"Of course you're not – I love you to take care of me and May."

May nodded in agreement.

Laura put her arms around his waist and gave him a hug.

"Want your tea now?"

"Hmm, want a letter now?" he said, holding her fast.

"Oh, you terror – where is it? I've been longing for one to arrive."

From somewhere behind his back Simon produced the letter, holding it just high enough for it to be out of reach. She struggled free, trying to catch hold of the corner of the envelope for all she was worth.

"Give me a kiss first, and then it's yours." He puckered up his lips and squeezed his eyes shut. Laura gave him a quick peck, and the letter was at last in her hand.

She ran into the garden and sat down on the grass.

"What about my tea then?" he called from the kitchen doorway.

May pulled him back into the kitchen by his collar.

"Come on Simon give the girl a chance, give her some peace do. You can start on the potatoes and then I'll find you another job," she said as she closed the back door.

Just holding the letter gave Laura's heart a jolt. She didn't open it at once, just held it close, savouring every moment. At last she drew out the cream coloured letter, allowing the envelope to fall beside her on the grass:

She saw the opening:

"My dearest, dearest love…" then she read on, hearing only James' voice in her head as she quickly drank in all his words, his voice becoming so real that it was as if he was sitting right next to her. She scanned the page, questions, questions.

"....could we marry on my next leave?....I hope to have five days in August...could things be arranged at such short notice?...I love you, do you still love me?.....the five days would be my next proper leave, but I hope to be home for a few hours on the twentieth of July. Could you arrange a meeting with Captain Fuller?.....I long to hold you in my arms again...do you feel the same about me?....Why are you there? Why am I here? I'm picturing you standing on top of the hill, with the wind in your hair...and your beautiful eyes, misty with tears, looking at me...happiest day of my life. I have often heard of love at first sight, but I would never have dreamed for a moment that it could ever happen to me, that I would experience the magical feeling for myself, how wrong I was. I was smitten from the first moment I saw you, all those months ago. My precious, precious Pansy, how I love you. My precious, precious Pansy say that you love me too...I know I'm no William Wordsworth, I give my apologies to him for the bad rhyming but the very first time I saw you with your salvationist's bonnet on, you reminded me of a flower...a pansy. It was the colour of your hair, your truly beautiful eyes and the dark bonnet framing your lovely face – it just reminded me of a sweet pansy's face. Will you mind if I call you Pansy when we are alone together? Do you think that I'm crazy? Well, I am crazy...crazily in love with you...Keep me in your prayers my love, and your heart. Oh how I hate this war that is keeping us apart, and more so because you cannot answer this letter. I'm on the move at the moment, and so by the time your reply caught up with me, I would probably be back here again after my flying visit...to see the preacher? Time marches on my dearest dear....My dear friend and love, I must go, whatever happens, I will love you to my dying day, you have my heart with you, hold it alongside yours until we meet again, my dear sweet Pansy, my love. Please don't mind being thought of as a flower, will you? Don't think that I'm being stupid.....Au revoir..."

Laura stopped reading and just sat there, clutching the letter to her breast. She spoke aloud,

"How can I ever think that you are stupid? I love you with all my heart, my dearest, dearest love".

She raised the letter to her lips, and kissed it. Closing her eyes, she pictured him; his face, his smile, his eyes and imagined his strong arms were holding her.

Suddenly she shivered, not in an ecstasy, but because the sun had disappeared behind a cloud, and the wind – even in the garden - was cold all around her. It took the empty envelope and whisked it high in unseen hands, and then having had it's fun, threw it down again, forcing it to tumble erratically along the grass until it finally came to rest on the sloping side of the shelter. Laura quickly darted forward and retrieved it from the podding arms of a wallflower before walking slowly back into the house.

Aunt Mary's letter came the next day. It started the morning badly for them in one way, because it held some sad news. Mary's brother had died in his sleep. He had had a short illness, brought about by worry, and old age, or so the doctor had said. She went on to say that as soon as the formalities and the funeral were over, she hoped to be coming back to Amleth on July twentieth unless they heard to the contrary. She also expressed a most earnest desire to meet the exceptionally handsome – exceptionally wonderful – exceptional – James, that a certain person had told her about.

Laura passed the letter to Simon and he said,

"That's wonderful. They will both be here on the same day – with a bit of luck."

"Yes. Won't it be good to see Auntie again?"

Simon agreed at once, he felt more than happy – and said so. His mind went back to the time when he had felt himself hovering between day and night, and to him – life and death and how, at that time, dear Aunt Mary had taken the place of his real long lost mother, when she had taken him under her wing, and simply loved him. Although he had known her for such a short time he couldn't have loved her more if she had been his real mother. After all Simon knew more than most that mothers were hard to find. He went on,

"Well, it's sad news in one way, but good news for us, isn't it? Wait till I tell Mr. B. this morning."

He glanced at the mantle, one look at the clock told him that he would be late if he didn't hurry.

"Gosh is that really the time? – I must dash or else I will be getting the sack!" With these words, he grabbed his things, and positively threw himself out of the house.

As the door banged shut, Laura turned to May.

"What a pity we can't find his own people May, it would be wonderful to give Auntie some good news about him, wouldn't it? He is such a love, but none of us is any nearer solving the mystery now than when she went away. How can a family just lose a lovely young man like him – and not try to find him?"

May shook her head, "Yes, it certainly is a puzzle – and no mistake. Still you are his real family now, aren't you?"

"We all are."

"He loves you so much, in fact I wasn't too sure how he would take to your James. Thank goodness for us all that he did, don't you think?"

"Yes, I must say that I was relieved myself. In fact, I think he's got on very well with him, and in such a short time too."

"They certainly hit it off straight away – mind you James is a very amicable young man, but then, so is our Simon.!"

The wireless that had been playing softly, was fading into nothingness but, nevertheless, there was somebody trying to be cheerful by singing… "Hey little hen, when – when – when – will you lay me an egg for my tea?" ….

"I still feel as though Simon is the mother hen… and I'm his chick."

Laura moved to the wireless and turned it off; turning it around she disconnected the wires from the top of the batteries. Then, taking the two accumulators out of their brown bakelite home, she stood them carefully on a newspaper.

"I'll take them into the shop on my way out."

"Before you go out, I'd like to talk to you for a minute."

"Yes, of course. You sound a bit serious though May. What's troubling you?"

"Well, over the last few days I've been doing a lot of thinking – especially about your Aunt. When Mary comes home again, it will be too much of a cheek for me to expect to stay here with you all. After all there are only the two bedrooms and I certainly don't have any intention of putting you all to any trouble. You have been so kind to me already – I don't know quite what I would have done without the support of you and Simon – but – I don't want to push myself in…"

"Please May, don't go on, don't be silly. I know that we only have the two bedrooms – but there is no problem there are all. Auntie and I always shared a room before, so we are not likely to change that..and..as for Simon, well you know full well that he will only sleep down here on the settee, he says that it was his first bed in this house, and he won't change that arrangement as we both know."

"Yes, dear – but what about when you are married? You are going to get married, aren't you? Or did I dream that?"

"No, you certainly didn't dream that particular piece of news…we will marry – not right at this moment though, and anyway…what with the war…and James not being here much….well let's say that we just don't know what is going to crop up in the future. Can we wait and see what happens – when the time comes? Meanwhile, there is no question at all in my mind – but that you will stay here with us for the time being….and I know that Auntie would be saying exactly the same as me. Surely…if anyone leaves the nest – whatever way you look at it – it should be me after all. Can you imagine just how long a time that particular manoeuvre would take?"

"Yes, but…"

"No buts…no more discussion – you're going to stay here. What would we do without you? Promise me that you won't think about it any more."

"Alright, dear, if you're quite sure."

"I am – and there's an end to it. Now can I go and put these into the shop? If I don't get over there to collect the others, we will miss out on the evening news – and ITMA."

"Oh no, that will never do – if Simon gets home in time and there's no Tommy Handley – we'll never hear the last of it, will we? You had best be off, thanks for listening to me- and I'll do as you say – for the time being anyway."

"That's the idea. After all life is too short to sit and worry about the future. Let's take each day as it comes – and be thankful that we have any day at all."

Laura left the house a few moments later, taking with her the all important accumulators. On the way out of the shop, the unmistakable wailing sound of the air-raid warning came to her ears. The droning of planes and the booming of the gunfire were chorusing well by the time that she returned home, and so was the rain."

"May, why aren't you down the shelter?"

"Well, raid or not, there's no way I am going down that shelter without some tea! It's done now anyway, and in two flasks. The basket is there by the back door, so it's just the blankets and our coats that are needed."

"I'll get them…."

May opened the door.

"Look at this lot – as if we don't have enough to contend with."

Laura threw the coat around May's shoulders and she hoisted it up around her, tucking blankets and flasks beneath it.

"I'll go first," Laura said, pulling her own coat up over her head.

She ran quickly down the path, through the downpour, taking the basket with her in one hand, leaving the other one free to be able to manipulate the awkward entrance. On reaching the top of the three steps, she negotiated them with care, for they were now quite slippery. She wrenched the makeshift door open with her free hand and pushed the basket inside, on to one of the bunk beds, then, turning, she quickly ran back up the path.

"Come on now, May, give me one of those blankets."

The two of them ran the gauntlet of the rain and gingerly descended the steps into the dark, dank smelling burrow, pulling the door shut behind them, making their self-imprisonment complete.

They switched on the torch at once, and lit Simon's clever light box. The light shone out its best, reflecting its glow in the shiny surface of the biscuit tin's lid.

Somewhere outside they heard the long whistling sound of a bomb, and the tremendous bang of its impact as it came to earth. The ground shook beneath their feet. It felt so very close. May let out an involuntary sound as it hit, and Laura quickly put her arm around the frightened woman, pulling the blanket tightly around them, to give comfort – and to ward off the damp feeling of their sanctuary.

More whistling…they held their breaths…waiting in expectation for the sound of the explosion, and then, when at last it came, it rent their ears, temporarily deafening them with its awful loudness.

More repeated and protracted gunfire followed rapidly.

"Hitler means business today alright. Let's hope that Simon is safely down the cellar at the shop…." May's last words were drowned out by the noise above their heads.

At the mention of Simon's name, Laura's thoughts went back to another day….a long, long time ago it now seemed, when nature's thunder had rendered him into a panic stricken state, and how, at that time, the noise (moderate in comparison to what was going on outside), had given him so much pain in his poor ear….

The strange whinings, explosions and non-stop gunfire from the local gun battery, plus the booming reverberations from the larger, though further off, guns made conversation very difficult – in fact impossible, so they just sat there close together, helping each other to be less afraid.

Suddenly, after what seemed an age, there fell about their ears a complete silence. They sat quietly, in anticipation – for quite what they did not know. Then May decided to make the most of the lull and poured out some tea for them both. They drank the no longer hot, but nevertheless welcome, liquid and were thankful that the bombardment had ceased for the moment.

There was one more extraordinarily loud burst of gunfire that rocketed their tomb once again and then....silence. After what seemed like another eternity – they heard the wail of the all clear.

They emerged like two snails coming out of their shells, only to find that it was still raining. There cowering on the bottom step was a small cat. Bedraggled, forlorn and frightened, it looked up at them.

"Hello, where did you come from?" Laura bent down and picked up the pathetic little bundle.

"We can leave our things here for the time being," May said as she closed the door across the opening. "I'll come back when the rain eases up a bit."

So the only things that they carried were – one empty thermos and one cat. Likewise, Laura thought, judging by the weight of it, neither the cat nor the flask presented any difficulties to them as they splashed their way through the unrelenting deluge, back into the comfort of the house.

The world may have looked the same, but they knew by the sounds and smell of acrid smoke in their nostrils without having to see the destruction, that their world had changed – and would never be quite the same again;.

Giving the bedraggled cat into May's care, Laura prepared to go to the ambulance station at once.

"You'll be alright won't you, May? Only I must get there as soon as possible."

"Of course, my dear, off you go and take care, and don't worry about me." She looked down at the wet bundle of fur that was now purring (with a vibrating rattle that she could feel in her hands,) and concluded, "We – will be fine."

Laura tightened the belt on her raincoat, pulled a beret down to cover her fair hair, and set off down the road as fast as she could on a bicycle that had seen better days

Simon, meanwhile, had been in the basement of the shop, trying, as usual, to be his old self. Consequently, when Mr. B. hand suggested a rather silly guessing game he had readily joined in. They did this, of course, to try to take their minds off what might be going on around them, and more closely – above them.

It was Simon's turn to speak, but before he had time to think, the guns had started their pounding. On and on they boomed, shaking the very foundations of the old shop. The sounds of the bombs whistling down as they found their targets, gave way to the sounds of deafening explosions, that reverberated, not only in the confines of the cellar, but more painfully within their heads.

Simon felt this pain more acutely than the others. He bent his head downward towards his knees, and sat with his hands covering his ears. He thought that his skull would burst, just like one of the bombs outside. As the pain seared through his ear, the blood drained from his face, leaving him with an ashen pallor that worried Rosie and Mr. B. very much. However, concern for one, soon turned to concern for all, as an almighty thud above them sent clouds of dust and plaster cascading downwards, on to the heads of the three prisoners – of war.

It was the first real air raid – the first of many that would change all their lives for ever.

When at last the all clear had sounded, they cautiously made their way up the narrow stairway into the shop, what was left of it. It had taken quite a pounding.

The whole of the front window had been blown in – and out. The plate glass was shattered, and lying across the floor amid all the other rubble. Some of it was hanging in chunks by its brown paper giving the appearance of pieces of broken toffee – stuck up in its own wrapper. Other slivers festooned the sides of the window, like so many icicles, the sorry remnants of a once beautiful pane.

Simon viewed the scene with disbelief. Then, rather irrationally, he started to laugh, pointing at the roller blind. It was hanging down and flapping across what was the door, proclaiming that the shop was closed.

Mr. B. nodded.

"Yes," he said…."I think we can safely say that we are closed – for the moment anyway."

Even he smiled at the silliness of the sight, although tears were not far away from his eyes, or the eyes of the other two onlookers. Simon looked around and then said,

"No, not much doubt about it at all, unfortunately…"

As he spoke, he caught sight of his reflection in a broken sign. He could see at once that his ear had been bleeding again, but he felt no pain from it now – just a numbness. He did, however, have a real corker of a headache.

"Thank God we are all alive," Rosie said, picking her way across the rubble strewn floor as she made her way to the gaping hole, that was once the front of the shop.

She stepped through the precarious door-posts and then, making a fist she shook it at the sky – shouting at it.

"You'll have to do better than this to beat us…you swines" she said, whilst wiping the tears and dust from her face with the back of her hand.

After the front of the shop had been boarded they stood, patiently watching, as the glazier put the finishing touches to the shop door. When it was completed, the roller blind, the only unscathed thing, or so it seemed, was ceremonially returned to its position on the new frame and pulled down.

The last job Simon did before slowing walking home was to nail a large notice on the boarded front, telling the world that there would be business as usual – on the next day.

His head was still thumping, and his eyes were not behaving as he thought that they should, in fact, he felt pretty dreadful. Going on duty tonight was definitely out of the question he realised, for he would be more hindrance than help, in his present condition.

He called in at the warden's station on the way home, but they already knew all about the raid and sent him on his way, with strict instructions to get himself fit before returning, and after exchanging hopes for a peaceful night, he resumed his painfully slow walk homeward.

When he eventually reached the house, Laura was out, but May was in, and he was grateful for that – for he had no wish for solitude tonight.

At eight o'clock the air-raid warning went off again, heralding the beginning of another long and shattering night. Simon found that he had a new friend to share his bunk, on that noisy night, someone who was warm and friendly, and possessing the very grand name of Little Raindrop.

"Hello," he said, rubbing under the chin of the little bundle, "I hear that you dropped out of the sky – just like me ….SNAP."

Book 1 – Chapter 7
Detective Work Takes Hold *August 1985*

Terri and father were in the garden and Angela could hear her giving him the benefit of all her worldly experiences: the young girl liked the old man, and kept up a running commentary whilst she was pottering around with her garden work. He never took any notice of her, except to ask her his old question of course, but she didn't seem to mind. It appeared to Angela that it did her some good in fact, for she was able to talk over her troubles, knowing that he could never tell her when she was wrong – or try to change her thinking, or her language, which was at times quite 'colourful'.

Knowing that all was well outside, Angela was able to take the opportunity of getting the dilapidated silver box out of the cupboard again. Then squatting on the floor, she tipped the photographs out and quickly started to rake through them. She had one purpose in her mind, and that was to find a particular photograph, the one that had the word Banjo written on the back. After a few moments of diligent searching, she found it. The young man smiled out at her as she remembered from the first time that she had seen him. She returned his gaze and said,

"Are you the answer my friend? Or even part of it?"

On closer examination she could see that it was not an ordinary snapshot for it was too posed for that, and on turning it over, she saw that there was just one hand-written word in black ink, 'Banjo'. There were some printed figures, and also some letters looking like some sort of code. Across one of the corners the year nineteen thirty six had been stamped, it was a studio portrait without any doubt, but unfortunately there was no name of the studio visible. She was still sitting amongst the photographs when Terri put her head in through the french windows.

"Bloody Nora. What a mess, the garden's tidier than in 'ere."

"Yes, I know, I reckon that there are about a hundred here, not that I have actually counted them. All this mess to find one particular one – this is it."

She held up the photo for Terri to see.

"Blimey, I've seen better. He looks like a chap that I saw in an old film on telly the other day. It was ....pathetic. I can't think of 'is name, mind you I don't think I ever knew it – anyway, he kept saying... 'turned out nice again…' and then started laughing a stupid laugh with a mouth full of teeth. It was unbelievably awful – and on top of it all he kept bursting into song – if you could call it a song. What a drip of the first order he was."

"What a coincidence. The man you are talking about, was a star in his day. His name was George Formby. He played a ukulele when he sang…"

"Yes – that's right, boy was it grim"

"Well, this man," she said, indicating the photograph, "this man, I feel sure may have played the banjo. I'm hoping that 'Banjo' was his nickname."

Terri was still mumbling on about the rubbishy film and that she couldn't understand anybody paying good money to see such tripe, as Angela began to tidy up the rest of the photos, not really taking much notice of the girl's tirade.

"Can I take the old boy for a walk around the block?"

Angela started listening at once, as the girl went on,

"Only I've done all I can in the garden today, and 'e must get bored just sittin' there. Well truth is – I get bored with him. Can I?"

Angela stood up, carefully stepping over the few snaps that were still strewn over the floor.

"Well I don't know Terri – that chair is not the easiest of things to manipulate you know and…"

"I know, you're making bloody excuses, aren't you? You just don't trust me, do you? Go on, admit it – you just don't trust me enough."

"It's not that Terri…"

"No? What is it then? I'm no damn weakling you know"

Angela knew in her heart she was making excuses and that any decision that she made wrongly, at this moment, might have far reaching consequences for Terri and undermine the good relationship that she had built up with her over the months. No, she had to give her a chance – perhaps it was now or never.

"Alright Terri – of course you can. I'm sure he will love the walk."

"Come off it, 'e won't know where 'e is, but anything 'as got to be better than just sittin' there enit? I'll take 'im out the back gate and just breeze around for 'alf hour, alright?"

Somewhat reluctantly, though she hoped that it didn't show to the girl, she nodded in agreement, as Terri rushed on saying

"I know how much you love the old boy, I'll take good care of him – honest I will, you can trust me you know."

"Yes, I know I can, I'll see you both in about half an hour, and I won't worry," she added putting her arm around Terri's shoulder.

They walked together, Terri collecting the old man on their way back to the back gate. Angela bent to kiss the expressionless face.

"See you later, my love..." and then instantly his mouth started to twitch in the old way...

"What...is....the....answer?"

"Not again mate, just you forget the bloody question – we're going for a walk," Terri said resolutely as she pushed the wheelchair out.

Angela closed the gate after them, and after watching for a while as they departed, she returned to the sitting room to complete her clearing up operations, still feeling slightly apprehensive, if she was totally honest.

As time was racing by, and although she would have liked to pore over the photographs for a lot longer, she knew that it was not on her side. Since she was going to put some advertisements in the national papers, she still had to work out exactly what she was going to say. By its very nature, it was going to be rather ambiguous wording. She sat there, working things out, and trying her best to avoid making the whole thing sound like abbreviated house adverts.

The words started to dance before her eyes, and she found her head swimming.

"What with my headache – and this headache," she tapped the paper in front of her, "I feel quite worn out, but at least this headache" she inclined her head towards the page of writing, "is nearly over. As for mine....it just seems to be my constant companion these days, I'll have to do something about it, but that's for tomorrow. This is for today." She finished talking to herself and made her way to the telephone.

After relaying and repeating the message five times over she was surprised to see that the whole operation had taken nearly an hour. Where were they? Worrying thoughts had just started to infiltrate her mind when she saw them coming into view through the french windows.

"Hello, we're back safe and sound – no need for you to send out the bloody troops."

Angela hurried out to greet them, and as she reached them father turned his eyes in her direction and said in his usual way,

"What ....is...the...answer?"

"Sorry, I couldn't give him the answer, but as you can see, I did give him an ice cream. I'm really, really sorry about the mess, but I had no idea how hard it was to feed 'im and keep 'im clean. That's why we are blee….." she started to swear again but corrected herself, thinking better of it, and just finished the sentence with the word "late".

"I've been trying to clean 'im up a bit for you." She bent down, "We did our best didn't we Pops? And you did like the ice cream, didn't you?" she added whilst still scrubbing away at his face with an old tissue that was, by this time falling apart. He looked first at Terri, then his eyes darted to and fro, finally coming to rest on Angela's face. The lips started to quiver once again.

"What…is…"

Before he could say anything more, Terri had joined in with him and they finished the question together.

The girl looked at Angela.

"I'm only 'ere once a week, but you're 'ere all the bloody time," and then putting her hand to her mouth as if to shield it from the old man's gaze, she almost whispered.

"Doesn't 'e drive you round the bend?"

"No. Strangely enough he doesn't. I guess that I feel too sorry for him most of the time."

Terri shrugged and said that she would have to be going.

"The garden's looking so much better for all your labours – it's a pleasure to look at these days. Thank you so much for all your hard work. I do know how trying father can be, and I really appreciate what you do for him on the days that you are here. I know that you don't have to so it makes it all the more kind hearted of you to care."

"Well, 'e can't help how 'e is can 'e?"

"No, he can't. But I know if he could speak to us, he would say thank you too. Since I've been feeling a little under the weather with my headaches I've been more than grateful for your help. Anyway, I mustn't keep you. Take care, and I'll see you next week."

"Yes – okay. See you next week, come hail, rain or shine. 'Bye Pops," she looked across at the still figure.

She made for the gate, with Angela following her, then, just as she reached it, she turned and quite unexpectedly called out (looking at Angela over her shoulder) almost casually, like an aside in a play,

"When my mum was…..under the weather….it was a sure sign that she was in the club." Then seeing the look on Angela's face, went on, "You know…up the duff…pregnant!"

The word pregnant rang in Angela's ears, sending bells ringing as if the word had been shouted at the top of the girl's voice, although, in reality, Terri's last words had been almost inaudible. After she had gone, Angela returned to the sitting room wheeling father in with her.

She felt her head buzzing as she changed the old man's clothes and generally cleaned him up. At last she finally settled him in the corner of the chaise longue, his body hardly having time to assimilate to the comfort before his eyes closed in rest. The afternoon's activities had obviously worn him out. Only once did he ask her his question, only once before his heavy eye-lids drooped – blotting out his unfathomable world.

As Angela gazed at him lying there so peacefully, she realised that she too felt worn out – and not at all like her old self. Pregnant. The word filtered through her brain

"Not possible," she thought, "How silly, thirty nine years old...and after all these years, no way."

She tried to push the offending word out of her mind, but why couldn't she stop the somewhat erratic beating of her heart?

She did her best to continue the rest of the day in a normal fashion, pushing all thoughts of pregnancy out of her mind whenever it drifted into her subconscious, which as it happened, was often.

When Peter finally came home, she didn't mention her headache – or the fact that she didn't feel like her old self. In actual fact, she had tried her best to convince herself that she did not have a bad head and that she was in no way under the weather. Therefore, it caused her some consternation and a little shock when Peter had remarked that she looked..."a bit shattered".

She tried to ignore the remark, and started to explain what she had been doing during the afternoon, with regard to the press advertisements.

"I had no idea how hard it was going to be – you would have thought that it would have been relatively easy wouldn't you? But it wasn't – in fact it was quite mind stretching. It all seemed so cryptic. It was worth a try, you do think so Peter, don't you?"

"Of course I do but let's face it – we are clutching at straws rather, aren't we? Any activity has to be better than none though, so well done m'love."

"Here is a copy of the final wording – what do you think? I know it's going to take you less than a minute to read it – but I can tell you it took a great deal longer to think it out."

"It's fine – we haven't tried anything like this before....so let's hope the right person sees it."

"Oh, somebody somewhere has just got to see it, I'm praying that...no matter how slender the chance, I'm just...Oh Peter, he's not getting better….I feel that he is slowly slipping away from us…and that he may never know…someone must respond."

"I know how you feel m'love, but I don't want your hopes to be too high. I want the same things for father that you do. You must believe that. But, well, we must remember that if we find this Banjo, if indeed there ever was a person of that name, well, he's bound to be as old as father: maybe even older – and, of course, there is a strong possibility that he might…"

"Don't say it, just don't say it."

She could not bear to hear the word 'dead', not in the same brain that was being bombarded with a neon sign reading 'pregnant'. She felt the tears well up in her eyes, and the comforting arms of her husband trying to shield her from the obvious pain that he could see on her face.

When she was in bed later that night, she tried to blot out all thoughts of being pregnant.

"I must definitely go to the doctor," she thought as she turned her head to look at her sleeping partner.

"I love you…so very much my darling. I love you more than ever," she whispered, as she leaned over the sleeping form, and placed a tender kiss on his cheek, without awakening him.

At last the new day dawned, and surprisingly, for she had experienced a very broken night's sleep, she awoke feeling happy and light-hearted. The thoughts of a response from one of the newspaper adverts kept her spirits up. Then in a rush, she thought about Terri's words again, and later wished she hadn't. The thought was outlandish…and yet it was still causing an unnerving fluttering in her chest. The conclusion that she arrived at was depressing to say the least.

"It's probably my age," she thought. Then the sparkle went out of the rest of her day.

The doctor was at the house reporting on father's progress, and it was good. There was no sign of a recurrence of the bronchitis, and his progress was very encouraging.

He was an understanding doctor and so patient with father, who, even as he was being examined, was asking his old question of the kindly man. Looking into the clear and still lively eyes, the doctor answered him.

"No answer for you today, my friend, except to say that you are fighting fit."

"Oh that's really good news doctor. How I wish that his mental anguish could be eliminated with antibiotics as efficiently as his physical condition was."

"Yes, my dear, the mind, in the main, is still virtually uncharted territory, and although the explorers in that field have made unquestionable leaps in the way of knowledge, it still remains a rather remote island. Never give up hope though, even in this technological age breakthroughs do happen, and sometimes they have nothing to with the wizardry of science, but are spontaneous, and quite beyond explanation."

"Well, I would love something like that to happen for him, for us all," she added rather dejectedly.

"You seem a bit down my dear, pop in to the surgery tonight, and cheer up, things aren't as bad as they seem. Anyway come along and see me – a chat with somebody on the outside of the family sometimes helps you know."

"Yes, I will come along, actually I was going to – I've been having some really blinding headaches…"

"Well, as I say, you come along tonight and we'll see what's what."

Whether it was the comfort of knowing that father's recovery was even better than they had hoped for, or whether it was her rather sleepless night catching up with her, she didn't know, but during the afternoon she did something that for her was quite out of character. She fell into a deep sleep. What had started out as a quick coffee break turned into something different. Having put the cup down, she had close her eyes for a moment. That moment had turned, unaccountably into twenty minutes of oblivion.

When she awoke, she felt awful, stiff and rather cold. Getting up and stretching, she crossed quickly to father's room to check on him, feeling a little more than guilty. When she peeped in she was more than a little relieved to find that he too, was cat napping.

A sudden chill went down her spine.

"What a stupid woman I am, allowing such silly thoughts of babies to carry me away on flights of fancy like that," she thought, and then sadly her happy bubble burst – and the rest of the afternoon found her rather depressed.

She was sitting in the surgery waiting for the coloured bulb above the door to light up indicating her turn, when she heard the back door of the consulting room close, and she knew that the last patient had left.

Suddenly she felt sick with anxiety, and when the light finally came on, she again felt the unusual fluttering in her chest.

Then curbing these false and real emotions she got up and crossed the room, knocking just once on the door.

"Come in," came the doctor's cheery voice.

As she entered he stood to greet her. Indicating the chair he went on

"Come in, come in and sit down, and let's see what I can do for you."

She went in and closed the door behind her.

All was silent in the waiting room, now that the surgery had finished and the receptionist had departed. It was empty and waiting .....

Book 2 – Chapter 7
Disaster *July 1940*

The day of the twentieth of July duly arrived. It was a Saturday so it was work as usual for Simon.

Everyone with whom he came into contact at the shop knew him for his bright and cheerful disposition, but today things were made easy for him in a way because Aunt Mary was due home, and James as well – double pleasure. Wider the smile!

The war, however, was taking its toll of all of them, and some days it took real effort to present the light-hearted approach to the customers, and as each day dawned – it just seemed that little bit harder, not only for Simon but for everybody. He found that his deaf ear was still a problem too. Under normal circumstances of course it wouldn't be, but the gun fire and explosions always put an intolerable strain on it.

He was still quite deaf, of course, and always would be, but to add to that misfortune he had the wretchedness of the acute pain that he always experienced during the times of loud noise. Since the raids were becoming more frequent, it seemed to him that he was often in more pain than not these days. It was because of this that his very deafness seemed to become worse. It didn't, of course, but it just seemed that way to him.

Because of this feeling he had, over the past weeks, begun to turn his head more noticeably to the good side to catch the words spoken to him. That birdlike movement, coupled with an almost perpetual frown, made the ladies that came into the shop quite worried about him, and they were always enquiring about his health. He, of course, loved to play up to them, making out that things were far worse than they really were. It was all done in fun, and today was no exception, happy banter was filling the air in the shop.

There was some good cheese in today, and as soon as the word was passed round, a long queue formed for this luxurious commodity, even the black, dried bananas took second place.

He worked deftly, clipping the coupons from the ration books with a small pair of scissors that were hung on a piece of string from the edge of the counter.

As it was eleven thirty, Rosie Bartholomew said that she would make them a quick cup of tea, as she was gasping. She only had the time to go through the back of the shop, hardly setting foot in the scullery when all at once the gun battery in the park started to fire. After a few seconds the all familiar sound of the moaning minnie started. The queue that had formed so rapidly such a short time ago, seemed to disperse with almost the same speed. There were only two women left in the shop now. One was young and she stood dithering at the open door and the other was elderly and frail. Simon was concerned with only one – old Mrs. Fitchet, who at that time was slowly and carefully putting her precious packet of cheese into her basket, dropping her walking stick to the floor as Mr. B called out loudly to his wife.

"Come on Rosie, leave that, and get down to the cellar." He shouted again as he quickly locked the till, cramming the paper money from it and the key into his deep overall pocket.

The droning of the planes could now be plainly heard above, and the guns were firing salvo after salvo, the shells bursting with monotonous regularity, bringing sounds to Simon that were almost unbearable.

"Come on Mrs. Fitchet, you must come with us now, down to the cellar," he said making his way around the corner of the counter, closing and bolting the door shut on his way.

Then he gently helped the old lady off the chair that she had been sitting on, kicked her stick to one side, and carefully steered her to the top of the cellar stairs, ready to descend.

Mr. B. had run into the scullery to get Rosie, and at that moment there was a deafening explosion. The sound of it hurled shock waves out in all directions, causing them to cry out as they both followed Simon to the open door of the cellar. They saw that he was part way down the stairs, carrying the frail old lady in his arms, when there was another explosion far worse than the last. The blast's after-wave hit Mr. B full on the back like a sledge-hammer propelling him both downwards and forward with terrific force. His wife took the full impact of both blast and her husband's body. She herself in turn fell forward, arms outstretched, embracing the air as if it would afford her some safety on her downward journey. Thus the weight of the two felled bodies landed squarely on Simon's back. He, meanwhile, unable to save himself in any way, was thrown downward and forward too. His legs unable to stand the strain buckled beneath him, sending him headlong into the dark pit of the cellar with the old lady in his arms defenceless against the impact that was to come.

During the seconds that they were falling, the beams above them became loosened with pressure and fell, bringing the ceiling down on top of the unfortunate group. White plaster and the dust of many years filled the air. Masonry, wood, and tiles bounced on and off their defenceless bodies. They all hit the bottom with a terrible and sickening thud. Although the whole scenario was over in only a few seconds, they were seconds that brought pain to their bodies, pandemonium to their ears, and darkness to their eyes – and their lives. The cacophony above was still at its height, but they lay there in a stupefied heap, the air from their lungs being squeezed from them, leaving them silently gasping.

The smell of gas pervaded the air and filled their nostrils with its unaccustomed sweetness, making their breathing even more painful. Unable to disentangle themselves, one from the other, they remained unmoving in that pitiful state. Then there came the sound of a voice, quiet, but nevertheless insistently repeating,

"I can't help you.....I can't move.....I can't help you...."

Rosie B. was draped over Simon's back, like so much gypsy washing hung over a bush, unmoving and unconscious. Both Simon's arms were trapped under the frail body of Mrs. Fitchet, pinioned not only by her inert body, but by the weight of the other souls on him as well.

All at once there was a series of tremendous explosions, causing what was left of the ceiling to do a little jig, completing its dance at the rafters where the movement stopped at a point somewhere above the heads of the still forms below. The gunfire that followed quickly, and another explosion, finally brought the whole precarious mess down on top of the tragic quartet. Simon was vaguely aware of the ack-ack's relentless barrage and the sound of ambulance bells in the shadowy distance but more than that he suddenly realised that he could see the face of Mrs. Fitchet, quite close to his own.

It was covered in a fine white dust, her small hat caught up under her chin by the elastic, it looked incongruously stupid, he thought. There was no sound or movement of any sort from her, and all he could see was the silent dust that clung to her face and lip. He tried without success to move his arms but it was impossible....in fact he could move none of his extremities, he felt completely paralysed. He spoke the old lady's name quietly,

"Mrs. Fitchet?..."

He waited for a reply, when none was forthcoming he spoke a little louder,

"Mrs. Fichet..."

Then an awful cold realisation dawned on him, and he lifted his head as high as his body would allow; and laying it back, closed his eyes, before letting out a long sad cry –

"Noooooo," as his tears made two pink rivulets down his white clown's face.

When he slowly opened his eyes again, he found that he could see soft daylight filtering down through a gaping hole that was once the roof. The light coming by way of the now non-existent floor of the shop, which was directly above them.

The guns were still pounding out relentlessly, their booming sounding closer than ever. Simon found himself having to deal with the pain in his head and also with the unmistakable smell of gas that was lingering in the air.

Mr. B. had stopped talking some time back, and Rosie had made neither sound nor movement since they had all fallen.

Simon's body, apart from his head, felt completely numb and - surprisingly – pain free. He felt claustrophobia sweep over him like a blanket as he lay there bearing the weight of the other unwilling prisoners, and this sensation was quickly followed by a hot feeling of bile that rose up from his stomach into his mouth uncontrollably, then the bitter fluid ejected like a fountain – all over the dead face of Mrs. Fitchet. The smell of the vomit combining with the ever strengthening smell of the gas, made him feel even more nauseated, and he retched again. The foulness of the air that he was breathing and the lack of oxygen made him feel quite light headed and silly. Then, quite suddenly, he felt a searing pain tear through his head, and the blackness of unconsciousness overpowered him.

Laura felt so happy this morning, happy and excited. Her darling James and dear Auntie both expected to arrive at about the same time – and soon.

Just after Simon had left for the shop, Laura too left home, riding on her bicycle, her hair streaming out behind and around her radiantly happy face. She pedalled as fast as she could, because she wanted to get to the Citadel as soon as she was able.

Today was going to be a special day too for a little family that were going to take occupation of May's house. May was more than happy for the family to use it than for it to stand idle. The mother and two children had been away to Dorset but couldn't settle down there and on their return to Amleth were distressed to find that, because of extensive damage to their neighbour's house, their own was made uninhabitable. So they were very appreciative of the help and temporary accommodation that the Salvation Army had given them.

Therefore, Laura's mind was fully engrossed as she pedalled happily along when suddenly all thoughts were blasted from her by the roar of the gunfire and the wail of the air-raid warning. Taking stock of her surroundings quickly, she made her way to a communal shelter that was near-by, leaving her bicycle at the top, next to a baby's pram.

She found a vacant seat and sat down. Opposite her was a young woman clutching a small baby to her chest. Laura smiled at her. The noise above was quite dreadful by now and getting worse all the time; the very foundations of the shelter seemed to judder.

"It can't go on for much longer surely?" somebody from the other end of the shelter said.

Laura was busy thinking about, not her own predicament, nor that of the other occupants of the shelter, but of Simon, and wondering how he was coping with all the ear splitting noise. Then she thought about Auntie, travelling on her own, and James...what about him? The explosions were devastatingly loud and Laura was not the only one to put her hands over her ears.

The young woman opposite was becoming more and more agitated as the situation worsened. She had with her the baby's mask as well as her own. The baby's was a cumbersome thing about two feet in length, made of black rubber with a see-through window at the front.

"Should I put her in?" she directed the question to Laura as she spoke, but before she was able to answer, a man's voice rang out.

"Not needed, my dear," he said, in an authoritatively superior manner... "We have had no special warning about gas."

"Well do you think Hitler will send us a telegram then just to give us a friendly warning?" The young woman, far from convinced, replied.

"I'm telling you, we...won't need them...they're ....stupid gas masks, I don't think that they would be any use in any case," the man confidently concluded.

"No use, no use, what are you saying?....."

The young woman was clearly terrified, she held the baby so close to her that it started to squirm and cry.

"Why don't you keep your big mouth closed?" an older woman interrupted... "Can't you see that the girl's in a state? We've got enough to contend with – without you causing a panic down here."

"I was only giving my opinion..."

"Well, we can all do without it – if you don't mind."

Then, turning to Laura she said,

"What a fool the man is, let her put the baby in...after all what harm can it do?" Going to the young mother, she said kindly,

"If you want to put her in, dear, we'll help you....won't we love?" she added looking straight at Laura.

"Of course", Laura said with a quick nod of her head. At that the woman winked at her and said, almost apologetically,

"I think that I had better go and made peace with old big mouth...after all...he is my old man...Twerp that he is."

"Oh dear...."

"It'll be alright – can I leave you to it?"

Laura nodded, and quick as a flash the young woman held out the now crying and unhappy baby to Laura. At last the baby was completely swaddled in it's black rubber cocoon and it's screeching sounds were, thankfully, muted to a degree by the mummy-case that surrounded it. The girl, having relinquished the black parcel into waiting hands, then pulled on her own gas mask, telling Laura that she should do the same. When it was adjusted and the baby handed back, Laura sat facing her, the green honeycomb base of the mask watching her, like the one eye of Cyclops. She could see the girl's eyes clearly through the perspex eye-piece, they were fearful.

The sound of the bombs falling and the ear splitting reports of the guns made the shelter and occupants .... quake.

"No wonder that the baby is crying so...how I wish it was all over..." Laura thought as she glanced at her watch.

The gun-fire was unrelenting. The young woman had calmed down now. Still sitting with her mask on, of course, but seemingly unconcerned that no other person had theirs on. She just held the baby close to her as she was able, gently rocking it and repeating the Lord's Prayer over and over again.

Two or three other people looked like they were praying too, although most just sat or stood motionless, waiting their fate – whatever that might be.

Laura herself was praying for her loved ones... and for all of them in that dim room...that could so easily be turned into a tomb. It wasn't like her to feel so despondent – but the raid had gone on for so long now, and the bombardment was so fierce…

They all remained there until the all clear's wailing note brought normality, and rational thinking to them all once again.

At last they filed up and out, out into the July day that was blighted by a cruel black stain that was slowly seeping across the once beautiful sky – and the smell of burning…

It was a landmine that had exploded in the park opposite the parade of shops. Perhaps it was aimed at the factories about ten miles away, or maybe the marshalling yards, that were a good deal closer – whatever it was supposed to do – it didn't. Its eventual destination was harmless enough, but the mayhem it caused to both people and property, was truly terrible.

The whole row of small shops had been affected, some more than others. The Bartholomews, tragically taking the full impact of the terrible explosion. The whole scene was one of utter devastation, and this was the sight that confronted Laura.

Her call to the Citadel was brief, when she eventually managed to get there. The young mother she was to install in May's house had been totally unnerved by the ferocity of the last air raid, and had decided that she would rather wait until the next day to make the move. So that is how it was left, with Laura promising to help her on Sunday afternoon.

She came out of the doors of the Citadel, and turned towards the village – and the shops where Simon was. Looking skyward in their direction, she saw the horrid stain of black smoke rising, and she knew in her heart, and with a terrible feeling of foreboding, that it was emanating from his direction.

She pedalled as fast as her legs would allow, in the direction of that devastated place – and Simon.

The smell on the air was all engulfing, and as she neared the intersection she was halted not only by a crowd of people but also by a rope across the road.

There was tremendous activity going on there. Tin-hatted workers from Civil Defence and heavy rescue were there; as were the Fire Brigade, Police and another group of workers that she soon found out were gas board officials.

An A.R.P. warden was standing with a notebook at one side of the crowd, talking to them and making notes. Laura quickly abandoned her trusty steed against the park railings, and slung her tin hatted gas mask case over her shoulder, before making off in his direction.

Just as she had managed to edge her way towards him, a solemn looking policeman approached the front of the crowd. He spoke to them with a voice that was both commanding and calming.

"Please disperse if you have no good reason for being here. There is very real danger still – as you can tell by the smell of gas that is about. The main has fractured – and it is a highly hazardous exercise to get it under control. Please clear the area at once - if you have no immediate and pressing reason to remain here. Go home, good people – go home whilst you still have a home to go to."

He gestured with his hands in a movement that indicated their departure from the cordoned area, and the people responded at once, and started to move away quickly. Some of them were in tears, some were comforting each other, but most of them were silent….

Only two were left now, talking animatedly to the warden, as Laura walked towards them. She could hear him reassuring them that the people of whom they were inquiring were thankfully safe. He then went on to say that incredible though it seemed, faced with the total destruction of the parade that was before them, only three people were in fact missing; all of them from the same shop. The phrase stuck in Laura's head.

"Which shop?" she heard herself cry out, "Which shop?"

The warden turned his head towards her, having not been aware of her presence before.

"I'm so sorry Laura, yes, it is Bartholomews".

"Are they alright?"

"Well, m'dear, it's difficult to say, at the moment, the gas main is the worse problem just now…when they have sorted that out, the real work of rescue can get started."

"Can I come through?"

"Not just yet m'dear, they are still sealing the ruptured main, it's far too perilous at the moment, there's always the risk of another explosion."

Laura looked so hopeless, he was moved by the sight of her anguish.

"I know it's a ticklish situation at the moment – but I've seen worse, as soon as I get the thumbs up I'll see what I can do."

Laura just stood and nodded to him

"Cheer up m'dear, it may not be as bad as it looks." He put his hand on her shoulder in an act of comfort, before moving over to speak to the policeman again.

The ambulances (one of which she was scheduled to drive that afternoon) had come down the hill and were now facing her, about sixty yards away. It seemed to Laura that they were on the other side of the world.

Suddenly she was aware of the silence. It chilled her more, standing there in the quiet, than it had before when the sounds all around her had made it hard for her to think. She welcomed the return of noise.

It was still a warm day, but the sun didn't warm her body or thaw the icy hand that was gripping her heart. The sound of a whistle blew shrilly on the air. The warden gave Laura the thumbs up sign as he walked towards her.

"Thank God, that means that the gas main is safe now, and the real work of rescue can start."

"Look," he said pointing to the rescue squad that was already making inroads into the chaos of what was left of the five shops.

"Can I come through now warden, please?"

"Give me just a moment m'dear, and I'll find out for you."

He turned and walked back over the debris picking his way carefully across the cluttered road to the rescue team.

As he moved away a woman, the only person left at the rope barrier, apart from herself, walked towards her and said,

"I don't know if it's important, but I couldn't help overhearing what the warden said earlier. He said that there were three people left in the shop…that's wrong."

"Wrong? What do you mean?"

"Well, I was in the shop when the siren sounded. I didn't rush out like everyone else did, because I knew that the old lady, Mrs. Fitchet, was in there, and I was concerned for her, and I was going to make sure she was alright… I've known her for ages, she's a lovely old soul…well anyway, I hung around a bit, but then I heard Simon say that he was going to take her to the cellar in the shop. Knowing that, well, I left and ran round to the shelter on the corner. I was lucky I came out of it alive I reckon, when I look at this lot. Anyway, I know that the old girl…is still in there."

Her voice slowed down and grew quieter as she said the last few words, and both women looked across to the remains of the shop.

"I think that you should tell the constable – and the warden. I'm sure that it's vital that they know about everybody's whereabouts in situations like this."

"Alright, I'll go and do it now," she said, as she moved away from Laura, and beckoned to the policeman. The warden who was on his way back to Laura was himself then called over by the policeman. They conferred for a moment – then the warden retraced his steps back to the group of rescuers, and spoke briefly to them. At last he turned again in her direction, negotiating the now huge pile of shop paraphernalia and rubble that was growing into mountains before their eyes.

He made his ungainly way back to her and, slightly out of breath said,

"They're busy doing a tricky bit at the moment m'dear – they're shoring up and making everything secure so that they can move around more freely. Just as soon as they have made the upper floor safe you can go ahead. They will start calling out the names then that's when we will start getting some news about the casualties. They won't mind you standing by then. Hang on a bit longer Laura, we'll soon know."

The wait seemed interminable to her. All thoughts of the happiness that she had started the day with had evaporated. The joy had been stolen from her – it was as if that joy had never existed. The thoughts of James and Aunt Mary had been cruelly replaced by a cold and harsh reality, a reality that was staring her in the face.

"Why?" she thought, "Why?"

A cry went up at last,

"We can see something now."

The stretcher-bearers who had been shuffling their feet became alert and ready to spring into action at any moment. Everyone becoming aware of the tense situation that was unfolding.

"Alright m'dear, under you come," the warden said as he held the rope up, and took Laura's arm as she scrabbled underneath it.

She picked her way carefully across to where the front of the shop once was.

"That's near enough love – don't come any closer for the moment" one of the men said.

"Can you see them? Are they alright?"

"Well, we've had a glimpse of something – can't tell you exactly what it is at the moment though...do me a favour, stick your tin hat on – we don't want a casualty out here too".

"Of course – sorry," she said apologetically.

"You know all their names don't you love?" the first man spoke kindly, "Tell me again."

"Jack Bartholomew…"

"Just their first names will do..."

"Yes...Rosie...Simon and Mrs. Fitchet. I don't know her first name..."

"That's all right love... right'o lads...let's have a bit of quiet."

A hush came over the whole group, and Laura found herself holding her breath.

As the work stopped, and the silence took over the airspace, all eyes were focused on the hole beneath them. One man's voice, clear and strong was heard shouting. He was lying on a slight incline, his head hanging down through the gaping hole that was once a floor.

"Hello down there. Can you hear us? Rosie? Jack? Simon?"

There was no reply. The whole procedure was gone over again...and again...

"Hear us, please hear us...please," Laura said, biting her lips in anguish.

He was in the land of twilight...he thought he was dead. He had no feeling in his body, and all around him was quiet.

"How peaceful," he thought, then through the haze of his tranquillity he thought he heard his name being spoken. Far away and distant the voice gently pierced his sensibilities. Eventually he opened his eyes and although they were sore and blurred he instantly realised where he was.

His name came to his ears again, only louder to him this time, and he thought,

"Somebody is calling me."

At that same moment from somewhere behind him, he heard an almost imperceptible groan. Who had made the meagre sound was beyond his comprehension, but one thing he did know, he had to do better than that. Mustering all the strength he could, he opened his mouth to shout. What came out was neither a shout nor a call of any sort, but a rasping grunt, his crushed words coming from his crushed body in painful monosyllables.

"Help us...help us.."

The effort of the two words was as much as he could bear. The pain in his chest was simply awful, he could hardly draw breath. The weight of his companions was bearing down on him like some mighty boulder.

The sight before him, which he had no choice but to see, was of old Mrs Fitchet, lying cradled in his arms, arms that had long lost any relevance to his being, and his body, once painless, now seemed to come alive with every sort of discomfort. Various stabbings, twinges and aches and pains seemed to engulf him. His mouth was full of grit and his eyes, the lashes of which were still full of plaster dust, were sore and smarting; and since they showed him nothing but destruction – he closed them with a hopeless and helpless sigh.

"Right lads, we heard something, let's get going as quick as we can."

"Who was it? Do you know? Was it a man's voice or a woman's? Was it Simon?"

"I can't really say who it was that answered love, try not to worry, we'll have them out in a jiffy now…just stand back."

Laura was trying not to be a nuisance as she stood there, fighting back the tears.

"I know it's terrible for you but be a brave girl, you're alright if you stay just there."

She stood pathetically silent, willing life's breath to those four entombed souls, hidden from her sight in the darkness below. She felt helpless, devastated and – alone.

She hadn't given poor May a second thought just recently, but now that she did she consoled herself with the thought that she could have got to the shelter without any difficulty, but she reflected, she was probably worried out of her mind about them both.

"We'll all be together soon," she thought "… no need to worry."

She tried hard to believe what she was thinking – she was willing to think of anything to take her mind off these last desperate moments.

The rescuers were a wonderful band of men. They tore at the rubble, securing it as they went along, speedily working all the while as a team. They worked deftly, each man seeming to anticipate the move of the next, without any words needing to be spoken.

The first person out of that dark hole was Mr. B. He was groaning loudly now that he had been moved. However, he was soon placed on a stretcher and being comforted by the crew. Laura ran over to see him, and she hated what she saw. His face was contorted with pain, he didn't open his eyes, he didn't seem to hear anyone either or make any sign that he knew where he was. He just kept moaning and occasionally let out a small whimpering scream.

While he was being tenderly moved into the ambulance, Mrs. B. was brought out.

"Poor Rosie," thought Laura.

The once happy and friendly woman was now lying on the stretcher, crumpled like a crushed moth, still and silent. She too was tenderly moved into the ambulance with her husband – each of them unaware of the other's presence as they were taken at top speed to the local cottage hospital.

Laura's eyes were now fixed on the gaping hole, waiting…waiting. At last, after what seemed an eternity, the tousled, white powdered head of Simon appeared from the abyss below and her heart leapt. He was gently laid on to the waiting stretcher as she ran to his side.

"Oh Simon – are you alright my dear?"

She could hardly choke back the tears as she gazed down at the bruised and battered body, the greyness of his skin being highlighted by the scarlet of his blood.

As she looked down on him, she felt that she was looking at part of her own life. When he was hurting, she hurt and when he was bleeding, she bled, not with a scarlet ribbon, but with an unseen tear, deep within her own heart.

She was at his side as the stretcher weaved its way toward the waiting ambulance. Once inside, and without opening his eyes, he said with almost an inaudible whisper,

"Hello beautiful eyes…I'm still here…this seems to be the story of my…life."

He managed, Laura convinced herself, a tiny smile before he lapsed into unconsciousness. She tenderly kissed first his forehead, and then his bloodless lips.

"Thank God," she said with relief, "Thank God."

She looked out of the open rear doors of the ambulance and saw the last sad victim borne out of that dark hole. A pathetically small person who was unmoving. The men quickly surrounded the figure that was now lying so still and bent on the blanketed stretcher. One man, Laura saw, took a handkerchief from his pocket, leaned forward and lightly wiped the still face. They looked at each other and shook their heads.

"Poor Mrs. Fitchet" Laura thought, as they brought her to the ambulance and put her on board.

Then they started up the hill for the short yet fast journey to the hospital. Laura looked from one to the other. She looked at Simon, his mind for the moment mercifully asleep, allowing him to forget the horror he had witnessed in the cellar. Then she turned to the dear old lady, Mrs. Fitchet. She too was sleeping, and would be...for all eternity.

Laura sat and put her head into her hands and cried, the tears were still streaming when they reached the hospital, and there was nothing anybody could do about it.

Book 1 – Chapter 8
There's Always Tomorrow... *Late August 1985*

How she drove home she would never know. After she had parked the car, she sat there for a few moments – quite still. She first felt disbelief – but then wonder filled her senses. Closing her eyes, she offered a silent prayer of humble thanks to God.

"I know that everything is possible with you dear Lord, thank you for hearing our prayers – and answering them."

When at last she entered the back door and walked into the kitchen, she felt the most warm and wonderful feeling pass through her body. Peter heard her come in and shut the door. He came to her at once, concern showing on his handsome face.

"How did you get on m'love? What happened? Come and sit down and tell me all about it. You look quite worn out."

"How's father?"

"He's fine, how's you? That's what I want to know." They made their way to the settee and sat down.

"Well? What did the doctor say?" He questioned.

"Don't look so worried darling, I may be a bit anaemic at the moment, but there is no need to panic. I have to go to the hospital tomorrow for a blood test...but that won't take me long, will it? Dr. Finch assures me that if there is some sort of deficiency, it can soon be put right."

"Oh I'm so pleased. I've been so worried about you, thank goodness it is nothing more serious."

"Well, there is something else too...." Angela took his hand and placed it on her chest.

"Can you feel my heart beating?"

"I think so," the worried look had returned to his face again, as his thoughts then turned to worrying about a possible heart complaint, or worse...

"Well, my darling, I found out today that it was ... beating for two."

Peter's face didn't register the words that he heard, at first – or the enormity of them either.

"For two?" he repeated, and looked at her quizzically. Then as he looked at her smiling face, she saw a look of disbelief spread over it.

"For two?" he said again, this time quelling his former feelings.

She nodded and stood before him offering her outstretched hands to him. He stood up at once and pulled her towards him taking her swiftly into his arms.

"Oh my love – are you sure? Quite sure?"

She nodded again and they kissed, cried and hugged each other for sheer joy.

Then he held her at arms' length and looked at her. Tired she may be but she had a certain radiance too; her eyes were gleaming, and her cheeks were blooming; and the lips forming the sunny smile made a picture that he would never forget. This moment would be forever etched on to his heart, he felt so elated, and his joy spilled out with love for her.

Happiness intoxicated them both, and they came together again in a warm embrace. She looked up into his eyes –

"God always hears our prayers, doesn't He?"

"Always."

"He has answered one of ours hasn't He?"

They clung together and she knew that the answer was – yes.

Then Peter suddenly stiffened and stood back, pulling her down beside him on to the settee again, a worried look showing on his face – replacing the one of happy elation. Shaking his head slowly he began to speak.

"With my feelings taken over from my senses, I am only just realising the implications for you my darling. It's late for us, a baby but for you it's…" his words tailed off.

"Hush, hush," she said putting a finger on his lips, "the doctor said that there should be no problems for me, I can have some special tests, if I wish to – but even that is not uncommon these days. These are the eighties not the nineteen twenties after all. I'm not afraid Peter, don't be afraid for me – I'm ecstatic."

She took his hand and placed it on her flat abdomen.

"There's life in here Peter, a life so small that we can hardly contemplate it, but it's there just the same. I never thought that I could feel so happy. We two have made such a precious thing. I know that God won't take it from us – I just know it. Tests or no tests, nothing is going to stop me having our baby."

Peter, listening to her as he was, couldn't spoil these moments for her or them with, perhaps his quite groundless fears, for her safety.

"Yes m'love, I know how precious life is, and I also know that our lives will never be quite the same again. I love you so much m'darling, I don't think that I could ever be as happy as I am at this moment."

They hugged again, and then he said.

"Let's go and tell father that he is going to be a grandfather, shall we?"

"Of course, love."

They tiptoed into the old man's room. He was fast asleep.

"There's always tomorrow...but tonight is ours," he said as they quietly closed the door.

Just fleetingly, Angela heard a small voice in her head.

"Pregnant" the voice said, the voice was Terri's. Slowly an almost imperceptible smile crossed Angela's face, perhaps it could not be seen, but she knew it was there just the same.

The next morning, early, they went to father's room again to tell him their news. They both knew that he would not respond in the way that they both would have liked, but they still thought it right to tell him. It was family news, and as he was a very dear member of the family it was only right that he was included in their happiness.

The only response that they received was the one that they were expecting, the old laboured question once again.

"What....is....the....answer?"

It had a weary sound to it and a despondency in the words that they were used to hearing of late. Under different circumstances they would have felt quite depressed – but nothing this morning could quench the excitement that they both felt.

Peter had agreed not to say anything to colleagues or friends officially, at the moment, and had at last left the house. Not before he had come back to her three times to kiss her goodbye. His face was a picture of pleasure, making him look younger than his years, with the great beam of his smile crinkling up the corners of his eyes, that were bright with hope.

"He looks like the boy I married, and somebody, somewhere is bound to guess that he has some sort of secret if he goes about everywhere with that huge grin on his face," Angela thought as she finally waved him off at the door.

She tried not to think about it too much either, but in the end had to give way to the pleasurable feeling that was engulfing her, why not? After all it would probably be the only time in her life that she would feel exactly the same emotions, that she was experiencing at this moment.

The old headache was still hovering around, but she tried not to let it interfere too much. The fact that her feet seemed to have sprouted wings made everything that much easier; after all – she thought that she was walking on air.

After father had been collected to go to the day centre, she was able to make her visit to the hospital, without having to explain to anyone what it was about.

After her visit was completed, she decided to cut through the park, it made a pleasant detour, and there was still a little time before father was due back home again.

The day was fine, and she walked with a spring in her step. She ended up at the children's playground. She sat down on a bench and watched the mothers with their toddlers, seeing at first hand how hectic life was going to be in a few years.

As she watched them laughing and playing, a cold chill ran through her, for she suddenly realised how difficult it was going to be with father and a baby.

"Will that mean that I will never be able to take them out together?"

She thought over the fact that the demanding routine of a child would cause many unforeseen problems for them all.

Sitting there in the sunlight, listening to the children's voices, her deliberations led her to only one conclusion: that it did no good whatsoever to worry about tomorrow, whatever tomorrow may bring, and that she would deal with each day as it came. Just one day at a time, and with the Lord's help everything would fall into place.

Wending her way home again her step was as sprightly as ever, and with her new resolution in place, she looked forward with happy anticipation – not fears.

She was at home, ready and waiting when the ambulance, carrying father, arrived. She stood looking up at him as he was put on the tail lift, and slowly brought down to ground level

"Hello dear," she said to him as she wheeled him off the metal plate with a small bump…. "Have you had a good time?"

He looked at her with watery eyes, his hair dishevelled and untidy. The saliva bubbles at the corner of his mouth were brown, and were the end result, as she quickly found out, of a well meaning piece of chocolate!

He looked so pathetic she thought, and as the coach moved off to deliver the other individuals to their waiting loved ones, he started his old labours once again. His eyes sought hers and at once he started to speak,

"What...is...the...answer...please?"

She touched him softly on the shoulder and answered him quietly.

"God is the only one who knows the answer father...I'm sure ... only God."

A few days later Angela was delighted to receive a letter in answer to one of the newspaper advertisements. Her heart was beating fast with excitement as she read it. It was from a woman, Mrs. Rowebotham, and she said that her late father was called 'Banjo' because he had played one during the war. It was a nickname that stuck! The woman also said that she was willing to have a meeting with her, and had enclosed a telephone number. Angela could hardly contain her excitement. The woman lived miles away in Leeds but it would be worth anything to get information from her – any clue, or, better still – an answer for father.

All the arrangements were made. Mrs. Rowebotham was due to arrive at two thirty, bringing with her some paperwork that she thought may be of some use.

"It's all happening so fast, I'm so excited Peter, are you? Just think of it, we may soon have the answer that we've been searching for – or maybe the beginning of one. Let's hope she will bring some good news for your father."

"I must admit I am most impressed with your powers of detection. To have received a reply, from such an ambiguous start, is nothing short of a minor miracle. I've got to confess that I had my reservations right from the beginning, but at least, it looks like it may be a start. Please don't be upset at what I'm going to say now, but I just feel that I must say it... Please don't get carried away with too much enthusiasm, just in case this all comes to naught. I don't want you getting upset, especially now of all times."

"I won't, I promise, but let's face it, at the moment we have no lead at all – no hope; and seeing your father's distress every day as I do.... I just want to try anything to help him. As for this lady, what have we to lose? Only the train fare from Leeds, the straw that we're clutching at is worth that, isn't it? Humour me at the moment, will you? It does sound so promising."

"I'll do anything for you…you know that." He took her hand and pressed it to his lips. "Of course, anything we can glean from this lady will be of interest. You're my clever little girl aren't you? … in more ways than one."

Shooting at Stars

Book 2 – Chapter 8
Aftermath *July 1940*

May had been in the bedroom preparing for her friend's homecoming when the raid had started.

She hurriedly began to take all the necessary steps for her journey to the shelter immediately, scooping up Little Raindrop from the bed where he had been asleep. Although she had felt frightened, the little scrap of fur had somehow helped to quell her fears by at least giving her somebody to talk to. As things were, he was the only companion that she was likely to have in the dugout this morning!

Once the terrible sounds of the air raid were over and she was starting to calm down and regain a normal heartbeat again, her heart took another jolt, for there, coming up the path was a telegram boy.

She waited, with some trepidation for the inevitable knock on the door. With her heart in her mouth, she fearfully made her way to answer it.

"Telegram for Miss Laura Anthony," he said, almost apologetically.

"Yes, that's alright, I'll take it."

"Shall I wait for an answer?"

"Yes, please, wait a moment."

She closed the door on the waiting boy and held the telegram to her chest.

"Shall I open it?" she thought to herself, and then not giving herself any time to think about it, she said aloud,

"Yes I must, it may be very important."

Fingers all of a tremble, she opened the buff coloured envelope, her eyes quickly scanning the words. With an enormous sigh of relief, she again opened the door.

"No reply son – no reply, thanks."

"Not bad news, was it?"

"No – not too bad anyway."

The boy smiled as he went off down the path, whistling loudly. May closed the door for the second time, and clasped the sheet to her with relief, the envelope slipping from her fingers onto the floor.

"No, thank God, no real bad news." She looked at the sheet in her hand again, and read... 'LAURA CAN'T MAKE IT TODAY. BE IN TOUCH STOP LOVE AUNT MARY.'

May bent down to pick up the envelope.

"Thank God," she said again.

The raid had been a bad one, she could tell. For quite apart from all the terrible bangs and crashes that she had sat through, she could see, by looking out of the sitting room window, a column of black smoke rising into the sky, and darkening it with its sheer size. It was slowly spreading its insidious fingers upward and outward, obscuring all of the blue sky to her left. She was thinking of Simon as she slipped on a jacket before making her way out of the house.

When she turned the corner and was confronted with the devastation of the parade, she felt sick. She shook her head in disbelief, the smell on the air and the sight of the havoc that was before her was almost too much to bear.

"Oh no, not the lad," she said to herself as she hurried towards the warden to try and get some news.

He was very understanding and it was with unbelievable relief that she heard from him that Simon had been taken to the hospital – and that Laura was with him. The fact that Laura was there made her decide that the best thing for her to do was to go home again, for nothing would be achieved by her going to the hospital at this minute. After all James was due home at any time, even if Mary was not, and what would he make of it if there were nobody there when he arrived?

Having made her decision, she turned and walked back along the main road. As she neared the Co-op store she could see the glass being swept up into tidy heaps, by the assistants. Some of the glass was still hanging by brown paper threads from the drapery windows and was being carefully removed by one of the members of the A.R.P. As she drew alongside the largest window, she saw Simon's favourite girl. She was laid, flat on her back, with her feet, now broken free from their moorings, sticking out, the black shoes broken away. The clothes had been ripped off the bottom half of her body, exposing thick pink legs and blue painted modesty knickers. The top of her body was covered in debris, with just the crooked arm, minus its fingers, showing.

She knew it was stupid, but as she stood there she started to cry.

"Oh Simon dear, I'm so glad that you can't see your favourite girl," she said, wiping her eyes, and then continuing to dab at them - all the way home.

When she turned the corner and saw the army car outside the house, she knew that James at least had arrived safely, and that made her shed a few more tears … of relief …

Laura looked up. Coming towards her along the hospital ward was James, concern showing markedly on his handsome face. Laura stood up at his approach and when he reached her he took her into his arms and looked into her eyes that were moist with tears.

"Oh James, it was so dreadful."

He hugged her and she leaned her head on his chest briefly before sitting down again at Simon's side. James found a stool under the bed, drew it out, and sat down beside her.

They both looked at the still figure lying there. Of course, Simon, immobilised by his injuries was seeing nothing and nobody. James, on looking at Simon, said in a quiet voice to her,

"How bad is it? He looks terrible."

"Well, of course he is in shock, and he's been very badly crushed – and because of that dreadful crushing the blood supply was cut off from his arms, that's why they look the way that they do."

Indeed his arms did look pitiful. They were exposed and lying swollen and blue on top of the stark white of the counterpane. The pale blue sheen left his arms and spread across the whole of his chest, gaining depth of colour on its journey. Laura continued,

"Incredibly," she went on, slowly shaking her head, "he has no broken bones, just cracked ribs."

Laura saw James was clearly upset.

"He will be out of action for quite a while I know, but I'm hoping that he will soon be back home again, and getting up to all his old tricks. I'm sure that they will let him come back as soon as possible knowing that there will be a trained nurse to help take care of him, don't you?"

At that moment Simon stirred on the bed which was a blessing to James because he didn't want to have to tell Laura that her Aunt Mary was not at home, and wouldn't be just yet.

"Hello – how long have I been here? Where am I anyway?"

"You're in hospital dear, the best, and only place for you after what you have been through. How do you feel now, are you a little easier?"

"I feel very strange… and I can't move." He had tried to move his arms, but it was both too difficult and painful for him, so he had given up.

Before any more could be said, a nurse came up to the bed. It was Netta Phillips. She was wearing the uniform of the Queen Alexandra's nursing order. She said,

"I was horrified when I heard about the terrible raid, and I had no idea that Simon was involved until just a few moments ago."

She bent over the bed, as she was talking, and stroked Simon's brow, with all the tenderness that a nurse should have. He was unaware of her presence because he seemed to have lapsed into sleep again. She stood upright and went on,

"I only came back this afternoon to say my goodbyes. As you can see by my uniform, I am now an army nurse. It all happened so fast. I applied, was accepted and transferred – all in two days. I've really had no time to tell anyone – let alone Simon ... and now I find him like this..."

"Don't worry too much dear. I'm sure you, more than anyone else, know that it's not always as bad as it looks." Laura commiserated.

"Perhaps I've done the wrong thing – perhaps I should have stayed here after all," she said, looking quite crestfallen.

James stood up and moved to her side.

"You're needed elsewhere, you can't tear yourself into different parts, can you? I don't think that you have made the wrong decision, but maybe I'm a bit biased?" He smiled at the girl, and she responded with a nod of acceptance to the words that he had spoken, without taking her eyes off the face on the pillow.

Another nurse bustled up to the bed and stood, smoothing her stiff apron.

"I think that it's time that you were going along now nurse, the transport has arrived."

Netta responded at once. She leaned over the now sleeping figure and placed a kiss on the quiet face.

"Goodbye love, see you soon" she said.

Then, taking Laura and James' hands into her own she made her brief farewells, before walking away from them, up the ward, and out of the door.

The nurse, with the stiffly starched apron, was speaking again.

"He's a very lucky young man. He'll be as right as rain in a month or so, just you see if I'm not right."

"So you don't know exactly when he can come home then?" Laura knew it was a stupid question to ask, but just couldn't help herself. All she really needed was the reassurance that he would be coming home, of course, and fortunately the nurse sensed what was expected in her reply.

"He's a strong young man, and I'm sure that he will astound us all with his rapid recovery. The waiting will seem longer for you, of course, but I'm sure you won't have to wait too long. Have patience my dear that's what we all have got to have isn't it? I think that he will probably sleep for a while now, so perhaps it would be a good time for you both to leave."

Looking at Laura, she went on

"You look quite done in yourself, maybe a rest would do you some good as well. Come up and see him tomorrow, you'll see a big change in him then, I'm sure he will be feeling a lot easier, and that will make you feel easier too."

Just as Laura and James were agreeing and preparing to leave, Simon's eyes flickered and then slowly tried to open.

He could see them both through a painful haze, for his eyes still stung and felt that they were full of grit. He heard Laura's voice, and although he could see them it was as if they were suspended at the end of a long tunnel…calling him.

"Hello lovebirds," he said almost inaudibly.

"Hush love, don't try to talk now, we'll come back tomorrow and see you – you'll feel much better by then. Close your eyes dear, and don't try to open them, they look so sore."

She stroked his forehead gently, and he closed them with great relief, but still spoke with a whisper to them.

"What about the others? What about the others? I've just got a horrible feeling…."

"Don't worry about them at the moment. Wherever they are, they are in good hands, just like you. Just rest and get better. We're going now, love. I'll see you tomorrow." She leaned forward and kissed him. James moved closer and said

"Goodbye old chap, I'll see you on my next leave, you'll be your old self by then, I know. God Bless."

"Cheerio lovebirds, take care of each other for me." He said the words with a quiet sigh and then lapsed into silence.

As they left the ward they stopped and looked back.

"He'll be fine darling, try not to worry too much," he said as he looked at her, " but I know that you will" he added giving her arm a squeeze.

They left the hospital, Laura leaning heavily on his arm. Since James had been fortunate enough to have the use of a staff car, it made the short journey home both speedy and comfortable. He knew that it would be best for Laura to know that her Aunt Mary would not be at home, so he gently broke the news to her at once.

"I was so looking forward to seeing her…"

Her eyes brimmed with tears, not only for that disappointment, but with all the pent up emotions of the day. Then she fell silent, considering the doctor's words to them.

Rosie Bartholomew was dead. Killed instantly by the blast. Jack Bartholomew had multiple fractures of his arms and legs and broken ribs, one of which had pierced his lung, again caused by the blast - but, at least he was still alive. His condition was quite poor, but because of it he had the shield of oblivion protecting him from the awful news of his dear wife's death. Lastly, poor Mrs. Fitchet. Dead of a heart attack, or so the doctors thought, and probably before she ever hit the floor, cradled in Simon's arms……….

Book 1 – Chapter 9
More Detection *September 1985*

Mrs. Rowebotham, a small, fur coated, heavily beaded lady, entered the room. She stood still for a moment, then, glancing at the figure in the easy chair by the french windows walked in that direction.

She stood and looked down at the slight figure of the old man, then she sank down beside him – and looked into his face.

His watery eyes looked into her dark ones as he said the laboured words to her.

"What…is…the…answer?"

She slowly shook her head, a gentle smile coming to her heavily painted lips as she tenderly touched his cheek; the scarlet talons riding high on her dimpled fingers.

"Eh me old love, I don't have the faintest idea at the moment, but you will have an answer – and very soon too."

He looked at her again, and before she had time to get up he had repeated himself once more.

Shaking her head slightly she stood in front of Angela.

"What must you think of me? I do apologise, please forgive my rudeness." She dropped her voice low and inclined her head towards the figure behind her, as she went on,

"I had such a feeling when I came into the room, I can't begin to explain it, except to say that it overpowered me, and I just had to speak to him first."

"Please don't apologise – it's perfectly alright. Let me take your coat, and do sit down. It's best if you see – and hear – my difficulties first – then perhaps you will understand my motives."

The woman sighed as she sat down and started to speak again,

"Eh lass I can see your difficulties."

The unaccustomed northern accent falling on to Angela's ears fitted the rosy cheeked lady absolutely, she thought, as the strong northern tones rang out again.

"I meant what I said to the old man though – he will have an answer in the not too distant future either."

Pushing herself up from the chair she stood again, this time turning herself about, twisting the beads at her neck as she did so. The fingers of her right hand winding and clicking the long strands in an agitated manner.

"The answer is in the house…not at this very moment but…"

She closed her heavily mascarred eyes for a second and then the spiky lashes sprung open,

"The answer lies in this house…I'm certain. Sorry if I'm embarrassing you, but I can't help these feelings that I get. I'm not a clairvoyant or anything like that, and I have never meddled in such things. I don't believe in interference of any sort myself, but it was said that my mother had a gift. I don't regard the feelings that I get as anything but that – just feelings. Sometimes they are strong, as they are just now, and sometimes they lie quietly – just out of my reach. I don't want to alarm you or worry you in any way – especially now" she added in a most off-hand nonchalant manner, as though not requiring any confirmation or answer, from the intrigued Angela; who, in fact, was feeling rather worried and more than a little mystified.

Questions were going around in her head, and she really, at this moment, didn't know exactly what to make of this rather eccentric woman.

"What on earth have I got myself into? What have I done? What on earth will Peter have to say about this?"

As she was thinking, she was more than relieved that Mrs. Rowebotham had, once again, sunk her more than ample figure down into her chair, her pronouncements for the time being it seemed – over.

"Well Mrs. Rowebotham…"

"Please, call me Bess"

"Well…Bess…I, well my husband and I, are so grateful to you for answering the advertisement in the paper…and for travelling all the way down from Leeds to see us. Before we get started, would you like me to make you a cup of tea or coffee?"

"Bless you, but there's no need for that lass, I'm quite comfortable. As for travelling down – well I'm more than happy to be here. I just hope that I can be of some help to you all."

She opened the large carpet-bag that was now engulfing her lap, and started to rummage around in it. At last she brought out a small bundle of papers secured with a wide elastic band, and putting her bag down on the floor at her side, she laid them in her lap.

"I'm hoping against hope that I can be of some real help. Shall we get started?"

"Yes, of course, I'm afraid that there is not much to go on from this end I must confess."

As she was speaking, Angela walked to the bookcase and picked the photograph up that was lying there. She came back and laid it on the coffee table in front of Bess, who quickly glanced at it. Then, removing the elastic band and snapping it on to her chubby wrist, she immediately began to rummage through the dog-eared wad that was now lying loose in her lap. She then drew out, with a triumphant look of satisfaction on her face, the identical photograph and laid it next to Angela's on the table.

"Snap, I think" she said.

"Well, there's no doubt about it, they're identical alright," Angela agreed.

Just before Bess Rowebotham started to speak again, a cloudy look seemed to cover her face.

"Two alike…and yet…different."

Then almost as if she had not spoken before, she began again.
"Two alike except one is black and white and one is a sepia print. Yours is a copy I know, because the one of mine belonged to my mother." Again she seemed distracted –

"Two alike but…" It was as if she was trying to remember something, without success. She then resumed her old composure again and looked at the two smiling faces before her.

"That's Banjo, my dad, no getting away from it. That picture was taken in nineteen thirty six. I was seven at the time."

"Was he in the services then? Was he in the war?"

"Bless you no…no sadly he had a disability, a club foot they called it…but although he wasn't in any of the services he was with them all the time. He was in a concert party troupe see? Well rather more than that really – he actually ran it. He used to get the acts together, and then, arranging through the brass hats, he was told where he could perform. All our family have been connected with the boards – one way or another."

She shook her head as she picked the picture up.

"Eh…he was a good old dad – and very talented too. Those photos were left in the places where they performed, with this." She turned to the sheets in her lap again, picked up a rather faded one and passed it to Angela.

It had on it the various acts and names of the artists, and also the places where they had performed. There were also instructions on how to contact 'Banjo', alias Fredrick Maycock for more information about the troupe. Angela looked a little crestfallen as she returned the pink slip to Bess.

"I had rather hoped that he would have been a friend of my father-in-law…and that we might have found out something else. Something to link them together in some way…something that may have given us a clue to the question…"

"Lass, the answer will be found here, please try to believe me," she said as she leaned forward and held Angela's hand.

"I'll try," she answered, a little half-heartedly. Bess looked down at the bits and pieces in her lap.

"I'm sorry that there is really nothing else here that is of any use. I have no diaries or letters either, not that they would have been much good, because they had to be careful what they wrote down. It's hard to us today to think of the restrictions that were in force during war isn't it? But that's how it was – or so I've heard anyway."

She thought quietly for a moment and then continued.

"There was only one incident that he ever spoke about, but there were no names ever mentioned even so. Quite a few in the troupe were killed by enemy action, they were frequently bombed and Dad took it very bad. He was lucky himself right to the end. I'm glad to say. It was as if the Almighty, knowing about his foot, gave him a long life to make up for it…where was I? Oh yes…he didn't talk about his own near misses – only this one situation. It seemed to stick in his mind so – mainly because he felt so helpless in the circumstances, I think. The troupe was in Scotland on this occasion, that much we found out later. It was all very hush-hush at the time. It was instilled in all of us that… "walls have ears." So of course we knew nothing about the place at the time as I've already explained.

Anyway, on this particular night Dad had gone into the gent's lav. It was, by all accounts, a large room, and because of that it had been turned into their dressing room too. Not the most wonderful of places, I'll warrant, still that's war for you… Knowing the dressing rooms that I did see, I'm sure that it was filled with all the props and clothes…oh and all the other paraphernalia that goes to make up a dressing room…. Anyway, in the midst of all this chaos a chap was sitting on a bench. He had his head in his hands, and he was crying – crying fit to burst Dad said. Of course he felt compassion for him – Dad was like that, he had a great big heart. Anyway, he sits down next to the chap, puts his arm round his shoulders, and asks him what his trouble is. All he could get out of him was that his brother was missing, presumed dead. Well, of course, Dad was sorry for the chap, but unfortunately this sort of thing was an every day occurrence during the war you see? Anyway, the only thing that he could do was to try to give him some comforting words, but he found it was very hard because all the chap kept saying was…"You don't understand – he's gone, I've tried to find him – but he's gone." Dad tried to tell him that if he was only missing there was always the chance that he would be found, but the chap seemed not to hear him, and just went on about him being – gone. As it was then time for Dad to go on stage, he had to leave him where he had found him. The last words that he heard him say were – "Only God can find him for me…"

Angela listened to the story intently.

"How extraordinary," she said, "Did your father ever find out anything else about the man? What was he like? Was he a serviceman?"

"He never said lass, but I do know that he never saw him again."

She picked up the picture of Banjo from the table.

"Can I show this picture to the old gentleman?"

"Of course you may – but I must say that I have tried it myself, not with much response I hasten to add, but do try. Meanwhile I will make us a cup of tea."

She left the room a little despondently, for the meeting had not borne any fruit as far as getting an answer for father, or so it seemed to her.

After putting the small bundle of papers on the table, Bess Rowebotham rose from her chair, then taking an upright chair, she placed it alongside the old man, facing him. He raised his eyes to her, his lips started to twitch, and once again the same laboured words came from his distorted lips – and filled the air. The kindly woman waited until he had finished speaking, and then held the picture in front of his eyes.

"It's Banjo, my old love, do you remember Banjo? He was a whizz on that thing wasn't he? Did you hear him play? Did you ever speak to him?"

She kept the questions coming fast, not really giving him time to answer them – even if he could. She wanted to bombard his brain, to wake it up into some form of consciousness. She finished speaking as abruptly as she had started, and waited for his reaction. If there was going to be one, it was now or never, she thought.

The old man looked steadily at the picture that was in front of his eyes. He turned them from the sepia photograph, to the one in the silver frame, then back to the smiling Banjo. Finally, he turned his eyes to the woman's face, and she could see that they were full of tears, his lips twitched and although no sound issued from them she thought she saw him mouth the word…gone. Was it wishful thinking on her part? The movement was so slight and was, of course, quickly followed up by the old familiar words "What…is…the…answer?" Just as he was saying them Angela came back into the room again.

"Same old words I hear," she said, setting the tray down on the table. Bess was sitting holding the old man's hands where she remained until the tea was poured out.

"Come and have tea now…Bess, and I will give father his" she said, picking up the child's beaker as she crossed to them.

When the tea was over, Bess started to put the small bundle of papers in order, prior to putting them back into her bag.

"Would you mind if I kept the pink sheet? Only I was wondering if there might be a name on it…well perhaps somebody that I could try to contact. What do you think?" Angela said hopefully.

"You can have the pink slip by all means, lass, but I know that it won't do you much good. I know that seven of them have passed away, not counting Banjo – and that only leaves two, Philip Topas and Dorothy Lane. Philip I know went to the U.S.A. after the war. I think he joined a circus, or the like. Dorothy Lane married a sailor and went to live in the West Country. She would be well over seventy by now, of course, and I have no idea of her whereabouts – or her married name either. Not much help, am I lass?"

"Well, it's disappointing I must admit, but of course it's not your fault...it's nobody's fault. I think I was expecting too much. After all everything I do will be such a long shot…won't it?"

She looked down at the pink slip in her hands, but before handing it back to Bess's outstretched one, she felt her face flush and hot tears spring to her eyes. She was absolutely helpless to stop them spilling out and falling down on to the paper.

"Eh lass don't take on so, it's so bad for you to get upset just now. Why not give up your search for the time being? I'm sure – certain sure, that the answer is here anyway. I feel it so strong – this house will have great joy and peace – believe me lass," she said, patting at Angela's hand with her podgy fingers.

While they had been speaking, they had both been aware of the sound of a car on the drive. Drying her eyes, Angela said quietly,

"That will be Peter my husband, he said he would try to get home a little early to meet you."

Angela stood up, and so did Bess, smoothing down the beads at her neck with both hands – ready to greet him.

Peter took over most of the talking for the rest of the time that Bess Rowebotham was with them. In fact, Angela became increasingly quiet. After she had made a light meal and cleared it away, she went and sat with father, listening patiently to him as he asked her the question over and over. She distanced herself from the other two deliberately, for she was feeling a failure. Although the failure was not of her own doing, it still hurt her. She just felt empty inside – inadequate and useless.

Eventually the time came for Peter to take their visitor to the station. Angela rose, and collected the heavy fur coat from the cupboard, where it had been hanging, and Peter helped the tiny woman on with it. It was totally unnecessary - for although it was September it was still warm in the South. In the North though, it could be blowing a gale, Angela thought, as she looked at the now flushed, fur-ball of a woman. As she came across to get her bag, and before she picked it up, she took hold of Angela's hands into her own.

"Don't worry lass, it will all turn out for the best – believe me – I just know that it will!"

Then, turning to Peter, she said in quieter tones

"I think it's hit your dear wife rather hard, I mean, us not coming up with something more positive. I've told her not to worry any more, but I know that she will, of course…and it's not good for her to have all this worry – or any upsets…not now that she is carrying," she added in a quieter voice still.

Peter was more than surprised that Angela would have confided in this rather overpoweringly strange woman (and he was right of course – she hadn't) so he ignored the remark saying,

"We are both very grateful to you for visiting us, even though it seems to have been rather a waste of your time…"

"Time? What's time? Time is not my master – I make time work for me…and I never waste it if I can use it".

Gripping both their hands tightly, she closed her eyes for a brief moment, and then opened them again saying,

"I just know that the answer is in this house – biding its time, you truly don't need to search any more."

She released their hands with a flourish and they all walked out towards the car. When they reached it, Peter held the door open, and Bess Rowebotham squeezed herself in and tugged at the seat belt.

As he walked round to get into the driver's seat, she wound the window down and beckoned to Angela saying,

“Don’t worry about the old gentleman lass. Everything will be alright, when the foreign lady gets here. Your husband will know all about it.”

The engine roared into life and Angela couldn’t ask any more questions of her. As she stood watching the car turn out of the driveway, the round faced woman called out once again,

“It will be alright.”

Angela made her way inside.

“What foreign woman. What did she mean, ‘It will be alright’.”

Angela’s head was spinning.

“I’m worse off than ever…now I’ve got more questions that I don’t know the answer to!”

She put her hands to her head.

“It’s all too much. I can’t bear it.”

She ran to the foot of the stairs, as she did so father caught a glimpse of her.

“What…is…the…answer?” he said yet again.

She felt sick.

“I don’t know,” she screamed at him, “and what’s more I don’t care,” she added, rushing up the stairs – and locking herself in the bathroom.

After he had left Bess Rowebotham at the station Peter made his way home, mulling over in his mind what she had said, as she left him.

“The foreign woman has the secret I’m sure, all will be well when she makes herself known to you,” she had said, as well as other things that he could make neither head nor tail of.

Apart from the fact that his father may have seen the Banjo troupe there was quite obviously no other leads at all. Certainly the story that Bess Rowebotham had told them about her father meeting and speaking to a highly distressed man, could have had no connection with his own father whatsoever, since he’d been an only child. That fact ruled out even that small possibility. Anyway, what was he doing, filling his head with these useless thoughts? When it was Angela he was most concerned about. She had seemed so upset by the whole exercise, which was what he had feared right from the beginning. All the meeting had done, it seemed to him, was to exacerbate the whole situation with his father, in fact, the situation seemed worse…. At last he reached home and Angela confronted him immediately he entered the sitting room. It was as if she had been lying in wait for him – ready to pounce.

"Are you expecting a foreign lady to come to visit you?"

"Not that I know about, it's been puzzling me too."

"Well, is it possible, that you may see a foreign lady?"

"M'love, I don't foresee such a meeting."

"Are you sure that you don't have any meetings coming up where there may be a foreign lady?"

"Darling, I don't think so."

"Think – don't think – you must know."

Angela was now so angry at his seemingly non-caring replies, that she felt that she wanted to hit him. He was just not helping her, and his refusal to meet her anger with anger of his own was too irritating. Didn't he care at all? She stood in front of him, clenching and unclenching her hands, the knuckles showing white in her rage. Peter was quite alarmed by her out of character behaviour.

"Angela…Angela, please, please don't get yourself so upset."

He stepped forward to comfort her but she pulled away – she wanted nothing of it.

"I am upset. It's too late for me not to be. I feel let down… useless…and what's worse you don't seem to know or care whether you are going to see this mysterious foreign woman – or not"

"M'love, this is getting totally out of hand. There is no foreign woman due to see me – that I know of…I can't be more specific than that. You know full well what type of work I do, and you know that I can't be sure, from one day to the next, exactly what might crop up. This situation is just what I feared right from the beginning. I was worried then that you might get your hopes up to such an extent that an unfavourable result would end in tears. As indeed it is doing. Your distress is cutting into me like a knife. Don't you think that I have the same feeling of disappointment as you?"

His question fell on deaf ears, because Angela was past consoling as she stormed off to father's room. After a moment he followed her, and by the time he reached the door she was sitting quietly, gazing down wistfully at the sleeping figure. Her demeanour was peaceful and calm. It was as if a phantom hand had turned a key, and in so doing, had changed a roaring lion into a docile lamb. It was as if she had been turned into someone that he didn't know.

"I only wanted to help him," she said tearfully, "I wanted to give him release…." she whispered.

He came to her side and took her hand. It was almost the hand of a stranger, he thought, for it just lay in his, without any response.

"Come Angela, come with me."

She stood obediently and walked with him out of the dim room.

He closed the door behind them and turned his attention to her. Her face, usually so animated and radiant, was showing no emotion on its lovely features – only a blankness that frightened him. It was completely expressionless.

"Oh my very dear love," he said, as he drew her to him. His large masculine frame enfolded her, but her body, taut against him, didn't respond to his touch. He drew back and looked deep into her eyes. They were empty and without feeling.

"Oh my darling, why did I let this happen to you? What have I done to you? Why did I allow that woman to come? Why did I encourage you?" he whispered.

He turned Angela to him again and tried once more to embrace her, but with the same result as before. He felt both powerless and helpless in those protracted moments.

He didn't know of any foreign woman. This person, according to Bess Rowebotham, who was going to somehow change all of their lives. It was all so much nonsense, he thought, and instead of bringing them hope she had brought despair.

"She has brought evil into this house my darling if she has left you like this" he thought as he held Angela's unresponsive body. All he wanted was that his dear sweet wife would be herself again. He looked at her; her arms were hanging down limply at her sides, and her eyes, though open wide, were sightless.

"My darling, come back to me, please…please. I love you so, don't leave me."

He bent his head and resting it on her shoulder – cried almost silently rocking them both back and forth slowly.

"Angela, please hear me…we can't find the answer for father…only God can do that, please love, please leave it to God. You are my life, please don't take that life away from me like this."

Suddenly deep within herself, into her void of despair, she heard his crying and his soft voice. She felt the closeness of him as he crushed the life's breath out of her, in his anguish. Instinctively, her arms went about him, and she gasped his name,

"Peter – Peter."

The vacuum that she had been in was suddenly released, a rush of words spilling out of her in an easy flow once she had sucked in that one deep breath of reality.

He reacted swiftly when he heard her call his name, releasing her body, only to cup her face in his hands. He saw at once that the light of life had returned.

"Thank God," was all that his voice could choke out. He pressed his mouth to the welcoming lips, and her sweetness filled his senses again. Younger lovers would not have experienced more intensity of feeling during those moments of heightened emotion, for they had come out of a black abyss – never to return there again.

There would be no more searching. Father's heavenly soul, earthly body and senses were in the hands of God…and there they would remain.

Time passed. Peter, busy as ever, never neglected Angela in the ensuing months, and to feel her gently swelling body next to him as they embraced, never failed to give him the most wonderful feeling of complete joy. Angela bloomed, and looked more beautiful than he had ever thought possible, and now that the sickness had stopped, she was feeling a happiness and contentment that she had never known.

Father was the same. The question was the same. But Angela was not the same. She could afford to be tender and compassionate to the old man – even more than she had been in the past for she knew that this was his present and his place in history was now, although her own vision was of the future, a tantalising and wonderful future.

Book 2 – Chapter 9
Preparations *August 1940*

May Davis had gone to Camberley. The last raid was, "Too close for comfort," her daughter had said and although Camberley was not exactly a safe haven, it was safer than Amleth, so, after much insistence, May had reluctantly agreed to go back with her.

The little family that was safely ensconced comfortably in May's house promised her that they would take care of it and her precious garden. So at least armed with that knowledge, May's departure was made happier than it could have been, given different circumstances.

Now it was just like old times again, Aunt Mary was back to stay, and that pleased Laura no end. The fact that Simon was home again pleased her even more. Now he was back, recovering well and in his old place on the settee.

"I seem to have done all this before – some time ago," Aunt Mary said, as she brought him a cup of tea.

"A lot of water has gone under our bridges since those days though hasn't it?" he replied.

"It certainly has. The whole world has gone mad. What a terrible place to live in. What will become of us? What with the rationing…blackout…and all the other hardships…"

"Like sitting in the shelter for hours?"

"Yes, listening to the bombing, and the guns is bad enough – but…oh…the terrible suffering…and the deaths…And look at you…you poor soul." She looked at him with great tenderness, "Your life hasn't been a bed of roses has it? Now this…."

"Oh I'm really on the mend now. I'll soon be back in the swing of everything."

He tried to sound a note of optimism in his answer, but the thoughts that raced into his mind brought a sadness to his voice that he couldn't disguise as he continued to speak.

"…the only pity is, that life can never be the same again can it? Not with Rosie gone, and Mr. B. so terribly injured – and in such a bad way…Yes, I'm the lucky one aren't I? Somebody must be keeping a watch over me alright…yes I'm the lucky one…but I'm afraid that I can't see it that way at the moment."

The cat stirred on his chest, and he slowly stroked the soft fur as Mary sat down next to him.

"Simon, it won't do any of us any good if we keep dwelling on the past. Life, no matter how dreadful it seems at the moment, is still ours, and no amount of trying to change it will alter one part…no matter what we do, it's over and done with. Of course, we will always remember what's happened, it's part of our lives, but to go on living we must try to leave everything where it is, behind us. The present is not all that hunky dory, and could get worse before it gets better, according to the news bulletins. We've plenty to worry about…but we've plenty to be thankful for too. You're safe and sound now, thank God, and dear Laura is to be married. It seems like only yesterday when she came into this house as a little girl…what happiness she has given me.."

"Not so little now though is she eh? What a cracker…and how I envy old James finding and capturing such a super girl."

"What about your love life these days? Laura told me that Netta Phillips was an army nurse now, have you heard from her yet?"

"Yes, I have…but she's miles away…and out of my life…for the time being anyway. So…it gives me plenty of scope for the other women in my life."

At the very moment that he was speaking, Mary bent down to retrieve the cup and saucer from his hands, and he promptly kissed her soundly on her cheek, after holding her in a very awkward bear hug first.

"Get away with you, I'll drop these, and then you'll be in real hot water my lad…I see that the arms are getting back to good working order and that your cheekiness is also making a good recovery…"

"Yes, hugging and kissing are part of my treatment, didn't you know that?"

He had a quizzical smile on his lips and his head was tilted, ready to catch her answer.

"Yes, of course I believe it. What makes you think that I wouldn't," she added with exactly the same tone as his in her own voice. They both laughed and he said,

"So you won't mind if I practice on you now and again, will you?"

"I think that I will be a bit too busy with the wedding plans to even notice what you are getting up to," she said with happiness ringing in her voice.

"I don't think that Laura wants too much fuss…," he said.

"Fuss? Fuss? Who said fuss? Just the essentials, we must have the essentials."

"I don't think that she wants a wedding dress...,"

"Not want a wedding dress? What nonsense...of course she will. All girls want a wedding dress."

"I'm almost sure that she said..."

"Leave it all to me Simon...you're only a man, and you wouldn't understand about such things. We'll manage somehow, coupons or no coupons – war or no war."

They both heard Laura's key in the lock. Aunt Mary put her finger to her lips.

"Not a word Simon."

The room became silent, and Simon continued to stroke the cat.

As Laura came in she said,

"Hello, you two, what have you been up to?"

"Up to? Nothing – what should we have been up to?" Simon said, shaking his head.

"Well, I don't know, but you both look rather guilty, and why are you so quiet?"

Aunt Mary said nothing, just smiled at her and Laura crossed the room to kiss her first, and then bent down to drop a kiss on Simon's forehead. As she leaned over him he immediately put his arms around her and said in his best theatrical voice,

"Kiss me again you delightful young lady."

She overbalanced, almost squashing the cat who, being annoyed at being disturbed, had jumped down in disgust.

"Now see what you have done." Simons said in mock reproach.

"Me? What have I done? Why youuuuu..."

She went to slap him, but stopped short of actual contact.

"If you weren't still recuperating I'd...I'd give you such a wallop. Even so, I am pleased that you are improving...your arms especially...and pretty fast at that."

"Just what I said to him when he went all silly on me before you came in."

"Oh he did, did he?" she said, smiling in his direction before going on, "It's quite clear that you will be able to be at the wedding after all – thank goodness. I'd have hated to cancel it because of you...," she said ruffling his hair.

"Well, whether I'm fit or not the wedding would have to go on. There's no way that I'd be a fly in the ointment for poor old James, let alone you. After all his leave won't be that long...and when you're coming home expecting to marry the most ravishing girl in the world...I don't think he would take kindly to holding the hand of yours truly...do you? It would be a teeny weeny bit of an anti-climax for the chap, don't you think?"

Laura didn't answer, just marvelled at this young man's words. She knew that he was still in pain, but she also knew that he was a past master at being able to cover his feelings – both physical and mental.

Simon adjusted his position on the settee and then continued,

"Don't worry Laura, I don't intend to miss the big day...even if some kind soul has to carry me there on a stretcher. Just you try keeping me away."

As he finished speaking a slow smile spread over his face until it was his usual grin, the face was still battered but the grin was irrepressible.

"I would never want you to stay away – you know it just wouldn't be the same without you and although the wedding will only be a small affair... without you, it would be non-existent as far as James and I are concerned – you know that though, don't you?"

Before he had time to answer, Aunt Mary's voice called from the kitchen,

"It won't be that small, will it Laura? Will it?"

She repeated as she came into the room drying her hands.

"Yes it will Auntie, I don't want any big show. As long as James' people, you and Simon are there with us as we make our vows...well that's all I care about."

She stopped speaking as she saw in the eyes of the older woman the hint of sadness.

"The war has spoiled everything hasn't it?" Mary said, the same sadness showing in her voice.

"It's not just the war Auntie dear. All I have ever wanted was to marry the man I love, in the sight of God. I've never wanted to waste a lot of good money on an outward show...not when it could be put to better use. You do understand, don't you?"

"What are you planning on wearing then?"

"My uniform."

"Oh," Aunt Mary looked crestfallen, slowly she went to a cupboard and drew out a small slim box.

"Does that mean that you won't want to use this then?"

As she was speaking, she laid the box on the table and removed the lid. Laura went to her side and watched as Aunt Mary gently peeled the tissue paper back - to reveal a dress.

"It was the one that I wore on my wedding day Laura, and I rather hoped that you would wear it too."

So saying she lifted the delicate lace out of the box and held it lovingly against herself.

Although Simon was watching the drama that was unfolding he had no part to play in it – and so remained silent. He couldn't, however, fail to feel the tense emotion that was in the room.

"Why, it's beautiful Auntie, the lace and silk are exquisite. Why have you never shown it to me before?"

"Well, although I have always hoped secretly that you would wear it some day, I suppose my own memories were still there wanting…to be left undisturbed…until the right moment came along…I felt that this was the right moment…but I see now that I was mistaken."

As Laura listened to her, she looked sympathetically at both Auntie and the dress. It was nowhere large enough for Laura, even if she had wanted to wear it; even with drastic needlework there was no way that she would ever have looked right in it. The silk underskirt had somehow dropped, and was hanging below the lovely lace, whilst the tightly buttoned-to-the-wrist sleeves were far too short for Laura's arms; and as for the waist!!

"Oh you were so much smaller than me Auntie…so petite. You must have looked really beautiful. The pictures of Uncle John and you on your wedding day don't do justice to this lovely thing at all."

She cuddled the older woman, whom she could see was clearly upset and very close to tears.

"Please don't be too sad, even if I had wanted to wear it to please you…I couldn't, could I?"

As she was speaking, she took the creamy lace between her fingers and put it to her face.

"It's so soft, and beautiful but both of us know that it is too small. I truly thank you for the offer of it, with all my heart. Bless you Auntie."

Cheering up a little, Mary said,

"We will still need a few extra coupons though, what about your trousseau? You'll want something new surely, remember the old rhyme?"

"Yes, of course, I will have something new, I would like a little summery two piece to go away in…that's if we get away; something that I will be able to wear for the rest of the summer, and next, probably."

"You can have my coupons."

It was the first time that Simon had joined the conversation since the beginning of the discussion,

"I don't need them you know, and as for smashing undies…well you couldn't go far wrong than by going to the Co-op," he said winking at Laura.

"That will be quite enough of that young man…any discussions that might be necessary with regard to undergarments will take place in private…so you just be seen and not heard if you please," Aunt Mary said with a withering glance in his direction.

"Yes, as I was going to say," Laura quickly went on, "I will be wearing my uniform with a white sash…and I will carry the Bible that my mother gave me and which she carried at her wedding….Yes, I will definitely carry my Bible. After all James will be in his uniform and the first time he saw me I was wearing mine… and it was love at first sight remember…and it's what's in our hearts that counts – not what we will be wearing. So don't mind too much Auntie, please try to understand."

"Well, if I'm honest about it, I suppose I'm as much disappointed about the dress as anything – but yes dear, of course I understand how you feel, it's to be your wedding – your day and I'll be the last one to interfere with your decision, or with what you want. Take no notice of me Laura dear, I'm just a silly sentimental old woman."

As she was speaking she was carefully putting the dress back in its box, and slowly folding the tissue paper over it. Then her face lightened,

"Maybe…maybe I will be able to make some sort of dress for a much smaller person…one day," she added giving Laura a knowing look.

"Oh Aunt Mary…. There's no way you're a silly old woman, sentimental maybe…but silly? Never. Just a very small woman – with a very large heart."

She gave her aunt a squeeze and then helped tie the string around the box before it was put into its former resting place in the cupboard.

Simon, witnessing the scene was far more concerned about what would happen after the wedding than to worry too much about what the bride and groom would be wearing, but he didn't want to bring that up… yet.

"Will there be any eats after we get back from the church?" he said, and his voice made Aunt Mary forget her disappointment about the dress, giving her other food for thought. She had exactly three weeks to throw together some sort of menu for the wedding breakfast. Although it wasn't to be a grand affair, it would still need all her ingenuity, but she wouldn't let it beat her.

"There certainly will be 'eats' my lad – or I'll want to know the reason why not."

Night raids had been increasing steadily over the weeks, and only two nights before the wedding the whole of Amleth had been quite devastated by incendiary bombs with the fires raging for hours.

Now it was the wedding eve, the siren had gone off like clockwork it seemed, and after the initial bombardment, there was a lull. During this welcomed lull James and Simon had found themselves standing together in the back garden of May's old house, where both of them had been banished for the night as Aunt Mary had warned,

"It wouldn't be at all right for the bridegroom to stay under the same roof as his bride tonight."

So under the circumstances Simon had decided to keep him company. Being in a house full of women on the eve of a wedding was far too much to cope with, he thought. Hence the two of them were now looking skywards. Their still tin hatted silhouettes standing out in dark contrast to the paleness above them. Their faces looking strangely ethereal in the reflected light that was coming from the sky and as they looked they decided that the docks were the target for tonight because the main glow was hovering in that direction.

The beams of the searchlights cut the sky into gigantic segments, like some monstrous cake. However, even the great cuts of light couldn't dim the rose hue of the sky.

The droning of the distant bombers could still be heard but the guns remained strangely quiet, as James' voice broke into the somewhat unnatural silence, saying,

"If only the beams could be made more powerful the gunners would have more of a chance…."

"How far can our latest guns fire…? If it's not a secret?"

"It's no secret old boy," he replied, not taking his eyes off the sky, "The fact is, it's an incredible eighteen thousand to twenty four thousand feet!"

Simon whistled as they both looked up, craning their necks even higher, whilst trying to catch a glimpse of the night raiders, without success of course.

"So if our gunners are missing them they must be flying even higher than that," Simon said whistling again before continuing, "The boffins had better get on with it then, hadn't they, if we are to stand any chance of knocking them down?"

James nodded in agreement, before answering,

"You know Simon, I suppose it's better for us not to think of men up there, after all, here we are – cold bloodedly talking about better ways of killing them."

"You're right, I suppose, but you know it's a strange thing…if the planes are German, I only think of the destruction that always follows in their wake….No…I only think of men…when it's our boys in blue up there… when they're struggling to keep the Huns off, even if it means bringing them down. I suppose it all sounds a bit curious really…."

"I don't know Simon, perhaps I do exactly the same thing myself…unconsciously…perhaps I do just the same," he sighed.

There was a sudden crack of gunfire and once started it pounded on relentlessly. There were to be no more lulls again this night. Simon looked at James, and put his arm around his shoulders.

"Well, it looks like our faceless enemy is back again doesn't it? So I think that I should get you under cover pretty quick, since tomorrow is your wedding day remember – and it's up to me to get you to the church on time. Well at least hand you over to your best man…turned out nice again hasn't it?" he said, laughing as they made their way to the shelter that was submerged beneath the trees.

Simon momentarily paused, "Let's hope that there are no air-raids during the service tomorrow….or you may even have to postpone it."

He tilted his head towards James in his old bird-like manner as a slow grin spread over his handsome face. Then they hurried on until they reached the door of the shelter.

"Never…I won't allow Hitler's rabble to be uninvited guests at my wedding. The only way they will spoil the day would be over my dead body…."

He was suddenly aware of the somewhat prophetic words that he had perhaps spoken, and said in a more serious voice, "I know what I'm about to say is a bit melodramatic old boy, but if anything happens to me…take care of her… will you? I know you're not going to be my best man…but that was something that was decided on years ago…at college…but you are the best man for me to ask to take care of the love of my life. She really is that you know… and no matter how long or short my life may be, I just want her to be part of it – to be part of me."

"I know how you feel, because she's a big part of my life too…without her – I just don't know where I would be…take care of her for me…will you?"

"With my life I will…and if the worst happens – I would like to think my very special brother would take over…agreed?"

He put his arm around the shoulders of the younger man, as they bent low to enter the darkened shelter.

"Agreed," Simon answered as they closed the makeshift door on the rest of the raging night.

They were just inside the metal structure, and growing accustomed to the dimness of the interior, when a bomb fell.

The children who were sleeping restlessly, awakened at once, and started to cry. Their mother was very grateful to have the sympathetic presence of the two men with her. The blast was so great that all the occupants of the dugout felt it, and the children started to shout out at once, their fear openly displayed. They needed a good deal of consoling from the adults that night.

"What a way to start a marriage eh?" Simon said with a wink at the woman.

"Yes, indeed," she replied with a smile that took all her courage to muster, "Yes indeed."

Book 1 – Chapter 10
Hope for the Future *September 1985*

Peter laid his pen down with quiet satisfaction and scanned the four pages of foolscap notes before him. Then he stood up, stretched, and gazed out of the window.

Looking down he saw the pale, sunlit garden, and then, turning his eyes towards the neat row of trees, he looked over and beyond the small confines of that quiet place to the narrow road that ran all around the perimeter of the house, finally veering off down the hill to the main road junction at the edge of town. What little noise managed to sweep up the hill was captured by the open arms of the box hedge, therefore keeping most of the traffic din away from the house. It really was an oasis he thought, "A gem set in concrete."

Terri's head came into view below him. She was manhandling his father in his chair with complete competence.

"What a godsend that girl has been to us all – and what a change has come over her now that she has a purpose in life," he thought as he watched her, fussing busily over his father.

His thoughts travelled back to the first time he had come into contact with her and he remembered how on that occasion, he had encountered – belligerence, and sullen hostile behaviour. Coupled with drug taking, she also had a growing need for alcohol. In short she had been a complete mixed up mess. His mind moved on to the rather one-sided second encounter he'd had with her, for she had known nothing about it!

She had been picked up by the police, who had found her lying in a pool of her own vomit, after she had taken, a near fatal night-time cocktail of alcohol and drugs. Only prompt action by hospital staff at that time had given her even a chance of survival, but the vision he had encountered in the hushed ward that night, was hard to forget. The sight of the white faced young girl, with the scraped back dyed hair lying in a caged bed – blaspheming loudly as her uncontrolled limbs flailed against the side of her cot, had saddened him beyond words. But all that was a long time ago. Later they were destined to meet yet again, under somewhat better conditions, when, taking all her circumstances into consideration, the powers that be had decided – in their wisdom – to give her another, perhaps last, chance.

So, under strict supervision she had, over the weeks and months made steady progress, getting both her health and her self-respect back.

After weeks of painful soul searching, she at last crossed the rocky bridge of her past life, and felt able to face the future of a new one. The next stage in her rehabilitation had been her obligatory work for the community programme, and it was on this programme that she had entered his household.

Looking down now on the shock of copper hair darting about, it was hard to picture her as the same pathetic creature of his previous encounters. Rough and ready she may still be, but her obvious caring capacity showed itself constantly and now positive love was showing in her life.

Angela's first months of pregnancy had not been all plain sailing and, when sickness had dogged her early days, Terri had willingly offered to give more of her time to them, more time than was expected of her on the scheme – so, it was agreed that she would come in every day now to help Angela in any way that she could. Her patience with father and general good humour made her a welcomed addition to the family, but what of her own?

Her own home life had been non-existent for years. The general break up had started when she had been quite young, and her father had started to drink.

However, all that was in the past, and now here she was in the present. A re-habilitated and whole young woman. Below him, the copper curls were still as she sat next to the old man, resting her head against his, and holding his hand.

"One life ebbing away and one just beginning to flow," he thought, as he looked at them sitting there. "If the world is her oyster, I wonder…what pearl lies hidden for her future?"

He turned and sat at his desk once more, then moving the small typewriter in front of him, he fed the paper into the machine and began to type up the notes he had prepared earlier.

He typed the words, 'What is the hope for the future?' It stared back at him from the white paper.

"At least I know that Terri has a future," he said aloud as he continued to type.

Terri heard the sounds of the clicking typewriter from the open window above her. She stood up, and walked into the sitting room through the french windows.

"Mr. Peter's hard at it again by the sound of it. Shall I switch the 'phone over, so that 'es not disturbed?"

"Yes please love, it's always better that he isn't bothered whilst he's typing, but he always conveniently forgets to do it himself, you know him…he never likes to let anyone down, and thinks that he should be on hand twenty four hours a day. People can be so thoughtless sometimes. Do you know that inevitably he will always get a call at meal times?"

"I suppose they always think they're bound to catch him then, after all he's got to eat hasn't he?"

"Yes I think that that is exactly what they must think. Thanks for doing it for me anyway. It'll save me from the effort of getting up."

"I don't think that you could get up with all that lot on your lap, you have managed to get yourself in a right mess" she said.

"Yes, as you can see, I'm no expert needle woman, and it's really not my thing, but I'm going to make this cover set for the pram… if it kills me."

"It probably will, if your face gets much redder."

"It's not redness Terri – just a warm glow."

"Well, if you say so…but I think that it's a condition brought about by too many pricked fingers. Anyway, I'll get you sorted out, and then I'll get back to Pops. He's well wrapped up, and can come to no harm for the couple of minutes that I'm 'ere straightening you out, I'm sure."

"You're such a blessing to me Terri, what on earth am I going to do without you?"

"Are you going to do without me then?"

"Well…" Angela paused and then went on. "I know that you will soon have to start thinking about your future, and you'll have to begin making some important decisions about yourself. I can't expect you to remain here with me for ever, now can I? I must be realistic, and although I will miss you very much, I know that you have a whole new life to live, and I want you to live every part of it to the full. It's a wonderful world Terri, but you've just got to find your own little niche. You haven't had too good a start I know, but that's all in the past now isn't it?" She took Terri's hand and added, "Now you have your future to consider and very soon your own life to lead."

Terri had become very quiet whilst Angela had been speaking and was obviously deep in thought.

"I have come to a decision. I was going to tell you about it when Mr. Peter came down, but well, I guess I can tell you first…."

"Oh Terri dear, don't keep me in suspense, do tell – what are your plans?"

"I want to be a nurse."

"A nurse?" Angela repeated, parrot like.

"Yes, that's want I want…if they'll have me. I want to work with old people…but I want to be a proper nurse. I never thought I'd 'ear myself say it, but I've really grown to love the old folks…but I want to be a proper nurse."

"That's wonderful."

"Do you think so?"

"Yes I do, it's a wonderful idea."

"I'm not stupid, you know."

"I know you are not stupid Terri."

"I got some C.S.E.'s Gawd knows how, and an O level in Maths. I'm pretty good at figures – I always have been: I put it down to playing darts with the boys." Her eyes drifted away to another time… "I really loved those boys," she added sadly.

"I know that you did dear, I know. Anyway, you're young so anything you may lack in qualifications can be put right with a little hard work and determination. I know that you will do whatever you put your mind to."

"I've been talking to the advisors at the unit, and they think that I've a good chance of becoming an S.E.N. That's nearly a nurse, isn't it?"

"That's not nearly a nurse, love, that is a nurse. Oh Terri you have no idea how pleased I am that you have decided on a nursing career, I loved every moment of it …. I loved being on the wards…"

Now it was Angela's turn to look a little wistfully nostalgic. Terri moved the material, and sat close to her. Suddenly she threw her arms around her and said, in a muffled rush,

"I do love you, you know," keeping her head buried in Angela's shoulder as embarrassment swept over her. Angela responded at once by clasping the girl to her. Then, speaking in a subdued voice said,

"I love you too, you know – you have been my treasure – and always will be."

Terri sat up, and without raising her eyes went on

"I don't know 'ow you could love me…I've been such a little bitch to you, and I know that I 'ave played you up something rotten…yet…you never came down on me… you've put up with such a lot from me, 'aven't you? Then…even if you did 'ave to bend my ear, you were somehow on my side…I was such a moron in those days. I can 'ardly bear to think about it…"

"Hush dear, it's alright…"

"No, please let me finish, I was so 'orrible and rude…just thinking about it makes me cringe…What about the time I threw all the china and broke best part of it…your lovely china, and then to add insult to injury… I just cleared off, leaving you to clear it all up? What a pig I was, and to you… you who had been so kind to me. Then there was the day I shut your finger in the door…" The girl's voice was slowly getting quieter with each word; her head was now in her hands, the face completely obscured from Angela's gaze. She was ashamed.

"All those things were not deliberate Terri, those moments of loss of control and anger are all over and completely forgotten as far as I'm concerned."

The girl raised her head and looked into the kind eyes that were looking at her with such compassion.

"I…I didn't want to come 'ere at first you know…not'ere of all places. I argued and argued till I was black in the face, but nobody took any notice of me, of course…after all I was the lowest of the low. Just the thought of coming 'ere put me into a cold sweat, and at that time I could of well done without that, I can tell you. The thought of it…no booze, no mates and stuck up 'ere, the back of beyond as it was to me then…the blooming back of beyond. For what? Gardening… to do the gardening, me to do gardening."

"Stop Terri. All that was such a long, long time ago. We all must have felt reservations at first…even me…"

"Well, I must say, at that time, I thought they would have done better by me, if they had locked me up somewhere and thrown away the key."

She was shaking her head with emotion as she recalled those early days at Oasis. The copper locks that framed the delicate features were tumbling about, as though being blown by the wind.

"Any reservations that I may have had at the time were soon dispelled once you were here and I started to get to know you. Let's say that you have had a pretty bad start, but now…well you have such hope for the future."

Terri made no reply, just sat silently, twisting and untwisting a piece of odd-cut material in her hands. Angela could sense at once that she had something else on her mind.

"What is it dear? I can see that there is something that you are not telling me. What is it?"

"I'm almost too frightened to tell you, and that's the truth of it, it's such a cheek…and well…it affects Mr. Peter too."

"Don't be too afraid to ask me dear…or would you prefer to wait until Peter comes down?" She looked at her watch. "He should be finished at any moment now, if you want us both to be together."

"I don't know…perhaps it would be better for me to speak to you first, at least if you say no, well I won't have to face you both will I?"

"Come on then – ask."

"Can I go to check on Pops first?"

"Of course you can."

Terri ran out of the french windows into the last sunshine of the September day. The sunlight, striking the copper of her hair formed a halo around her head as she bent down to check the blanket on the old man's lap. The twisted lips started their old movements again as Terri wiped the dribble that was coming from the corner of his mouth with a tissue.

"What …is…the…answer?"

The question seemed weary, but without waiting for a reply, was repeated.

"What …is…the …answer?"

"I don't know Pops, I haven't asked yet. I'm just working up the courage to now. Keep your fingers crossed for me won't you?"

She kissed his brow, and ran quickly back into the room.

The question that Terri had put to them both eventually was a little surprising, but not wholly so. She had explained to them both that when her time at the hostel was up, she wouldn't have anywhere to make a home, until she was able to take up a live-in training place in Norwich, where she hoped to lay the foundations down for becoming a nurse. However, this move to Norwich couldn't take place until the October of next year, leaving almost twelve months when she would be virtually homeless. She explained that what she would dearly love to do, was to come to live with them, during that time, and be a mother's help, both before and after the baby was born. She felt that she was quite capable of looking after a new baby, because that is exactly what she had done for her mother when her own sister, the youngest, was born. Her mother had not had a good birth and virtually rejected the poor baby, so for a few months Terri had taken over mother's responsibilities, with both looking after the new little one, and the other day to day chores. She had finished up by saying that she hoped that Angela could find it in her heart to give her a chance to prove herself and that Peter could also trust her.

Since Peter had broached the subject of a home help some time back, it seemed to him that it must rest with Angela for the final decision. For it was she who would have to make the final choice between a qualified nanny or, without any reservations, trust Terri with the job. Angela took very little time to make her preference known.

As she said to Peter,

"If she is half as good with the baby, as she is with father and around the house, I will have no worries whatsoever."

They didn't keep Terri in suspense for very long, and the girl was overjoyed. She hugged Angela, and couldn't thank her or Peter enough. Then she raced into the garden, her blue jeaned legs almost tripping her up in her haste, and knelt down at the old man's side.

"Oh Pops," she had cried, "I'm going to come and stay with you soon, I'm so happy".

She kissed his cheek and turned his chair towards the house and started to push him inside. Before she had gone very far she had heard the old question yet again…

"What…is…the…answer?"

Bursting with joy and inner pride, she had confidently replied…

"It's yes, my old dear…it's yes."

Shooting at Stars

Book 2 – Chapter 10
For Better for Worse *August 1940*

James stood back and surveyed the damage. The back of the citadel had received a direct hit and the high sloping roof had smashed down into the body of the church.

Captain Fuller came up to James shaking his head from side to side, and gazed at his beloved citadel – or what was left of it. He said a silent prayer of thanks for the miracle that there were no casualties.

"My dear fellow," he said as he laid his hand on James' shoulder.

"What a disaster…" the words that came from James' mouth were no more that a hoarse whisper.

"I know that it's dreadful, but please don't worry about your wedding. I've made arrangements for the ceremony to take place at the local parish church. Reverend Bush is more than happy for us to go there, in the face of such a calamity…it's dreadful…dreadful," he added sorrowfully shaking his head in disbelief at what lay before him.

"Laura will be disappointed," James said, hardly hearing the Captain's voice. However, before the Captain could elaborate further, Simon had joined them, accompanied by four friends and the chief warden.

"Look James, I know that it looks pretty hopeless now, but I've been talking to the lads and they think that they can do enough clearing to make it fit for the wedding – after all – Laura would rather be married here than any other place …wouldn't she?"

James was still looking out at the mess of the beautiful little sanctuary, unable to speak, when the warden came up to him.

"Look Major, we all know how much it would mean to Laura – and to yourself, or course, if we were able to pull it off. I must say that Simon here has had a pretty desperate morning, he's been dashing around, sounding people out and rounding people up to help, if that's what you decide, of course…it's up to you. For my lads and my part, I think that so long as old jerry keeps his distance for the next few hours…well, we're in with a good chance, and we're all more than happy to do what we can."

The warden paused briefly and looked at his watch.

"The heavy gang will be here in a few moments anyway…what about it? Shall we give it a go? After all, what have we got to lose?"

The warden looked across at Simon, who was talking animatedly to his friends.

"I know the lad feels a bit guilty about the fact that he is not strong enough himself at the moment to be much good with the heavy stuff…but believe me, he's doing all in his power to get us going."

James didn't answer the warden at first, just nodded to him as he turned his eyes towards Simon before walking towards him, and started to speak as he put his hands on to his shoulders.

"What can I say? I've been hearing about what you have been doing this morning for Laura and me…How can I thank you? What would I have done without you?"

Simon quickly returned his question with another one of his own as well as a cheeky grin.

"Well, you can't can you? If you really can't manage without me, perhaps you had better take me along on your honeymoon too?"

He jumped away from James as he spoke, feigning off an imaginary blow to his chin, laughing all the while with his wide smile.

Captain Fuller looked from warden to church, and then back to the two men at his side before speaking,

"Do you really think that something can be done?"

Simon by way of an answer looked at the small crowd that had assembled with them.

"Well what do you think folks? Shall we give it a go?"

The response was immediate. One, because most of them knew Laura anyway, and two, they all felt that Hitler's bombers were not going to get the better of them. Consequently there was much nodding and murmuring throughout the crowd of a distinctive 'yes'!

James felt overwhelmed by the response.

"Thank you all," he said simply.

Somebody shouted from the back of the crowd,

"Don't thank us. Let's get started."

So with much ado, they broke into groups and were all hard at work in no time.

James again turned to Simon,

"Don't tell Laura too much about the devastation here when you go back to report to the women folk, will you old man? Play it down a bit, will you...?"

"I will be the height of discretion never fear, leave it to me."

"Oh, on your way back will you check the trains for me too? I want to know that they are still running. My Ma and Pa are due in at about a quarter past twelve, if all goes well…but I'm a bit concerned now because of the raid…"

"I sure will partner, leave it to me." With that he turned and made his way back to the house, smacking the rear of Laura's bicycle as if it were his steed.

"I'm only going to be away for three nights Auntie, you seem to have a terrific amount of things for my case…."

"No, don't you worry about a thing dear, I only have the essentials here," she said, and disappeared through the door.

"There's no stopping her is there May?"

"Oh she's loving every minute of it – as we all are."

Laura had pressed her uniform and it hung still and dark on the picture rail. Her bonnet and the wide white sash of satin that she was to wear lay on the sideboard, next to the small black Bible. The table in the centre of the room had been covered with a lilac coloured satin bedspread, and that in turn had been overlaid by Aunt Mary's best white lace tablecloth, a treasured heirloom of her mother's. The effect was quite beautiful, and enhanced all the more by a beautiful bouquet of summer blooms, a present from the happy groom.

Because Aunt Mary was not able to indulge herself with a white wedding, she was making up for the loss by using all her ingenuity and inspiration with the wedding breakfast. Austere in one respect, but certainly not in love and preparation. It was truly wonderful how even perfect strangers, when they heard about the wedding, had rallied around with precious irreplaceable groceries and other things to the delight of Aunt Mary, who had only allowed herself to break off from the task of adorning the table like a 'bride' long enough to organise Laura's going away case. She was, as May had said earlier, ' loving every minute of it'.

"You will be carrying your Bible today, won't you Laura?"

"Why yes, of course," she said, picking up the small black book, "It was my mother's before me you know. It's been well used over the years by us both, but it will give me great joy to use it, especially today."

"I was rather hoping that you would, because I took a chance, and a bit of a liberty, I suppose…" She opened her handbag as she was speaking and drew out something wrapped in tissue paper. She handed it to Laura, who was quite mystified, "With all my love, dear, I hope that you will like it."

Laura sat down on the edge of a chair and carefully peeled back the tissue. There inside lay a white bookmark, not an ordinary one though by any means, but one that had been painstakingly and beautifully made. There on the shining silk lay a perfect cascade of pale blue flowers ….forget-me-nots: their tiny blue faces spiralling downwards, entwining themselves with the pale green of delicate leaves. It was exquisite. It took Laura's breath away.

"Oh May…it's perfectly lovely…"

"Well, I wanted to make you something as a keepsake, and when I thought about it, I remembered the day that your James first came to the house … how you tended those little flowers with such devotion, and how sad you were when you finally had to throw them away."

"What a perfectly sweet idea…of course I'll use it…it's so beautiful…the little flowers are so intricate…and they look so real…they seem to jump right off the silk…it must have taken you hours to make…I've a confession…" she said as she opened the Bible and held it out for May to see. In the open page lay just one tiny blue flower and leaf.

"So you pressed one…you never said."

"No, well I felt just a little bit silly really…but I knew that I loved him even then May, I just knew…even then I knew. In fact I loved him from the very first moment that our eyes met…"

"Well, he must have felt exactly the same way too. Mustn't he? So these early dreams for both of you have come true, haven't they?"

Laura nodded and then slipped the delicate silk between the pages and closed the book. She held it in front of her, where it hung down like a beautiful blue and white waterfall, spilling out of the Bible's closed pages.

May looked at it, and at the look on Laura's face. All the hours that it had taken had not been wasted for the look told her that each stitch had been more than worthwhile.

"Come on then, give me a hug, my girl." Laura came and put her arms around her.

"Thank you...thank you May, I will treasure it for ever, bless you…dear, dear May."

"Oh stop that now or you will have me a-weeping before the wedding service."

Aunt Mary opened the door.

"What's to do here then?"

"Just look Auntie, isn't it beautiful?" She held the Bible with the white cascade out towards her aunt.

"Oh what a pretty, pretty thing. That must have taken you quite a time to make May…you kept it dark, didn't you?"

"Yes, I guess I did keep it to myself…but that was because I thought that maybe I wouldn't finish it…for one reason or another. Nevertheless, from the first time I saw the flowers, in a vase on the kitchen table," she answered, smiling a knowing smile at Laura, who really could hardly believe her ears, "I knew then that it would be James for you. What I say is, that you only see a certain look on somebody's face once in their lifetime, and I saw it on Laura's face that day. Later on, of course, I saw it on James' face too, the look I mean."

She made a sudden grimace.

"Oh my Lord…Oh my dear…I haven't made anything for him!"

The other two women took up May's look – in mock horror.

"Weeeell…. I think that he will forgive you…just this once," Laura said, and they all ended up laughing.

They were still chuckling about May's forgetfulness when Simon came in.

"What's going on here then? What have I missed?" Laura quickly hid the book behind her back.

"Nothing that you need worry yourself about love," she said.

"Then what are you hiding behind your back?" He made as if to look, but Aunt Mary quickly stepped in saying,

"Nothing for you to see just now my lad…all in good time, you'll see…all in good time."

Then, as she went on, her voice changed in tone, and was filled with a mild apprehension as she thought what his reply might be to her next question.

"What news of the bombing Simon? It sounded really close and yet the pall of smoke in the sky was up the hill," she indicated the direction with a nod of her head. "What was hit?"

"I'm sorry to be the bearer of bad tidings…but I'm afraid the Citadel took a bit of a bashing last night."

"No," May's mouth fell open.

"Oh dear," Aunt Mary said as she sank into a chair.

"How bad is it Simon?" Laura was the last one of the trio to speak, and as she did there was a hint of anguish in her voice.

"No, don't get upset, there's no need to worry yourselves, and certainly no need for you to worry beautiful, the wedding won't be cancelled or anything like that, if that's what you're thinking. You can't get out of it that easy; you'll soon be walking up the aisle, into the arms of your beloved, never fear."

"It honestly won't affect the wedding?"

"No, it honestly won't."

He walked to Laura and put his arms about her slender waist. With relief she laid her head on his chest. The other two occupants of the room, sensing that this might be a last private time between them, quietly left, making their way to the kitchen, thus allowing the two young people to have their conversation in peace and quiet. Both Aunt Mary and May were well aware of the intricate bonding that existed between them, and they both knew that Simon had been the lost sheep, and that Laura had found, befriended and come to love that lost sheep in a very special way.

When they were alone Simon spoke,

"You'll be a bride today – never fear. James is a fortunate chap…I don't quite know what I'm feeling at this moment…except to say that I want you…that is I want both of you to be very happy. I guess I'm putting this badly and I almost don't know how to explain it...but…I know that James will love and cherish you as his wife…for ever…but I just feel that I have loved you for ever, that is to say, my forever; and that part of me will be with you forever….even though you will be married and perhaps miles away from me…Do you understand what I'm trying to say? Not very clearly, I know. You know already don't you that I will love you, with a special love, till the day that I die?"

"Simon dear, don't go on so. I do know exactly how you feel – because I feel just the same way. You're not putting it badly, I know full well what you are trying to tell me. James is well aware of my feelings towards you…my very special feelings. I can't start to tell you what I feel deep down, but I think James understands how I feel, and just how much I care for you. He cares deeply about you too, and we are both agreed that for as long as you want us…well…we will be here for you. You are our ready made family dear, and where we go, you will go too."

They stood still together, holding each other's hands with a childlike innocence. Laura went on speaking looking into his clear eyes, brighter now with unspent tears, and to his head, cocked to one side, to catch every word with his good ear as usual.

"Our lives will not change much at the moment, they will just be different that's all. You must know that I will never give up the search for your real parents and real family, but until that day comes along, we, that is to say, all of us here are your family. You do know that, don't you?" He nodded his head. "There is something else you must know as well…of everyone in the world, next to James, you are the nearest to my heart."

She finished speaking, and there was a lump as big as an apple in her throat, and she couldn't have uttered another word.

"Yes, I guess you're stuck with me after all," he said, trying his best to be light-hearted because he could see that Laura was on the brink of tears. "Thank God," he added, giving her an affectionate kiss.

At that moment there was a knock.

"Who on earth can that be?"

"We'll never know if we don't answer it, will we?" Simon said as he made his way to the door glancing at the clock that had just given a ting for half past nine.

"It's pretty early for callers I must say," he added as he opened the door.

"Hello, Simon. I'm sorry to trouble you but do you think that I could have a short word with Laura?"

He quickly stepped outside the door, pulling it to behind him, almost closing it.

"It's not to do with the bombing – and the awful damage to the church is it? Only Laura – well any of them in here – don't know just how bad it is around there."

"No m'dear, it 's not to do with that…. Although it's coming on a real treat. People have come from everywhere – or so it seems. The lads have done wonders already…even the children are helping…it'll be grand…but no, it's nothing to do with that," she whispered.

"Righto…just a mo…" "Laura" he called, as he pushed the door open. "Fay Bain is here to see you." Then he turned back to the waiting woman and mouthed the words, "So glad it's good news – thanks."

Laura appeared at the door in the next instant so he went back inside leaving the two women alone. Fay Bain was flustered and a little agitated, as she started to speak.

"So very sorry to bother you Laura, today of all days…and I wouldn't have come if I could have avoided it…"

"What is it Fay?"

"Well, I need to go to the warehouse for clothes and more blankets…and well…one way or another the keys seem to have taken themselves for a walk. Since I know that you hold some I wondered if I could borrow them for a time?"

"Of course, you can have them. Come in, will you?"

"No, m'dear I'll sit in the car, I'm sure it's all of a bustle in there – I know what weddings are like."

"Alright, I won't keep you waiting long". She went inside and was soon out again and running down the path. Simon came out at the same time.

"See you later, Laura, I've quite a bit to do, and I've to run an errand for your bridegroom as well, so I'll be off," he said, jumping on to Laura's old bicycle and pedalling down the road in the direction of the station. He waved to them both, his tin hat and gas mask bumping about on his shirted back all the while looking most uncomfortable.

"Here you are Fay," she said as she handed the keys through the passenger seat window, "there are two as you know, one for the top and one for the bottom, the top lock is a bit tricky to turn now, mainly because the key is bent. I'm surprised that you are on your own. Who's going with you? How much do you intend to bring back?"

"Well, m'dear, we are pretty desperate for just about everything at the moment, so I'm going to bring back as much as I possibly can, as for somebody coming with me…well that's another story. You see everyone is so…tied up at the moment…and so busy…I've decided to pop along myself…and just do what I can. I'll be quite all right, don't you fret. I have been there before, so I know what to expect."

Laura looked at the face of the elderly lady, it was beaming, and she looked very happy, but Laura herself was not very happy with the situation.

"Fay, you can't go on your own, I don't understand what Captain Fuller is thinking of…is there nobody free to go with you?"

"Oh don't worry so…I'll be fine, I'll be there and back in next to no time…you see, so promise me that you won't worry your pretty little head about me…there's honestly no need – and especially today. I'll be back for your wedding, there's no way that I will miss that, believe me."

"I've an idea Fay…wait," she called out as she disappeared into the house again. Once inside she started to change her shoes.

"I'm going out Auntie," she called.

Aunt Mary and May came in from the kitchen.

"Out?" May's face was a picture.

"You can't go out," Aunt Mary said aghast.

"Yes I can – and I must – I just can't make out what they are thinking of, sending dear Fay to the storehouse on her own. I'll go and help her load up, then she can drop me off again on her way back to the hall. I hope that by then somebody will be available to help her unload…I just can't imagine what they were thinking of in the first place. I know that she can drive…but all the lifting? It's just too much for one person. It takes two…and I'm going. Don't worry, I'll be back in plenty of time."

She turned and looked at them both as she reached the door.

"If you could see yourselves…close your mouths…or the flies will get in," she added, smiling.

As she left them, the two women flabbergasted by the whole business just looked at each other in disbelief. Laura was quite right, their mouths were open.

There had been no more raids, thankfully, and the day was perfect. The sky was a beautiful shade of blue, with a few wispy clouds drifting slowly across it. It was just as well that it looked so calm, because this was the view that James saw as he raised his eyes heavenwards through the open roof of the damaged Citadel.

Inside, the church had been masterfully transformed by many willing hands. The result of Hitler's hatred had been healed by the clever disguise of white sheeting that was now draped over the ugly scars of war. The masses of flowers that the children had brought made the metamorphosis complete. The result was truly incredible; in fact James thought that it looked even more beautiful without a roof than with one!

Now he sat waiting – waiting for his bride. At his side sat his best man, who had arrived breathless, his twenty-four-hour-pass, ticking away fast. Behind them, also on a twenty-four-hour-pass, sat Netta Phillips, who was en route for Singapore. There was no sign of either his mother or father yet, or for that matter Simon, but the rest of the church was filling up fast.

As they sat there, composed and still, his best man, David Winter said,

"Who'd have thought it?"

"Who'd have thought what?"

"Who'd have thought that we would be sitting here together, for you to be married... to a girl I have only seen from the back!"

They left the house in a flurry of rice and confetti, James holding on to Laura's hand tightly as they ran the gauntlet of the garden path. Both of them were laughing as the gentle breeze lifted and swirled the coloured paper shapes up into their happy faces. Then they were in the car. Having given one last kiss, one last pose for Aunt Mary to take just one last snap with her box Brownie. At the turn of a key the engine roared into life and the car slowly pulled away, leaving the little group waving frantically, as it started on its journey. It was bedecked at the front with ribbons…where they came from Laura never did find out, and at the back, two old boots and a couple of cans…handiwork of the best man and Simon, bouncing off the still hot tarmac with a clatter.

About two hundred yards up the road, and well out of sight of their friends and relations, James pulled the bridal car into the kerb and stopped. Turning to Laura he said,

"I think I'll get rid of the boots and cans, what do you think?"

"I think that I love you Major James Aston…"

"I think...you're beautiful."

He leaned forward and pulled her towards him. She looked more like a sweet pansy than ever, he thought: with her eyes so big and bright and full of vibrant colour, and her fair hair gently curling, framing her lovely features; and on top of it, the cutest, silliest hat, he had ever seen, made entirely of frothy burgundy veiling, just tipping down on to her forehead in a tiny V point. He kissed her strongly on her gently parted lips, and whispered,

"Pansy, Pansy, I adore you."

As they were kissing, another car passed them and honked it's horn, the occupants calling, "Watch it!!"

After that James made short work of removing the noisy dangling appendages from the back of the car, and settled back into his seat again.

"I think that we can thank David and Simon for those knots" he said rubbing his hands together.

"Don't forget Netta…I think she aided and abetted them…I think she enjoyed herself – as much as the two boys."

He answered her with a nod, and then, just as he was about to start the car up again, he noticed the ribbons on the front.

"Oh no, I forgot about the bows."

"Please darling, don't take them off yet, leave them there. They will stop me from having to pinch myself every moment, to make sure that I'm not dreaming. I want today to go on for ever."

"It will my love…it will go on for ever."

She settled back in the car as it gained speed and watched the fluttering ribbons, recalling the day.....

Maybe she had been a little rash accompanying Fay to the warehouse but she did get back in plenty of time to prepare herself for the wedding, although to hear May and Aunt Mary...she had... 'left herself no time at all!' Plus the fact that both the women left at home were, she found later, 'having kittens' all the morning until she had arrived back again.

What she could not have prepared herself for was the sight of the Citadel when it had come into view. Her heart had missed a beat, with her fingers tightening on her Bible, as she had seen, quite clearly, that it had been quite drastically bombed and obviously had no roof! However, as the car had pulled up at the entrance, dear Auntie, who was to give her away, had gripped her hand and had told her to ... "Brace up" also saying that she was sure that everything would be ... "Alright".

In fact it was alright, more than alright. It had been quite beautiful. As she had walked up the aisle towards James, she had been aware of the scent of flowers and the warmth of the sun that had been shining out of a picture book blue sky. As she had looked, there had seemed to be flowers everywhere, and as she had drawn closer to James, she had found her heart pounding, so much so that she had been quite sure that everyone else around her had heard it too. When he had turned to look at her, she had found herself experiencing the same old feeling that she had felt in the past. It engulfed her, rapidly sweeping from her toes, upward...upward towards her face. For one split second, she had closed her eyes thinking to herself...

"Is this really happening to me? Am I really here? Dear Lord, is it only a dream?"

Her eyes had remained closed for only a little longer than it takes to blink, and when she had opened them again, she had seen her love looking at her...he looked so handsome in his uniform, with the sunlight shining on the leather straps making them shine in competition with the sheen on his brown hair. When he had smiled at her, she had just melted inside...she loved him so....

Suddenly the car gave a jolt as it ran over a rough patch in the road. The bump brought her down to earth, and she realised that she had been day-dreaming with her eyes closed.

"Sorry my love, did that wake you up?"

"No, I wasn't asleep James, just remembering today. It was wonderful, wasn't it? The outcome was lovely for me to see, but you must be completely worn out, with all the hard work that you put in to get the place usable for us."

She leaned towards him and rested her head on his shoulder adding,

"I know that you did it for me…bless you my darling," and planted a kiss on his cheek.

"Well, I must confess that I worked with a goal in mind…and of course you were that goal, but the others…they were fantastic, they all worked as if it was for their wedding day too. You're some girl, I didn't know that you had so many fans, but I'm the chief one though...don't you forget. I'm just dying to hold you… but I know that we must press on…if only you knew what you are doing to me…just by sitting there…wait until I make the last stop for precious petrol…then I will sweep you off your feet and into my arms…."

"Will you have any energy to sweep me off my feet? Perhaps I had better do the sweeping!"

"Well from what I heard from Aunt Mary, your day has not been without the physical strain of lifting – shifting – and packing at the warehouse… so I guess that we had both better…sweep together!"

"I guess so…desperate times mean desperate measures, don't they? It's all the fault of this hateful war."

"Don't let's think or talk about the war…not for the next three days at least. I expect it will still be there when we get back but…just let's think of us…here and now, this is our little snatch of time, our little place in history, let's not spoil it. We have so much love and so little time."

He took his left hand off the wheel and laid his arm gently around Laura's shoulders, she still had her head resting on him, making contact with him as he drove. She loved the feel of his strength and protection as his arm tightened about her.

"At last we are together, and for all the years to come…please God." He added smiling at her.

"If I live to be a hundred, I will never forget how the church looked today...the scents, and the sounds of our wedding. Oh and just everything…it will live with me for ever. So if I seem quiet…it's just that I'm remembering…I want to go over each moment and relish it, it's so precious to me…just like you are."

"That goes for me too you know, if I'm quiet I will be thinking about my beautiful Pansy…and how she looked when she became my wife… and what a lucky chap I am. Although I really know that luck didn't have any part in it. God sent you to me on that first meeting…and after then well…it's all history. I never did have any time for a drink that night in the Moon, you know. I just went along there with David because we had some time to kill, and it was bitter out…"

"With no bitter in then?"

"No…you're quite right, we were just sitting there commiserating with each other on our lot when Simon and you came in… funny I never thought about it much until now."

"Of course God had his hand on us…I was sent, just to make sure you didn't get that drink." He wouldn't have wanted you to end up being drunk and disorderly would He? That wouldn't have been a very good way for us to have met, would it now?"

"No it wouldn't because when I saw you with my clear head and eyes, my world stopped… and I fell head over heels in love."

"He tightened his grip on her shoulders as he finished speaking.

"So did I my darling…so did I."

Laura's voice became a whisper as she stopped talking and they continued the rest of their journey in silence, each with their own memories of that day…

James' memories went back to the first moment that he had seen the ruins of the Citadel, and how devastated he had felt at the time. Then his thoughts turned to the elation when at long last it had been finally cleared and finished. Another flash came to mind when he remembered the moment that the car had drawn up outside the church. At that moment he had found that his mouth had suddenly run dry. How was Laura going to respond to the sight of the damaged church? Perhaps she should have been told the truth? Was it all going to be too upsetting for her? But he knew he need not have worried, because all the hard work that everyone had put in to the gigantic clear up had paid off, of that there had been no doubt.

Even the children had done them proud by bringing the flowers. Flowers that had hidden a multitude of holes beneath them and which had made the final result quite unbelievable, when he considered the complete devastation of the morning.

Then again in his mind's eye, he was watching Laura as she approached the gap that had once been the main doorway. He had been aware of the flowers and blue sky above and the lilt of the bridal music but he was seeing her as he had done all those months before in the 'Moon'. He had not been able to take his eyes of her then and at that moment he was still not able to. She had walked towards him slowly, the sunlight sweeping down through the open roof, glinting on the white satin band across her breast… then at last she had been at his side; looking at him with love-light shining out of those beautiful violet blue orbs...she was his friend... his love... and at last his wife. The vision would remain with him all his life. It had been the most blessed and joyous day.

The sky had been changing its colour as they had been making their way south. It had started with the clear blue that had given them the canopy for their wedding, and had slowly graduated through the blues into pale aquamarine. Now that the sun was beginning to dip into the dark line that was the horizon, pale orange fingers of flame were spreading out horizontally in front of them, darkening to deepest orange and, as the colour deepened, so did the whole sky, imperceptibly, it seemed, then with a last quiet gasp, the colour was snuffed out.

"Our day has gone" James said at last.

"Our day may have gone, but I can see the first of the evening stars, shining brightly for us on our first evening together James."

"For our first night too, my love, how I wish my hands were not on this wheel, how I long to hold you close to me. In fact..."

As he was speaking, he drew the car to a halt at the side of the deserted road.

"I can't wait a moment longer to hold you – come to me Mrs. Aston."

He leaned towards Laura, who readily enfolded him into her waiting arms.

They clung to each other, neither wanting the moment to come to an end, but at last James pulled away, reluctantly, from the embrace.

"Only a couple of miles more now, my darling, and then we will have all the time in the world to be together."

He made as if to hold her again, but fighting off temptation, he started up the car, and they slowly moved off, into the now deepening night.

Shooting at Stars

Book 1 – Chapter 11
The Long Night *October 1985*

Terri came to 'Oasis' in late October. She was filled with energy and life, and was like a breath of spring in the household. She soon had a good rapport with the frail old man of the house, and clearly wanted to do all she could to make his life as comfortable and pleasant as humanly possible.

Angela's morning sickness, that had seemed to go on for ever, was at last abating, and after four months, she was glad to be free from it. Unfortunately though, migraine had taken its place instead. There was no regular time for the terrible headaches – and no relief either, for, from the very beginning of the pregnancy she had decided that she would not take any drugs for fear of damaging the tiny life that was solely dependant on her for its well being.

Therefore, because she would not take any medication for the symptoms, she had informed Terri, that she intended to… "pray them away!"

Terri was going to need a good deal of convincing that prayer by her – and maybe her friends, would have any effect whatsoever on the condition. However, she respected Angela's beliefs, so, when on this particular day the headache had started with unaccustomed ferocity, she had almost come to the point of uttering a prayer herself, even though her thoughts of God were rather sketchy! She helped Angela to her bed, drew the curtains, putting a glass of water at her bedside before quietly withdrawing from the darkened room.

Before getting Pops his afternoon cup of tea, she stood quietly at the bottom of the stairs, and looked across at the old man. He was sitting as usual looking towards the garden, his eyes glancing upward from time to time, to view the photograph on the bookcase. Terri walked over to him.

"Hello my old love," she said, as she dropped a kiss on the top of his head. "Poor old Mrs. Angela, she's in a poor state again today."

"What …is…the…answer?"

"I wish that I knew Pops, at the moment, a dark room and sleep seems to be favourite."

"What…is…the …answer?"

"Having the baby…that's the real answer."

"What....is....the....answer?"

"Oh my poor old dear, you just haven't a clue, have you?" She said, wiping his mouth of the never-ending drool.

She looked into his eyes, they were clear today, darting about and taking everything in that they could, but finally always coming back again to home base – the photograph. During the lull, from his repetitious speech, Terri beat a hasty retreat from his side into the kitchen. The old man finding himself alone once again, retreated, back into the unknown depths of his own mind. His gaze coming to rest this time – on the view from the window.

Just as they were finishing their tea, the telephone's shrill sound filled the air. Terri jumped to her feet and raced to stop the noise of it's ringing.

"Hello...Oh hello Mr. Peter...oh...well....no she doesn't, anyway she's lying down at the moment...yes she's in the throes of one of those bad heads again....about an hour I would say. No it'll be no trouble at all... no I can get him ready in no time...Oh I'll make sure of that, don't you worry about it...no there's no worry. Yes I could do, hold on whilst I go upstairs."

She laid the receiver down at the side of the 'phone, and bounded up the first flight of stairs to the first floor landing where the study was. Then, taking hold of the large wooden acorn knob on the end of the handrail, she jumped down the next flight of stairs in one leap, like a springing cat. She had the movements down to a fine art, and never missed her timing.

Reaching the landing between the two flights, where the bathroom was, she repeated the bounding movement and was soon at the top, running soundlessly along to the bedroom where Angela lay, and pushed the door open.

The figure on the bed stirred. Terri moved closer, and because there was so little light, had to bend over and peer down at the sleeping woman. She was unprepared for the sound of Angela's voice, and gave a little jump when she heard her name

"Terri?"

"Oh yes, it's me, I just wanted to see how you were getting on now."

"I'm much better now dear...although I still feel as if I've been kicked in the head by a horse."

"Well, Mr. Peter is on the 'phone. He has left some important papers in his study evidently and he would like me to post them before five o'clock if that's possible."

"Oh that's alright dear, you get off, I will be fine now, but would you mind taking father with you too?"

"Of course I'll take him, he's no problem at all, so don't worry."

"Thanks – you are a love."

"I'd best be going then, see you soon."

She went out closing the door quietly behind her. Turning her attention to the study door, she reversed all her previous movements, and was soon reaching for the extension 'phone.

"Hello, so sorry I have been so long…no she is feeling much better…yes the worst is over now, so you can stop worrying about her…yes, they do take quite a bit of getting over it seems. I'm looking now…no sign of them on the desk… are you sure you left them here, and not in the other office?"

Her eyes quickly searched the area.

"Oh…it's okay, I've seen it," she said, retrieving a large brown envelope from its resting place…it had slipped down behind the typewriter…one large envelope addressed to somebody in Poole, yes?…Right'o, bye for now, yes first class, see you tomorrow, 'byee."

She returned the telephone to its rest and hurried from the room, jumping down the stairs with all the expertise of an athlete; her feet picking their way down the last few, as if she were walking on hot coals. Reaching the bottom, she quickly replaced the other receiver and flicked on the answer 'phone.

The clock said a quarter to five when they finally left the house.

"This is a turn up my old friend, isn't it? We didn't think that we would be stepping out together tonight, did we?"

Her companion in the wheelchair, who was well muffled up against the elements looked at her, but for the first time in a long time didn't ask his old question.

Angela heard the dull thud of the door as they went out. The sound didn't pierce her skull like a hot spear now so she knew that the worst of the headache had passed, for which she was very grateful. Her eyes still felt sore and her head was extremely fragile and, she concluded, it would take the next couple of hours to be really free of her non-alcoholic hangover.

As she lay in the still darkness of the room, she let her hands move slowly over the rapidly expanding girth of her body. She felt the silky tautness of her underslip beneath her fingers and decided that she couldn't possibly wear it any more, she felt enormous.

When at last her hands came to rest, she said,

"I've been in the darkness like you, my baby, but not in the special darkness of your world."

As she spoke the words, she felt a movement, one kick – and then another: two of them in quick succession. She gave a gasp of delight.

"You clever little baby" she said.

She lay hoping with all her might that she would feel a kick again, but she didn't.

After a few moments of quiet, she was aware of how dry her mouth was. Reaching out in the dimness, she propped herself up on one elbow, and put her hand out for the glass of water that Terri had kindly left. Unfortunately, she misjudged it, and the glass fell to the floor. It missed the carpet, and found instead the only six inches of parquet flooring that was visible – where it broke, showering the floor with water before bouncing it's broken fragments back on to the carpet's edge; where they lay invisible to the eye.

"Oh what a nuisance," she thought, "too easy to land on the carpet without breaking I suppose."

Sitting herself up, somewhat unsteadily, she pushed the duvet away from her legs and manoeuvred them over the side of the bed. Her head was not painful, but most definitely woozy. Steadying herself, she prepared to stand up. Since her eyes were still feeling rather sensitive, she avoided switching the bedside light on, which in hindsight was a bad decision for, as she stood up and her bare feet touched the carpet, she knew at once that she had found an elusive piece of glass.

"Ouch, oh no," she said, flopping back on the bed. Lifting her foot up with difficulty she ran her hand along the bottom of it.

"Well there's nothing sticking out anyhow, that's a blessing."

Cautiously, she put her foot down and wriggled both feet into her slippers. Having accomplished this, she made her way somewhat unsteadily to the door. As the light in the hall hit her face she quickly covered her eyes, having no wish for the old pain to start up again.

"I do feel so sick" she mumbled under her breath, "I must get to the bathroom."

Whether it was the dizziness – not seeing where she was going – the sudden pain in her foot as she put pressure on it, or a little of each of these contributory factors, was never known; for, after walking about three steps – she fell.

The scream that escaped from her lips went unheard as she fell headlong down the small flight of stairs. She threw her hands out in front of her in a desperate gesture to protect, not herself, but the delicate life within her. The efforts that she made were to no avail, because there was no protection forthcoming. She felt each sickening jolt as her body lurched down the four stairs, knocking the air out of her before finally sending her spinning into unconsciousness……

"Feverfew, that's it. I'm sure that's the herb that's good for headaches Pops. On our way back, I'm going to call in at Masons, he's a good chap in there, yes, that's what we'll do."

With that she turned from the post office and looked up the road.

"Not many people about, good, let's have a bit of speed."

With that she started to push the chair with all her might to get it going to the speed that she wanted until she brought it to a gentle stop outside Masons Pharmacy. She quickly applied the brake, and disappeared inside the shop. When she came out again she looked dejected. The old man's eyes looked in her direction.

"What …is…the…answer?" He asked, his voice muffled by the scarf covering his mouth.

Terri bent down and removed it.

"The answer is - no! They don't recommend it for pregnant ladies, what a blow, I'm really disappointed Pops. I did so want to do something to help Mrs. Angela with those awful heads of hers, but it's no go I'm afraid." She added despondently.

She had a habit of speaking to the old man, as if he understood every word that she was saying, and sometimes, in a very peculiar way, their conversation even made some sense.

"What….is….the ….answer?" he said again with more clarity now that the offending gag had been removed.

"I wish I knew," she said, "I really wish I knew."

The old man didn't speak to her on the way home, which was just as well for she didn't feel much like talking.

By the time they had reached home the mist had come down. It gave the house an eerie look. It swirled about at knee height, and the trees seemed to be dripping moisture, although there had been no rain.

"Ugh – I don't like this weather one bit, do you Pops?" she said whilst not really listening for a reply.

She made her way along the uneven surface of the stony pathway, the chair's wheels making hard going of her efforts.

They were soon inside the warm welcoming rooms. Terri quickly pulled the curtains all round against the encroaching gloom and locked the doors, knowing that the master of the house was away for the night. When this was done, she ran to the bottom of the stairs, and listened – all quiet above, the only sound she heard was the sound of the clock ticking away merrily on the mantel shelf.

"That's good Pops, she's still resting," she said, flicking the answer 'phone off after checking that there were no incoming calls.... "Let's get you and me organised."

After settling the old man in the corner of the chaise-longue and bringing the treasured photograph within his sight, she made her way to the kitchen to start the evening meal. She switched on the radio as she started to prepare them all a cup of tea, the news bulletin had just finished and there was a sporting quiz game on, but she was only half listening to the programme.

She put a cup of tea and a biscuit on to a small tray, then flicking the dial until she found some music playing she turned the volume up a little, before making her way through the sitting room to the bottom of the stairs.

"There you are Pops, you can hear that, can't you? Sounds like golden oldies, right up your street. I'm just going to take this up to the invalid, and see how she is, then we will have ours."

With that she started to climb the stairs, two at a time, which by her standards was disastrously slow. She reached the first landing, but before she could ascent the next flight – she found Angela.

She had landed at the bottom of the stairs, lying face down on her stomach, one leg was bent back, almost nonchalantly, over the still body. There was blood on one foot, and it was running down the leg and dripping scarlet droplets on to the white of her underslip, which was rucked up showing both of her thighs. Her hands were beneath her, and her chin was turned to one side, pointing upward. The eyes in the pale face were closed, as if in sleep, and the hair, usually so well groomed, lay in a tousled mess around her head.

Terri moved slowly, as if in a nightmare. She put her tray down on the floor, not taking her eyes off the unmoving form. Then, as if released from an unseen fetter, she leaped down the stairs to Angela's side, not knowing at first quite what she should do. As she bent over the still body, her own hair shining and curly, covered both their faces as she strained with all her might to hear the blessed sound of breathing. She was crying now, and saying softly,

"No God....please...please..no..no."

Breathing was there, slow and shallow, but it was there. Jumping to her feet, tears blinding her eyes, she bounded up the stairs, to the study phone and dialled 999.

"Why don't they answer?.... Ambulance, ambulance... please hurry...it's a pregnant woman...I think...she's dying..."

She gave the rest of the required information as coherently as she could and then turned all her attention to Angela, who had not moved.

She raced up the stairs to the bedroom and returned carrying a duvet and pillows in her arms. She didn't want to move her but the sight of the distended stomach being put under so much pressure made her mind up for her. She gently pushed the pillows beneath the pregnant stomach and in so doing released Angela's arms a little and as they moved, they made the angle of the head alter, causing Terri to panic a little, fearful that she had done more harm than good.

However, the breathing was no worse, if anything it seemed a little better. As she laid the duvet over the now rapidly cooling body, she became aware of something else, telltale signs of blood on the front of the underslip. The blood on the back of the slip had been accounted for, but on the front? A horrible foreboding swept over Terri. Surely it could mean only bad news? Should she try to staunch it? She decided against the latter, after all, there was not a profusion of blood – just a small patch, and in any case, the ambulance should be with them very soon now.....

She crouched there hardly daring to breathe, close to Angela's head whilst holding the duvet down around the inert figure in order to keep the warmth in.

Terri was openly crying now, and between muted sobs said,

"God if you are there, don't let this thing happen, hear me...see us...please God."

For the lonely young woman, it was the beginning of one of the longest nights of her life as she felt again the same traumas that had blighted her in the past. She was distraught and fearful once again of the future...but this time...not her own.

Book 2 – Chapter 11
Starshine and Glow-worms *August 1940*

It was quite dark when they finally arrived at the country house where they were to spend their three precious days. James had heard about the place years before, and although he had never stayed there himself had known others who had, and remembering how they enthused about the special uniqueness of the place, had vowed long ago to visit it himself, and now, with Laura he believed it would be perfect.

He turned the car into the wide drive that was heavily wooded on both sides, and followed it snake-like until it finally came to rest at the side of a large house, the whole of which appeared to be covered with some sort of creeper making it hard to distinguish masonry from the flora, and one suspected – fauna, that may have been lurking unseen.

Leaving the car's side-lights on he helped Laura out. The dimness of them did nothing for the visibility, nor would have the one blackened-out slotted head lamp, had he left that on for, even the matt white painted on the running board was completely invisible in the darkness that surrounded them. They stood close together, their arms entwined.

"We've arrived at last my sweet, I do hope that you're going to like it here – this place comes highly recommended."

"How could I not like it? I'm going to be with you – and that's all that matters to me." She turned her head and listened to the night sounds.

"We seem to have a welcoming committee as well, don't we? Did you arrange that too, my clever husband?"

"Every hoot, squeak and snuffle my sweet – of course."

As they stood there a light from an upper window shone out briefly, giving him just enough time to see the tiny coloured shapes that had been caught in the trap of net, that was Laura's hat.

"Oh Laura, I love you so, this all seems so unreal…are you really mine?" His lips sought hers with a sudden urgency.

"For ever, my love, for ever." She gasped, returning his kiss equal to his own as he held her body tightly close to his.

"Well, hello out there. I thought I heard a car, and since we don't get many of those in these parts now, I guessed that it must be the newlyweds, come along in do."

The seemingly disembodied voice issued from the direction of a dimly lit front door.

"Am I speaking to Madame Vadera?" James asked, as they made their way towards the light.

"You are indeed...Major Aston?"

"Yes, that's me Madame, and may I present my wife, Mrs. Laura Aston, to you?

He took Laura's arm and gave it a squeeze as he propelled her forward to meet their jovial host. Madame Vedera, took Laura's hand into both her own, and patted it,

"My dear, it's lovely to have you here. I get so few guests now because of the war...so I am most excited about you both being here. Come right in dears, and welcome to the Garret."

The voice of Madame was somewhat musical. It's soft undulations having something to do with the fact that she switched from speaking English one moment to rapid French the next with such ease. It was fascinating to hear her. At this moment she was calling out to her husband in French, a dialect that James could make neither head nor tail of – although he had always considered himself pretty fluent in that particular language himself. The voice snapped back into English once again,

"Now I know you must be hot and dusty after your long journey Mrs. Aston dear, but there is plenty of hot water for bathing. I'll take Mrs. Aston dear upstairs whilst you see to your cases Major Aston dear. I'm very sorry that my husband can't help you, but he keeps very poor health these days. Leave the door open and follow us up do. Just keep coming up the stairs as far as you can, you won't get lost Major dear."

Laura gave James a funny little look, and then dutifully followed the fulsome, yet sprightly figure, that was already moving swiftly upwards in front of her. Madame Vadera and Laura made their way up the apparently endless stairs, fifty of them, she informed Laura, as they approached the last twenty (or so) that twisted their way into a steep spiral.

Laura heard a door bang somewhere below them just before they reached the top and she was puffing slightly as Madame led her into the room that was to be theirs for the next three days.

"Here we are Mrs. Aston dear," she said and as she spoke Laura noticed that there was not a hint of breathlessness in her voice.

"She must be fitter than I am..." she thought, as Madame ushered her into the spacious room. There was a large brass bedstead and the floor was of dark wood with loose-woven carpets covering the best part of it. As far as she could make out, there was a small table at the far end, with a lamp and glowing wall lights, but before she could see anything else, Madame had thrown open another door saying,

"Through here is the bathroom Mrs. Aston dear," she indicated to Laura that she should follow her, so obediently, she did so.

"I'll turn the old geyser off now, but the water's lovely and hot, and it will still be lovely and warm in the morning too. The system's old, but very efficient. I'm afraid that there is no gas laid on in here but this oil lamp gives a good light, don't you think dear?"

She indicated the glowing bowl on the wash-stand, then not waiting for an answer, she moved quickly on, opening another door with somewhat of a flourish.

"And this is the penny house."

"I think that I can make use of that almost at once." Laura said with a smile.

"I feel that embarrassed Mrs. Aston dear…to say that there is no light in there…but the lamp light should be alright if you leave the door open a bit. There's a low high window in there too, and if the moon's out – it's as bright as day," she added, laughing.

"Everything will be fine Madame, it's such a pleasure to have only the sounds of the country, and the peace, instead of the constant bombardment that we get at home, and the thought that we will be able to see the moon without it being overpowered by searchlights, is wonderful. The rooms will be perfect for us, thank you so much for being so kind, or should I say, merci. The extent of my French I'm afraid Madame."

"No need to speak to me in French my dear Mrs. Aston, I'm as English as a ten bob note. I know that we are a little unusual but I do hope that your stay here will be a happy one, and that all the memories that you take back home will be lovely."

As they came out into the bedroom again, James appeared at the door

"Well, my dears, you get settled in, and then, when you are ready Major Aston dear, come downstairs and collect a supper tray. I'm sure that you would like to be private for your meal, and not come down to the dining room…"

She looked across at Laura as she was speaking and smiled at her. As she did, Laura felt her cheeks colour and become hot, but there was absolutely nothing that she could do about it!

Then turning away from the two young people, Madame made her way out and down, calling out as she did so,

"See you in a couple of minutes then Major dear?"

The door closed. James looked at Laura.

"Well Mrs Aston dear"

"Well Major Aston dear?"

"Just one thing Mrs. Aston dear…what on earth have you put in your case? The stairs were bad enough…but your case, well…what are you trying to do to me?"

"Honestly love, I'm not guilty, I had nothing to do with the actual packing, in fact Aunt Mary did it for me, all I had to do was lock it…and that was only to stop that joker Simon from getting to it and doing goodness knows what! I didn't even put it into the car."

"Well, just you feel it now Mrs. Aston dear, and you'll see what I mean."

"My goodness, what on earth…?"

"See what I mean? Anyway, where shall I put it for you?"

"In the bathroom please, love, there is a hanging wardrobe in the recess in there, strange though it sounds."

She pushed the door open to the inner room as she spoke.

"I may as well put both of them in there then…heck…only an oil lamp. I'm so sorry Laura, I never thought it would turn out to be so antiquated as this."

"Oh don't say that James, I love it. It's so quaint and quiet. By the way," she paused and pointed her finger to the door at the end of the room, "that's the penny house Major Aston dear."

James pulled her to him, twirled them both round and gave her a long lingering kiss.

"How romantic Major dear, my first kiss… in a bathroom!" She laughed, and threw her head back, giving James the opportunity to kiss her again, this time on her slender neck.

"You're so very dear to me. I love you so much Laura."

He was kissing her again, when they heard it. The voice seemed to float up to their ears from the bowels of the earth.

"Major dear," it said "Come down for your suppers."

They both started to laugh hysterically and James, trying hard to control himself, called back in as normal a voice as he could,

"Coming Madame…right away!"

Giving Laura another quick peck, he turned and fairly galloped down the stairs.

When he had gone, Laura became properly acquainted with the bathroom by turning her attention to the large geyser that hung over the end of the deep, white cast iron bath. As she bent to push the plug in, she wondered how on earth they had managed to get the huge thing up all those stairs. That was quite a mystery. She turned the cold water tap on first and then twisted the brass tap of the geyser. Nothing happened at first, but then, with a hiss and a bang the water shot out – stop – start – stop – start.

"Come on old lady do your best for me…there's a good girl." She said patting the enormous belly hanging there. That one pat seemed to do the trick for after it, the water gushed out in a constant stream, without any further hiccups.

Soon there was enough water for her needs, and she turned both taps off. The room was warm and steamy by this time, and whilst the water had been running, Laura had undressed, taking a large towel from a glass fronted cupboard at the end of the room, wrapping it around her.

"Oh yes, very Dorothy Lamour-ish I must say," she said to her reflection as she rubbed the steamed up mirror with her hand, "or on second thoughts, do I mean Esther Williams?"

She turned to her handbag, which was hanging over the edge of a wooden chair, with her hat. As she wrestled with the handbag strap, and the hat's elastic, it sprung upside down, releasing its confetti captives as it did, allowing them to flutter to the floor. She looked at them for a moment before returning to her steamy reflection, then looking at herself in the mirror, she said

"I'm married, and I can't quite believe it. I'm married".

Still in this bewildered state of unbelief, she turned her attention to the bath again, there was a bottle on the side of it which she picked up. There was just one word printed on it, 'Roses'; she unscrewed the bottle and the pink liquid spilled out into the water foaming slightly as she swirled it around with her hand. Replacing both cap and bottle carefully she undid the towel that was wrapped round her and let it slip to the floor, stepping gently into the bath she lowered herself into the water.

James heard the water splashing as he entered the room, but his thoughts were centred at that moment on the tray that he was attempting to manipulate. It was both heavy and awkward. He had already put it down once on the difficult journey up the winding stairway and he didn't want to do so again. Having successfully negotiated his entry, he kicked the door shut with his foot, and quickly walked the length of the room depositing it with a good deal of relief on the table. Finally, having carefully removed the bone china from it he stood the ugly metal against the wall, covering its blackness with the tray cloth.

He walked back undoing his jacket, finally throwing it across the foot of the bed and gazing upwards towards the ceiling, what there was of it! The apex was almost above him, and from there it fell at an angle, quite steeply, away from him. He allowed his eyes to travel the whole length of the flowered curtain, which was covered (at one end) by some strange ring patterns. The ring shadows were thrown up by two gas brackets that were fixed to the end wall. They were the only other illumination and not very effective on the whole in the vastness. The brackets themselves were exactly like the ones that were seen in theatres, little globes protected by imprisoning black metal baskets, and it was the shadow of these metal rings that were so clearly defined.

He moved over to the side of the curtain. It ended about five feet from the edge of the bed at floor level. After a brief inspection, James looked pleased with what he saw, and smiled a quiet smile to himself.

He could hear that the sound of splashing had stopped, so he made his way to the bathroom door and tapped lightly on it.

"Supper's ready my lovely, may I have the pleasure of your company... soon?"

Laura was in a mild state of panic. The key, so carefully taken from the mirror compartment of her handbag and so painstakingly guarded against all and sundry during the day – had disappeared. She remembered quite distinctly placing it on top of the marble wash-stand, but now it had vanished from the face of the earth. The reason she had taken her eyes off the key was because she had been briefly distracted by a large and very beautiful winged moth that had flown into the room from the window of the 'penny house'. It had started to flirt at once with death, as it tried to get to the flame of the oil lamp. Laura had been horrified, and there had followed a frenetic chase between them, Laura doing all she could to save the moth, who seemed bent on self-destruction in the flame. Finally she was able to pick the tired and somewhat dazed creature up, as it was sunning itself beneath the warm light of the lamp. She put it out of the window before closing the door of the little room behind her, thus being able to prevent both the return of it and other winged creatures with the same death wish.

Now, ready to don her nightdress, she went to her case, and of course, found it locked. Going back again to the wash-stand, where she knew that she had put the key, she was dismayed to find that it had gone.

She hunted everywhere. She crouched on the floor and searched the rush matting more than once. She felt like crying.....

"I wanted everything to be just right – what am I going to do?" she said to herself.

There was no choice. She slipped her petticoat over her head again. It was made of cotton and rayon, and had small flowers embroidered on each side, the leaves turning into two thin straps that went over her shoulders. It came to just below her knees and although the evening was still warm and she needed no other wrap – she felt quite naked, as in fact she was beneath the petticoat, but at this moment she felt completely naked.

Shyness made her take her next action, bending over James case, she found, thankfully, that it was not locked. She lifted the lid. There on top – pyjamas. Quickly, taking the top out, she closed it again, feeling a little like a thief. She was putting it on when she had heard James knock and call out.

"I'm coming darling," she said, as she opened the bathroom door and sheepishly entered the bedroom.

Having heard what had happened to Laura, and her antics with the moth, he had promised her that he would find the key when he went in there. She still looked ravishingly beautiful to him, no matter how she was dressed he thought, but seeing Laura's obvious distress at not being able to get to her clothes, he was more than determined to find the key at all costs.

The supper Madame had prepared was delicious. They ate the chicken salad, and home-made bread with relish. The pudding was utter delight, some sort of pancake, that had been rolled, and stuffed with fresh fruits, and luxury of luxuries – a small jug of cream. Cool lemonade finished the meal, with plenty left over for later.

"That was superb Madame, you have done us proud, superb food – even if it's only for a little while."

"Oh James, how I wish that we could forget it for good."

"Now don't you start worrying about the war, remember what we said... Just relax and let me look at you... you look so fresh and pretty and I don't want to see your face clouded by any worries... not tonight," he said as he squeezed her hand. She felt an uncontrollable warmth rising to her cheeks as he continued, "You look so cool and lovely, whilst I...." he looked down at himself... "I feel I am welded into this wretched uniform."

He came and stood at the back of Laura's chair, slipped the jacket from her shoulders and kissed her neck on both sides.

"You are so beautiful," he murmured, "Give me ten minutes and then I'll be back... with myself – and the runaway key!"

Whilst the water was running into the bath, James made some preliminary forays to each corner of the room.

"System that's what is needed here, system."

He did his best, but unfortunately his best was not good enough. All his attempts were in vain. The key was nowhere to be found. After he had finished bathing, he looked again, but in the end felt that he was on a wild goose chase, and abandoned the search. The last conclusion he came to was that perhaps the thing had gone down the plug-hole, for on close inspection, the hole was found to be very wide, and quite capable of swallowing the tiny key. If that were the case, it would mean that he would have to break the lock...but that could wait.

He hung his uniform next to Laura's dress in the hanging space. It gave him a feeling of real joy, seeing them hanging there together, he knew it was a silly thing, but somehow very intimate...

The pyjamas felt cool on his skin, and, as it was a very warm night, he opened the window of the 'penny house' to it's fullest, allowing any breeze full access to the interior of the apartment.

As he extinguished the oil lamp, he felt the first light current of cool air touch his body as he made his way back into the bedroom, making sure that he left the bathroom door ajar so that the night air could be appreciated by both of them.

Laura had turned the already dim gas lights off completely, so that there was only the soft glow of the oil lamp left in the room. She was lying in the large bed, with just a sheet covering her. The flowers on each breast rising and falling with each breath she took, accentuating the contours of her body with each movement.

He crossed to her side, lying on top of the sheet, next to her. He turned her to him, and she put her arms about his neck as they came together. He kissed her lips, her cheeks, her ears, her brows and finally her eyelids.

"Close your beautiful eyes my darling and keep them closed. I'm going to turn the lamp out and open the window to let in some more cool air. Don't open them again until I tell you...promise?"

"Promise," she said. She relaxed on the pillow, the bed was soft and comfortable, and she was so happy. So much had happened in such a short while...she felt herself begin to drift...it had been such a wonderful, though hectic, day … All at once a strange sound came to her ears, and cut across her thoughts.

"James?"

"It's alright Laura, take no notice of the noise, it won't last for much longer, no peeking."

"I'm so curious…can I open my eyes now?"

"No, not yet, not until you feel me lying next to you…not until then."

She waited patiently, the odd sound stopped and a second later she felt James' body slide under the sheet next to hers. He took her hand in his and lifted it to his lips.

"I love you so very, very much," he said softly, "you can open your eyes now."

To have prior knowledge of an event allows a person to be prepared. Laura had no such prior knowledge – no warning – no hint from James of what he was planning for her. Therefore, she was not prepared for the sight that met her gaze; and her eyes opened wide with amazement. The whole of the curtained side of the room had disappeared – and in it's place – sky.

Not an ordinary sky, but one that was made of black velvet, studded with a myriad of stars. Small and large, some twinkling, some not. Some were in tiny huddles looking like minuscule pin cushions, and some in elaborate shapes... but all were breathtaking, their outlines sharp and diamond clear.

"Oh James, it's just too beautiful for words. I have never seen anything quite like this…ever before.. I'm speechless."

"I must admit, I did pray for a night such as this, otherwise my whole plan for bringing you to this place would have been a complete disaster. Even if the moon had been about at this time, we would never have been able to see the stars shining so brightly for us. It is a majestic sight, isn't it?"

He put his arm around Laura's shoulders, and she snuggled herself to his, each of them experiencing the unfamiliar touch of another body lying close and giving them complete contentment as they lay in each others arms. Laura spoke,

"What tiny specks we are in God's universe…we are but two microscopic beings in such vastness…there must be millions of stars out there…."

"Don't forget the millions that we can't see either."

"I know…it's truly quite unbelievable…and so many of them have names too."

They lay gazing outwards into the boundless depths of space that unfolded before them, taking in the unforgettable sight. Knowing that it would stay as an indelible mark in their memories for ever. The air in the room was warm, yet comfortable, the bed offered welcoming comfort; the stars, breathtakingly beautiful, continued to shine down, as they had done for centuries past. Shining through the miles of outer space to light the earth and at last finding the large glass window pane of the garret to pass through, before finally coming to rest on the large bedstead, wherein lay husband and wife. Their hands were locked together in physical one-ness, with spiritual one-ness hovering above and around them, when exhaustion and blissful contentment finally overcame them.

They had drifted slowly and silently into deep sleep, closing their eyes on one of the happiest days of their lives.

'To sleep; perchance to dream....'

The hammering that Laura heard in her head, disorientated her for a brief second. Was she dreaming? Or was it a RAID? She awoke with a start, hitting James in her panic – at that point he awoke too.

The brightness of the room was incredible. They looked at each other. Each made to speak, but before either of them could do so, the hammering at the door came again, this time quickly followed by a voice that they instantly recognised.

"Major Aston dear.....Mrs. Aston dear...I have your breakfast here.."

Laura started to giggle, and hid her head under the pillow, pulling the sheet over her head. The voice came again,

"Major Aston dear...coo'ee Mrs. Aston dear..." the voice was undoubtedly softer in tone the second time.

"Control yourself," he said, trying to restrain his own laughter, "it's alright for you...I'm the one that has to open the door before she knocks the thing down!

He slipped out of the bed and went to the door, swallowing hard he composed himself in the best way that he could before opening it. Full of apologies he said,

"So sorry to have kept you waiting Madame..."

"Oh that's alright Major Aston dear, think nothing of it, I quite understand," she said smiling a knowing smile as she handed the tray to him; it was covered with a white cloth, which could not hinder the delicious aroma that was escaping from beneath it.

"Thank you Madame, this smells wonderful."

"I hope you both enjoy it," then dropping her voice to a whisper she went on confidentially, "the sky was perfect last night wasn't it? Has Mrs. Aston dear seen the view from the window this morning yet?"

James shook his head.

"She'll love it, mark my words…magnifique…" ...and then rather louder she called, "Bon appitit, Mrs. Aston dear," as she closed the door behind James.

He walked the length of the room like some overgrown page at a wedding, carrying the tray as if it were a silken cushion, with a precious ring upon it. After putting the tray down, he turned and looked at Laura. She was leaning up one elbow, watching his every move. In the brightness of the room the coverlet was strikingly colourful, making Laura appear quite delicate and pale. He made his way back to her, jumped on the bed, and knelt beside her. He looked into her outrageously vibrant, violet blue eyes,

"Laura, can you ever forgive me?"

"What's to forgive?" she said lowering her head and her eyes from his penetrating gaze. He tilted her head up towards him and her eyes met his gaze once more.

"You know that I love you more than anything else in the world don't you? And you know that I want to love you more than anything else too…please say that you forgive me."

It was James' turn to avert his eyes now. She lifted his face to hers.

"There is nothing to forgive…I fell asleep too remember.. and I love you with all my heart. I look at you and I'm on fire with the love that's in me.. but we've got the rest of our lives ahead of us haven't we?"

They came together, each drawing the other to an embrace – experiencing the absolute closeness of the others body. They were still in this tender attitude when…suddenly, from outside the door, Madame Vadera's voice rang out shrilly.

"Major Aston dear, don't disturb yourselves from your breakfast…but I forgot to mention that I have made up the picnic basket as you asked me. I know that you want to get away as early as possible, and so I've done it already…it's ready for you both when you come down. It's a beautiful day Mrs. Aston dear. Le soleil sourire Major, le soleil sourire," she concluded as she made her way down the stairs…once again.

By the time Madame Vadera had finished speaking they had both collapsed again with laughter. James called out (as normally as he could)

that they would be down shortly. As he had been speaking, Laura had slipped out of his grasp and made for the bathroom. As she glanced at him, he made a grimace at her – in obvious disappointment, frustration and regret.

When Laura had gone, he walked over to the window and looked out on a truly glorious sight…then, taking the large handle at the side on the wall – he cranked it. The curtains above him moved slowly down until he stopped them about two feet above his head, and finally he opened up the window to its widest, allowing the warmth of the day to bring its sweetness into the room. Just as he was pouring out some coffee there was a shriek from the bathroom.

"I've found it…I've found it," Laura's voice sounded jubilant… "the key…I've found the key, at last I can open my case and get to my clothes."

"I thought that it had been washed down the plug-hole love, where on earth was it?"

"In my hat. I can't believe that I missed it. I can even remember moving it whilst I was searching. My hat, of all places."

As James removed the cloth from the tray, the scent of real coffee had filled his nostrils and wafted down the room.

"This breakfast looks sumptuous Laura….just like you." He added as Laura emerged, dressed, refreshed and joyous. She ran barefooted into his waiting arms. As he twirled her around, she caught a glimpse, for the first time, of the view from the window.

She took him by the hand and they walked over to the enormous glass pane.

"James, it's incredible." And it was.

Looking down, and away from the house, across the top of the trees, was the sea; shimmering and sparkling in the early sun that was slicing through the morning haze that was still visible. She moved closer and stood by the open window, feeling the warmth of the new day, and the sweet scents on the air, that flowed in.

Breathing in deeply she closed her eyes and sighed. James came and stood up close to her, slipping his arm around her slender waist.

"Well, Mrs. Aston dear, is it to your liking?"

"It's beautiful.. beautiful…just like you," she added, turning to face him, threading her arms through his, she held his strong, bare chest closely to her as she kissed him tenderly. It took every ounce of his self-control to disentangle himself and pull away from her embrace.

“Stop tantalising me…Mrs. Aston dear…all at the right…and yet, wrong moment. You know that the dreaded Madame will pounce on us at any time…and…much against my better judgement…I must beat a hasty retreat.”

As if by some preconceived plan, there was the familiar knock at the door. He swallowed a quick mouthful of coffee, as he ran past Laura to get changed. As he dashed by her, he kissed her ear and whispered,

“The dear friends that told me about the Garret and its artists and sculptors, never once mentioned dear Madame.”

Laura smiled at him sympathetically as she went to open the door.

When they had motored down to the coast later that morning, and abandoned the car far behind them, they had walked hand in hand…and just talked. Above them the gulls wheeled and cried their plaintive cries, soaring high to catch the warm air current that was keeping them aloft. They hovered, spread out like so many air-borne feathered fans in the almost cloudless sky.

They talked about everything…about James’ parents and the fact that they had failed to arrive for their wedding. About Mr. Bartholomew, who did manage to arrive, even though he had to use sticks to walk with, of May’s gift and of dear Aunt Mary, packing two stone hot water bottles in her case, with a note that said… ‘nights can be cold… even in the summer.’ They spoke about their hopes and fears, both for the present and the future, and against their better judgement… the war.

The real fear of separation that it might bring, sooner than later it seemed, was in both their minds.

He told Laura that just before they had left the Garret, Madame Vadera had given him the latest news bulletin. It has not been good. The south-east was taking quite a pounding, and the pace of the Battle of Britain seemed to be warming up. The docks and London being high on the Luftwaffe’s list it seemed. That, coupled with the advances that the German forces were making, made for very bad news indeed. It was depressing and horribly worrying.

They continued in silence for a few moments.

“There’s nothing we can do about it, love,” James said, “We can’t blot it out completely… but let’s try not to think about it too often. We won’t have many days like this, will we?”

Laura nodded her head in agreement.

They continued in as light-hearted a way as possible, and, of course, Simon featured strongly in their resumed conversation. Whilst they were talking about him James put his hand into his pocket and drew out a folded piece of paper.

"I found this in my case by the way. I almost forgot about it until now. The accompanying letter expressed a wish that he, 'Simon, the best brother-in-law in the world'......didn't want us to be bored so he has given us a couple of conundrums to keep us busy."

"Oh he's hopeless...what are they anyway?" She was smiling as she put her hand out to James, so that she could share the piece of paper. They both looked at it.

"That first one's Chad, I reckon, what do you think?"

Laura looked at the paper.

"Yes, I think that you are right... nosey boy... with nothing, yes I think it must be Chad... the other one.... let's think ..." she pondered for a while.

"Well, I guess that Simon would be laughing his socks off now if he could see us – on this glorious day – on our honeymoon – thinking about his stupid riddles."

"I know...it's too silly for words really, but anyway... I do think that I know the answer. My guess would be Fuller's Earth."

"How on earth..."

"Well, what with reference to babies and garden forks, it must be Fuller's Earth powder. Anyway, that's what I think, and I'm sticking to it," she added smiling, "and what's more, I'm <u>not</u> going to think of it any more."

James was carrying the wicker picnic basket, empty of food now, but filled instead with madam's pride and joy; two real woollen rugs.

"They are the real thing.... from Edinburgh," she had told them as they had left the house.

So, of course, they were guarding the precious cargo with their lives.

"I hope you know where we are James," Laura said, as they started to climb slowly up a grass track that showed two white grooves that had been worn into it, exposing a bright chalky surface which was acting like a beacon for their feet.

"Yes, I do know where we are, all the land around here, used to be my home ground, when I was a boy. I just hope that it's not changed too much that's all. If it has... well, I've made a big mistake," he added to himself... "Just hold on to me and you won't go far wrong – I won't let you get lost."

They had been walking for the best part of the day, exploring the cliff tops, the nooks and crannies and fossils on the beach. Holding hands they had walked on narrow paths cut through fields of wheat. The wheat, being waist high, undulated around them like golden ripples on a pond, all the while singing its special melody to accompany the silver sounds of the sky larks as they veered above them into the cloudless sky. But…now the blue of the day had gone, and the evening was closing in and, as they climbed even higher, the twilight's blush turned into early night.

As they turned the corner, a tree with over-hanging branches touched Laura's arm and she moved closer to James,

"Where are we going?" she asked in a whisper.

"It's a surprise," he answered in the same whisper, "but I don't know why we are whispering – there won't be anyone up here except us, we're well off the beaten track now… and quite alone."

Arms still linked together they rounded one more bush… and then Laura stood stock still. Her eyes and her mouth were open wide in wonderment. There dancing before her, and indeed everywhere she looked, were pale green luminous pinpoints of light drifting up and down in the air, sometimes coming delicately to rest on the banks, glowing all the while.

"What are they James? I've never seen anything like them before."

"They're Lampyrine – Glow-worms… silly name for a beetle isn't it? I've yet to see a worm that can fly, but for all that, they <u>are</u> worms, and very shy ones at that, because if you get too close and disturb them, they can switch off like magic… look."

He moved to the side of the bank, and sure enough as he extended his hand into a group of phosphorescent lights, they all seemed to disappear.

Coming back and standing behind Laura, he put his arms around her waist, encircling it completely and drawing her to him, bending down he put his lips to her ear and whispered,

"Pretty, aren't they?"

"Oh yes – so very pretty."

"They don't look very pretty in daylight, but at night – well… it's a different story."

They stood there silently, watching the pageant of lights as they flitted to and fro, then James started to speak again,

"They all glow, males and females alike… even their little eggs glow too… of course the females glow just that little bit brighter, to catch their mate, the poor unsuspecting things.." he added with a hint of wry humour in his voice.

"I don't expect that they mind being caught by a mate… one.. little bit," she teased, " I know that I don't mind being caught…. one little bit. What about you?"

There was no spoken answer from Laura – just a kiss.

They continued their upward climb, passing more of the enchanting glow-worms that were on the chalky banks, and slowly veered up the hill and away from the dancing lights. Laura looked back once, just before the trees of the hollow obscured her view, back down the hill – for one last look at the flecks of luminescent fire.

"You have looked down my sweet, now – look up."

Laura, obeying him, raised her eyes to the heavens. The stars were there, just as they had been the night before, but this time without glass interrupting their vision, they were more dazzling to the eye than ever. They took the blankets out of the basket placing one on the ground, and the other they rolled up like a bolster, placing it beneath their heads.

They lay silently, on the springy moss covered turf, gazing at the unclouded clear brilliance of the cosmos. They scanned the whole heavenly body above them; sweeping their eyes from cluster to cluster, some of which looked like gigantic diamond rings. The light from the bright stars overshadowing the countless constellations in the distance that they had no knowledge of but just gazed upon – with awe. Laura was quite star struck again.

"What makes them twinkle so James?"

"Oh it's all to do with the earth's atmosphere, it sort of shakes the light around as it passes through the air, all quite complicated stuff."

"What's the brightest star in the sky?"

"The sun," he teased.

"No – I mean a star – a twinkler."

"Sirus – I think. It's never very high up when we get to see it in Britain, but it does have exceptional brilliance. Laura – I'm only telling you one more thing about the stars tonight."

They turned their faces toward each other.

"Oh…what's that then?"

"It's a little rhyme, all to do with the heat of the stars."

"Go on - tell me – what is this little rhyme?"

"After I've told you… no more questions about the stars?"

"No I promise, what is the rhyme?" she said a little impatiently.

James looked into the deepness of Laura's eyes, and at the stars reflected there. He stroked her hair and then began to draw an imaginary line with his forefinger, around her brow, down her cheek, finally tracing slowly round her lips.

"Oh be a fine girl, kiss me," he whispered tenderly.

"Is that it? Is that the rhyme? Or are you trying to make fun of me, by making it up?"

"No, of course I'm not making it up, and you know that I wouldn't make fun of my best girl – and no more questions – you promised me."

He repeated the rhyme again, "Oh be a fine girl, kiss me…"

She welcomed his kiss, his touch. For the waiting was over. They were free of the world and it's troubles, and for a short time they were free of everything but their love; and there, in the seclusion of that warm and welcoming hollow, with the canopy of stars above them – they yielded to one another's passion. The precious gift from God to man and woman was theirs, and their ecstasy was complete as two heartbeats became one.

The moon rose silently, dimming the glory of the shimmering stars, as she spread her silvery light like a glorious counterpane on the contented lovers' marriage bed.

The kisses that were freely given and taken, and the whispered words of endearment, could only be heard by the scented night air, as they were caught up on a breeze of enchantment, finally being captured within the melodious sounds of the night.

This was their fragment of history, there would never be another moment quite like it for the rest of their lifetimes. All the feelings and all the words of love that they spoke that night, would remain locked in the haunting and evocative store of their own private history book….for ever.

Book 1 – Chapter 12
Waiting *February 1986*

The months that had passed between Angela's accident and now, had been like some slow and silent nightmare. The actual night of the fall had now been consigned to past history, the weeks that followed it, however, would always be remembered by Terri and Peter.

When Angela had fallen all those weeks ago, she had knocked herself completely unconscious for quite a few hours. Thankfully, the baby had managed to survive, its heart beating loud and strong even though Angela had bled quite profusely for a considerably long and worrying time. However, because of the state of insensibility Angela had, mercifully, not really known the seriousness of the situation that had befallen her.

Peter's father had gone as a temporary measure, into a local short stay nursing home so that when Angela finally came back again, it allowed Terri to start very early nursing duties with her first patient! Complete bed rest was the order of the day, and Terri made sure that, without any exceptions, that was just what her patient received!

On the occasions that Terri had visited the old man, she had started something new with him. To stop his perpetual questioning, she had started to read to him from a book taken from his room at 'Oasis'. She had found that he reacted in a very peaceful way and she felt that, even if he didn't understand much, at least he was calm, and that, she felt, was preferable to his usual state of agitation. So visiting times were not so painful as they could have been.

Many weeks had passed and Angela was at last up and around again. She was always telling Terri that she was… 'worth her weight in gold' especially now that she felt particularly large and cumbersome.

Pops had returned too, and Terri had taken him over for practical purposes, all the time. He was, of course, no weight, so he presented no great physical strain on her, but he did need a good deal of tiring and time consuming care, coupled with infinite patience as well, which Terri had now lovingly acquired.

"I know that the church needs a new roof…and I know all about fund raising…but does it really have to be you that has this party? Please let me ring somebody and call it off."

She directed the question at Angela who was counting and stacking cups and saucers in front of her. Stopping what she was doing she turned to Terri and, with a smile playing around her lips, she playfully patted the girl's cheek,

"It's not a real party Terri, you make it sound as if I will be dancing and doing high jinks or something…it's only a Tupperware party.. I wouldn't say that was particularly rollicking… and just think of all the commission we will get for the funds…hopefully."

"Yes, but thirty people… maybe more…it's all going to be a bit of a strain for you…I still think it's a bit much."

"The more people that come – the more sales – and, more commission…"

"It's a pity Mrs. Pelhagen, who arranged it all for you didn't have it herself…. She should have given some thought to your condition… what with the baby due in a few week's time."

"Don't worry so love, I could have said no…"

"Pity you didn't then if you ask me, it's all too much."

"Please Terri, I've felt so…so out of it lately…and I do feel so well now…please don't be cross with me."

"I'm not cross – just concerned … you make sure that there will be no lifting – and no bending either."

"Yes nurse, I quite understand. I will be really sedate."

"Well, just you make sure that you are… I'll help with the tea when it's time, but there's no way I'm going to be around for the chit-chat; I'll take Pops out then, and afterwards I'll read to him for a while… but definitely no chit-chat."

As she was arranging the table and room for the visitors, she finally sat astride one of the high-backed chairs that she had been arranging, resting her arms on the top, before speaking,

"You know when I read to Pops, wonder of wonders, he never interrupts me, well not until I stop that is. We're not any nearer to the answer to his old question though, are we?"

"No dear, no nearer… but as for you reading to him – well it was a very clever thing to think of… why Peter and I never had the same thought, I just don't know… we could have started to do it years ago. It just took brains to think of it, don't you think?" she added with a smile, putting the final cup and saucer in its place. "I think I'll go and have a lie down on the settee for a bit… Thumper is really kicking me today, although I don't know how he's finding the room."

" I'm glad to hear it. That baby knows that you need the rest even if you don't!"

Terri had helped the 'Lady', arrange the table with goods – opened the door at least ten times, taken coats and ushered people in, and had generally made herself useful until the moment had come for the chit-chat to begin. At that moment she made herself scarce.

A wind had sprung up out of nowhere, and there had been some odd flurries of snow during the morning so, instead of walking Pops, she decided to stay inside – and read to him instead.

Once in his room she sat down beside him at the window, and gazed out at the beautiful contortions of the snowflakes. After a little while the old man spoke,

"What …is…the…answer?"

Terri was aware of his faltering voice, but for once she didn't answer him straight away, continuing instead to stare at the flakes, that were, it seemed, multiplying by the second. She was sitting up close to the old man so that he could see her face clearly.

"What…is…the…answer?"

The voice assailed her ears once again, but this time she was aware of a soft touch as the words were spoken, at least she was almost sure that she had felt something. She turned and looked at him. His head was on once side as usual, and the ever present saliva was nestling in the corner of his mouth – making a cluster of bubbles. She looked at his hands. The fingers were curled up, and the nails (thankfully kept short) were pressing into his palms. They were motionless.

"Pops? Now it's my turn for a question, did you touch me?" she said, taking his hands into her own. "Did you…?" she asked. The old man's mouth started to twitch again.

"What …is…the…answer?"

Old words finally coming laboriously out once more.

"S'alright Pops, I'm imagining things, of course you couldn't move that much… could you? Let's look out of the window again…pretty sight eh?"

The wind had blown a few gossamer flakes on to the windowpane. They stuck there, their intricate shapes clinging on for life, then sadly they melted away before their eyes.

"So perfect they were Pops, and now there's nothing left of them," she added wistfully, looking at the sky that was now completely grey.

The snowflakes looked like so many little black dots, on their way down, and the wind, that had strengthened, had started to whip them up into neat piles at the corner of the sill.

Terri stood up and looked out at the garden, the driveway was full of cars and everything that she could see was covered with a light dusting of snow.

"What…is…the…answer?"

"The answer is that I think I should go and warn the ladies in the sitting room that the weather looks as if it has set in….and that it could get a good deal worse."

She left the room, and the old man raised his eyes, blinking at first as he watched the descending feathery flakes. Then, as he closed them two imprisoned tears were released from his eyes and slipped slowly down his cheeks.

Terri burst into the room calling out

"Back again Pops" and then as she moved towards him she saw his face.

"Oh what's up – did you miss me?"

She made light of the two wet lines as she wiped them away because she had seen them so often before. As she wiped his face and mouth his eyes flew open again and he started to speak,

"What…is…the…answer?"

"This is the answer at the moment I think," she said holding a book aloft, "look we're on a new chapter now."

She sat down and flipped through the book until she came to the place that she had left the marker in. As she began to read, the old man became silent and his ever roving eyes became still, fixing themselves on Terri's face, watching it avidly. All seemed at peace until she came to read a certain passage in the book.

'…..so at last he came to the top, and sat down on a little pointed rock, and looked up at the broad yellow moon… and listened to the owl's hoot, and the snipe's bleat .. and smelt the soft perfume of the birches and the wafts of heather honey…'

All at once Terri was aware that the old man's head was hanging down at more of an angle than ever, and he was quiet – more quiet than ever, and he was crying. Not the usual two droplets this time, but real and profuse tears. She snapped the book closed at once, and quickly knelt in front of his chair.

"My old love," she said, wiping his tears, "Did the book upset you? I thought that you liked it… I definitely won't read any more from this one if it's going to upset you.

His tears were still flowing.

"It's only a story you know, Tom's alright in the end… and he's happy and free." She looked at him and thought to herself, "More free than you are old man."

She heard the hilarity of the departing guests, for the clearing of the snow from the windscreens had turned into an impromptu snowball fight. At last the happy retinue (although slightly wet) began to make their way cautiously out of the drive. She stood and watched them go at snails pace, down the hill and away from the house slowly melting into invisibility.

She was thankful when all the noise and fuss was over, for it just didn't seem right that some should be so happy, when Pops was clearly so depressed and sad. The tears were still falling in a steady stream. They had only been falling for a minute or so, but they upset Terri very much. At last he raised his head to her,

"What ….is…the…answer?" he said softly again. She put her arms around him and gave him a long hug.

"I wish I knew my old love, how I wish I knew, tomorrow we may know, tomorrow love," she sighed into his ear.

Angela came into the room bubbling with happiness,

"Terri you'll just never guess the amount of commission we…." Her words trailed away when she saw them both.

"Whatever is it? Whatever is the matter?"

"Nothing to worry too much about…it's just that Pops is so sad...and I think it may have been me that has upset him…it could have been something in the book….I don't know…something upset him, touched him on the raw. Whatever it was it made him cry… and seeing him like that upset me too." She shook her head as she spoke, and sighed deeply as she looked down at the frail old man in her arms.

Angela walked slowly to them,

"I know exactly how you must feel Terri, because I've had the same sort of experience myself… over and over. I understand the hopelessness and helplessness you are feeling… believe me. I've been there myself.." she added, stroking the girl's bright head.

Father raised his eyes to her as soon as she was in his vision, and he heard her voice. Then, after what seemed an eternity –

"What…is…the…answer? Tell…me…now."

Terri looked at Angela and Angela looked at Terri, both of them with the same look of total disbelief at what they had just heard. Then they both looked at the old man. Terri spoke gently to him first,

"What is the question love? Do you remember it? Do tell us – if you can."

Angela leaning her arms on the side of the chair, also implored him,

"Try to tell us the question Father… please try…please," she added as the tears welled up in her own eyes.

She could no longer see the old man's face clearly, for it had disappeared into the watery mists of her own sight, so father's reaction to her pleas, if there was one, went unnoticed by her own sightlessness.

Terri saw Angela hang her head and sway slightly, so she quickly jumped up, took her by the shoulders and led her back into the sitting room where she made her lay down again.

Terri made Angela as comfortable as possible, but the bump, which seemed to increase in size by the minute, made comfort very difficult. After placing a few cushions in strategic places, Terri gave the mother-to-be's huge mountain a gentle pat.

"Not long now baby, make the most of your cosy place 'cos the world out here is just a bit on the cold side," she added with a smile, indicating the garden through the french windows, now completely obliterated by the white wet blanket. Angela's eyelids were drooping,

"Yes, it does look rather beautiful, doesn't it?"

"When I'm looking at it from the warmth in here, yes, but I've no desire to go out in it at the moment though – thank you very much!"

At that moment the wind blew a strong gust forcing the snow to pile up even higher against the windows. She looked at Angela's face. The eyes were closed.

"It was too much for her… look at her, she's tired out."

She shook her head with disapproval, and the copper curls that were tied at the nape seemed to nod in agreement. She covered the sleeping form with a light rug, then stepping back, looked long and hard at her. Angela was, without any doubt, a lovely looking woman, and the pregnancy, although it had been thwarted with difficulties, had done nothing but improve on her serene beauty. The lovely blush on her cheeks, and her pretty hair (worn longer of late) made her look even more youthful. Crouching at the side of the sleeping woman, Terri placed a soft kiss on her forehead.

"Thank you for being my good friend all these past months. Thank you for giving me your love – a home and a second chance and, by way of a thank you Madam, I'm going to nag you silly over the next few weeks, to make sure that you do nothing that would make you lose this much wanted and loved baby or endanger your own precious life. I'll tell you all this when you are awake, but at least for the moment I've got it off my chest."

She stood up and looked in the direction of the window again.

"Gosh it's dark…I'd better see about Pops… and the tea before Mr. Peter gets back – or I'll be getting my cards."

She spoke to the air in general as she resumed her duties.

"At least the party guests have cleared up…. that's a help…"

Book 2 – Chapter 12
Time Changes Everything *August 1940*

Madame was kindness itself. She had treated them like very special people... and had implored them to return as soon as they possibly could. She also made sure that she provided them with the most appealing meal that she was able to, when it had become time for them to go.

James, having packed the cases away came to the front door to meet Laura who was saying her last farewells to Monsieur and Madame Vadera. Once they had set off, Laura looked back and waved for as long as she could see the couple, watching them until they were overshadowed by the trees that lined the long driveway.

"Monsieur Vadera didn't look at all well, did he James? So drawn and grey..."

"No. Madame confided in me last night that he was desperately worried about his family in France. The reports that they have been receiving have been so erratic and confusing...he just doesn't know what to make of them...or what to believe...and what with his arthritis...he's very low."

"How stupid and thoughtless of me. I suppose that I've been too wrapped up with us, to really give others a thought. Poor man, I feel so guilty...and Madame has been such a love to us...I think that she actually helped me forget the war.. and all that it entails... and because of that, our few days here have seemed so much longer.. almost like a lifetime in a way."

"She wanted us to forget the war...that's why she went out of her way not to talk about it, and for that I am very grateful – we'll be in the thick of it soon enough. The thing I am going to miss most about her... are her little taps on the door – and how! Are you happy darling?" he said, glancing sideways."

Yes, my dear, I am blissfully so, I feel that I'm caught up in a wonderful bubble of happiness at the moment...but I realise that I'm in for a shattering awakening when we get home, then my lovely bubble will burst. But until that time comes I'm content in my bubble with you – my angel," she said as she tweaked his ear.

"No surely not? You are my angel."

"Am I? I always thought that angels were men."

"Well, they can't be, because you definitely are my angel – angel. I do love you so much, I feel as if I've known you and loved you all my life…you'll always be my friend won't you?

"Your friend and love, for better for worse, always and ever."

He took his eyes off the road for an instant and looked at her,

"My sweet Pansy," he whispered.

She sighed,

"I know Madame would like us to go back there one day, but I don't want to, not ever again. It could never be the same, and I could never feel the same either. No, I just want to remember everything – everything as it was for us. The Garret…what a super place it was…so different and beautiful; you were clever Major Aston dear to find it for us!"

She threw back her head and laughed her sweet giggly laugh, and James joined in – this time their laughter did not have to be suppressed.

When they brought themselves to order at last, James explained that before the war the place was used extensively by painters and sculptors. Taking what he called 'working holidays, away from the smoke….' It was hard to even think about smoke whilst travelling under an almost perfect blue sky. A sky darkened only now and again by the appearance of the odd bird or two in it.

"I expect when the war is finished and normality takes over, there will be plenty of artists ready and willing to take our room, and make the most of the wonderful light coming from our window." Laura said wistfully.

"I'm sure they will love, and who can blame them?"

"I will always remember opening my eyes on our first night and seeing the sky and then, when my eyes had adjusted to the beauty of it all…oh…it just took my breath away."

"As you did mine, my own dear love."

"I want to close my eyes and picture everything, the gulls, the sea, the fields, the birds….glow worms.. oh and that wonderful, wonderful night sky… and our room on top of the world…"

"Eh, what about me? Where do I fit in this picture of yours? Have you forgotten me already?"

"Oh, I'll never forget you, you are my most blessed memory…and if you weren't driving…I'd cuddle you this instant."

"That I can quickly arrange, my dear Mrs. Aston." he said, slowing the car to a halt at the side of the deserted lane.

As they approached Amleth from the south, the sky took on a glow but it was not the glow of any beautiful sunset but was instead the reflection of slow burning fires. The searchlights were on and spinning and the night was still dark, but fully alive.

As they drew up outside the house, and the car engine was silenced, they heard again the harsh reality of war. The anti-aircraft guns were blasting away from all directions, filling their ears with most unwelcome sounds. An A.R.P. warden was pedalling furiously down the road towards them and drew along side.

"Come on mate…this one's set in for the night.. get yourselves under some cover…"

As he looked in at James, he suddenly changed his manner,

"Oh evening sir," he said, touching his tin hat with his hand in salute.

Just then they heard the sounds of heavy droning above them.

The warden was making off again calling out and imploring them to…'jump to it'.

They were quickly out of the car, through the front door, and feeling their way through the darkened house then out into the garden finally standing at the door of the air-raid shelter.

Shouting loudly to make herself heard above the din of the pounding guns, Laura called out,

"It's us Aunt Mary, can you make room for two more?"

Amid the fumblings and gratings as the door was prised open, they were welcomed in by the familiar voice,

"Bless your hearts. Of course, come on in and hurry yourselves up do."

Once inside they hugged one another in turn, long before their eyes had become accustomed to the dim interior of their second home. However, they were soon able to see the care-worn look on the older woman's face, such a different countenance from the happy one of a few days earlier. At last she spoke.

"This has been going all day on and off. Six times I've been in here would you believe? Six times? What a homecoming for the pair of you. Did you have a lovely time my loves?" she said shouting.

"I'll tell you all about it when all this racket has died down. Where's Simon?" Laura said.

They found themselves lip reading as much as listening because the noise outside was so loud.

"He's on duty at the moment," Aunt Mary mouthed, "can't think when he will get back. Oh, I nearly forgot, this came for you this afternoon, James."

She reached into her pocket as she was speaking – drew out a telegram and handed it to him. He leaned close to the light, tore open the envelope and scanned the paper. He shook his head and sighed as he crumpled it up, and thrust it into his pocket.

"What is it James?" Laura asked, looking intently at his face.

"News that I was expecting love, I'm afraid. The war waits for no man… and certainly not for me. I've got to go….now."

"Oh."

The little sound that escaped from Laura's lips came with the realisation that this moment, was the moment she had been pushing as far out of her mind as she could, in the past few days. She had known all along that it had to come to this. James was a soldier, after all. She had known that fact from the first moment she had seen him and she had known it on the day that she had married him too. Now she had to be brave, and show true, old fashioned, British grit. She knew all of this, of course…. She knew how she should be feeling all right, but that did nothing to help how she was feeling, or what she could do about the terrible wrenching that she was aware of in the pit of her stomach.

He drew close to her, whispering,

"It's the moment that I've been dreading love… but it's what we both expected …. isn't it?"

He tilted her face to him. She closed her eyes and nodded, fighting back burning tears as he continued, "I'm going to get your case in, and bring down some extra bedding for you."

Then taking his gaze off her anxious features he said,

"I've got to be going Auntie, do you want me to bring anything else down from the house before I go?"

What had been needed had been brought, and James had gone before she knew it. A hug, a kiss, a smile from that handsome face – his usual… "Au revoir" and lastly the sweet whispering in her ear…. "I love you ….and God Bless"….then – he was gone. Her own voice had broken when she had responded with her last words of blessing and love and she wondered if he had heard any of them.

She turned to Aunt Mary and putting her arms about her, buried her head in the kindly soul's shoulder. Aunt Mary, in turn, put her arms about Laura, patting her gently, in an effort to console the unhappily weeping young woman.

"Oh Auntie, how I hate this war…how I hate it…"

September

Late ~~October~~ 1940

Strangely enough mothers and children had begun to arrive back in Amleth, slowly at first, and then with growing momentum – to the consternation of officialdom!

Much of Laura's time lately had been taken up with the organisation of new classes in the already battered school. Only two classrooms and a very small hall were in use at the moment, so timetables had to be constructed with a good deal of thought, planning, and meticulous care because there was only Laura, the headmaster, and one other part-time member of staff available to teach.

A completely full school day was of course a thing of the past… but they all did their best with the resources available to them. Most of the children thrived, although of course some leniency had to be allowed for the sleepy faces and sluggish responses, brought about by the particularly long and trying night raids that were being inflicted upon them.

Winter was well on its way and the darker nights made people's minds equally coloured, with overwhelming feelings of foreboding. Everyone tried to put a brave face on things, and the children – not being aware of the severity of the terrible situation, did much to raise the spirits of the all too frequently depressed adults around them.

Night raids had been Laura's constant companion since she had arrived back from the all too brief sojourn of her honeymoon – but tonight there had been no warning blasting out – so far, enabling her to retire to the luxury of her own bed.

She was hoping for a peaceful night for a change and perhaps some pleasant dreams, but whilst she was lying there her thoughts turned inevitably to James.

The ongoing dangers he was constantly in kept going over and over in her mind, making the depth of sleep she had hoped for an impossibility. Bomb disposal… the very thought of it sent shivers down her spine, and made her draw the covers closer to her body, in a vain attempt to blot out the fear that she felt for him.

She slept fitfully and awoke to the tones of the moaning Minnie and Aunt Mary's voice. Quickly saying a prayer for them and her beloved

James, she hopped out of bed, pulled a siren suit over the top of her pyjamas and gathered up a loose blanket.

"I'm coming Auntie....here we go again..."

It had been a long, terrible night and the next morning neither of them had been surprised to hear that the docks and arsenal had been very badly bombed. The local railway station and bus depot had also been hit, and there was extensive damage to both.

The German planes had used the same tactics that they had been using on the few days that Laura and James had been in Dorset. However, on last night's showing they were even more indiscriminate in their target bombing. They firebombed everywhere.

Thus making everything – and everybody, a sitting target for the heavy bomber's sights. Sadly they heard that there had been a great loss of life, with even the risk of many more casualties impending. For a landmine had drifted down into the middle of a housing estate nearby, demolishing the first house that it came into contact with (killing the occupants), before finally and almost silently, burrowing its way into a self-made crib of brown earth, and lay there – unexploded.

Aunt Mary was distraught.

"Oh Laura, what will become of us...? Where will it all end...? And you just married an' all...the world's gone mad..."

Because Laura was working at school and also giving her time to God's Army of workers at the Citadel, plus driving ambulances (whenever the need arose) and generally making herself available (like most people) for anything else that might crop up, she had less time to dwell on the fate of James and his companions which she knew was a blessing. Simon was kept extremely busy too, with his full time job at the Co-op, and the A.R.P. duties, plus any and every other job people asked him to do and him, being the good-natured soul that he was, did all that he could to help everybody, even if the physical strain showed sometimes.

Even under these circumstances, he still found time to cheer Laura up whenever he could, but just lately even that was proving somewhat of a problem, for it seemed that their paths crossed and missed so often that it sometimes took a good deal of believing that they actually did live in the same house! Some weeks were worse than others in this respect, with poor Aunt Mary acting as a go-between, but tonight was different.

"Wonders of wonders…who are you?" he said, tilting his head towards her for her reply.

"I was just about to ask you the same question myself!"

"What manner of being are you, pray tell me?"

He came closer to her whilst she was fumbling to get the key out of her shoulder bag. Her coat collar was pulled up high around her ears to keep the cold and damp away, obscuring part of her face from him, but when at last she found the wayward key, and reached up to push it into the lock, the collar slipped down exposing her complete head.

"Oh…the snood…what a wonderful contraption.. I say, did you knit it yourself?"

He put his arms loosely around her, holding her back briefly from opening the door. Disentangling herself she said with a smile,

"Simon…pack it up.." as they entered the dark hall.

As soon as the outer door was closed they entered the little sitting room. Aunt Mary had drawn the familiar blackout (and the floral curtains that covered it) and there was a glowing fire in the grate. That coupled with the gas lighting gave the room a cosy feel.

Simon turned Laura round to face him, and with his head held quizzically on one side, he drew her towards the brightly lit globe. Tilting her head he rapped out, in an exaggerated Sergeant Major's voice

"Inspection time Madam…there are a lot of strangers about…and I must be sure of your identity – please."

"Oh Simon, don't be so daft," she said, trying to wriggle away from his grasp.

"H'mm.. yes.. just as I thought," he said, gazing into her eyes, "..it is Mrs. Laura Aston without a doubt.. nobody but you could posses such beautiful eyes.. they are much better than any identity card."

Then changing to his normal voice, and releasing her from his not too tight grip he said,

"Do you still love me?"

"Idiot".

"That is not the answer I require…proper answer please."

The old Sergeant Major's voice took over once again.

"Of course I do…I do…I don't know how the world would go on turning without you."

She made to grab him as she was speaking, and tried to hold him, but the thickness of coats between them made that task impossible.

"It's like trying to hug a bear," she said.

"Except that I'm better than any old bear.. aren't I?"

Before she could answer one way of another, Aunt Mary came in to the room from the kitchen.

"Laura, when you have done with hugging one man, there's a letter from another on the mantelpiece and," she said, looking in Simon's direction… "there's one for you too, it's got a foreign type mark on it as well. Do you think that it's from Netta?"

They broke away from each other's grasp, Laura running straightway to the fireplace. Simon went the other way taking that much more time to reach his long awaited letter.

"Yes..." he said, answering Aunt Mary at last… "it is, I've been waiting such a long time for this…"

He read the two pages quickly…

"That's great news, she hopes to be coming home soon…for good, she can't say when the leave will be…just that she hopes to be home in the near future…good news, eh?"

"That'll be lovely, she's a sweet girl," Aunt Mary said with approval.

Laura meanwhile, although nodding at Simon, had hardly been listening to him as she had taken her own envelope into her fingers, recognising James firm writing at once. She started to unbutton her coat with one hand, finally throwing it off into a chair, without taking her eyes off the letter in her hand for one second.

"Any message for me?" Simon said, casually glancing in her direction.

"Hang on a moment – I haven't opened it yet…" she said sitting down on top of her coat, and tearing at the envelope. She kicked off her shoes as she was scanning the pages and curled her legs up under her. Aunt Mary viewed this with surprise and said,

"That won't do your coat much good, my girl, remember it's the only one that you have and they're not easy to come by these days you know…" she finished, sounding a bit cross.

"It's love Auntie. When love takes hold, every other sensible thought flies out of the window; but never fear, old Simon's here."

He moved over to Laura who was still engrossed in her letter. Without disturbing her too much he moved to the chair saying,

"Lean up your Highness, if you please…" And obediently Laura moved herself, first one way and then the other (again without taking her eyes off the paper in her hand) thus enabling him to retrieve the offending coat from beneath her. He shook it out and hung it up putting her shoes in the cupboard at the same time.

"There you are Auntie, no need for you to panic."

Aunt Mary just nodded and tutted as he looked at her.

"Yes, alright Simon, I suppose I am being a bit of a grouch, don't know what's the matter with me .....really I don't"

He went to her and put his arms about her shoulders.

"It's the war Auntie…just the war..it gets to us all in the end."

Suddenly the sound of the dreaded siren started up. Aunt Mary raised her eyes to the ceiling

"Hmm, I thought it was too good to last," she said with disgust, "I'll pack up some food for us, then I guess it's down the hole again…"

Simon looked in Laura's direction, she appeared not to have heard the alert.

"It's that man again Laura, and I don't mean Tommy Handley either," he sang out, crossing to her, "Any message for me by the way?" he added playfully, pretending to read the page upside down.

"Yes alright, there is something for you, but have a bit of patience do..did I hear the warning?" she added with a sigh.

"You sure did..and you know that patience is not one of my good qualities."

As she stood up, she started to walk towards him, carefully tearing off a strip of paper from the bottom of her letter and handing it to him.

"Good-o, but you really shouldn't have gone to all the trouble of tearing is off – I wouldn't have minded you giving me the whole thing!"

Laura made a grimace at him as she folded the letter putting it into the top pocket of her blouse.

"Think yourself lucky indeed that I allow you any space in my precious letter, any more of your cheek and I'll put a stop to your old messages."

Simon followed her into the kitchen carrying a pillow in each hand.

"I must say…if old jerry found the cryptic messages that James and I send one another.. they would find it all very mysterious…wouldn't they?"

"No, they wouldn't…they would think that you were both totally mad. and they wouldn't be far wrong.. especially about you anyway," she added with a smile…. "As for James…well he's a different matter, of course," she said, dodging the pillow sized – outstretched arms, and taking refuge behind Aunt Mary's back.

The lull that had ensued after the warning had gone (giving the fighter planes time to get air-borne) was over, and the guns had started up, their shattering noise bludgeoning it's way into their ears once more.

"Come on you two, listen to that...help me...don't hinder."

Although she may have sounded a little cross, in her heart Aunt Mary was pleased that the two of them could still find something to laugh about. Fun. There was precious little of it around these days after all....

~~October~~ September 22 1940. Laura had just written the date on the blackboard and started to write the word 'Composition' when there was a tap on the door.

"Come in" she called. Mr. Philip Jones, the headmaster, came into the room grim-faced. She knew at once that something was terribly wrong.

"What ever is it Mr. Jones? What ever has happened?"

"There's somebody to...to see you Laura.. I'll take over here."

"It's bad news, isn't it?" she said, hardly daring to breathe.

There was a deathly hush in the small classroom, not a movement or sound from any of the children.

"I'm sorry Laura, Simon Moon has all the details, he's waiting for you in my room."

Laura's heart missed a beat as she ran out of the room and down the short corridor as if in a dream. Stopping outside the door for a second or two she swallowed hard and took a deep breath before taking the door knob into her shaking hand. She stepped into the room. Simon had his back to her and was looking out of the window. Her mouth ran dry, and she put her hand out gripping the edge of a table for support, she swallowed again.

"Simon?"

He spun around to face her. She saw his face contorted with grief, with tears spilling down his cheeks. As she crossed to him, her own feelings were being crushed by the weight of his obvious sorrow. They held on to each other in a wordless embrace. Stepping back at last, she looked into his face, a face that was filled with sadness.

"Oh Laura... I can't believe it..."

"Simon," she said, mustering all her courage, "you must tell me what has happened... when did it happen? Where is he now? Simon – I must know what has happened to James? I must know... please tell me?"

She took his shoulders and shook him gently.

"Oh no …no Laura, it's not James," he said wiping his face with the cuff of his coat. Laura gasped, and then stepped back from him in disbelief.

"Not James? – I don't understand. Thank God it's not James…but who…? What…? What is it then?"

"It's….it's Aunt Mary…. Laura I'm so sorry," he said as he started to weep again, "….she's dead."

The words reverberated in her brain. "Dead? How could that be?"

She sank into a chair that was beside her, and putting her head into her cupped hands, swayed to and fro, slowly. Then, all at once, she sat bolt upright, and looked unblinkingly at the tear-stained face that was before her,

"What happened Simon? Was it an accident?"

"No…. it was a heart attack, I was there – there was nothing anyone could do…she was in the garden. She was just standing in the garden…when she.. she went down like a stone. I ran out to her and held her Laura.. just like she once held me.. she just…died."

He looked down at his arms, and held them out to her, as if he were tying to show her the invisible form of Aunt Mary in them, shaking his head, he looked into their emptiness and then, raising his eyes, said,

"She just died in my arms.. in that damp and miserable garden…"

His voice broke with emotion, and Laura stood to comfort him.

"Hush dear… it's alright, hush…"

"I loved her Laura… she was all, and everything to me.. she was like my own mother… she was my mother.. the only one I have ever had. She knew that I loved her, didn't she?"

Laura nodded, whispering gently to him,

"Of course she did, of course love."

Simon went on speaking as if he had not heard her, his words rushing out in a breathless stream.

"She was so low this morning when I arrived home. Evidently she had just heard the report on the wireless about the factory girls that had been killed in their works shelter.. and the fact that one of them was only sixteen seemed to upset her so much.. she said she felt as if all the stuffing had been knocked out of her… I couldn't cheer her up…Oh Laura, I couldn't help her… she just walked out into the garden .. and died…I'll miss her so …"

"We'll both miss her love, she knew how much we both cared… I'm so glad you were there with her."

Laura, whilst trying to comfort Simon was struggling with her own feelings, for the sudden death of her aunt had brought the memories of her own mother and father's death flooding back into her thoughts; the tight gripping in her stomach; the hot knives burning into the back of her eyes, the feeling of loss – emptiness and sickness, were gripping her whole being, but, somewhere in the depths of her own despair, she saw the forlorn frame of Simon. Once again he was looking as he had done all those months ago, his face, taking on the drawn whiteness of a long ago memory.

"I couldn't do anything to save her... I felt so useless..."

"But you were there – holding her... Simon dear, you did all you could – don't blame yourself for something that was out of your control.... and she loved you as much as you loved her, believe me."

"She has gone to a better place.. to a better world than this – hasn't she?"

His head tilted on to one side as he questioned her, and his eyes sought hers with a look that demanded the complete reassurance of hope.

"Oh Simon... I know we'll miss her very much, but yes... she is in a far better world than this, and she is with her Friend and Lord. One thing is for sure, she would want us to look after each other more than ever now."

"And we will," he said, regaining his composure again.

Laura echoed his words as she grasped his hands tightly in her own, "And we will......."

The funeral had been a miserable affair, the weather setting the mood at the outset by being damp and cold. The keen east wind attacked the spiky outstretched arms of the trees that surrounded the perimeter of the cemetery, and made them shed their last leaves of autumn on to the soggy ground beneath, before swirling them away in all directions.

This was the picture that confronted the little group as they made their way to the graveside. The sombre black of the mourners reflected their feelings exactly – even the brightness of the flowers did nothing to elevate their sadness.

As they stood at the graveside, the wind biting into their bones, the group of friends looked across at Laura and Simon. They were both standing arm in arm, white-faced and tearless, unlike those of them who were trying vainly to subdue theirs and, finding it impossible, were now, one by one, drawing out handkerchiefs in order to dab at their wet and wind stung faces.

Simon and Laura seemed to be remote from the other mourners, their thoughts being far away from the distressing scene before them. They were standing there, not showing any outward sign of emotion, both of them having done their weeping for Aunt Mary days before. Now they stood, brave-faced against the wind, with no outward sounds penetrating their inward thoughts. Laura was remembering how her Auntie always told her never to wear black, so for that reason she was wearing a bright scarlet scarf at her throat. The wind had caused it to escape from her collar and it was now fluttering up the sides of her face – but she made no attempt to control the gambolling ties. Perhaps people would have found it in bad taste if they could have been aware of her thoughts, for, try as she may, she couldn't stop herself from thinking of all the funny, silly things that had been part of her life with Auntie for so long. Yes, she would miss the happy presence of her, but she knew that she had a niche in her heart where happy recollections could never be erased. Somehow in a strange way, Laura suddenly felt elated. In fact, although she didn't realise it, in that same brief moment it showed in her face.

Much to Laura's distress, James had not been able to get any leave for the funeral. So that evening, when she and Simon were sitting together mulling over the events of the sad day, she expressed her undying thanks to him, for – just being there.

"If it hadn't been for you," she said, sitting up close to him, "I would have felt quite devastated at being alone. Oh I know how kind everyone was, May and her daughter especially, but without you love, I would have felt quite desolate. Bless you for your strong arm that I was able to lean on." She finished speaking and they sat silently.

"I don't know what to say, he said with a quiet reserve, "It was like a dream… sort of unreal, and yet, at the same time real. It was as if I was watching, and yet taking part – all at the same time. Yes, I was conscious of the cold wind and you… but Aunt Mary? She certainly was not there in that coffin. How could she be there in that cold ground I asked myself? No, she's free. Free from the worries of the war, pain and death. Her spirit has long gone to heaven. She was an angel to me whilst she was on earth, should I complain now that she has gone to be an angel in the heavenly realm?"

He broke off for a moment and laid his arm about Laura's shoulder.

"No, I may feel sad for myself, but not for Aunt Mary. Do you understand what I'm trying to say, Laura?"

"I know exactly what you are saying, and strange though it sounds, I feel the same way."

They had no more time to commiserate with one another, for right on time the warning sounded, and the guns started almost at once, soon becoming incessant. In a few moments more explosions could be heard very close.

"What a night for me to have to leave you alone, I'm so sorry, but you know I have to go…"

"Don't fret about me.. I think I'll go and see if I can be of any use round at the hall…."

"Oh no you won't…whatever would James say? And what would he think of me if he managed to get home on the quick to see you? Only to find that you had taken yourself off somewhere during a raid?" Then he added, " And a pretty nasty one at that, by the sound of it. Nobody would expect you to go there tonight anyway, you're off duty… remember?"

The sounds of the bombs falling and the subsequent explosions seemed to be getting closer.

"Come on, I'm going to see you safe inside the shelter before I go on duty."

He started to get the things together, and since Florrie Smith had claimed Tabby Raindrop as her long lost puss he didn't have to play hunt the cat. All he had to remember was – to make sure that Laura's Bible went with her, also her knitting (that had been unpicked more times than he could remember) and a packet of biscuits.

Laura picked up the basket that was standing in its usual place by the kitchen door on her way, and they ran up the garden path. The noise of the shells bursting above, the guns on the common booming out their never ending thunder, and the frightening sounds of explosions…were as much as Laura could stand, and her head felt like bursting.

"How on earth are your poor ears up to all this deafening roar?" she said when they were safely in the shelter. He answered her as he was lighting the candles,

"Well, I always stuff my ears out with cotton wool these days…mind you it doesn't do an awful lot of good 'cos the bad one still bleeds and gives me a bit of pain. I guess it always will… but the cotton-wool helps keep some of the racket out… don't worry about me I'm alright.. mind you some of the really big bangs do reverberate around in my brain..

stop…I know what you're going to say next," and they both ended laughing and saying together, "What brain?"

He gave her a hug and left her, pushing the door firmly shut on his way out. He hated to leave her there – all alone in that living tomb, but he prayed that her enforced imprisonment would soon be over….

The day of the funeral was well behind them now and of course, life had to go on. Simon was back at work and keeping himself busy, for he knew that Aunt Mary would want him to do just that, so now, it was up to him to carry on as usual and… get on with it.

Laura had been given some time off, which was a blessing, as she had been very busy the last couple of nights with ambulance duties. And those, coupled with her school work and work around at the Salvation Army hall, meant that she had found precious little time to be at home; and there were things that she knew she had to do there. So the time off was most welcomed, and the fact that James was also due home at any moment, made the prospect even more pleasurable to her.

Laura was upstairs emptying Aunt Mary's cupboards and drawers when James had knocked at the door. She had been busy all day, and when she heard the knock, she broke off the sorting that had occupied her attention for a good few hours and ran down the stairs, pleased to have an interruption from her sad task. When she saw James standing there, love surged up inside her as she threw her arms around him in a wild embrace, almost knocking him off his feet. Then averting her eyes from his face, she fled from him and rushed upstairs again.

James, not experiencing this sort of behaviour from his wife before, felt both concern ….and hurt. Leaving his case, great-coat and hat in the little hall, he followed her up the narrow staircase, taking the stairs in his stride, two at a time. He stood at the bedroom door, and looked at her. She stood with her head bent over an old battered suitcase; her hair dishevelled and hanging down, obscuring her face from his view. Her white jumper had ridden up, exposing a small strip of pink underslip at her waist every time she reached for another garment to pack; and that was in itself a useless waste of time, for the case was overfull – and as more clothes were pressed down on top of the lower ones – they just slipped out. Making the whole exercise a repetitive journey to nowhere.

He watched in silence and sorrow for a few moments, as she continued with her unsuccessful labours, before crossing to her. Standing at her side he reached out his hand and touched her hair as he said,

"Darling, you haven't spoken to me yet, I know that you're busy, but please, please let me help you…now that I am here. You've let me into the house.. but you haven't let me into your grieving heart.. you've locked me out .. let me in.. please. I loved Aunt Mary too, you know… I know that it wasn't for very long… but I still loved her.. can't you stop long enough to comfort me? Even for a second?"

Laura was hearing his voice and trying to be both sensible and brave.. but both of these activities were falling short of their objective. There was just no way she could stop the build up of red hot tears that were engulfing her eyes, causing the clothes before her to swim,

"Stupid – stupid clothes," she said, for no matter how she tried to cram them into the bulging case .. they just kept falling out again. As they fell for the last time, she lifted her eyes and looked at the blurred outline of James.

"Oh James," was all that she said as her body slowly crumpled into a heap on the floor at the side of the bed. Instantly he bent down beside her, his arms clasping about her trembling body.

"My darling, I'm so sorry… so very sorry," he said tenderly.

Laura was crying loudly in his arms, but at last the tearful sounds lost their force and became intermittent.. and finally stopped altogether. She turned her tear-stained face towards him, her eyes looking like violet-blue pebbles washed by the sea of salt tears, and said,

"Oh James forgive me….that was the first time that I have cried for myself – for my loss – for me… I'm sorry I shut you out, please forgive me… I'll never do it again, I love you very much and I need you so."

As she finished speaking, she kissed him, not with passion, but with true and tender love.

As they sat there on the floor, their backs resting on the side of the bed, they were (without realising it) both discovering solace and peace from the sheer presence of one another. They gained much in these fleeting moments, and by allowing each other to share in the grief and sorrow; were able to give and receive comfort, in a way that they had never encountered before.

What did become clear to them later was that in sad or lonely times they needed – more than anything else – the comforting touch of another human being. They had known this fact for a long time, of course, for there had been many occasions when they had both given love and help to others, but this time they were both on the receiving end themselves, living out the very actions that they had in the past so freely given.

"For better or worse darling…. If this is the worse, things can only get better for us," he said at last.

"Yes, you're right. Auntie would call me a right useless lump if she could see me now.. useless to myself.. and to anyone else as well. Self-pity never did any good to anybody. Help me up love, my legs have gone completely to sleep, and I feel cold right through."

Once on her feet she clung to him terrified to move as the tingle crept up both her legs, the sensation of it feeling both pleasurable and painful to her, all at the same time. She was laughing through gritted teeth as James attempted to rub some life back into the offending limbs and squealed as she begged him not to, as for a moment or two she stood there hardly daring to breathe. She became colder than ever for the little room was without heat, and her light jumper was totally inadequate for the sudden drop in temperature as evening approached.

"I'll pop downstairs and get the matches to light the gas, then I'll help you to get all this cleared, it won't take long. You do want to get it all done today… don't you love?"

"Oh yes, clothes are in a desperately short supply at the moment and I know that it is what Auntie would want me to do, and with you to help me.." Standing on tiptoe she reached her arms up and put them about his neck before drawing him close to her…"I know that we will soon get it finished."

His hands went around her waist, and he felt the silky strip and the warmth of her body beneath it as he held her close. He kissed her passionately.

"Can I make a date with you tonight beautiful?"

"I think that it could be arranged, Luftwaffe allowing, of course"

"Luftwaffe, or no Luftwaffe – can I have my date?"

"Of course…you…can" she answered, kissing him after each word and then adding, "Auntie worked like a beaver getting our room ready for us.. and you haven't even seen it yet. I promise, whatever happens.. you will see it tonight, and you will get your date. I'm only sorry that she isn't here to thank…"

"But she would want us to be happy, wouldn't she darling?"

"We will sweetheart, I know we will…."

Towards the end of James' leave, he confided in Simon that he had acquired two tickets for a show in town. He had never taken Laura out to a theatre, or any sort of show, apart from some recitals that they had managed to get to before they were married (Laura subsequently bought two records after those expeditions, and played them to death on a rather ancient gramophone) so the trip to town was meant to be a real treat for her. However, since he had planned the outing long before Aunt Mary's death, he felt (because of the unfortunate circumstances) that the best thing to do was to give them to Simon to use – or for him to pass on to a friend.

"Not on your life, James – you take Laura ... and enjoy it."

"Oh...I don't think that she would like to go...not now.. and I don't want to risk upsetting her...."

"Listen.. I'm telling you – take her. It will do you both good... and I bet she'll love it."

"But it's a light-hearted musical...you know, 'Me and My Girl'...I just don't think she will want to go."

"Leave it to me James, I'll have a word with her when she gets in, you just make yourself scarce for a couple of minutes. Life's too short chum...you must take her. You've both to live a bit, promise me, if I can explain how you are feeling...will you take her?"

"Of course I will – I just don't want her to feel I'm uncaring ...I only wish that you could come with us..."

"Not on your life – I'm not known for being a gooseberry old man, Now if Netta were here... well that would be a different story. She's due home after Christmas some time you know, I'm really looking forward to seeing her again. She's got a little surprise for you too... but that will come later on..."

They heard Laura's key in the lock.

"Give us a mo James – I'll call you as soon as we've had our little talk."

"Of course, you're a real pal Simon – but don't upset her will you old boy? I'll burn them rather than hurt her feelings."

"Leave it to me... leave it to me, it won't come to that – I've a way with women – well Laura anyway," he laughed, as James beat a hasty retreat into the kitchen.

They did go for their night out. Hitler's Luftwaffe did their best to interrupt the night's proceedings, but all the audience sat tight. It was a bright and breezy show with catchy tunes. They had heard the songs before on the wireless of course, but to see them performed was most enjoyable. The colourful costumes and high spirits of the cast lifted the mood of the onlookers, and by the time it came to the Lambeth Walk number – all the theatre joined in with the members of the cast, singing loudly at the top of their voices. This, in turn, helped to block out the sounds of an air-raid that were filtering in through the walls. Fortunately, before the show had come to a close, the all clear had sounded, allowing both cast and crowds to depart in safety.

Although they arrived home on the last train – and were late, they still managed to be in the house before Simon and that gave Laura the opportunity to make up his bed on the settee as usual, before retiring herself.

Whilst Laura was busy, James wrote Simon a note:

"Dear Simon – don't wake us up in the morning – we're going to have our last lie in. The show was great – all thanks to you. I may not see you before I go tomorrow, so if I don't – take good care of yourself – and my lovely Laura, and I hope to see you in about three weeks (if I'm lucky). Leave me a couple of brain teasers please, if you have any ... they do break the monotony when I'm on standby. In return, I will send you a real diabolical one – when I've thought it up of course. Once again, take care of my special girl – special brother, and yourself. Au revoir for now, James."

He folded the paper and stood it on the mantelpiece, next to the clock.

"I've left a note for Simon – just in case I don't see him in the morning," he called out the Laura.

She came in from the kitchen, carrying a brown paper parcel, and placed it on the settee.

"Oh, I could have added something to it .. but never mind, I'll do my own and put it in the parcel. It's not very important, but it's just that I want him to make some decision about his old clothes, and if I leave them for him, at least he'll have to think about them."

She finished the note, pushed it into the fold of the paper and placed the parcel on Simon's pillow.

At last they were in the comfort of their own bed, but only for a couple of hours, because once again the wail of the siren sounded in their ears. Laura gave a final kiss to James and stood up. She walked to the end of the bedstead and held it, the brass striking cold under her hand. She looked back at James, who had made no move to extricate himself from the warmth of the bed. He in turn gazed at Laura whose outline was clearly visible to him. The sky beyond the uncurtained windows had been lightened by the sweeping searchlights, giving her the appearance of a silhouette, which James was quick to see.

"Don't move," he said.

"I must, I've got to get some clothes on… I'm freezing out here."

"No, please – not for a second…"

"It's alright for you … you old bed bug, I'm the one that's freezing and getting my death of cold."

He continued to look at her.

"You look like one of those paper cut-outs, and so beautiful – have I told you lately that I love you …?"

"Yes, you have my darling, but have I told you lately that I'm FREEZING?"

"Come back to me again and I will warm you, there's nothing doing outside at the moment, please Pansy love, it is my last night after all. Have pity on a poor old soldier…"

She was almost seduced by the sound of his beguiling suggestion and the abject pathos of his voice, almost – but not quite. As she reached for her clothes, she said

"Stop it, you old faker, I will not succumb this time ….. I know…"

She didn't have time to finish the sentence, for an enormous explosion interrupted her. She clung on to the bed, as the windows rattled at the force of it. James leapt up at once and soon both of them were dressing at top speed.

"Sorry love, of course, I want you to be safe, old jerry's timing is about as good as Madame Vadera's. Here we go again…"

Four hours later they managed to get back to the luxury of their own bedroom. The alert was short, as alerts went, and with the possibility of separation looming large in their minds, they hoped that the rest of the night would pass without incident for them. In some measure they both had a strange feeling of guilt worming it's way into their thoughts, for the night, or early morning as it was now, had come alive to the sounds of hectic activity. Activity that they themselves were usually involved in, and therein lay their feelings. Their lack of involvement with the said activities made each of them feel as if they were shirking their respective responsibilities to the outside world, sheltering as they were in the safe cocoon of their room.

Neither of them had spoken, they just lay together, listening to the sounds outside their small world, and watching the sky (alight now with the glow of incendiary bombs) as it cast an almost ethereal entry into the privacy of the small room. As the wind blew it brought a variety of different sounds to their ears. At first sounds of fire fighting bells and ambulances, then, as the wind changed its direction, a new, harsher set of sounds floated in. The clinking and rasping of trucks in the goods yard as they ran over the metal points; the screech as the wheels came to a halt; back and forth, back and forth; more clinking, more rasping of wheels as they came to a sliding stop, and the series of thuds that came as they bumped into each other….The sounds seemed to go on for ever, then miraculously, they were all borne away – to be replaced – intermittently with the sounds of bells and rescue again.

Laura found that her hidden feelings were conjuring up pictures that were hard to shrug off, and she felt her thoughts rising inside her breast and brain, until she could contain them no longer. As she opened her mouth to speak, she was amazed to hear – not her own voice but that of James. As they both began to speak together, James gave way to Laura, but he felt as if she were reading his mind as she said,

"Why do I feel so guilty? I feel as if I should be somewhere else… I feel like a naughty school child who has been caught playing truant.. it's a most odd feeling…"

"Yes… I know because I'm having the same sort of feeling sneaking up on me… but honestly, we shouldn't feel guilt because we are taking a little time for ourselves; time out of the madness we find ourselves in. This time that we have, is God given I'm sure… and we must take it; make the most of it; after all – tomorrow both of us will be in the thick of it again; in our own battle; in our own ways; so let's not begrudge ourselves these precious moments together."

"Yes, you're right… I'm just being silly… but I still fear for you especially, and for all of us. What sort of world are we making I wonder? I think of the war as some horrific monster – and it wants to gobble us all up, nobody spared; good – bad – saint or sinner – all of us… it's such a terrible thought … and how long will it last?"

"I pray that it won't last too long love, but before the whole world is at peace again, I think that we are going to witness a long and bloody battle," he said turning his head to look at her… "and I do fear for you, my sweet, sweet thing, and I do know how much you love me – it's that knowledge that keeps me going… but I'll admit that I'm frightened too. Oh I'm not a coward, but I do get frightened sometimes about the future, but it's there Laura; like an unending horizon; spreading out before us; a time without fear and terror."

She kissed him and said, "But now, we'll be together, wherever we are, whatever we are doing, whatever the time is... we'll always be linked – by our own thoughts and love."

She leaned over him... "Promise me that you will always think of me... that way I will never die in your heart."

"You're not going to die... don't say such things... we've lots of time in front of us before we see those pearly gates."

He kissed her and she flopped back again into the warmness of the bed before he spoke again.

"Time... what a strange and unfathomable thing it is. We can't see it... feel it...or touch it, but we all acknowledge it, it's always there. It's a bit like having a faith in an invisible God isn't it?"

"In one way I suppose... yes."

"We all look at our clocks and watches and they tell us what to do with our time, but where is it?"

"Well, we know that in a brief second it can produce a life – or destroy one. It flows over us all, like some unending river, gathering us up in it's arms, and tossing us through it, for good or evil... and there's nothing we can do about it. We use it, abuse it, waste it."

James caught Laura's vision of this invisible ogre, and said,

"And lose it... but when we have some to spare, we count ourselves lucky – and we call it precious, don't we?"

"You're right, and we make it.... get behind it..."

"Find it..."

"Give it..."

"And take it ... don't forget we always want more..."

"And always end up with less..."

"What about overtime? Does that count?" he said smiling.

"Well, I know a great deal of people who have been using an awful lot of it, trying to find out about Simon. He admitted to me once that he felt that time had stood still for him, he has no recollection of any time before now... so what happened to his time, I wonder."

"Well, I'm glad that he's in this time – with us. He's a smashing chap, we've had some really ..." Before he could finish Laura added....

"Good times?"

He nodded in agreement as he looked at her. Her eyes were dark, and strangely beautiful, the wonderful violet-blue being replaced only until daylight returned the colour to them – colour that could only be stolen by the night.

"The second I saw you… I knew that I loved you," he said.

"But was it really a second? We're back to time again, and don't forget that in the Bible it says that… 'a twinkling of an eye is a thousand years in God's sight…' so where does that leave us?" she whispered.

He gathered her up in his arms and as she held on to him, she felt the powerful force of love welling up within her; and spilling out, washing over her limbs and down through her arms, culminating in the pressure of her hands about his strong and powerful body.

"With all this talk of time, it's going too fast for us, can you spare me some of yours? Share it with me… please… time is our enemy, let's use it up in the nicest possible way…I love you so much my dearest wife."

He kissed her with a gentleness that she could no longer resist.

"And I love you, my dearest, dearest husband. All my time is yours… love me."

They came together into the fleeting void of love that felt timeless.

Simon arrived home at six o'clock in the morning. After making himself a cup of cocoa, he came back into the sitting room and collapsed on to the settee, thankful that it had been made up for him – he was about ready for a couple of hours sleep.

As he savoured the steaming brew he noticed the parcel that was sitting on his pillow.

"Aha… what have we here?" he said putting the cocoa down. He drew the lumpy package too him. As he opened it a note fell out, and he recognised Laura's writing. He read it quickly, there were only a few lines, and they were all about his old clothes; what did he want to do with them? Did he want to give them away?

Peeling back the brown paper, he saw at once that he was looking at the clothes that he had been wearing when he had first met her, on that cold winter's night in 1939.

"That's nearly two years ago," he thought to himself, "I'd almost forgotten all about them… I wonder where she dug them out from?"

He shook them out.

"Hmm… maybe I'll try them on again now – hey-ho memories, memories – and the lack of them too," he mumbled under his breath. He tried them on. They seemed as baggy as ever,

"I don't seem to have grown at all, not even outwards" he added, pulling the jacket out in front of him.

"There's enough room for Laura in here with me."

He shook his head as he pulled it first one way and then another. Finally he gazed down at his feet, the trousers were too long, covering the best part of the old shoes.

"Yes," he mused, "I think the time has come… first thing this morning – you have to go," he said, plucking at the collar of the ageing tweed coat.

As he had been speaking, he noticed the note that was propped up by the clock. He crossed to it, holding up his droopy trousers on the way. Sitting down to read James' note.

"Ha ha, I bet he didn't think that he would be half the night in the old shelter – poor old James. They will surely need their lie in."

At that moment there was a rattle at the front door,

"Good, the post, let's hope it's exciting," he said as he quietly bent to pick up the one letter that was on the mat. It was for him.

"Oh great," he said as he went back and tore the letter open. He read it quickly with interest. He nodded as he reached the last page.

"Ah, just what I've been waiting for. Right James, let's see how you get on with this".

He walked to the kitchen and returned with a pair of scissors. He then proceeded to carefully cut a strip off the bottom of the letter, putting it absent-mindedly into the pocket of the baggy jacket. Next he folded the letter in half again, and stood it on the mantelpiece, for Laura and James to read later on.

Soundlessly he moved to his drawer in the sideboard and took out the last letter that Netta had written to him, as well as an ink bottle and pen. Then, sitting down at the table, he took James' letter, turned it over and began to write:

'S.B. James, if this doesn't rattle your brains – then nothing will!"…

Then he copied, with the greatest care, thirteen words from Netta's letter, on the last one the pen spat and made a small blot.

"Oh no… don't say I've got to start all over again," he said, blowing gently on the offending blue bubble. "Saved – that's alright – good."

He smiled to himself as he propped the note up next to the letter. Having finished with the old one he put it back into its envelope and meticulously started to tear it up into tiny pieces. Lastly, he caught sight of the empty envelope still lying on the table. Flipping it over he wrote quickly in block capital letters. 'YES, THEY HAVE TO GO AS SOON AS POSSIBLE, PLEASE.' As he propped it up with the other two, he thought they looked like a row of flags awaiting some celebration.. he yawned.

"Let's get these clothes off" he grumbled, sitting down to remove the shoes first.

He yawned, then stretching for the brown paper, pulled it on to his lap. He yawned once more and closed his eyes.. it had been a long night.

The clock on the mantelpiece ticked relentlessly on, pausing only to ting at the half hour; the sound echoing around briefly; before continuing its rhythmic and melancholy pulse into the empty room. Simon had gone.

Shooting at Stars

Book 1 – Chapter 13
Alpha…and…Omega *March-April 1986*

Of course there was no magic answer to father's question, the years of fruitless enquiries had long ago proved that. So for him, life went on in the same way as it had done in the past. Angela's life on the other hand was not at all like it had been.

Although she was having to rest more, she was also making the most of being in her own home, because she knew that, in a very short time, she would be whisked off to the hospital. Of course, she understood the reason for her having to go into hospital to have the baby. After all, her age was against her; it was her first baby and she had encountered some difficulties when she had fallen. So…it was quite understandable, but in her heart she would have loved the baby to have been born at home. However, the idea of a home confinement had brought such dissent from both her doctor and midwife that she never broached the subject again after her first tentative enquiries.

"I really don't know how to sit or stand today…. I feel that uncomfortable."

"In that case you must have a proper rest… in bed. Come on I'll help you up the stairs."

Terri was insistent this time because Angela normally shied away from getting into bed during the day, preferring instead the settee, or father's chaise longue, but this time Terri could see that she was ready to lie down – properly.

Once she had settled Angela – and checked up on father, Terri decided that the garden needed some of her attention. The daffodils were making a beautiful show, but the winds had been rather strong lately and had thrown leaves, twigs and other bits and pieces around on to the paved area by the french windows. The flowers were holding their own, albeit they were almost flattened, but the bird table, Angela's pride and joy, had been blown over. So taking the opportunity (whilst Angela was in bed) she intended to get it upright again, and securely in place before its demise was spotted by the eagle eyed mother-to-be!

She was still in the garden when Peter came home. He saw her, and called out on the way to the house.

"Where's my lady, copper-knob?"

"Lying down upstairs for a change… she really did look done in this morning."

"I'll pop in and see her then; thank goodness she will only be feeling like this for another few weeks! I have got to go out to a meeting this afternoon, but I'll leave a contact number on my desk for you… I shouldn't be late anyway. She is alright though isn't she… no headache or anything?"

"No, there's nothing like that, in fact, do you realise that she hasn't had a migraine since that awful day she fell?"

"Yes I know, we were only talking about that yesterday, pretty incredible we thought… but rather a harsh cure we decided….Well I'd better get on and let you finish, because it looks to me as if it's going to pour with rain any moment now."

He made his way into the house, crossed the sitting room and looked in on his father. The old man was asleep.

"He looks so peaceful," he thought as he walked up the stairs to the bedroom. Opening the door quietly, he stepped into the room.

"Hello love, I'm not asleep." Angela's voice greeted him at once.

"So I see. Have you had a doze though?"

"No. Not at all yet. This baby of ours seems to be playing football, tennis or I suspect – both."

Peter moved to the bed and sat on it. He put his hand on the now huge mound that used to be his wife's slender body.

"I really do feel extra ugly and cumbersome today, I don't know why."

"You're always beautiful to me… never ugly m'love."

"You do love me, don't you?"

"What a question."

"Am I being silly?"

"No – just very pregnant and I suspect, very close to making me a father… you're not frightened are you darling?"

"Frightened?…No. I've never thought of the pain of the actual birth, or anything like that, I've only ever thought of the baby... our baby… and it's well being."

At that moment Peter's hand felt a terrific movement under it. He shook his head in wonder.

"It's just incredible thinking of the life that's hidden from us. It's so near yet so far; I'm so proud of you my angel."

"I'm trying so hard to be patient… and I know that it won't be too long now… but it does get harder each day, and I'm getting so impatient…I want to meet little… Thumper, and see the feet that keep pounding me, God's brought me along this far and I know that He won't desert me at this late stage… It's just that these last weeks seem to be dragging by so slowly."

Peter lay down on the bed next to her, and leaned up on one elbow. They looked at each other with a depth of meaning that needed no words. Looking at her, he saw her hair, damp and curling at the temples and her skin that held a sweet blush on her cheeks. He smiled at her, and she returned his smile with a bright-eyed one of her own. She was, to him, a picture of radiant happiness.

Looking deeply into her eyes, he bent his head and kissed her on her soft welcoming mouth. Oh how he loved her. He longed to hold her close and protect her as an overpowering feeling of love enveloped him.

Angela herself felt a strong desire to be held and loved by her husband, a strong and strange feeling that turned itself into a sensation that started at her feet, and then rushed up finally engulfing her whole body with its heady sweetness.

"Oh my darling, darling, thank you for loving me … even now," she added indicating her large lump.

"More than ever now if that were possible. What could be a more wonderful or beautiful sight to me, than you carrying our much longed for child, under your heart?"

He kissed her again and caressed her cheek with his hand. As they lay together she felt the dress that was unsuccessfully trying to hide her swollen abdomen, pull taut across her, with a strange tightening. The contraction, for that is what it was, came and went like a soft wave, dying away as quickly as it had come, it's gentleness belying the strength that it was capable of, and would be capable of, in the not too distant future. It wasn't an unpleasant feeling… just unfamiliar…

The 'phone rang.

"I'm sure that will be for me," he said and a second later Terri's voice confirmed his words.

"Mr. Peter… it's for youooooo…" she called.

"Alright Terri I'm coming," he answered, then turning to Angela again he said, "I've got to go my lovely. Hopefully I'll be home in an hour and a half. You'll be alright and Terri has a number that she can contact me on … at any time…"

"Off you go… you can't keep people waiting, although I love you here with me, I do understand that you have to be somewhere else too. When you get back… we can start to go through the 'Names for Baby' book…again. I don't think that any child would relish going through life with the name Thumper! Off you go… it's the 'phone first…go."

He took her face into his hands – kissed her tenderly, and left the room.

Terri had never read from the book of the Water Babies, since the time that Pops had become so upset. These days she had taken to reading to him from the daily paper. The world was in turmoil as usual, so she always chose the passages to read with care. It was as she was quietly reading to the old man that the sound of the 'phone burst into their quite time. She jumped up at once and ran to quell the shrill noise. When she returned to the room again, she stood at the side of the old man's easy chair, and looked out of the windows. The strong wind had dropped now she noticed, and the once flattened daffodils had managed to drag themselves upright once more and were busily nodding their windswept faces at her.

Turning to the occupant of the chair, whose gaze was also on the window, she started to speak.

"That was the library for Mr. Peter. The book that he has been waiting for - is finally in and I'm thinking that perhaps we could go and collect it for him … you'd like that my old love, wouldn't you?"

She took his hands in hers and leaned forward, looking into his face as she was speaking. The steely eyes met hers and the mouth immediately started it's old twitching again, the bubbles welling up at the corners,

"What …is…the…answer…please?" he said, for the umpteenth time that morning.

As she stood looking at him, she thought back to the time that she had first met him. She could still remember clearly how he had nearly driven her mad, asking the same old thing over…and over again. Now, however, knowing him as she did, she was able to view him with different eyes, she understood, and so was able to tolerate the repetitive words with compassion and sympathy. She bent forward and wiped his mouth, not showing the least surprise at the extra word – please – because it was tagged on with some regularity these days. The sentence, however, never progressed any further, unfortunately, and the question, even if he remembered it, was never spoken.

Although the room was warm she could feel that his hands were quite cold. Thin hands that showed numerous, dark blue veins meandering lazily beneath the paper thin skin. She adjusted the rug so that they lay more comfortably beneath the warm wool. The pillow at the side of his head had become flat, so she deftly plumped it, angling it as she did so, with one hand, whilst tenderly supporting the ageing head with the other. Then, glancing at her watch, she quickly left the room and bounded up the stairs to Peter's study. Once there she crossed to the desk and, finding the telephone number that she needed, started to dial. The bell on the other end rang for some time.

"Oh…I wasn't expecting you to answer in person… I was all ready to leave a message for you… no…no… she's quite alright…no don't worry so… don't go on… it's not about our lady-in-waiting, it's about your book…no…the one you have been waiting for…yes at last it's in. I know that it's important, so would you like me to collect it for you? No. It's dropped now, no it wouldn't take me long … yes, we would be back in about half an hour …. No, she will stay put till I get back. Okay… see you later, sorry if I've disturbed you. 'Byee."

Peter replaced the receiver and looked quizzically at it, almost expecting it to ring again. He continued to sit in the high-backed chair for moment – gazing into space, his mind filled with both relief and slight disappointment. At last he stood and made his way out of the room, fully intending to go back to the meeting that he had absented himself from. He crossed the cold hallway and put his hand on to the door handle, but before he could turn it, he stopped – changed direction – and crossed back into the ante-room again – before he had realised it. Picking up the receiver, he quickly dialled. After only a few seconds, Terri's voice answered.

"Terri – I've changed my mind. I will go and collect the book myself on the way home. I don't want to drag both you and father out … plus the fact that I will feel a whole lot happier if you stayed there with Angela… yes, she is getting a bit down….I would hate anything to…no alright. Thanks for the idea…well yes, but it will only be a little later than I thought… yes, just tell her for me, will you? … Thanks. See you later."

He hung the receiver up and purposefully crossed the hall entering the room opposite, with apologies once again coming from his lips.

The meeting seemed to drag on. He knew that he was inattentive, with his mind firmly… somewhere else… and it was not like him at all, in fact it was completely out of character. It didn't help his frame of mind either, that half of the people that should have been present – had failed to arrive, making the meeting a rather ineffectual and time wasting one, and one that, in the end, had achieved hardly anything. He sat there feeling restless and fidgety, consequently he was much relieved when the proceedings were drawn to a premature close.

In a very short time, he found himself in the car park of the library, and once there he walked quickly up the steps, and into the red brick Victorian building.

The warmness that enveloped him like some gigantic blanket when he entered the building felt stifling to him. The coat collar that he had turned up to protect his ears from the wind, was just as quickly turned down again – and the coat unbuttoned – as he walked into the spacious hall.

Most unusually, Miss Veronica Applebury was not in her accustomed seat. The chief librarian was nowhere to be seen. In actual fact, there was nobody around. He wandered in and out of the aisles, making his way towards the reading room, hoping that he would see - or hear – some sign of life. Suddenly a girl's head popped out from the section marked 'Reptiles'. Both Peter and the girl were startled at the sight of the other, and she gave out an involuntary gasp.

"Oh, sorry I startled you," he said, "I received a telephone call earlier… about a book that I have been waiting for. Can I give you my name and the details… only I'm in a bit of a rush?"

The girl looked sheepishly at him, and with considerable embarrassment said,

"I'd much rather you didn't – if you don't mind: I'm new you see, and I really don't know much about anything at the moment. I don't think that I can help you at all. Miss Applebury will be back directly… would you mind waiting for her? I know that she will not be long... She knows that I'm on my own, and she will only be a second or two…."

He looked at his watch, he felt somewhat thwarted, time was racing past he knew, but although he was on tenterhooks about Angela, he just felt that he should wait for the book. In one way it was an irrational feeling – after all, he had waited all this time for it, another day wouldn't make the slightest difference to him. He could leave at once, and call again tomorrow… Then why didn't he? No, he just knew that he had to wait…

"Well…yes, I will wait, but I am in a hurry… will you give me a call as soon as she gets back, please?"

“Yes, of course I will, I know you won’t be kept waiting long,” she apologised.

“I’ll just go into the reading room…please don’t forget me will you?” he added smiling, trying to put the girl at ease, for he could see that she was very embarrassed and quite agitated. Regaining her composure, and swallowing hard she replied,

“I will call you the instant that she returns.”

He turned away from her and entered the reading room. He made no attempt to put the light on, for he had no intention of reading. Walking over to the desk he stood behind it, and looked out of the window. It was getting dark outside now, and the street lamps were on, most of them were still red; but some of them had already turned the customary yellow.

“I seem to have seen all this before,” he mused as he turned the captain’s chair around to face the window. He sat down, and gazed out at the lights of the town and the car’s lights as they sped down the hill. He found the inner voice in his head praying.

“Lord…please keep my Angela safe in Your sight whilst I’m here…Thank you for helping us to cope with my dear father… For giving us understanding and patience … for sending Terri to us, to help take the burden from my dear Angela. I’m ashamed to say that I have felt … and do feel despair… sometimes…but in my heart I know that You are in control… and You will see us through….”

There was no sound in the silence of the room, except Peter’s regular breathing, and no light, except that which filtered up for the distant town. Miss Veronica Applebury – chief librarian – entered the building precisely three minutes after Peter had arrived.

“Oh I’m so glad you’re back Miss Applebury, there’s a gentleman waiting in the reference reading room. He has come about a book that he was to collect. He said he had received a telephone call about it. I didn’t want to get involved myself because I knew nothing about it – sorry.”

“That’s alright April, that will be Reverend Aston, give him a call for me, will you, there’s a good girl… I’ll have it ready when he gets here. He’s a bit on the deaf side, so give him a good shout.”

April Longman needed no further instructions. She was still feeling her way around the old Victorian building, but by dodging in and out of the bookshelves she soon found herself standing outside the large oak door of the reading room. The door stood ajar, and she could see that it was dark inside. She tentatively pushed it further open, and made as if to enter, then she hastily came out again. Stepping back away from the doorway, she glanced up at the sign above it. Reference Library Reading Room, it said.

"Well, I thought that I hadn't made a mistake," she mumbled to herself as she stepped into the room again, this time putting her hand on the light switch, and flipping it on. The old fashioned chandelier that hung low in the centre of the room flickered into life, its glass facets flooding the dark room with light. Looking towards the desk, she could only see the back of the head of the occupant seated in the chair, the form was silent and unmoving. Cautiously she walked towards the desk. Clearing her throat she said,

"Reverend Aston? … There was no response from the still figure. Trying again, but louder this time, she called out,

"Reverend Aston?… Your book is ready for you."

She was nearly level with his chair by now, when suddenly he spun round in it so fast that he frightened poor April, and as his eyes flew open she gave a gasp, and rapidly started to back away from the suddenly animated figure. Peter rose and came towards her, smiling as he caught sight of the petrified look on her young face.

"You're a wonderful girl," he said as he ran from the room. He ran past all the rows of books and then he ran past Miss Applebury.

"Your book Reverend…" she called out to the fleeing figure, and then louder… "Don't forget your book…."

Open mouthed she watched the receding figure on its soundless flight from the building and then looked down at the large volume held in her two hands. She could hear his voice saying thank you, thank you to the air, but he had in fact made no attempt whatsoever to take the heavy book from her.

As he ran out of the building, he could still be heard calling out to the air, "Thank you….thank you," over and over again; his arms outstretched before him, as if he were breasting some invisible tape…at the end of a long race.

He ran on blindly, not even casting so much as a glance in the direction of the car park. He ran - and ran - and ran. The clouds of his breath going before him in the cold air, like a panting steam engine. He only paused briefly when he reached the bottom of the hill that led to his oasis. He stood there looking in the direction of the house, trying to unscramble the thoughts that were going around in his brain. The one long last breath of air he sucked into his panting body, helped him to choke back the tears that were making a large lump in his throat, and gave him enough strength to start the run.

He reached the top, and rushed through the gate. In his blind haste he fell as he was climbing the few steps that led to the front door, and slipped heavily on to his knee. Openly, and unashamedly he found that he was crying... Not for the pain of the fall, for that was minimal, but because the fall had acted like a catalyst allowing emotions - that had been welling up inside him – to burst forth and be free. Sobbing in this way he fumbled, through blind eyes of tears, with his key, and at last entered the house.

He flew through the room, oblivious of the incredulous Angela and Terri, his mind and body focused on only one intent... to find his father.

When he reached the old man's side, he put his hands on the frail shoulders, and looked at his sad face. At once his father's eyes sought out those of his son; his lips started to twitch, as they had done – many, many times before, their slow movements, still making the simple job of speech very, very difficult – and so painful to watch.

"What...is...the...answer...Please?" he said, with the tears in his eyes, clearly visible for his son to see.

"I know the answer father...it's... it's.... Madame Butterfly, can you hear me? Do you understand...?"

He shook his father's shoulders gently, tears spilling from his own eyelids, turning his father into a hazy blur....

"Father...father... it's Madame Butterfly..." he said again, with an earnestness that was coupled with unbounding relief.

His father didn't take his eyes off his son's face, then after sitting quite still for a few seconds, his head was raised, as if by some unseen hand, at the same time his shoulders relaxed and his face was filled with obvious joy. Sitting there, erect and unsupported, he looked at Peter – and without any hesitation in his speech, and with a serene comprehension of the words that he was able to speak, he said in a firm voice,

"I'll tell Pansy..."

He closed his eyes and as he did, tears fell from them – for the last time. He slumped forward into his son's waiting arms – and died. Now he was free at last from his distorted, twisted and imprisoning body, Peter thought, as he sat sobbing – rocking the body of the old man.

Terri knew at once that Pops had...gone, but Angela didn't seem to comprehend – or even understand what had happened at first – or her mind didn't want to. Then as the cold realisation dawned on her, she felt a shiver run down her spine, and she started to shake. She looked across at her husband, cradling his father, and said in an almost inaudible voice…

"Why did he do it…? Why did he kill his father…?"

Terri couldn't believe what she had heard Angela say and was about to answer her, when the usually composed and pretty face contorted with the onset of labour pains. The baby was coming...early.

The evening of the death of James Aston (Col. Ret'd) would never be forgotten. It was both a time of acute sadness and a time of tantalising anticipation – for all of them in the household. Peter, for all his strong and caring personality (when dealing with other people's bereavements and problems) was completely overcome by the set of circumstances that he found himself face to face with. On the one hand he couldn't assimilate the swiftness of his father's death; and on the other, he found the onset of his coming fatherhood almost unbelievable. He didn't know whether to laugh – or cry. He felt frightened – not for himself, of course, but for his dear wife. The baby was making its presence felt with a vengeance there was no doubt about that, but it was too soon – that much he was aware of.

Terri was wonderful, both practical and capable. It was she who took up the initiative, by telephoning and making the arrangements that had to be made – not Peter, and it was she that led him away from his father, comforting him yet at the same time confronting him with the urgent reality of the impending birth. The escaping moans from Angela's lips and the pained expression that swept her face from time to time – brought him back to the substance of the moment, with a heartfelt jolt.

Because of the empathy between them, he couldn't bear to see her discomfort – even in these early stages. Angela, however, was feeling no such empathy. She was unconcerned about her husband's feelings, and was in a time sphere – all of her own.

She didn't appear to need him – or the comfort that he so willingly wanted to give, and to that end, he felt that his feelings were being trampled under her feet. He felt useless. He felt rejected and desolate. He was feeling the same emotions that he had always held towards her – but she? She appeared to neither need him nor indeed even be aware of his presence, as he sat there holding her hand.

The arrangements had been finally decided upon, and Terri would be staying with her beloved Pops, whilst Peter went in the ambulance with Angela. Staying with Pops held no problem for her at all. She had loved him in life, such as his life was, and now in death? Well, love was not something that you could turn off, like a tap…even if she wanted to – which she didn't. In any case, this was a very small kindness that she was about to do for them. It didn't begin to repay the debt of gratitude that she owed them both. They had simply changed her life. From the shabby no-hoper of the early times with them, she had been brought, by their kindness, care, tolerance and above all else their love, to a new understanding of her own true worth.

It was a little enough thing that she was giving in return this evening, she loved them both dearly and hated to see them so sad – at a moment in their lives when they should be rejoicing….. Angela's sudden rush into labour at the exact moment that the old man died was quite cataclysmic, and everyone in the room seemed to be in their own state of personal shock to some degree.

At last, after what seemed an eternity, the ambulance arrived. Angela's waters had broken just as she was placed on to the stretcher, just to add a little more confusion to the situation, but at last she was safely aboard, and ready to go.

Peter went to his father's side as Terri went to the ambulance, carrying the case that had been ready, and waiting, for this moment to come.

"Well, Mrs. Angela – this is it. I'm going to be staying here, but I'll come and see you just as soon as I can. I want to hold that bundle almost as much as you."

"Oh Terri, I feel terrible…not because of the baby…but because of Peter…why did he hurt his father so? Why did he…kill his father?" she whispered.

"No – you don't really think that do you? How could he? He loved his father – truly loved him… and he wouldn't have done anything to have hurt him, please believe me…put that thought right out of your mind…promise me?"

"But he died…after he spoke to him…he died."

"Yes, I know, but didn't you see him? He came alive too, somehow Mr. Peter found his answer for him…I didn't quite catch them myself, but when Pops heard the words, his whole face lit up…he came alive… and he understood, I'm sure of that…"

"But Terri…he died…he died." She bit hard into her lip as yet another pain swept through her body, she couldn't control it, any more than the tears that were cascading down her cheeks.

"Come along Miss, we had better be off now, is the father-to-be coming with us?" The ambulance man's voice had an urgency about it as he spoke to them.

"No." Angela immediately responded.

"Yes, of course he is," Terri replied, nodding at the man's head as he peeped in on them.

"You'll be OK Mrs. A, easy as falling off a log my mum used to say. You once told me that you are never alone, because you have a Friend that never leaves you…well I know that He is with you now, and that He'll look after you…for all of us; but give Mr. Peter a chance will you? And try to remember what I said about Pops."

She bent forward as she finished speaking and placed a kiss on Angela's damp forehead.

"God Bless," she said before quickly running back into the house.

The couple of moments that Peter spent with his father were poignant to the point of pain, as he cradled the inert body within his arms.

"Forgive me my dear father, forgive me if I hurt you…I didn't mean to – I loved you always, even all those years that I was growing up and we were apart…I understood – and I loved you. I don't know, or understand myself quite why those words came to me – two words that shattered out lives…but I do know that God has forgiven me, if in fact I did hasten your death…I hope that you will too, my dear, dear father. I know that your spirit is with God now, and that you are gone from this place…but I will miss you so much…we all will…"

Terri came up quietly and touched him on the shoulders.

"Leave him with me…Mr. Peter – don't stay here any longer," she whispered, "Go to Angela, she needs you more now – even if she doesn't know it, and she's waiting to go."

He stood up and clasped Terri to him, trying hard not to cry as he said,

"Thanks copper-knob, what would we do without you?"

"Go – go. Don't you understand? Your baby is going to be born… go NOW."

He made his way quickly to the door, glancing back over his shoulder just once, at the still figure of his father; then entered the waiting ambulance. The double doors closed, and they were soon speeding away.

The fragmentation of time that had occurred during those brief traumatic moments had now rejoined, allowing a tranquillity to descent on that quiet sitting-room. A peace that could only exist with the finality of... death.

Within the confines of the fast moving ambulance though, there was no such peace. Only an air of joyous anticipation for the new being that had begun its perilous and somewhat early journey into the blinding light of life. There were some things in common that the room had with the electric atmosphere of the speeding vehicle however; there was no speaking in either place; but both had the sounds of crying. Crying that filtered its way upward to be dispersed into the noisesome and uncaring world, the same world of which the new being would be a small, but important part.

At last he was able to be at the bedside. They had planned, right through the long and difficult pregnancy that he would be present at the birth, and now that moment was drawing near he wanted to help and encourage her as much as he could. The responsibility he felt for her was overwhelming; and he was praying for a safe and uncomplicated delivery of their long-awaited child, as he took her hand. Her face was flushed and she closed her eyes as yet another birth-pang passed through her. When it was over, and she was able to speak to him, her words cut into him like a knife.

"Please go," she said.

"But love, I want to be here with you…."

"Please go…" she said again, as another pain started, "please go…oh…oh…oh…"

The last sounds were panted out, rather than spoken. He felt deflated and dismayed. A nurse came up to the bedside and smiling at him said,

"I'm just going to take your wife's blood pressure but there's no need for you to go Reverend."

"Yes there is Peter…I want you to go…" Angela's voice sounded agitated and breathy.

The nurse looked at him and said quietly,

"Perhaps it would be best if you did go – just for a little while – you will be able to come in again later on. You go and get a coffee, there's a machine in the waiting room up the corridor; I'll give you a call – don't worry – this often happens. Best laid schemes and all that," she added smiling.

Peter kissed Angela's cheek, and then walked dejectedly out of the room. Rejection – stupidly he was feeling this emotion twice. His poor head was in a turmoil. Rejection by Angela at one of the most precious times in their lives was bad enough – but his father too? How could somebody reject you when they are dead? He questioned his own feelings. Just by the act of dying, he decided – by quitting this life and leaving such an empty space in your heart – that's how, his brain irrationally tried to convince him.

"How stupid," he thought, "Here I am, a grown man of forty-five – about to become a father for the first time, please God, and I'm behaving like a child with all these unreasonable thoughts, it's so unreal."

But then the whole situation felt unreal. His feelings had been split down the middle by the two people in his life that he loved most – and now both of these people had left him alone, Angela by choice, and his father…? Did he unwittingly hasten his father's last act? The act of dying? His misery was not relieved by the thought of Angela's words coming into his head,

"Why did you kill your father…?"

"Kill my father? Surely not – my God – oh my dear Lord…surely not?"

He buried his head in his hands as he thought these dreadful thoughts.

"But why did the words that I spoke to father come into my mind…? What did they mean…? What does it all mean…? I thought I had the answer to all our prayers, I just knew that I had the answer to his question – for some inexplicable reason, I just knew; and, when I told him, I just knew that he understood…"

His thoughts raced back to the moment when he had uttered the two fateful words in answer to his father's pleading question, and the elation and delight that his father obviously felt, when he heard them.

Madame Butterfly – it sounded ridiculous when he had said them, but there was no doubt in his mind that his father knew what they meant – and that he had complete understanding of their significance. Then for the first time since that moment he recalled his father's reply, with no hint of stuttering hesitation, no drooling from his mouth; just the overwhelming look of happiness.

"I'll tell Pansy," he had said.

"Pansy? Who was Pansy?"

It meant nothing too him – nothing at all, what did it all mean?

Now Angela's decision to shut him out seemed to be the last straw to break his spirit. He let out an audible sigh.

"Is it your first one mate?"

Peter raised his head in the direction of the voice, his face filled with sorrow and his eyes red with both shed and unshed tears he looked a broken man.

"Yes…" was all that he could manage as a reply.

The man noticing the collar around Peter's throat, and his obvious distress, thought that something terrible had happened, or was about to happen – and that he was here on 'official business'. He chose his next words with care – not wishing to make matters worse.

"I'm sorry vicar, is there anything that I can do to help? Is it bad news? Can I call somebody for you?"

The man's voice seemed to break into Peter's blackness – and brought him back from the abyss of the incomprehensible – to reality. He sat up, straightened his shoulders, and after wiping his eyes on a much crumpled handkerchief, stood up, and walked towards the man.

"No, I don't need any help…but thanks for your offer. It's just that I've had some bad news…and it's shaken me up rather…and now to add to my troubles – my wife seems to want to do without me too…I just can't win today….."

"Oh my wife never wants me around, which is just as well – and this is our third."

"But we planned to be together – that's what hurts me."

"Well I reckon you have had a narrow escape. It's not my idea of a fun experience – no way!"

"The nurse did try to cheer me up by telling me that some women do react in this way…but you see my wife did have a terrible shock before she came in…and I think she blames me for everything…"

"Well vicar, if you don't mind me saying…I guess she had every right – yes?"

As he was looking at Peter, a grin spread over his face. Peter took his meaning at once, and a beaming smile spread over his face too. He walked forward, proffering his hand.

"Well I didn't exactly mean that…but yes I guess you're right. My name's Peter Aston, by the way, and as it seems we're in the same jittery state we had better become acquainted."

"Philip Thompson, and I'm very pleased to meet you Reverend Aston."

"Please do call me Peter, and by the way – that help you offered me I think I can do with it now, so picking your brains, how long do you think it's likely to be?"

"Well, I can only speak from my own experience of course…not good news, when you're talking about the first. Mine took an age, or so it seemed at the time. So, however long it is for you – you can rest assured that it will feel twice as long…sorry about that, not much help am I?"

"I think that I would rather know the truth, but I must admit it doesn't give me too much comfort. I just wish that I could be with her. I'm supposed to be rubbing her back….I've been practising all these months.. and now I'm no use to her. I'm utterly redundant."

"That feeling won't last mate, not when the little squeaker arrives home."

"Mr. Thompson," the nurse's face was beaming, as she called through the door, "you can come through now, the baby has arrived."

"Great – great, what is it?" he said, rushing to the door.

"Well in a second or two your wife can tell you – how's that?"

Philip Thompson followed her out of the door pausing only long enough to call out to Peter.

"Best of luck Reverend, I hope all goes well with your missus."

Then he was gone.

Things were speeding up considerably in the delivery room, and Angela was in the final stages of her labour. It had not been easy. Much as she had wanted to experience the birth without the use of painkillers, the nursing staff, with her permission, had intervened. The drug had helped her to relax more, and consequently things had become somewhat easier.

Quite suddenly Peter came into her thoughts. She wanted him. She needed him.

"Can my husband come in?" she asked.

"Why of course my dear. He has been patiently waiting so long for this moment, I'll go and get him for you."

She made a quick exit; collected Peter from the waiting room, took him to be gowned up and shepherded him into the labour ward, in next to no time.

He went to Angela's side at once and took her hand, lowering his face mask at the same time. He kissed her dry lips.

"Darling, darling, I so wanted to be with you, is it very bad…?"

Before she was able to answer him, a great contraction surged through her body and she gripped his hand with a great strength. What could he do? He still felt pretty useless.

The little nurse that he had spoken to when they had first arrived at the hospital came to his side.

"Bathe your wife's face for her, it will cool her down," she said indicating a small bowl on the side, "then you can put some salve on her lips that always helps because they get very dry. Don't look so worried, everything's going alright," she added patting him on the shoulder.

Another contraction, even more powerful that the last took hold. Angela let out a loud moan.

"It's alright love, everything's alright," he said echoing the nurse's words.

Coming from him they sounded futile, he thought as he looked at her face – she looked so distressed. He never thought it would be like this – he was totally unprepared for the sight of her pain. More contractions followed, getting stronger – and closer together. Small amounts of gas and air, that Angela was sucking in at the very last moment, seemed to take the edge off the pain for her, but it left him a wreck. He could feel the sweat running down his back, his face was awash, and had been for some time, and he felt quite drained. Angela looked at him, smiled, then said,

"It's me having this baby you know – not you. Don't look so wo….woo….."

She never finished the word.

"Quickly Reverend, the baby is coming…"

Choking with emotion, he watched as the most intimate and wonderful sight unfolded before him. His mouth, behind the mask, fell open at the sight of the newly born infant, as it slipped soundlessly into the midwife's capable hands.

"It's a boy…it's a boy darling. It's a beautiful – perfect little boy."

He moved back to be at her side, and kissed her parched lips.

"Oh you clever girl," he said as he looked into her face.

He thought that it would show some sort of elation – but it didn't. Instead she gave out another moan and gripped his hand again. He didn't understand, had something gone terribly wrong? Then he realised that he could still hear the monitor at his side. Ping…ping…ping..it went.

"Sister, there's another limb – there's another baby!"

The little nurse sounded ecstatic. Peter was in a mild state of shock – twins…? They had no idea that it could be twins.

"Come on then, mother: just a little more effort, and you'll have two for the price of one…not much longer now, you've done all the really hard work…just a little more effort…that's a good girl…now push…gently now…come on father quickly now."

The next baby came into the world feet first, and they all saw that it was a little girl before her head emerged. Peter was speechless.

"It's a little girl mother, and she's a beauty, a real little poppet" the midwife said, cooing over the new arrival.

Peter walked back to Angela's side again. She was beaming, and in her arms she was cradling her son.

"Our son darling," she said as she looked first at Peter and then the baby.

"And your daughter," the little nurse said, handing the pink bundle to her, "aren't they beautiful?" she went on, "the little lad weighed in at five pounds one ounce, and the sweet little girl weighs four pounds twelve ounces, and what a surprise packet she turned out to be…."

Both Peter and Angela looked at the babies with awe.

"Oh Lord," Peter said aloud, without closing his eyes, "thank You for all your blessings, for the babies…and the staff…oh Lord I'm speechless…truly my cup runneth over…."

The midwife Sister spoke.

"I'm afraid I will have to ask you to leave now Reverend, your wife needs rest, as well as a little tidying up. You look like you could do with a little break yourself too. Why don't you go home; get some sleep, and come back later on?"

Peter agreed and after kissing all three of them, left the hospital.

Philip Thompson was on his way out of the hospital when the overjoyed Peter nearly knocked him over. Unlike Peter (who had been awake all night) he had managed to go back home and have a night's sleep before coming back this morning to see his wife and new daughter. Now he was off to work – to hand round the cigars – he had said to Peter with a new father's pride shining on his face. Then, rather than the other enthusiastic father ringing for a taxi, he had offered him a lift home, after all it would only take a few minutes of his time, and the poor Reverend did look slightly done in, he thought.

He wasn't a church going man himself, and in fact this was the closest that he had been to a vicar since his marriage some ten years earlier. He was pleasantly surprised to find that Peter Aston seemed such a human chap who, like himself (the first time around), had been bowled over by the birth of his children.

"Here we are then Reverend, get a couple of hours shut eye I should, your wife won't want to see you for a couple of hours herself, so make the most of the quiet life while you have the chance....One new baby is bad enough when it comes to feeding time – but two! Good luck to all of you."

It was nearly six a.m. when Peter stepped into the house. It was silent, but not for long. Terri's footsteps could be heard running along the landing, then she bound into view, her red hair billowing out around her face.

"What's the news? What's the news? What is it? A boy or a girl? I can't wait any longer Mr. Peter. Tell me please?"

She stopped in front of him – and breathlessly stared into his face.

"Yes," he said.

"Yes? What sort of an answer is that? Yes – what do you mean? Is Mrs. A alright? Is that what you mean? What about the baby?"

"Yes, I mean Angela is alright, and yes; brace yourself, we have a boy..."

"Oh lovely, a little boy...what did he weigh? And does he look like you?"

"....and a girl." He finished his sentence and looked at the face of the incredulous girl before him.

"And a girl? You mean twins?" Her eyes opened wide and her mouth dropped open, "I don't believe it – two of them? A boy and a girl?"

"Yes, I know how you must be feeling – and I saw both of them born...yet I can hardly believe it myself. Isn't God good? He's given us double of what we longed for – two children instead of one... it's almost unbelievable..."

Terri threw her arms around him and they laughed for sheer joy.

"Oh yes, it's wonderful; wonderful; wonderful. I just can't wait to see them. What did they weigh? Can you remember?"

"I do remember...the boy is five pounds something and the girl is four pound twelve...Oh Terri they are so beautiful..."

He sat down on the settee, exhausted, and realising for the first time that he had been awake for twenty-four hours. His eyes strayed to the french windows, where the early morning light was flooding in on his father's chair, as it stood outlined in the brightness of the new day.

Terri had gone into the kitchen to make him some breakfast, telling him that he really did look 'done in'.

He stood up and walked to the window, when he came to the chair he rested his hands on the back of it, turning it towards the light.

"This is one of the happiest – and one of the saddest days of my life," he said, gazing out into the bright windswept garden, "but you live on father, you live on because…because of mother and you, Angela and I are blessed with two new lives…your grandchildren…parting brings such sorrow father…but now..for us - a new dawn is breaking…"

Book 2 – Chapter 13
Sudden Departure *September 1940*

Laura and James crept downstairs hoping not to awaken Simon. As they entered the dark sitting room, they crossed it carefully paying little attention to the bed on the settee. Once in the cold but light kitchen they closed the door quietly behind them.

"I'm so sad that you have to go darling," she said as she picked up the kettle. James came and put his arms about her slender waist as she was filling it, resting his head on her shoulder.

"I know…it's beastly leaving you ," he turned her around to face him "but keep your chin up…it won't last for ever…"

"I know, it's just that…" Her words trailed off as he kissed her lips squarely to prevent her from speaking.

She finished lighting the gas under the kettle and as she laid the matches down he took both of her hands, and holding her at arms length – looked at her. Her beautiful eyes looked back at him with such tenderness and he knew well what a terrible wrench it was going to be for him when he had to go. How he hated the thought of leaving this lovely being. Inwardly he feared for her safety, because the bombing of poor old southern England seemed to be unending and getting progressively worse. How he wished he could persuade her to go to the country with his parents… but of course he knew that she wouldn't. He just had to be patient and wait until her, "Later love.." turned into, "I'll go now." He wouldn't hold his breath for that moment he decided.

They continued to look at one another for a few more moments, unspeaking and fearful – one for the other, each of them thinking that this <u>might</u> be the last time they would see each other….. Laura pushed these thoughts out of her mind as she looked at him and said,

"You look so handsome love – just as you did when I first met you – but remember, you are a married man now – I've caught you in my web."

He pulled her to him again and wrapped his arms about her.

"I'm caught alright and I can't, and don't want to ever, get free from your lovely clutches."

He started to sing quietly into her ear:

"Me and my girl, made for each other..."

They started to dance noiselessly in a small circle, enjoying the all too brief moment of sanity in an insane world.

"Lovely as this is darling...it won't get you any breakfast, will it?" she said, turning the kettle out that was steaming up the kitchen as fast as it could. "Look" she went on "we didn't even see how steamy it was getting in here..."

"That's because I'm always steamed up when I'm around you Pansy dear...and don't bother about anything for me...I wouldn't have time to sit and eat it anyway...I guess I'd better think about going..."

"Oh surely you can stay a little longer?"

"No, I don't think so."

"Of course, you're right," she nodded "you must get going...come on then...we must be careful not to wake our sleeping beauty – he's got another hour or so yet to dream...."

She opened the sitting room door quietly. The blackout curtains were still drawn.

"I'll leave this door ajar so that we can see a little," she said in a whisper.

While crossing the room they both instinctively looked in the direction of the settee. They stopped in their tracks and peered hard.

"Simon isn't there," James said at last, " so there's no need for us to do all this creeping about."

He strode to the window and threw back the curtains. Sure enough, there was no sign of Simon – anywhere. Laura looked perplexed.

"His bed hasn't been slept in," she said in a surprised voice.

"His clothes are here on the chair though – how odd."

"Wait a moment, there are some notes on the mantle," she said crossing to them. "Oh, this one's for you," she handed it to him, "One for me...and this one. Oh, this one's from Netta so I guess it was meant for both of us to look at."

She returned Netta's letter to its place on the mantel and quickly read her own note.

"Well mine doesn't say much...it's only telling me that he does want to get rid of his old clothes, you know the ones I mean, the ones we raked out of the bottom of Auntie's wardrobe when we were sorting out the clothes – the things that he first came in, you remember them, love, don't you? I left them for him to have a look at last night...well he obviously did look at them, but he just says that he wants to get rid of them...he doesn't say anything else. What does your note say? Any clue as to where he is?"

"Well not really – look for yourself," he said holding it out to her, "See? He just waffles on about the conundrum that he has given me ...and how hard it is...but that's it more or less – nothing else is there?"

Laura turned the note over,

"How very peculiar"

She looked down at her own note again and then at the brown paper that was lying on top of the eiderdown. She bent to pick it up,

"But the clothes are gone – just like him. Where has he put them for goodness sake? And where on earth is he?"

"Do you think that he could be down the shelter?"

"What a brainwave James...yes of course that must be it – that's where he is alright...what a joker...I'll give him what for later."

"Do you want me to go down there to make sure?"

"No I'm alright now, I was a bit shocked when I didn't see him there but I'll be fine now. I think that – perhaps he just wanted us to have the whole house to ourselves last night – you know he does get some very funny bees in his bonnet.... And it was your last night wasn't it?" she added, blushing slightly.

"Well if that was his reasoning....he's growing up fast."

"Look, love, all this is delaying you so, and much though I regret it, you must be off...I don't want anyone to think that you've gone missing too."

At eight fifteen Laura decided to wake Simon. Making her way down the path she pulled the door away from the opening of the air raid shelter,

"Rise and shine Simon...sorry to wake you but it's a quarter past eight..."

The slightly musty smell wafted over her as she stood there looking into the gloomy interior. Simon was nowhere to be seen. She came back into the kitchen and looked first at the teapot and cups that were on the kitchen table, and then at the plate of tomatoes on toast that were under the grill keeping hot. Disbelievingly she shook her head.

"Where on earth..?" her words trailed off as, for the first time she realised that she had not even checked out Aunt Mary's old room.

"Of course – maybe he went upstairs to sleep after all…I know it's unheard of but – maybe…"

She ran up the stairs to check the little room. It was cold when she opened the door, cold and empty.

Dejectedly, she returned to the kitchen and sat down at the table. Where is he? Her mind was in a quandary. Where has he gone? Why had he gone out in such peculiar circumstances? And what on earth was he doing wearing those awfully shabby clothes? Yes, she had double checked, the only clothes that were missing were the ones that she had parcelled up for him to look at. What was he playing at?

"Just wait till I see him," she thought, as she drew out the breakfast plate from beneath the grill, and placed it before her. "I know that I didn't want any breakfast… but I can't afford to waste it either…I know it's your favourite food Simon…but, under the circumstances…" she reluctantly ate the food and cleared away the things.

The first thing she did on entering the sitting room was to go over to Simon's drawer. On opening it, she was surprised to find that it was empty.

"That's very curious. Where have all his papers gone? Unhappily she sat down by the small fire, that was throwing out warmth and brightness into the room – unfortunately she felt neither warm nor bright. Her eyes fell on his clothes that were hanging on his usual chair. Yes, his clothes were there…and worse still – so were his shoes. As she shook her head, she had a strange feeling in the pit of her stomach. Surely he hadn't put those awful clothes on to go to work? No- not at seven o'clock in the morning – and most certainly not without his overcoat, gas mask and tin hat. Nothing seemed to be adding up. She sat there with an unexplained sense of foreboding – a feeling that she had never had in her life before. Standing up she walked to the front door, opened it and walked to the front gate. She looked both up and down the road, but there was no sign of anyone. She felt unbelievably restless, in what appeared to be the calm of an unseen hurricane – waiting to move and expose her to the cruel winds of truth.

She became aware of the sounds of droning only split seconds before it was blotted out by the wailing tones of the siren. She gazed up at the overcast sky…

"Oh Simon I'm so worried about you..where are you…?" she mumbled as she turned back to the house.

As she crossed the room she was tempted to curl up on the settee in front of the glowing embers – that would not now be made up with more coals – but the sounds of the guns spurred her into the usual routine of activity – signalling her departure to the shelter once again. On her way through the kitchen her eyes alighted on her ration book ….her ration book…Simon's book was not there. All at once she felt a ringing in her ears…sick….she thought…I'm going to be sick….

At five o'clock the all clear sounded, and Laura was out of the shelter as fast as her legs would take her. A quick look around the small house soon confirmed her innermost fears - Simon had not come back.

She threw her coat on as quickly as she could and deftly tied her hair in a turban. As she stood at the mirror, fiddling with the loose strands of hair, her eyes stared back at her, the dark circles beneath them, together with her pale face – did nothing to cheer her up. She looked dreadful she decided as she turned away from her reflection. Then after grabbing her bag and gasmask case she made her way out of the house into the darkening street.

Later on whilst she was making her way home, she had been praying that he would have returned, but no, the house was just as she had left it. After walking for nearly three hours she felt cold, worn out and sick inside. Sitting herself down on a chair at the fireside, she grabbed Simon's jacket and held it to her in an unrelenting grip.

"Come home Simon, please come home," she said gazing into the cold ash strewn hearth, "don't do this to me…it's just not funny….where on earth have you gone to…?

It had been exactly six weeks since Simon's disappearance. He had not been seen since his last duty at the A.R.P. station on that fateful morning, and he had never returned home.

The worry of it all was making Laura quite ill, but Captain Fuller and his wife had been most supportive and had done everything in their power to try to trace the wayward boy. Unfortunately they were having no more success with finding him than when they had tried to find his long lost relatives all those years ago.

Laura couldn't settle to anything, she went mechanically through the days, hoping against hope that she would hear some sort of news – good or bad, she was quite resigned to either, and had reached the state that any news would be a welcome relief to her. She had lost all interest in cooking for one – let alone eating. In any case whatever she did manage to swallow down was soon up again. Having reached such a low ebb she knew that she couldn't keep the news from James any longer, so reluctantly she put pen to paper. Although she didn't want to worry him unnecessarily, she just needed to share some of the heartache she was going through.

As she finished the letter, a peculiar sensation of light-headedness engulfed her and as she laid the pen down and stamped the envelope she had the feeling that she was hungry, which was unusual to say the least, considering how she had been feeling just lately.

It was only toast but it fared no better than anything else she ate for, no sooner had she swallowed it, than she was off and running again. Looking into the bathroom mirror after she had wiped her mouth she took a long hard look at her reflection. Pushing back her hair, she spoke aloud to the distinctly rough reflection.

"I guess I must take myself in hand. What with the raids; the worry about Simon; not sleeping properly and this persistent sickness – I feel just dreadful – and look it too. I must say…I'm glad you're not here to see me James. I look terrible…"

As she was dressing to go to the doctors the next morning, she noticed that her skirt was more than a little big.

"I'm fading away fast…just like my lovely Simon," she said in a whisper. Then she sat on the bed and cried – and cried – and cried.

He was a comfortable old doctor, and he had a comfortable old surgery. His desk was covered with books and papers, as were the cupboards behind him. He himself was the personification of neatness, with his little bow-tie almost exactly mimicking the shape of his singularly well cut moustache. Laura had known him since she was a child, and he had seemingly never changed, except for the colour of the perfect moustache. When she had first met him it had been a flaming red – with the bow-tie to match; now it was pure white, and of course, as usual, the bow-tie matched it.

The doctor had prescribed a tonic – but he had done more than that. He had told Laura that she was pregnant. At first she could not believe it.

"But Doctor Lambert, I'm so thin…how can it be…?"

"My dear Laura, a good many ladies lose weight before they eventually start to put it on again, it's quite normal.. so that is one thing you don't have to worry about. That mystery boy seems to continue to give you worry but you must try to relax. Simon will turn up I'm sure….I'm only sorry that your dear Aunt Mary is not here to see you through all of this...but you do know that you can come and see me whenever you like....and talk to me about any worries or fears that you might have…don't you…? I mean it Laura. I know that you have lots of lady friends to confide in…but there may be some things that you would rather talk over with me.. now you won't forget, will you…?" He looked across at her and gave her a wink.

After giving her the forms of supplementary rations and telling her to get sorted out at the food office, he told her again not to worry. He knew all about Simon from his partner Dr. Andrews and about the desperation that Laura felt with regard to him, but went on to tell her that his personal philosophy was that… 'Happy and contented mothers, make for happy and contented babies…'

"So no more tears. Go home and write to your husband, let him share your good news…I'm sure that he will appreciate that."

"I will doctor… when do you think that the baby will be born?"

"Well, from what you tell me, and my examination, I would say that it will arrive next May….it's very early days at the moment so I don't want you doing anything too strenuous.. no driving ambulances…I don't want you taking any silly chances," he added, looking at her over the top of his gold rimmed pince-nez. "You're a healthy young woman and I see no difficulties if you heed my words…May, yes…that's a lovely time for babies. Let's hope that May 1941 will be a good month for you, the baby and all of us. I want you to come back and see me before Christmas, take care. Oh and by the way, congratulations to you and Major Aston, of course."

Laura left the surgery in a happy daze. She drew her coat tightly around her for it was quite cold now. Outwardly, she may have felt cold…but inside? That was quite a different matter. Warm feelings doused her body when she thought about the new life within her. Stupid things came into her mind as she walked head down looking at the cracks in the paving stones….

When she was a child the cracks presented an unknown and secret quality…and to tread on one was …unthinkable…. It was seeing the doctor and remembering him as he was that re-kindled her thoughts of childhood, she decided. And now there was going to be another childhood; a child for her and James. A child so tiny within her, that only God could see it….

That night she went to the Citadel. She walked past the Holiness table with the open Bible lying on it, reminding her of the everlasting presence of God, and made her way to the mercy seat. As she knelt in prayer, she thanked God for the delicate and most precious gift of life that she was now guardian of. She was conscious of the smooth polished wood beneath her arms as she continued to kneel there, but nothing else. She allowed her love to flow out and God's love to flow in and over her. She needed this special time to talk and listen to God, and when at last she stood up she felt a lightening of her heart. She stood there straight and tall, her lovely features composed; with her beautiful eyes shining out of her pale face with renewed hope.

Simon never did return to Amleth, and although it was quite a time before Laura could think of him without a dreadful draining feeling of emptiness, she resigned herself to never seeing him again.

James took Simon's disappearance very badly for a while. Laura thanked God for the new baby that was coming – for it was the thought of this new member of their family that kept him going. Had it not been for that… As it was James had been overjoyed at the news, and had found himself more powerfully in love with Laura than ever, the child was just an added and most blessed bonus of that love. He was longing to take her in his arms again...

Towards the end of 1940 there was a disastrous raid by the Luftwaffe. From Amleth, London had seemed to be one great ball of fire, the sky turning from pale pink to blood red in an incredibly short time. The incendiary bombs from the first wave of planes, lit up the targets for the bombers and made the hours of destruction that followed go like clockwork.

Sitting in the shelter, Laura felt very frightened and was more than grateful that Mary Fuller had insisted on staying with her, the clicking of their knitting needles drowned out by the sounds above.

"It's certainly bad tonight Laura…and it was so cloudy today…I had hoped that we would have missed out on this packet tonight…"

Throbbing sounds of gunfire raged about them, with the sounds of explosions getting nearer by the minute – or so it seemed. Sleep was definitely out of the question, so they just sat there knitting and singing for what seemed like an eternity…until the bedlam was over.

It had been, as they found out later, one of the worst nights of the war so far. Fires raged on for hours before they were brought under control, and hundreds were made homeless and very many more were without power and were unable to cook or light their homes. There had been chaos at the local hospital too, with surgeons having to complete essential operations by candle light and amid dust. It was a terrible, terrible way to end the year. The outlook for 1941 was also decidedly gloomy; and Laura, instead of looking forward to the birth of her first child, felt nothing but an overwhelming apprehension.

"What sort of a world are you coming into my sweet baby?" she said as she turned the new calendar to January 1st. The baby – unconcerned – answered by showing it's willingness to survive, by giving her a resounding kick….

Book 1 – Chapter 14
Semi-circle... Autumn 1986

Father's funeral was long past, but of course, they all still felt sadness at the irreplaceable gap that he had left. So, it was like a sunburst on a dull day when, only a few weeks after that occasion Terri had announced to Peter and Angela that she too had become a Christian thus bringing a new warmth into their lives. Therefore, when the time had come for the christening of the babies, she had been thrilled to be asked to be their godmother. So, on a warm May day in 1986, James Richard Aston and Laura Sally Aston (they were being named after all their late grandparents) were duly christened.

The days and months that followed were hectic. The house had never seen such comings and goings before, with mainly happy sounds filling the rooms. The twins were a joy to everyone, even the interrupted nights were soon forgotten in busy light of day. Angela had taken a good while to get over the births, but because of the safe arrival of the totally unexpected pair, and the ensuing delight that they engendered, the news that she would not be able to have any more children, receded into the background and became – both to her and Peter quite inconsequential. As far as they were concerned, their family was complete, later in life than they had hoped maybe but, nevertheless, it was complete.

Now it was November and the days were dark and short. On the morning that Terri was due to leave them, the sun had managed to break through the early rain of the day. As Peter was carrying the cases to the car he glanced up at the sky and what he saw made him call into the house. The two women on hearing the urgent sound of his voice hurried to him.

"Whatever is it?" Angela said.

Peter said nothing – but just pointed upwards. They both followed the line of his finger.

"Oh it's a rainbow," Terri smiled.

"I can hardly believe it. I don't think that I have ever seen one so late in the year before – have you Peter?"

"No, I don't believe I have either love, mind you I don't think that it will be around for much longer – it's fading all the while. It's almost; going, going, gone."

Angela put her arm around the young woman's shoulders before saying,

"It's a sign of a new beginning you know Terri ....so although we are sad to lose you, we're ready and willing to accept that our ray of sunshine is going somewhere else... Right Peter?"

He nodded before saying,

"Whatever part of the world you end up in...well we know you will make it a better place. Whatever you tackle we know you will do your best and come through with flying colours, we're quite sure – aren't we darling?" he said putting his arm about Angela's waist.

"Yes – yes we are dear," she agreed.

"Well," Terri said, "I'm sure that God wants me to be a nurse now – so I'm willing to die in the attempt ... and if I should fail – it won't be for the want of trying."

"You won't fail love – you'll make a super nurse," Angela said giving her arm a squeeze.

They all stood for a second more looking at the fast disappearing rainbow, then Terri said quietly,

"I must go and kiss the babies goodbye..." then, trying to conceal her tears, she hurried back into the house.

At last the moment had come, and Terri was in the car, and winding down the window in order to give Angela a last kiss.

"I can't believe that I'm really going," she sniffed.

"Well you are, and your adventure is just beginning."

Peter started the car engine up and as they moved off Angela called,

"God Bless," and waved her last goodbye.

Peter didn't speak as she sat glassy-eyed beside him. It was a strange feeling she felt, both of sorrow at leaving the part of her life that she had both hated and loved behind, but also, at the same time, a tantalising feeling of anticipation – of the new life that she was embarking upon. She took a deep breath and said...

"Look out world, I'm coming."

Two years almost to the day that Terri left them, a letter had arrived at the Aston household, sent by Mrs. Jennifer Piper. As she looked at the invitation card, she fleetingly thought of Mr. George Piper, and the reports she had heard about him, but then returned to the invitation again. Terri was to be married! They had known about Gregory for some time of course, but here it was in black and white. The wedding was to take place in Scotland at the beginning of December. When Theresa Piper was to marry Mr. Gregory McAlastair. As she placed the card on the shelf and looked at it, she thought about their commitments and hoped that they would allow them to go, because it was one wedding that she did not want to miss! And about Terri, and what a walking disaster she had been when she had come into their lives – all those years ago…. The house was quiet, unusually so, because the children were out at a party, and she was not expecting them home again until four o'clock.

"I've an hour to myself…what bliss," she thought as she walked to the french windows and looked out.

George Piper, newly released from prison, stood outside the towering gates and breathed deeply of the heavily polluted air – a free man once again. The little money he had accrued was burning a hole in his pocket.

" What I need is a drink," he thought to himself.

When in reality it was the last thing he needed. Amazingly, the awful memories of the night that he had been arrested – and the subsequent days of drying out that he had endured – seemed to be so far in his past that he had totally forgotten them.

Yes, prison was behind him, and his life was his own again to do with as he wanted and it was not now controlled by the do-gooding morons of authority that had ruled it for so long. The do-gooders who had tried to paint such a rosy picture of his future and the wonderful new life that was waiting for him on the outside.. Idiots!

He caught sight of his own reflection in the blackened out window of a betting shop. He saw the image of a nondescript man in his mid-fifties, with thinning hair receding at the temples; making him look far older than his years, and exaggerating the almost skeletal facial bones, that gave rise to sunken cheeks. His eyes that were lifeless pools stared out of darkened sockets with dormant rage. This was the reflection of a man who had had no hope as a child – and now as a man – no hope and no future. He felt the smouldering anger niggling at him.

"Yeah a great future lies ahead for you – don'et? What I need is a drink – something to take the taste and smell of prison away…that's me plan, for me future, you snotty do-gooding bastards…"

He made a vulgar gesture, defiantly with his hand at the pathetic reflection, that returned the gesticulatory symbol with exactly the same hatred.

Determinedly he walked on to the pub. A place that he knew would be inhabited by people like himself – living in the real world. A world of unemployment, dole and giros; and sad reality. True, getting drunk was not particularly on his agenda, but he could hold his liquor couldn't he? All he needed was a boost to his self-confidence…something to steady his nerves, before he made his way back to the home he had walked out of all those years ago. After all – he felt fit, and completely in control of himself. Just a couple of quick ones before he faced Jenna…

It was a good coming home party for George Piper – unfortunately! For his so called friends turned out be worse enemies. He ran the gambit of emotions; from depression, sadness, happiness and incoherent ecstasy to verbose shouting and swearing; it was the usual pattern of events. His old nightmare was returning – and he couldn't see it, he was on his usual roundabout, that only some sort of miracle could halt.

"Go and sleep it off George, get yourself away before you get into trouble again..and don't bother to come back here unless you can get it together, don't be an idiot George," the landlord added.

With a series of hand movements indicating the door, he urged the so called 'friends' to remove their companion forthwith. George answered by way of an inane laugh (that made nobody else smile) as he danced towards the circular windowed main doorway.

"Yess sir…you're all right Jack…I'm all right Jack…"

He shouted,

"I'm all right Jack," again as he lurched into the street.

His 'friends' having happily drunk almost all his money away escorted him to the doors, but declined to go with him any further. In fact, none of them cared a jot for the overpowering, quite violent and often frightening man, whose appearance was sometimes totally deceptive. Oh he was quite amiable at the moment, but they all knew how quickly his mood could change, and discretion being the better part of valour, they decided they were better off staying away from him..and this they did – to a man.

Once outside in the air, he felt somewhat worse than he had done in the confines of the smoky bar. He staggered a step or so, putting his hand on the brickwork to support himself. The brown paper parcel that he had carried from the prison slipped from his grasp, and fell to the ground at his feet. He gazed at it, swaying slightly, trying hard to keep his eyes focused on it; in an attempt to gauge it, he slid slowly down the wall and then knelt before the dreaded thing. As he looked at it, it seemed to him that it changed its shape. He blinked his eyes, then he lunged at the paper.

"Gotcher," he said, with a strong hint of annoyance creeping into his voice. His rising from the pavement and his subsequent journey to his old home was made laboriously …one erratic step at a time.

He reached Vincent House and gazed upwards. Even the dull grey of the sky hurt his eyes.

"Jenna…good old Jenna…" he said. "Good old Jenna, I'll be alright…GOOD OLD JENNA," he shouted.

He felt for the half bottle of White Horse in his pocket, a 'gift' from one of his well meaning friends, bought with his own money! Then, unscrewing the top he took a swig of the amber coloured fluid and afterwards replaced the cap with meticulously dainty movements before falling down on to a low graffiti-covered wall. After a while he was up on his feet again and making his unsteady way to … his Jenna.

Entering the lift that stood open he lurched inside and peered at the panel of numbers that were dancing before his eyes. He was confused, - but only for a moment. He hadn't forgotten the position of the button he needed – which was just as well – for there were no numerals visible on the battered plate. He pressed it and the doors, rather hesitatingly closed. The lift was filthy. Crisp papers and coke cans littered the floor, and felt pen graffiti covered every inch of the walls. There was also a dark patch on the floor, spreading its tentacle like arms from one corner to the centre. The stench in his nostrils, and the sudden jerk of the lift made him feel sick and his mouth filled with water.

Suddenly he felt confined in that small space – his imprisonment was back. He beat his hands on the metal of the door as the lift moved relentlessly upward. Before he had stepped out at level twelve, vomit descended on to his jacket front and down on to the floor where it had mingled obscenely with the urine of his newly acquired cell. The doors had opened briefly – once. When they did a youngish woman had stood there holding the handle of a baby's pram. She looked in at the disgusting sight, screaming,

"You revolting old pig," as the doors hiccuped closed again.

He left the lift and made his way to the door of the flat. He stood there feeling slightly nauseous, and more than a little unsteady. Banging on the door with his fists, in rapid burst, he called out his wife's name in a loud voice:

"Jenna.....Jenna.....open up and let me in...Jenna..."

All of a sudden the door opened and a tall well built man stood there, a glowering expression on his face. He was wearing dark blue trousers, a none too clean vest that exposed tattoos of every shape and colour, and he towered above George Piper. As he looked down he raised his fist saying,

"Shut your mouth, what the 'ell are you 'ollering abhat...?"

"Jenna.....I want me Jenna...who are you...?" he added suspiciously, peering up at the man.

"I live 'ere mate, and there aint nobody 'ere by that name."

"Where is she then?"

"I don't know, I've never even 'erd of 'er, don't ask me....Jean," he called over his shoulder, " come and speak to this idiot will yer?" he said, turning back into the narrow hallway.

A woman squeezed past his tattooed bulk as she came to the door. Her too blonde hair was piled up on top of her head and scraped back from her rather high forehead – startlingly wide by virtue of the fact that, long ago in pursuit of beauty, she had removed every trace of her eyebrows. Pillar-box red nailed fingers lifted a cigarette from an equally red lipsticked mouth as she spoke to him, her eyes peering at him through spiky mascara and her last exhaled net of smoke....

"What's your trouble?" she said keeping her distance from him as her nostrils caught his offensive smell.

"I want me Jenna...where is she..?"

"I don't know her mate. We've lived 'ere eighteen months now...and I've never even 'erd of 'er....We all keep ourselves to ourselves along 'ere...Have you tried next door.... They might know something of 'er. Mind you, I wouldn't want to see you if you were my old man, not in the state that you're in...Why don't you go and sleep it off somewhere....?"

George's eyes narrowed into a cruel stare, and his hand flew out and held hers, twisting her fingers as he tightened his grip.

"Hey – what do you think that you are doing? What's your game..?"

"I want me Jenna," he slurred.

"I don't care 'oo you want...'ere pet come quick.."

'Pet' came back to the door, and grabbing George Piper threw him backwards on to the concrete floor of the walkway where he lay stunned.

"Clear off you disgusting pig – and don't show your face 'round 'ere again, this place is bad enough as it is – we don't want the likes of you littering it up….get up…and get out…now."

As he finished speaking, he bent forward in a menacing manner, brandishing his fist in George's face, before going back inside and slamming the door shut.

Other heads had appeared along the landing, intrigued by all the commotion and as they looked at the inebriated figure on the ground, whom they all knew of old, they quickly closed their doors; not wishing to become involved with him again. The days were gone when they had rallied around him…and his long-suffering wife Jennifer. Now they had, and showed no feeling of pity for the drunken and often violent man now lying flat on his back. The doors closed in quick succession – thud – thud – thud. George Piper was alone and angry.

Down on the ground once again, he sat on the wall and drowned his sorrows with a few more swigs from his friendly bottle. Three youths started to approach him. It was their intention to have some sport with the pathetic looking man. He watched their approach through slitty eyes as he slowly screwed the top on the bottle sliding it carefully into his pocket.

"'Ello dad, 'ad a 'evy day 'ave you?"

As the boy was speaking he leant forward and ruffled the sparse hair on George's head.

Too late he realised that his attention to George's head had been a mistake…

George, enraged by his touch, jumped up and caught the offending boy's throat in a tight grip.

"Don't come the funny boy with me sonny," he hissed through almost closed lips, hiccuping loudly at the end of his words… not for an instant releasing his grip on the helpless young blood.

Without moving he looked with steely eyes at the other youths, who were standing motionless, and visually shocked – behind their friend. After what seemed an age he released the frightened boy from his grasp….throwing him into the arms of his startled companions like so much rubbish, and went on,

"and that goes for you others too, I've eaten the likes of you for breakfast…so don't get any other fancy ideas about comin' the old acid with me."

He hiccuped again, and this time the force of the expulsion of air caused him to totter backward and slump once again on to the broken wall.

At last one of them spoke,

"You're George Piper, aren't you?"

"So?"

"Nothin mate – it's just that I – that is – we, we didn't realise who you were …not at first."

"So now you know….watsit to you?"

"Well I knew you 'ad been away…"

"Well…I'm not away now am I clever boy? The only people 'oo are away are me wife and kids…"

He hiccuped loudly again.

"Oh yer, I remember your wife and kids all right … a big posh taxi came for them…."

"All of them? What about me Ginger?"

His eyes looked at each of them in turn as his head started to roll. The boy who was still rubbing his sore neck said quietly,

"Oh I remember 'er all right… she was taken to 'ospital when she O.D.'d…. yer I remember 'er all right…."

The quiet words of the boy had a sobbering effect on the older man who was obviously affected by them. He looked from one to the other, and then said pathetically

"O.D'd? You mean…you mean… she's…..dead?"

He rose from his position on the wall as he was speaking, and shakily moved towards the boy who had last spoken and who now defensively put his hands up saying quickly

"Na…na…nothing like that…she's not dead."

George sat down again with a bump as the boy went on,

"Na…she was in 'ospital for a long time I remember…she never came back 'ere again..she went to some other place.."

"Place? What place?"

George's patience was getting towards breaking point now and with some inner strength he made a lunge at the lad, who once again put his hands in front of his face to protect himself as he side-stepped the angry drunkard.

"'ang on dad…'ang on, gimme time…I'll 'ave to think abart it…"

"What abart me Jenna and the other kids?"

He made another abortive grasp at the boys, who were by this time standing just out of his flailing arms reach. George, having started to turn as he threw his arms about, was caught up with the momentum of his own body weight, and after transcribing a full circle, fell down landing neatly cross legged in front of the open mouthed lads. His first thought on reaching the ground was for his friendly bottle – and its safety. Slipping his hand into his pocket, he quickly drew it out. Relief spread all over his face when he saw that it was intact – almost empty now, but still intact. He carefully unscrewed the top and raised the bottle to his lips, sucking greedily at the last of the amber whiskey.

"Where's me Jenna?" he said pathetically to the now empty bottle, " and me gel?"

He raised his head and looked sorrowfully at the watching lads.

"Let me think dad, it's a long time ago now…I need to think…I'm sure I'll remember..but I need a bit of time."

They helped him up to the wall again where he sat swaying, his face flushed with both drink and latent anger.

"Look mate, you can't stay 'ere…come along wiv us..there's a lock-up that we go to wiv some of the boys..to have a smoke.." as he gave George a nudge and a wink, "know what I mean?"

George didn't grasp the full meaning of the boy's words, but readily agreed to go with them, surrendering at once to their suggestions. They steered him to the garage and took him inside. There was a sweet almost sickening aroma in the airless, windowless box, then when the door was closed, somebody pulled a switch and a light from a naked bulb flooded the room. There were a few old easy chairs, which, like George, were a bit worse for wear, some upturned boxes and a littered table in the centre. Empty beer cans, some old take-away fast food trays, matchboxes and aluminium foil festooned both the table and the grubby floor. Large garish posters were on three walls, but the doors were adorned with graffiti pictures, beautifully executed by some unknown, yet perhaps potentially worthwhile artist.

The now subdued man sat on one of the upturned boxes.

"Look mate, you need some grub…got any money?"

"Where's me Jenna? Where's me gel?"

The boy with the sore neck ran his hands through his thick bleached hair before saying,

"Look dad, I'm off now to find out what I can for you.. gimme a bit of time…"

After they pooled their money, the large African boy said,

"There's just enough for some pies and cans, my man, you sure look like you could do with something.. do you want lager or beer?"

George knew that the question was directed at him, but before he had time to give an answer the black boy went on,

"We can't run to the hard stuff, but beer is good," he added flashing his white teeth into a broad smile."Good, then beer it will be my man," the boy said, giving a mock salute and little bow to him, before turning and going out of the door quickly followed by the other two.

"We won't be long George…take it easy…you're a free man now…good aint it?"

The door closed and a key turned. He was alone. He sat in the midst of the squalor of the filthy place, oblivious of the degradation that he was in. He smelled of sick ….. and he had urinated down on to the floor..yet he sat there unconcerned.

"I'm free Jenna..Jenna," he called, his voice echoing slightly, "Good en'it?"

Book 2 – Chapter 14
Firstborn *May 1941*

The battle for Britain was still on and raids were becoming longer, stronger and more devastating. James reaction, therefore, to the thoughts of becoming a father were twofold. He was both overjoyed but more worried than ever for Laura's safety. His pleas for her to go to his mother in Wilthsire became more urgent in every letter he wrote to her and as time went on, he became increasingly more frantic for her. At last she had to admit things were getting more than a little difficult. However, due to the fact that she was well advanced into the pregnancy, she had decided to wait until after the birth before making the move.

Mary Fuller had been a tower of strength to her all the way through, and had encouraged her to stay with them at night and, undoubtedly getting in and out of the Morrison shelter in the Fuller's dining-room was a far easier task than the old Anderson at the bottom of her garden; although the thought of being squashed under it had to be blotted out of one's mind, or else sleep, when one could sleep, would have been impossible.

She was as busy as she was able to be during the day, but the presence of her rapidly expanding girth confined her to walking rather than running as was her want. The flowered smock stuck out in front of her - in no way hiding her bump – but as she said it did warn people that she was coming. She likened herself to one of the R.A.F.'s barrage balloons, and wrote to James in one of many letters,

"...I may look like one of the balloons, but there is no way that I could float as they do. How I wish that I could, oh my aching feet..."

As time went on and the child within her grew, her love for her absent husband grew as well. How she longed for him to be with her. Sometimes when she was lying in the solitude of her room she would daydream about the first time they had met...and it still sent tingles down her spine – even after all this time... However, solitude was in short supply and after a very long and particularly noisy air-raid during the night, she found herself walking away from the Fullers to do a little essential shopping, before returning home to catch up with some well needed rest.

Unfortunately, Hitler's Luftwaffe had other ideas. Having managed to do some shopping, she was having to spend the rest of her morning in a public shelter, feeling extremely tired and more than a little depressed. Her feelings whilst temporarily entombed were not helped by the presence of a rather stout lady in black who was the possessor of a loud rasping voice, whose words cut into Laura like a knife, since she was the only one in the shelter that they could have been aimed at. The glance that she had given the woman showed her to be sitting about five feet away on the other side of the shelter. Her head and shoulders were above those of her companions by virtue of the large hat towering above her, looking like a large black cake and adorned with an enormous bunch of bright red cherries. It was perched precariously and looked as if it were about to fall with each nod of the owner's head.

Looking disparagingly at Laura's girth the woman sniffed and said,

"Gun fodder that's what I say it is...gun fodder. If women stopped having children there would be no more wars...no killing, no men to kill. Gun fodder...that's all he'll be if it's a boy ... more gun fodder." Hardly giving herself time to breathe she went on,

"Restraint that's what women have got to have...restraint..."

She sniffed loudly again after the pronouncements and tossed her head from side to side, making the cherries tumble and dance. People around her looked distinctly uncomfortable and looked at their feet, shuffling them about in embarrassment. Laura was in no mood for an argument, in fact she had tried to take no notice of the voice. However, the words had hurt her more than she realised. They had not angered her – just hurt. Tears had sprung to her eyes as she sat there but they had not made their escape beyond her thick lashes. The woman's tirade went on and on. Her offending opinions were delivered vibrating the ears of the captive occupants of the shelter – distracting them, to a small degree, from the raid outside that was later to have the dubious honour of being one of the worst carried out in daylight.

".....gun fodder...no...we do not need any more gun fodder thank you very much...mad men all of them. The way things are going there won't be any of the world left for any of us..."

She shot another withering dart in Laura's direction before closing her mouth and pursing her lips into a hard straight line.

At last the all clear sounded, adding its plaintive wail to sounds of fire engines and ambulances outside. Most people had scrambled for the doorway as soon as they had been able, but Laura didn't. She preferred to wait until there was more room. Finally the only person remaining with her was the woman, the cherries lying unusually still on her hat. Laura stood up and spoke for the first time.

"I believe that a baby is God's way of saying that He wants the world to go on…I'm sorry that you don't share the same opinion as me."

They emerged from the shelter together and the woman suddenly took Laura's arm gently, saying to her, in a voice strangely bereft of harshness,

"I'm truly sorry dear…please forgive me.."

Laura looked into her face and saw that the harsh lips had softened and her eyes were full of tears.

"Of course I forgive you – we're all frightened you know…all of us.. frightened and tired of this war, but the human race has to go on. Doesn't it?

The woman nodded, dabbing her eyes with her gloved hand, then turning away from Laura she started to walk away, the cherries swaying to and fro. She walked slowly out of their lives, for they never met again.

Having arrived home, relief turned quickly into tiredness and at last, very thankfully she was able to lay down, barely having time to pray for her love before her eyes closed in sleep. The baby kicking actively during the air-raid, was now calm – and maybe sleeping – as was his beautiful mother.

The Amleth Cottage Hospital – not too far from Laura's home, had been turned into an extra maternity wing, because the large hospital had been badly damaged during earlier bombing raids. Consequently when Laura had gone into labour, her journey up the hill was a short one, far shorter than the labour which had turned out to be very long but uncomplicated. Peter George Aston was born at last, announcing his displeasure with the world when his little bottom was smacked unceremoniously by the midwife. He was brought to Laura tightly wrapped in a shawl, with just his face and head showing. As she gazed down on the now silent face, overpowering love filled her.

"You little darling," she said with the pain of the last few hours quite forgotten as she kissed the top of his downy head.

Continuing to gaze at the new life in her arms, her thoughts turned to James, and the moments of tender love they had shared….and how that love had crystallised to form this new and perfect being who was… their son.

She awoke from sleep, it was dawn – and the blackout was open. Pale light filled the small ward as she looked around. Lying there she realised that the bed place that she was in was the same one that Simon had occupied after the air raid at the shop. Over the past months it was as if he had never existed, and yet now, here she was actually reliving part of his life in her memories.

"How strange," she thought, "how very, very strange…"

Book 1 Chapter 15
The Wages of Sin….

Angela picked up the pile of clean clothes from the kitchen table and made her way upstairs to the twin's bedroom, which was light and airy but a little cold. Laying the clothes down she crossed the room and pulled the window shut. She was fixing the latch and straightening the curtains when she heard knocking.

"Bang – bang – bang – bang."

"All right, all right, I'm coming.." she called as she hurried down to the door.

There on the step stood a hollow eyed, scraggy individual, whom she could see, and smell, was plainly the worse for drink. He had stepped up to her before she could say or do anything, and thrust his face to hers making a beery smell waft into her nostrils. At the same moment, he pushed her backwards into the house, followed her and quickly slammed the door shut behind them. The anger on the man's face coupled with his action made her feel terribly afraid.

"What do you want? Why have you come here?" she asked trying to keep her voice as calm as possible.

"You the vicar's wife?"

She nodded.

"Where's Jenna?" He spat out, his eyes flashing. He clearly needed an answer.

"I don't know anybody by that name…"

"Liar"

"No – really, I don't…"

"I know you know…I don't want lies."

He grabbed Angela's wrist and pulled her forward. He was breathing into her face again. She turned her head sideways in an effort to avoid the smell of him, trying to break loose from his grip, but it was hopeless. As she moved her head he quickly caught her hair with his free hand and forcibly turned her around to face him.

"Me Jenna's gone…I wanna know where…now," he pulled her hair hard, "tell me where…now," he pulled on her hair even more. "Tell – me – where – she – is?"

Tears rushed to Angela's eyes as she answered him,

"Please – you must believe me, I don't know anybody…" she started to say again.

"Lies…all bloody lies. I want me Jenna and me gell…and you're goin' to tell me where they are…Mrs. High and Mighty."

He released his grip on Angela's head and pushed her with such force that she fell heavily over the arm of the settee, then he came and stood menacingly over her. The roots of her hair were smarting painfully, and her whole head was hurting as she brushed the tears from her cheeks with an unsteady hand.

"Girl? Girl? Could it be that this awful man is… George Piper? – Terri's father?" She was about to speak when his hand flew out hitting her head with such viciousness that it tipped sideways, forcing her to cry out in pain…

"Aagh."

"Me gell – Ginger – where's me gell?"

"She's not here any more..she's gone away…"

"Where?" then, without waiting for a reply he hit again, the ferocious blow striking her in the mouth, splitting her lip.

"Answer me you stuck up cow," he went on, his thick speech slurring his words together.

"She's up north."

"Doin' what?"

"She's training to be a nurse," Angela replied truthfully.

"Some 'opes.. do you expect me to swallow that?"

He made a grab at her hair again, catching hold of it and pulling it upwards in a wrenching movement.

"Aagh…it's true…it's true," she sobbed trying desperately to release herself from his steel like grip.

"Like where M'lady?"

He slapped her again.

"God help Terri," she thought to herself, "and God help me too."

"Northampton," she said aloud, "She's at a hospital there. I have an address."

She reeled back as he flung her down again.

"Get it," he commanded.

She stood up and slowly crossed to the writing desk. Pushing back her hair, whilst trying to control both pain and fear, she shakily wrote on a piece of paper. When she had finished she walked back and offered it to him. He snatched at it and put it into his pocket.

"Right M'lady, now…where's me Jenna?"

"Oh no, not that again," she thought, but then realised that he must mean Terri's unfortunate mother, so she again replied truthfully that she didn't know.

He made his way towards her with hatred exuding from his every fibre… She started to back away but he quickly caught her again, this time holding her tightly by the shoulders. Then as he spoke, he viciously shook her with each word.

"I…want…me…Jenna…where…is…she?"

His voice rose in decibels to a high cackle.

She felt limp and knew that she couldn't take much more of his treatment. Her head was reeling, and her face felt as if it were on fire. She slipped downwards out of his grasp, as he momentarily slackened his grip.

"I don't know where she is, you must believe me" she whispered almost inaudibly.

He stood, feet apart, hand on hips looking down on her threateningly. As she looked up at the figure towering above her, she saw a man distorted into huge proportions, as if by fair-ground mirrors…She cowered at his feet, a position George Piper liked to see his women in. They were at his mercy then, and he was in complete control. As he felt the power surge through him a leering smile crossed his lips. Angela's thoughts were racing wildly through her head…

"The babies…Sarah…what's the time…Oh Lord".

The blow to her ribs as he knocked her knocked the air out of her lungs and again she cried out.

"Please….please stop.."

The cry fell on deaf ears.

"I don't know where she is.. nobody does." She ended weakly.

"Shut it you whining cow," he said as he punched her again. "I wanna drink..you got some?"

He staggered a few paces from her.

"Not really.."

"What?" He made to cross to her again.

"Only some cooking sherry," she gasped out quickly before he reached her.

"Where?"

"In the kitchen."

"Get it then," he said with mounting annoyance.

She tried to rise but pain shot through her,

"I can't," she whispered hardly moving her lips.

"Useless bitch," he mumbled under his breath, "where?"

Angela pointed in the direction of the kitchen.

She heard the sounds of crockery being broken and cupboard doors banging, and then ......silence.

As she sat on the floor shivering with fear and pain the 'phone started to ring. She looked towards it in desperation – knowing that she could never reach it. On and on it went, the shrill bell unrelentlessly piercing her already painful head. Then he was there again, making his way unsteadily towards the offending instrument.

"Shuppup," he said, knocking it off the table with one sweep of his arm, before pulling the wire connection from the wall. He looked towards her, "Just in case you get any fancy ideas," he said.

As he lurched forward he caught sight of the printed invitation on the mantelpiece. Peering at it he said,

"Scotland...Terri's in Scotland..."

His speech and temper were deteriorating fast. He turned to Angela.

"You lying ...lying bitch."

She shook her head with fear, and shaking from head to toe cried,

"No...no...she is in Northampton at the moment."

With dim realisation he said,

"Scotland, Jenna's sister lives in Scotland... and that's where they are."

His speech was almost incomprehensible now and his movements slower as he crossed to Angela's pathetic form. The effort he exerted in giving one last blow to her head, which rendered her senseless, made him fall backwards in an unconscious stupor. The vile stench of him filled the whole room, but neither of them knew of the odour which surrounded them. The clock struck four – but neither of them heard it.....

.....Is Death.

The nightmare had died away gradually, as Angela's mind and body healed. Now, knowing the rest of the jigsaw of that awful afternoon, she found that understanding the series of events finally helped her to be able to dismiss the horror of it. She knew now that Sarah had tried to ring her because she was going to be late, but that she had been cut off, and to make matters worse had been further delayed by a bad road accident involving an articulated lorry. She knew too that her attacker and the man killed by the lorry were one and the same person…George Piper…

"A drunken man… trying to hitch a lift," the police had said…

Now that Angela had returned to the peak of fitness the children were home again at Oasis, after their 'little holiday' with Sarah with whom they had been staying during Angela's convalescence.

They were full of life as ever and excited at the thought of 'going away' again with Mummy and Daddy, for preparations were well in hand for the journey to Scotland – and Terri's wedding. The night before they were to leave, Angela and Peter managed to snatch a few moments together.

"Seeing Terri won't bring back bad memories of a few months ago, will it darling?"

"No dear…not at all, that's definitely behind me now.. a thing of the past well and truly. All I can think of now is the wedding and Terri's happiness…If she's just half as happy as the day I married you…"

Standing up Peter pulled her to him.

"What about now?" he said circling his arms about her.

"Would you marry me now, knowing me like you do?"

"Since I still love you, and can't think of life without you, I think the answer can only be…..yes."

Slipping one arm away from her body he ran it along her back, cupping her head in his hand and drawing it to him. His lips quickly found hers and they kissed.

"I do love you Angela Aston…I've been so blessed…first with you and now with the twins…you're such a clever, clever girl m'love."

"It wasn't all me, was it? I think I may have had a little assistance from their father. The fact that I made love with him may have had something to do with their appearance…what say you?"

She laughed and threw back her head as they hugged one another again. Then suddenly a faint cry came to their ears.

"That will be Jamie, he always wakes about now for a drink. I'd better go and do my motherly duty I think."

Then another cry joined the first, and the two sounds blended in unison.

"And that will be Laura, trust a woman to get into the act," he said smiling. "We had better get them settled down again or, before you know it they will be really awake and raring to go!!" she said, rubbing Peter's nose with her own, like an Eskimo.

"But the night is young," he said, winking at her.

"Not that young," she answered darting out of his arms, and running up the stairs with a laugh.

"Well, it's quite young," he said following behind her, covering his ears with his hands as they reached the bedroom door.

The duetists voices reached their top crescendo.

"One of the joys of parenthood," he said grinning "and I love it."

"So do I love…so do I," she answered as they entered the room.

This time when the clock struck the room below was empty so of course nobody heard it.

The house in Scotland was large and rambling, but very welcoming nevertheless, and was owned by Gregory's father – a doctor. Part of the house was a surgery usually, but at the moment, it was filled not with patients - but with wedding guests.

After the introduction and wild exclamations about the twins, Angela was, at last, able to meet and talk to the woman she had only heard about – Jennifer Piper. After their chat together Angela was pleased to learn that she had, with the help of her sister and family, managed to regain not only her health and self-respect, but also a feeling of complete freedom from her past life, which gladdened Angela's heart.

At last, after all the initial chatting was over, the women and very excited band of children left Peter to his own devices.

"Men always feel rather surplus to requirements when it comes to wedding preparations," he thought as he finished his coffee. Except that he was feeling even more marooned in a woman's world, by virtue that both Gregory and his father were absent from the house.

Peter stood and looked out of the window. The snow, as in the carol, was falling ' snow upon snow' lacing its way downwards even harder as the day wore on. There was another person that he was eager to meet, and that was Gregory's grandmother. He knew that she lived in an annexe, but as he peered into the blinding white of the scene outside, realised that it was going to be quite a feat getting there. He made his way through the house to the kitchen – and the side door, where he looked through the glass panel. Sure enough he could see the annexe and the pathway to it piled high with snow.

"Hello"

A voice spoke behind him and he turned around.

"Oh hello," he responded to the smiling face.

"That's Grandma Jay's house," she said, moving next to him and looking out.

"Yes, I guessed it was."

They both stood looking out with the girl pressing her nose to the glass pane.

Without moving she asked, "Why are you looking at it?"

"Well, I was just thinking that if I wanted to meet the lady, I would soon need a snow plough."

"Oh she's not in there," she said, again without moving. Kate Piper had spoken with an air of superior knowledge that only comes when you are twelve years old.

"No?"

"No," she said moving away from the door "she's in the study having a nap."

"Will you do me a big favour Kate?"

"Depends, I can't stay here too long. I'm helping with the babies."

"Are you?" he teased, looking around for them.

"Well…I'm next to help, actually…" She made to go.

"Please Kate, just show me the study..will you?"

"Yerrs, but you won't disturb grandma….will you? Or I'll be in trouble with everyone", she added, puffing out the last word with the feeling of somebody who was rather used to being in trouble.

"Of course I won't, I promise."

"All right, then….come on."

She led him down a long passage to the back of the house and stopped outside a large door.

"This is it", she said "but I'm not going in. I'm off, I'm sure to be needed now."

She turned and ran silently from him, back along the passage.

"Thanks Kate," he stage whispered but his words fell on to deaf ears for by the time he had uttered them, she was out of sight and hearing.

His turned his attention to the door and the large, round brass handle. Would it squeak? Perhaps he could open it a crack and peep in? If the old lady was clearly asleep, he would shut it again….perhaps she would be sitting up?…perhaps she would be lying down..

"This is ridiculous, just standing here perhaps-ing."

He reached for the handle, it twisted comfortably and silently as he turned it. Gently he pushed the heavy door open, just enough for him to look in. There was nobody reclining or sitting. Instead there was the figure of a woman standing at the far end of the room, where the tall windows, reaching almost to the floor, had combined with the snowy backdrop to turn her into a bold silhouette. He soundlessly entered the room, squinting slightly against the brightness,

"Mrs. McFarlain?"

He tilted his head in her direction in anticipation of her reply. Jay McFarlain, tall and elegant, was gazing at the emerald on her finger and miles away in thought when she heard her name called. She turned around immediately, her long hair, loosely held by a brown slide, catching on her shoulder. There was a smile on her lips ready to greet the person that accompanied the deep voice.

The mainly unlined face, tanned by the celtic winds froze in the middle of the smile. She looked long and hard at the figure in the doorway with the brilliance of the snowlight shining on him. Again, he spoke,

"Mrs. McFarlain?"

Her throat was dry, her mind was spinning – where were her words? Why was she dumb-struck? She knew why…and her stomach heaved. The man in front of her…older, larger maybe, but the man in front of her was… He was walking towards her now, his hands extending to hers in a gesture of friendship.

"Hello…I'm…"

Before he had uttered another word he had reached her. Her hands, slim and cool, were in his.

"Simon?" she said in a voice that was almost inaudible.

"Peter," he corrected her gently.

"Simon?" she said again, her voice regaining it's volume.

He shook his head and smiled at her,

"No, it's Peter, Peter Aston."

They stood looking at each other. For a brief yet fleeting moment he thought he recognised the face before him but no, no, he was sure he had never met this charming lady before..and yet…?

In some sort of disbelief, she repeated the name,

"Peter Aston? Peter Aston?"

"Yes, that's right, perhaps you recognise my name?"

She held on to his hands tightly.

"Forgive me please" she said in a soft lilting Scots accent, "I just, I thought…I know you….knew you…"

She shook her head.

"I'm being silly, please do forgive me, it's just …I don't know – I can't explain."

She shook her head again and they made their way across the room and sat down in front of the fire. She looked into it, her left hand across her mouth, again shaking her head whilst at the same time holding on to Peter with her other hand as if her life depended on it. She glanced at him, her eyes bright with tears. Then she resumed her head shaking as she looked once more into the fire. He was shocked to see her reaction to him. He felt uncomfortable and awkward.

Many times in his ministry he had found himself face to face with sadness and despair, in fact, all types of distress, even death, and always he had found himself able to cope – in a professional and caring way, but this….? How could he cope with this? He didn't know in the slightest what he was dealing with. He said a quick prayer to himself.

Almost immediately, a thought came into his mind,

"Perhaps you knew my father, I was thought to resemble him a little…"

He was clutching at straws he knew, but at least he had her attention.

"His name…"

"His name was James Aston."

"Yes!"

"And your dear mother lived in Amleth many, many years ago?"

Peter was dumbfounded, but then he thought for a moment.

"I see Terri has kept you well informed."

"No, my dear, she has had no time to tell me anything about you, except to say what lovely people she had worked for, we've not really had the time for your family history. Where is your dear father now? What with all the coming and goings I lost touch with him…" she spoke slowly her voice fading away.

"Well, I believe he is in heaven now, for he was called home earlier this year."

She stiffened.

"Gone…all gone then…gone."

Still looking at him with some disbelief, her lips turned into a soft smile.

"Can I ask you a very personal question?"

"Well, I'll answer it if I can of course."

"Are you at all deaf?"

He looked at her quizzically, his head slightly on one side.

"Well, yes, as a matter of fact I am, I don't know quite how it came about, but I have a burst eardrum, I think I must have been born with it..."

She shook her head again.

"But how on earth do you know such a thing?"

"I knew your father."

In her heart she said, " and I knew you," but she realised how stupid the idea was... and yet she was positive – the wide grin – the eyes – the head held on one side as if to catch every word –

"Simon, you've come back," she thought. Aloud she said,

"What a stupid old woman I am. Here I am asking you these sillinesses, when as unbelievable as it sounds, and after all these years, I'm meeting the son of a man that I knew, and nursed."

"Nursed?"

"Well, I was one of the nurses that took care of your dear father, after the terrible explosion, but you know all about that, of course."

"I'm sure that I only know part of the story. I know that after the accident father never resumed full active service, and that he was eventually invalided out of the army with a breakdown. I don't really think that he got over the shock of losing my mother, let alone being blown up by a 10,000 pounder. He moved away down to Salisbury to be with his parents at first, and I was in boarding school....frankly, I never had what you would call a father and son type of relationship with him, as the other boys seemed to do; I always felt that I had missed out, but I just blamed the war, and made the best of it."

Jay McFarlain listened intently as Peter poured his story out.

"I had a great love for my grandparents, and holidays, when not spent at boy's camps were always spent with them. Father was becoming more and more of a recluse, in a way it was as if he had given up – I can't explain it..."

"I can understand," she said, patting his hand, "life can be so cruel, and that cruelty can spread nasty roots into a heart once full of passion and life and slowly crush it beyond repair – I know, because I saw it happen to many a fine young man."

"Where did you meet my father?"

"Oh many, many years ago in Amleth."

"That's where he met my mother..."

"Yes, and that's where I met him. Your mother and I attended the same church in those days....she was a few years older than me...Laura, a very beautiful young woman, made even more beautiful by the love for your father...."

"My grandparents always told me that they lived for one another."

"Yes, that's so true; they met, and I can tell you that it was love at first sight. I know that sounds a little melodramatic, but it's true. From the moment they met they had eyes only for each other, and they never stopped loving each other – not even for a moment."

Peter sat silent. It was a strange feeling talking to this lovely woman, a stranger, and yet, a woman who perhaps knew more about him and his family than he did. Suddenly she was talking again.

"When your father was tragically injured whilst defusing that large bomb on the housing estate, they rushed him to the military hospital at Woolwich, he was blinded you know..."

"No, I didn't know, I had no idea."

"Oh yes, quite blind...eventually he was sent to the army convalescent home, Charteris House in Dorset and it was there that I saw him. He was in deep shock and of course heavily bandaged. You don't mind me telling you this, do you? I don't want to bring back old memories that might hurt you, especially at this happy time."

"Oh no, please do go on, it's rather wonderful hearing all about my mother and father, not to say intriguing. My father was such a broken man during the last years of his life, more than ever after the stroke..."

Clearly, Jay McFarlain was not seeing the man that Peter was describing to her. Her mind was far away in the past, a past that a broken old man had no part of. She sighed a long sigh and continued her story.

"He was such a lovely man, handsome and tall, with eyes that lit up whenever your mother appeared."

"Please go on, I must know everything," he said giving her hand a little squeeze.

"Well, it was many months before he could see of course, but thankfully he did regain his sight, although it was weakened. It was during his time at Charteris that your dear mother...my friend was...was gunned down by a marauding German fighter plane....her and the baby, your brother, gunned down in broad daylight...a mother with a baby in a pram...." Jay's voice broke with emotion at the thought.....

Tears fell from her eyes, Peter who also had a lump in his throat, raked in his pocket for a handkerchief and gave it to her.

"Thank you, I'm so sorry, it's as if it were yesterday, just thinking about you and your father and mother had brought it all back."

The lilting burr finally fell silent. Peter's own heart was deeply moved, more so because most of the story was new to him; he couldn't remember the last war, but he was aware of the effects of war....but he still needed to know the rest of the story, and he needed to know it all.

"Please, please, dear Mrs. McFarlain, please do go on if you can."

He took her hand and held it to his lips.

"Will you? Please say you will?"

She nodded, "Of course, I will my dear.....dear Peter...?"

The voice raised questioningly, as though still doubting the name of the man who was imploring her. Still doubting?

"Well James' bandages were at last removed but his eye lids had been stitched down. It was all to do with the healing process you understand?"

He nodded as she continued.

"Well, as I knew him it was felt better that I was present when the stitches were taken out, so with my heart in my mouth I stood, desperately willing him to recognise me, for he had not spoken a word since the explosion. Well, when the last stitch was cut, and everyone else stood back, I looked into his dear face and called his name, and his eyes slowly, oh so slowly, opened and alighted, not on me, but on a photograph propped up on his locker, a photograph that had followed him around – that he had never seen, a photograph of your mother, you and the baby. It had been posted just before she had been killed, and before the explosion."

Peter remained silent.

"Anyway his eyes alighted on the picture and a slow smile of recognition spread over his face. He just said one word "Laura", then his eyes closed again. He cried and cried, and slowly started to come out of his depression and shock."

"He didn't know that my mother was dead at that time, did he?"

"No, no it was quite a time before that terrible news was passed to him – by me, sadly. I will never forget that day as long as I live..."

She paused and her eyes looked, he thought, into the past; seeing pictures that he couldn't see, and didn't want to see...At long last, he could understand his father's obsession with the picture. That picture had been the first, and yet the last sight of his wife and children. The hard lump in his throat gave Peter acute physical pain, as pictures of his father skimmed into his thoughts. Jay spoke again,

"Eventually James left the nursing home and went down to Salisbury, to finish his recuperation, with his parents, that's where your story fits in, doesn't it? As I was an army nurse, I had to go where they sent me, and it wasn't long after your father left that I was posted to a hospital in Scotland. Well, the war grew worse, and although my life became very hectic, as you can guess, I did manage to write to him once or twice but he took ages to answer and the last time I heard from him was just after I was married. I had written to tell him earlier that I was to be married to David Marsh his best man who had also lost touch with him. Later on I wrote to him again and invited him to the wedding, he didn't come of course, but I did receive a letter and a little parcel from him, offering David and me his best wishes. The post mark was obscure and he didn't put any address, so sadly I lost all contact.

"Yes, that must have been at about the time that he became a complete recluse. He lived on his own when his mother and father died, staying on in the family home; then not many months after, he sold up and moved into a small house on the borders of Exmoor. I saw very little of him over the years. By then I had taken the decision to enter the ministry and thankfully he was happy about my calling and gave me his blessing. He even said at the time that my mother would have approved, too. On that last occasion, just before I went off to college, he embraced me, it was about the only physical contact that I can remember from him. Of course our lives moved away from each other, as you can imagine, and my pastoral duties took me to different parts of the country, I tried to keep in touch with him, but he wouldn't have a telephone under any circumstances and he wouldn't answer my letters. He was a very obstinate man. Even when Angela and I decided to get married, he wouldn't answer letters. He just didn't want to know. He wouldn't have any of it. It was hopeless. We did go down there to see him once…Angela was so patient with him. She was a real pal to me and to my father, but even she never managed to break through his darkness."

"Sad, how very, very sad, he was such a lovely, charming man, how I wish you had known him…" her voice trailed off in a vague way, then gathering her thoughts together again she said,

"How sad that it should have ended like that."

"Oh that was not really the end, seven years ago he had a massive stroke."

"Oh no!"

"Unfortunately, yes, at first we thought that he wouldn't get over it. Then, after a relatively short spell in hospital and since they could do no more for him, Angela and I took him home. I must admit that at the time I did consider a nursing home for him, but Angela wouldn't hear of it. She said she wanted to look after him."

"How on earth did you cope with your busy life?"

"Well, Angela felt that as she had been a nurse ever since we had married, and since we had not been blessed with any children, it was just meant to be, and that father had been given to us, so that we could give him a special kind of care – a special kind of love. A love that he had missed out on for all those sad years spent on his own. Frankly, she truly believed it was God's will, and I think I felt that way too, once he was at home with us. Can you understand?"

"From two such caring people? Yes I think I can, nevertheless, it was still quite an undertaking for you both, she must be quite a girl, that sort of nursing is no easy matter, I know from my own experience."

"Well, I must say that Angela was and still is one in a million and I love her dearly."

He paused to look at his watch.

"I thought she would have been here by now actually but I guess things must be even more hectic than I thought! What with the dresses and the children to cope with, I think I'm, well we, are well out of it!"

"I think you're right, but I must say I am longing to see these famed twins. This wedding will really be a white one, we were supposed to be going by pony and trap...."

"In that case I hope there are plenty of umbrellas for us all, the snow hasn't let up once has it?"

"No but it is about right for this time of the year, so I think we knew what to expect. I'm sure it will be a lovely wedding...some day I'll tell you about another lovely wedding that I will never forget."

"You mean mother and father's?"

She nodded.

"I'm still utterly stunned by all the things that you have told me, and how puzzling it is, though rather wonderful, that you are somehow linked to my past – and me, all this has really come as a bolt from the blue...You said that you married my father's best man, a David Marsh? But your name?"

"Yes, I did marry David, we were together only six weeks when he was sent to France."

"Oh, I think I can guess – he didn't come back to you?"

"That's right, I was truly devastated. There I was a young girl looking as so many did to a happy future; with perhaps, in my dreams, roses round the door.. Well it was not meant to be, not at that time anyway. I remained in Scotland for the rest of the war, where I met my second husband. He was working at a cipher station in the wilds when I met him. He had to come into the main hospital once a year for a medical, there always had to be one cheeky one, doesn't there?"

She smiled at Peter as she spoke.

"It was he who decided to call me Jay – only because I had a letter J on my handbag – he saw it, and called me Jay from that day. The fact that my name was Jannette made no difference to him whatsoever! Thinking about it later I came to the conclusion that it was right for me. After all I was starting a new life with him, what about a new name? I was used to nick-names anyway, very few people ever called me Jannette, it was nearly always Netta. So when I married, a new me – Jay McFarlain was born and later on I became the mother of Elle and much later – grandmother to Gregory, and here we are. My own dear Angus passed away five years ago, a truly wonderful man. I still miss his presence very much, But I rest easy in the knowledge that he is with the Saint's in heaven. That makes death and parting easier to bear doesn't it?"

She looked at Peter for his reassurance, and got it without a word being spoken.

"So, that's my story, young man."

"I can hardly take it all in, just so many coincidences, fancy you knowing my father and mother. I still can't get over it, you knew my father…"

"I can picture him now with your beautiful mother, what bestiality war was."

She shook her head slowly and sadly.

"At least he spent the last years within a loving family, so that's one blessing."

"Good that he was with us maybe, but he still had a trial to live with and through, because sometime later he had another stroke and his condition worsened. He became totally dependent on both of us, but on Angela particularly. Those days were so difficult, he appeared to be in a world of his own most of the time, - helpless – apart from being able to look at the photograph constantly – the one you described. He appeared to get no joy from his life whatsoever. No matter what we did or how we tried."

"Oh dear."

Jay McFarlain was clearly upset.

"The worse and most trying thing was that he was not able to speak to us, I mean a proper conversation, all that he managed to do was utter one sentence, and that with great difficulty. I'll never forget it as long as I live, he repeated it over and over again, and drove Angela and me to distraction; as soon as he saw one of us he would start grappling for the words. It was so hard for him to speak you see, so painful, so distressing."

Jay McFarlain sat and listened, trying for all she was worth, to equate the picture of this ailing old man with the man she remembered – the strong and handsome James.

"What was it that he said?"

"Well, it was more of a question; a question incidentally that drove Angela and me into the depths. I prayed so much at the time for the answer that I think that God must have switched me off!!.... 'What is the answer?' That was it – simply.... 'What is the answer?' We were in despair, Angela more than me really, after all she was with father, day in and day out."

His voice dropped away as he remembered.....

"What is the answer?"

Peter nodded.

"Just that, nothing else, no other clue?"

"No nothing more, just....that..."

"What happened, did you ever find out the answer?"

"Well, the whole thing was very strange really. Angela and I spent a great deal of time writing to different people, trying to contact old army friends, we tried all sorts of things, all without success I might add, all we came up with was – nothing – absolutely nothing... No response from any quarter and this went on for a couple of years. The main difficulty was that he had virtually dropped out of all society, so that even before his stroke he was cut off, by his own choice of course, but nevertheless not much help to us."

"So what happened? It must have been dreadful for you both."

"Well, there was nothing until a very strange and inexplicable thing happened."

He stood up and walked to the window. It was still snowing and the sky was darkening rapidly.

"What sort of strange thing?"

"I hardly know how to explain it, or at least to describe it...it was so strange....I still can't understand it or give any sensible explanation...except to say that it will haunt me for the rest of my life."

She stood and went to his side. Both stood in silence looking out of the window.

"Please try to tell me what happened if you can, of course I'll understand if it is still too painful for you to speak about."

"Maybe it might help me to talk about it, I know that I can never forget it, for it is with me always and I think it always will be, it's with me all the time."

"Does it hurt too much to tell?"

"No, not really, in a way it's quite a wonderful story, but for me… it was simply the most earth shattering experience of my life. It all started when I was standing in the library waiting to collect a book… Father was on my mind of course, but then he always was, he was getting more and more distressed at us for not helping him, all we had to do was to find the elusive answer to one simple question, not much to ask after all! It was simply breaking our hearts….. I was looking out of the window… praying maybe – I don't know what was in my mind exactly when suddenly without any warning…. two words came into my mind, two words out of nowhere, two words that I just knew were the answer for father. I didn't know anything more, but I knew without any shadow of a doubt, that I had the answer. My head and my heart knew. Well, I flew home, I ran all the way. I didn't even attempt to use my car… I just ran and ran and ran, all the way. By the time I arrived I'm not ashamed to say that I was crying and in fact I was in a terrible state. I ran into the house and straight to my father's side, knelt beside him…I'll never forget the look in his eyes… 'What is the answer?' he said in his usual way with his eyes full of tears. 'Madame Butterfly' I said 'Madame Butterfly."

Peter didn't look at Jay Mcfarlain as he was speaking, had he done so he might not have continued.

"Father for the first time in three years smiled at me, really smiled and spoke sensibly for the first time. He held me with his hands, hands that had been incapable of movement, he thought for a moment, and then, without any hesitation said…. 'I'll tell Pansy...' He looked at the photograph of mother, slumped forward into my arms… and died."

At exactly the same moment that Peter stopped speaking, Jay McFarlain fell to the floor at his feet, in a dead faint. He was horrified, quickly bending down he scooped her slim body into his arms and carried her to the settee. He was reaching for a cushion when the door opened and Angela entered the room.

"Peter?"

"Yes, love come quickly, she's fainted," then he added apologetically "It's all my fault, I was telling her about father, how he died…"

Angela was speechless at first, then when her patient was reviving she said in a low voice,

"Peter how could you?"

"She knew my father." …Lamely he added, "She asked me."

"Did she? Well even if she did…fancy telling her how he died, that's awful."

"She wanted to know – honestly."

Jay McFarlain started to open her eyes.

"Hello."

"Hello, you must be Angela my dear."

"That's right, how are you, what has my silly husband been up to?"

"I'm fine," she said trying to sit up.

"Here let me help you," Peter said leaning forward.

"I think that you have done enough damage for the moment, don't you?"

"Oh, don't tell him off my dear, it's all my own fault. I'm a silly old woman, it was just my imagination, and the miracle."

"The miracle?" Peter said.

"The miracle?" Angela echoed.

"Why yes, most definitely, a miracle."

They all looked from one to the other.

"But I don't understand," Peter said, "What do you mean?"

"I mean God answered your prayers, didn't he? You prayed, both of you didn't you, constantly and often, for the answer to your father's distress and the answer to his question? And He gave it to you, didn't He? From what you tell me it quite clearly was the right answer, how else could you have guessed? ….. I'll tell you…..never."

"I never thought of it as a miracle, I don't know why, but I never did."

"Maybe we should have then darling, don't forget, we were…well I was so distressed at the time.. the only thing that I could think of was that you.. you had killed your father."

She reached up and buried her head in Peter's jacket, as he put his arms about her.

"No, my loves – you were both part of a miracle, there is no doubt in my mind whatsoever."

Jay McFarlain was completely recovered. She knew, that in all the world there were only two people on earth who knew the answer to James' question; Simon Moon and herself…and, of course, God.

The door flew open and two little people ran in,

"Mummy – Daddy, Mummy – Daddy," they chorused as they crossed the room, closely followed by Terri.

"Grandma, here they are, and so excited, aren't they adorable?"

Jay looked with love at the twins as they scrambled up on to their parents' laps.

"Steady on, don't knock us over," Peter laughed.

Angela took a child's hand and said,

"Come and meet Terri's Grandma." Leading her towards Jay she said, "What about giving her a kiss to say 'hello'?"

Full of confidence, Laura Aston flung her pyjama clad legs on to the welcoming lap and snuggled down making herself at home, the smell of her sweet scented body filling Jay's nostrils. She leaned herself forward and placed a moist kiss on to the waiting cheek.

"'Lo," she said and turned her face to Jay who looked into the trusting eyes of the child on her lap. They were blue – a special violet blue – vibrant. They took Jay's breath away. She had seen those eyes before in another time. They belonged to another Laura. The first Laura Aston.

"Laura?"

"Laura" repeated the child, nodding.

The Circle is Complete

It was one month after the wedding and the Aston household were back at Oasis. The door bell rang. It was the postman. He gave Angela a small package, that was addressed to herself and Peter. The postmark was Lanarkshire. Angela's first thought was Terri, but when she turned the packet over she found that it had been sent by Jay McFarlain. She was tempted to open it at once, but finally decided that it would have to wait until Peter came home. After all it was bath time, so she would just have to put her curiosity on hold for the time being; therefore, on her way to the nursery she put the packet on the sideboard next to the silver framed photograph – which still took pride of place.

Peter was home. The children had had their kisses and stories and were now hopefully – in the land of nod. At last it was time to open the packet, and Angela was as impatient as could be.

"Bring it over m'love, I'm curious as you are, so let's see what it can be."

How is happened she didn't know. She reached for the packet – and then as if in slow motion, the silver frame; with the smiling woman and children's faces; slid across the sideboard, twisted and then fell to the floor almost at her feet.

"Oh no. How on earth did that happen? Peter I'm so sorry."

"Don't worry darling, it's only glass. It won't take a moment to clear up," he said as he walked over to her.

"I'll go and get the dustpan…I'm so sorry…"

"Don't keep blaming yourself. It could have been me – it was just an accident that's all."

Angela went off to the kitchen and Peter bent down and picked up the frame. He carefully took out the last piece of glass and drew the picture and the black cardboard backing out.

"I'll measure the size in a moment or two," he said as they made their way to the settee.

He rested the frame on the arm of the seat and sat next to Angela, who by this time had taken the outer paper off the packet. The bubble pack fell away – and they saw a small black bible. Peter picked it up, underneath was something else, wrapped in tissue. Angela quickly pulled the paper apart, they both looked at the beautiful thing before them.

"Oh Peter, it's absolutely lovely."

Peter gazed at the white silk bookmark, with its cascade of blue flowers.

"Yes, I have to agree m'love, it is beautiful."

"The embroidery is exquisite, they're forget-me-nots aren't they? Oh it's so very pretty. Look there is a letter here Peter," she held it out to him, "do see what it says."

Peter took the letter and read it. Then his face lit up.

"Oh Angela – the Bible belonged to my mother, and her mother before her, my father sent it to Jay years ago, just after she was married, saying that he thought she would like it as a keepsake, knowing how fond of her she was. The bookmark was used by my mother on her wedding day. It was evidently made for her by an old friend. Jay goes on to say that she thinks its rightful home is here with us. She would like us to give it to our Laura, when she is old enough to understand."

"That's lovely, darling – it's a lovely story."

"Here you are love, you read the rest, there is more."

As Peter passed the letter, his elbow knocked the frame from its perch and it fell to the floor once again.

"Oh no, this thing has a mind of its own tonight and no mistake," he said as he leaned over to pick it up. As he did so, his eyes alighted on a small piece of paper sticking out between the photograph and card. There was writing on it, and full of inquisitiveness, he drew it out, to read. Angela was silently reading Jay's letter and Peter was silently reading the slip of paper when they both turned to each other and started to speak at exactly the same time. They stopped – then started again, but once more they spoke together. They were agitated now, one with the other.

In desperation they both held their respective papers aloft, and then to each other. Both were speechless yet overpowered by unspoken words. Each read the other's paper in silence. The gist of both, and at the heart of both were the following thirteen words… "Intricate and geometrically beautiful oriental construction with female overtones (as flowers are needed)."

On the paper that Peter had been reading, and that Angela was reading, there were two other sentences. 1….. 'S.B. James, if this doesn't rattle your brains – then nothing will…' and 2…..'I'll give you the answer to this conundrum when you get back on leave again….' Apart from a small blot on the last letter of the first sentence there was nothing else written. Angela's mouth fell open – she didn't know what to say. What did it all mean? Peter meanwhile was reading the second part of Jay McFarlain's letter.

In it she explained that during the last war she had met a very nice young man called Simon Moon, and that she and Simon were in the habit of dreaming up riddles for each other (to lighten their spirits); all pretty silly stuff, but harmless. When she became a nurse they had started to write to each other, and were in the habit of writing a question – riddle and so on, at the end of the letter, promising to send the answer on in a subsequent one if it was not guessed correctly. She then went on to say that as soon as James came on the scene, Simon had started to plague him with the puzzles as well. James, being the chap he was had joined in quite willingly.

At one time, evidently, he had the whole of his bomb disposal crew trying to work the things out. She added that looking back on it, they must have driven everyone mad! However (and this was the part of the letter that made the hair on Peter's neck bristle; and a strange ripple run along his spine), Simon was getting too clever by half, so she decided to make something up that was of such an obscure nature that he wouldn't have any chance of guessing it, and therefore would have to admit defeat. Then followed the SAME thirteen words that were on the paper that Angela was now holding, the paper from behind the photograph. The only difference came at the end of Jay McFarlain's letter. Because at the end of her letter, she had put the answer. The answer is – Madame Butterfly. Peter was speechless, as his mouth dropped open in utter disbelief.

"Read on – read on dearest, don't stop now, read on." Angela implored him.

At that moment the gently cry of a child broke the silence.

"I'll go darling, do read on, read, read" she pleaded.

Peter nodded and returned to the letter, whilst Angela slipped away. In it Jay McFarlain explained that only two people in the whole world knew both question and answer, and those two people were herself and Simon Moon, the mysterious boy who had appeared out of nowhere and had disappeared in the same way after staying with his mother and her aunt for nearly two years. It was during that time that she, Janette Philbeam, as she was, had met and made friends with Simon. She had found him to be a kind young man, with a lovely nature. When he had disappeared, Peter's mother had been devastated and had made herself quite ill worrying about him.

Jay explained that she had found all this out later, as she had been posted away from Amleth at the time. She went on…

'About three weeks after Simon had disappeared, she (Laura, his mother), had found out that she was pregnant, with Peter. It was almost as if Simon had moved out of Laura's life – to make way for the baby. For the time that Simon had disappeared coincided, as far as one could tell, exactly with the time that the baby had been conceived. Simon was never seen again….'

Peter tried to come to grips with the information. He sat silently for quite a long time. "But she called me Simon…could it be? Me Simon? Lord, I just can't understand….but then I'm not supposed to."

Omega

The last line of Jay's letter was a P.S……

'By the way, Simon was deaf in one ear….' Peter continued to look at the paper in disbelief. The clock chimed loudly – too loudly. Peter realised with astonishment that he could hear in both ears, for the first time in his life.

Epilogue *September 1990*

Billy Norfolk, gentleman of the road rummaged through the jumble of clothes on the table. Suddenly his eyes spied the sleeve of a jacket.

"Lovely," he thought, that's just what I'm looking for."

He pulled at the tweed material and the rest of the garment came into view. Billy shook it out and held it against himself.

"It's a bit on the large side for you Billy isn't it?"

The lady behind the table said.

"No, it's just what I want," he answered pulling the coat on over his existing one.

"I've never had patches before," he said caressing the cracked leather lovingly with his gnarled brown hands. "Lovely," he whispered.

"Ten pence then and it's yours."

Billy's weather-beaten face lit up.

"Ten pence well spent, I reckon," he murmured as he handed over the coin to her.

On the way out of the hall he manoeuvred his rucksack on to his hunched back and did the jacket up, leaving his hands free to push into his pockets, where he found, and drew out a crumpled paper.

As he reached the road he stopped to examine the tattered strip in his hands. Without the benefit of his glasses, the words were hard to make out, so he squeezed his eyes up and held the paper close…

"The dancer is," he read….. "Matron Butterly…"

………..THERE ARE MORE THINGS IN HEAVEN
AND EARTH, HORATIO, THAN ARE DREAMED
OF IN YOUR PHILOSOPHY.

HAMLET ACT 1 SCENE V

THE END